With the sixth lash Serle cried out at last, an awful ragged sound. Bron knew what the loss of control must cost his brother. The lash fell again; again, Serle cried out.

With that second cry, the pressure in Bron's head broke. Deep inside him, in the darkest spaces of his secret self, something arrowed forward. His barriers yielded like shredding cloth. The thing tore up through the layers of his consciousness, flooding his mind and body as if he were no more than an empty vessel. Still it swelled, like an endless breath, until he was no longer able to hold it and it exploded outward, a cataclysmic burst that almost took his consciousness with it, a tidal wave of power sweeping irresistibly over the crowd, the square, the entire village.

Time stopped. Every living thing was frozen. All but Bron.

THE ARM
STONE OF THE ONE

VICTORIA STRAUSS

AVON · EOS

AVON BOOKS
A division of
The Hearst Corporation
1350 Avenue of the Americas
New York, New York 10019

The
Vow

One

T WAS Bron's oldest memory, the telling of the Tale. Throughout his life, if he reached behind his barriers toward those childhood moments, it was as if he were there again, the firelight warm on his family's faces, his mother's husky voice filling his ears with the phrases he knew by heart. She had learned the Tale from her mother, who had learned it from her mother, who had learned it from hers, and so on in an unbroken chain stretching back more than a thousand years. The words never varied; the cadences of her voice, her emphasis on certain phrases and even her pauses, were always the same. Yet each telling made the Tale anew, a vivid and living thing, rebuilding with words a world long since gone to dust.

"Long ago," the Tale began, "when the worlds were one, our family lived in a wondrous palace, high on a rocky cliff above a swift-flowing river. We were not then as we are now. Then, we had wealth and power. We commanded a rich and fruitful land that stretched further than a man could ride in seven days. We were known across the wide world for the strength of our rule, the justice of our governance, and the prosperity of our people. At the time of the Tale, the head of our family was the noblest and most powerful man ever born of his line. His name was Bron."

There was always a pause here, long enough for Bron's mother to smile toward him, long enough for Bron to feel a fierce responsive surge of pride. The ancient name, like the Tale itself, was passed down the generations. It was the task of the women of the line to tell the Tale; it was the task of the men to bear the name.

"Tell us about the lords and ladies, Mother," said Bron's younger sister Elene. The interruptions of the Tale were as hallowed by habit as the narrative itself. "Tell us about the banquets, and how they danced for days and days."

Bron's mother smiled again. She had been beautiful as a girl, and when she told the Tale it could still be seen. Her features were strong and symmetrical, her eyes dark and very clear. Her hair, once ink-black but now as gray as pewter, fell straight and heavy past her waist. She combed it as she told the Tale; it crackled softly as she did so, fighting the comb, wrapping itself around her fingers.

"Our Ancestor Bron had a wife and three sons. He had two brothers and three sisters, all with husbands and wives and children. There were cousins and uncles and aunts, courtiers and ministers, scholars and scribes, soldiers and servants—so many people the palace was more like a town than a dwelling. Every night there was a banquet. Every week celebrations were held to mark birthdays, weddings, christenings, the harvest, a hundred different feasts and festivals. Travelers came from leagues away, from other countries and from across the sea, to receive our Ancestor's hospitality. All were welcomed with honor and gifts—rich or poor, noble or common, man or woman or child.

"Yet no matter how much he gave, no matter how great the celebrations, our Ancestor's wealth was never exhausted. His riches were beyond calculation, and because of his wisdom and good governance, they constantly renewed themselves, like a tree that grows new leaves when old ones fall."

For a moment the family sat silent, the dazzling images filling up their minds: the palace's soaring towers and spires, its rooms and corridors heavy with tapestry, its tables thick with shining plate and crystal goblets, its banquet halls gilded with torchlight, its lords and ladies turning in the intricate patterns of the dance.

"Now of all the magnificent dwellings and objects and lands and gold and gems our Ancestor possessed, no single thing was as precious as the Stone."

The whole family—Bron, his two brothers, his two sisters, and his father—breathed in unison: "The Stone."

"The Stone," Bron's mother echoed. "No one knows what the Stone is or how it came to be. We know only that it is the most powerful object in the world. It sees and understands all things—people and animals, stones and trees, cities and towns, storms and avalanches and the changing of the seasons, everything that happens, everything that lives and dies, everything that *is*. There is nothing the infinite focus of its vision does not touch, nor any place the timeless continuum of its contemplation does not reach. He who shares the Stone's understanding is the wisest man in the world. He who possesses it is the mightiest."

"And our Ancestor was the wisest and mightiest man in the world," said Bron's younger brother, Olesin.

"He was," Bron's mother said. "For the Stone belonged to him, and through the strength of his Gift he was able to send his mind along the flow of its perception, and share its knowledge."

"The Stone," Elene said fiercely. "The Stone was ours!"

"Now, the Stone's being contains a paradox. Its power consists wholly of its vision; it has no physical attributes with which to defend or move itself. And so it has always been subject to the will of humankind. For centuries before our family rose to power the Stone passed from hand to hand, sometimes understood and sometimes not, sometimes serving good and sometimes evil. The Stone suffered, for it detests wrongdoing and prizes stability. When at last our Ancestor's five-times-great-grandfather captured the Stone in battle, it recognized his honor and strength. Here at last was a man fit to hold it, fit to shield and protect it. The Stone and our family swore a pact. Our family vowed to defend the Stone, never to use its power for evil. The Stone promised that through their Gifts all the descendants of our line would share its knowledge, and gain wealth and prosperity and all good things. There was only one condition. The bargain must remain a secret. Though all the world knew of the Stone, none must know where it lay. The Stone was weary of fighting. It wanted no more battles, no more campaigns, no more transferences. It wished to be at peace.

"For six generations, the contract between the Stone and our family held. But in the time of our Ancestor Bron, a man was born who lived his life by a single burning purpose: to find the Stone and make it his. The name of this man was—"

"Percival." This was Bron's interruption. The name was ugly in his mouth, three syllables invested with the entire legacy of hatred that had bound his family for a thousand years.

"Percival," his mother repeated. "Percival the Deceiver. Percival the Traitor. Percival the Destroyer. This evil man spent his life scouring the world for the Stone; he was no longer young when he reached the court of our Ancestor. As was his custom, our Ancestor offered the hospitality of his house. Through the corruption of his power—which was perhaps as great as our Ancestor's own—Percival divined that his quest had ended. Cloaking himself in invisibility, he stole away into the night. Our Ancestor never recognized who he had sheltered, nor suspected the knowledge that had been stolen. Not until he next consulted the Stone did he learn the truth of Percival's treachery.

"When Percival returned a year later, accompanied by the army he had raised, our Ancestor was ready. Our forces were strong, as strong as the powers of hand and mind could make them. But the armies Percival commanded were stronger. Slowly, Percival's troops advanced. Behind them, the once-prosperous fields spread charred and barren. The towns lay crushed to rubble, and the dead rotted unburied in the streets.

"At last Percival reached our Ancestor's palace and set siege to the walls. It was a terrible battle, fought hand to hand and mind to mind. Our Ancestor used all his strength, but he could not hold against the twisted forces Percival invoked. In the end Percival and his men breached our fortifications and entered the palace no conquering force had ever taken."

"No!" cried Elene, as if her voice could reach back through time and mend the broken stones.

"Our Ancestor, defending the palace gates, was one of the first to die." Bron's mother stared into the flames, the comb idle in her hands. "Percival cut off our Ancestor's head with his own sword. He impaled it on a pike and gave it to his squire to carry like a banner. They say that when the squire took up the pike the Stone cried out, a shout that was heard to the far corners of the earth, so that for a moment every breathing creature shared its grief.

"Percival's army slaughtered every living thing in the palace. They raped and tortured, they hacked away arms and legs, they skewered babies on their swords, they even killed the horses and the swine and the ladies' little lapdogs. At last, when there was nothing left alive, Percival entered the hall where the Stone lay. With his own hands he took the Stone and placed it in a leather bag. He marched his army out of the palace and set fire to the wreckage he had made. He and his men watched as it burned to ash. Then, their horses' hooves crusted with the blood they had spilled, they rode away across the blackened lands."

The fire hissed softly. The shadows trembled, devouring the corners of the room. Within them, Percival's horsemen seemed to leap and grimace, blood-drenched and brutal, triumphant.

"Now, in the time of our Ancestor the Split was well under way, the violent dividing of reality that was the result of the struggle between the two great powers that shape the world."

"Mindpower," said Olesin.

"Handpower," said Elene.

"Each power, equally, is man's birthright. For centuries they existed in harmony, side by side. But while it is the nature of the skills of mind to be stable and unchanging, it is the nature of the way of hands, the way of tools, to grow and develop. In time a thing called technology was born, a discipline of devices and machines whose capacity to alter the world was so awesome its adherents believed no other power was necessary. Slowly mindpower fell from favor—at first neglected, then pushed aside, at last hated and feared. Those who had ceased to understand it renamed it, calling it magic. They hunted and persecuted its adherents wherever they were found, seeking to wipe them from the face of the earth.

"But mindpower is rooted as deeply in the soul of humankind as handpower is. Man cannot destroy a part of himself, no matter how he seeks to do so—he can only divide it from his understanding, drive it deep within him to a place where he can no longer see it. As the holocaust of handpower's hatred raged, those who clung to mindpower began to vanish from the world, together with the places where their ways survived. A village might disappear with all its people, leaving only empty land behind; a forest that held a sacred glade might overnight be replaced by barren rock, or a lake with a hermit's hut beside it turn to desert from one day to the next. Yet these people and places did not become nothing. How could they? They were living beings, living powers. They simply went . . . elsewhere. No one truly understands the how or why of it, nor exactly what or where 'elsewhere' is. We only know that in the end, where there had been one world, there came to be two— the original world, now ruled entirely by handpower, and a new world, in which the ways of mind survived."

"Our world," Elene asserted. "Where Percival took the Stone."

"Yes. Those who followed the path of technology were barely aware of the Split, of the falling away of powers that once were as common as tools had become. Many who held to the ways of mindpower, however, understood what was happening. Percival was one of these. Evil he might have been, but he was also greatly Gifted. He saw that the Stone—a thing of power, the greatest Gift that had ever been or could ever be—had no place in a world of tools. He led his followers into the world of mindpower, carrying with him the captive Stone. In the jagged mountain range that rises at the center of the middle continent, he and his men built a Fortress surrounded by high black walls. They placed the Stone at its heart, in a prison-room they made to hold it—a room without doors or windows, a room only they could enter.

"The world of mindpower, just emerging from the Split, was still incomplete. Its people and places were like leaves scattered across an expanse of water, pieces of familiar territory connected by great expanses of emptiness, flat and featureless and clad in mist. There was no government, no authority; the people were frightened and without direction. Percival and his men used these things, their own Gifts, and the power of the Stone to conquer the world of mindpower as they had once conquered our family. There was no one strong enough to oppose them. As the new world rose to completion, the mists receding and the blank places acquiring detail, they consolidated their dominion. In the end they ruled all the lands, all the nations. They called themselves *Guardians*." Bron's mother spat the word, as if it were acid on her tongue. "Guardians of mindpower, Guardians of the Stone. As if they had the right to guard what they had stolen. As if they had the right to protect what was gained by trickery and treachery and bloodshed. As if they had the right to possess what *was not theirs*."

She stopped, breathing deeply. The family breathed with her. The ancient rage moved in them, shaking them, defining them, making them one.

"Now, Percival and his men believed they had slaughtered our entire family, every single person who could lay rightful claim to the Stone. But they were wrong. When he learned of Percival's treachery, our Ancestor took his little grandson, the child of his heir, and sent him with his nursemaid to a safe place outside our lands. When the nursemaid heard the Stone's shout, she knew that all was lost. Faithful and true, she guarded both the child and the secret of his heritage. It was she who first told the Tale, so that the boy might know who he was. It was she who, when the boy married, taught the Tale to his wife, so that the knowledge might be passed on. From that time to this we have lived in hiding, guarding the precious secret of our lineage. As Percival robbed us of our wealth and high position, so time has robbed us of our mindpower. The Gift that once filled every member of our line to overflowing is all but vanished from among us. A spark remains, enough to build the barriers that hide the truth of our heritage, but that is all. The greatness that defined us in the time of our Ancestor is lost to us—a shadow, a memory, nothing more."

There was anguish in her voice. Of all the family's dispossessions, none was so terrible as this. Wealth could be gained again, land recaptured, but no human endeavor could bring power back.

"But there's hope, Mother." Elene's voice was small. "Tell about the One Who Comes."

"The One Who Comes." Bron's mother took up her comb again; once more it traveled crackling through her hair. "It's said that some day power will be reborn among us, a Gift even greater than that of our ancient Ancestor, a Gift whose like the world has never seen. The One who owns that Gift will avenge our ancient wrong. He will breach the Fortress's walls, as our walls were breached; he will cast down the new Percival as the old Percival cast our Ancestor down. He will destroy the prison-room that holds the Stone, and restore it to its proper place among us. No one knows when that day will come. We have waited ten centuries, and perhaps we will wait ten more. But it will arrive. When it does, the Stone will rejoice, for it will be unbound. Our world will rejoice, for the Stone will be free. And we—we will rejoice also. For we will be again as we were, our Gift reborn and our might restored, without peer among the nations of the world."

"As we were," echoed Elene and Olesin, in rare accord. Their faces were rapt; behind their eyes the spires of the Ancestor's palace rose from the wreckage of the Tale, reborn to the glorious future. "As we were."

Bron's mother dropped the comb, and held out her hands. Bron's father reached to join her, and the others, a small circle gilded and shadowed by the dying fire.

"We call now to the One Who Comes. We call as we have called this thousand years and more, across time and distance, with the power of our minds, the power of our lineage, the power of our hope. Come to us. Come to us. Come."

Her voice was no longer only a sound, but a thing that could be felt, running like light through the family's joined hands. It bound them not just to one another, but to all the centuries of their hidden heritage. For an instant it was not merely the seven people in the firelight, but the whole of the ancient line that reached out along the pathways of the future, in search of their promised restoration. For a thousand years they had searched—in houses and hovels, tents and caves, on land and on sea, in a dozen different countries and a hundred different languages. For a thousand years, the future had offered them nothing more than it did tonight: words spoken in darkness, a hope nursed out of sight, another ten centuries, perhaps, of waiting.

"And so the Tale ends in silence," Bron's mother said softly. "I have told it this night, as all my ancestresses have done before me, so that we may always, in our deepest souls, know who we are. In secrecy we guard our knowledge; in concealment we preserve our hope. So it must be, until the day of our deliverance."

It was the signal for the raising of barriers. Their hands still linked, the family began the process of closing the doors they had opened tonight, carefully folding the Tale away behind walls of thought, far below the level of everyday consciousness. It was painful, this disguise, but necessary. The skill of barrier-building had been passed down for as long as the Tale itself; the children of the line began to learn it as soon as they could speak, and not until the skill was perfect in every respect were they allowed to hear the Tale.

Barriers complete, the family went about its bedtime tasks. Bron's mother mixed the porridge for the morning; his sister Annis banked the fire. His older brother Serle and his father made the rounds of the house and barn. They might have been any ordinary peasant household, preparing for the night. Yet, hidden or not, the secret of their ancestry could not help but mark them. Since their fall from power, the men and women of Bron's line had been in exile, not merely from their power and their birthright, but from the world in which they lived.

The crowing of the cock in the chicken run outside the barn woke Bron, as it did every day. Beside him, on the straw mattress they shared in the hayloft, Serle was still sleeping. The rising sun poked long fingers through the unglazed windows, its light almost solid with the dust that hung in the air.

Bron elbowed Serle in the ribs. Serle muttered sleepily and turned over, pulling the blanket over his head.

"Wake up, Serle," Bron said. He kicked his brother softly.

"Leave me alone," Serle said.

Bron kicked him again, harder. Serle erupted with a muffled roar, seizing a pillow and pressing it over Bron's face. They struggled for a few moments, laughing. Then Serle abandoned the pillow and rumpled Bron's hair.

"Enough," he said. "You go in—I'll be along soon."

Shivering in the early-morning chill, Bron pulled on his clothes. He climbed down the ladder to the main floor and pushed open the wooden door that divided the barn from the house. The house was a single unpartitioned space built of roughly dressed stone, with a thatched roof and a flagstone floor. A huge fireplace took up nearly half one side; opposite, behind a curtain, stood the big bed in which Bron's parents slept, the truckle bed for Annis, Elene, and Olesin pushed out of sight beneath it. The long plank table and benches had been made by Bron's father, Jevon, as had the coffer chests near the bed, the wooden cupboards, and the carved armchair beside the hearth where Jevon spent his evenings. Bunches of herbs and strings of dried fruit hung from the smoke-grimed rafters; sacks of grain and barrels of ale and salt meat were ranged neatly along the walls. The air was dim, for there were only the fire and two small windows in the front wall, covered by greased parchment in the summer and wooden shutters in the winter, to provide light.

Bron's mother, Alse, stood by the hearth, stirring a kettle of porridge for the morning meal.

"Where's Serle?" she said. "Not still asleep?"

"He's coming." Bron sat down at the table. Alse portioned out a bowl of porridge, adding milk still warm from this morning's milking and a generous dollop of honey from the family's hives. She set it before her son and returned to the fire.

"Mother, make her stop!" It was Olesin, his voice plaintive. "She's pinching me again!"

"Stop it, Elene," Alse said, without turning around. "Or you'll feel my hand on your backside."

Elene assumed a wounded expression. "I didn't do anything! He's a horrible little toad to say I did!''

Eight-year-old Elene was a strong and vibrant child, with rosy cheeks and a shining mass of red-brown hair. Olesin, two years younger, was fairer and more slender, with translucent skin beneath which the blue tracery of his veins showed like a map. Different in most ways, in the strength of their wills Elene and Olesin were much alike. Disciplining them, separating them, or silencing them was a constant task.

"Be quiet, Elene," said Annis. At seventeen, she was a plumper version of her sister, with a glossy braid that nearly reached her knees. She was engaged to be married next November to the younger son of the village innkeeper—a match much better than the family, with its uncertain position in the community, had a right to expect. "Eat your breakfast, and leave the rest of us in peace."

Serle came in at last, his hair wild, his eyes puffed and bloodshot from lack of sleep. He was apprenticed to the town's blacksmith, who had offered him a partnership if he could pass the Trade Examinations and gain membership in the Blacksmiths' Guild, and for the past few weeks he had been laboring long hours to complete his Master's project. Neither Alse nor Jevon had dared hope for so much for their oldest. Serle was handsome and clever, a loving son and a kind brother, but he was also willful and impulsive, with an intolerance of discipline and an explosive temper that had gotten him in trouble again and again during his school years. His parents had feared he might spend his life as a wastrel, or worse, that the attention he brought upon himself might turn toward the family as a whole. But smithing, for which he had a talent, seemed to have given Serle a focus. Since his apprenticeship he had settled down considerably.

"I'll be late again tonight, Mother," he said, through mouthfuls of porridge.

Alse nodded. "I'll keep something warm for you."

Serle laid his spoon beside his empty bowl, took the packet of bread and meat his mother had prepared for his midday meal, and was gone. Jevon pushed back his chair and got to his feet, moving with care. Alse spoke quietly.

"Shall I pack up some of my cordial for you today?"

"No, no," Jevon said. "It's only a twinge. The walk will ease me."

Jevon suffered terribly from pain in his joints, which swelled and ached in spite of the liniment Alse applied each night. Like his father and grandfather and great-grandfather before him, he was a copper miner. He had been handsome once, with the reddish hair and blue eyes all the family but Bron had inherited, but his trade had taken all but the memory of it away. One side of his face was badly disfigured by a narrow escape from a mineshaft fire, and welts of scar tissue marked every part of his body, attesting to slips of the pick, falls, flying slivers of rock, and the myriad other hazards of a life spent underground. He had always been unshakably determined that none of his sons would follow him into this brutal trade, and for years had put a portion of his tiny wage aside in order to buy apprenticeships for them. For Bron, who was clever with his hands, he had purchased a weaving apprenticeship, to begin next autumn when his schooling was complete.

Alse's eyes rested on the door as it closed behind her husband. Bron could read the worry on her face as if she had spoken it aloud—which, of course, she would never do.

"Come, the rest of you," she said briskly. "Bron, Elene, and Olesin, it's time to be off to school. Annis, I'm going to take the eggs to market today. You can stay here and take care of the house."

Annis's lips curved in a small, secret smile. Bron knew she would take the chance to see her fiancé; the bread would be burnt tonight, and supper overcooked.

Alse handed out lunch packets, and Bron, Olesin, and Elene set off. Half an hour's walk brought them to the village. Greshing was the largest habitation for many miles, boasting four cobbled streets, a central square with a fountain in the middle, a Town Hall, several shops and an inn, the smithy where Serle was apprenticed, a Guardian Residence, and a Guardian School. The School, to which the Residence was attached, took up two sides of the square. Like all products of Guardian architecture it was massive, a precise assemblage of straight lines and pure angles. The unyielding symmetry of its design, dictated by Guardian law, was duplicated in thousands of other towns and villages across the world.

Bron and his brother and sister joined the procession of children trooping through the School's big double doors. Once inside, they separated: Elene and Olesin to the Babies' Class, for children between six and eight, and Bron to the Seniors' Class, for eleven- and twelve-year-olds. There was also an Intermediate Class, for children of nine and ten. Every child in the world was required to attend Guardian School three days a week, six months a year, from the age of six until the age of twelve. The Schools taught basic reading and writing and figuring, the history of the world and of the Order of Guardians, the Guardians' language, rudimentary mindskills for those who could master them, and most important, the Limits—the Guardian-authored rule of the world that, since the time of Percival, had protected mankind from the consuming evil of handpower.

Children learned of Percival in Babies' Class: how, battling the chaos and anarchy of the splitting worlds, he and his men rescued the Stone from those who held it prisoner and carried it safe into the emerging world of mindpower; how these first Guardians came to understand the true cause of the Split, and banded together to bring their wisdom to others. Today everyone knew that it was the uncontrolled pursuit of technology that had ripped the worlds apart, nearly destroying the powers of the mind in the process; a thousand years ago, however, there were few who grasped this fact. It took nearly a century, a hundred years of tireless traveling and teaching and sacrifice, for the Guardians to convey to the new world the truth they had always known.

High in their mountain Fortress, Percival and his men swore a solemn oath to the Stone. Never again would the ways of mind be threatened by the lust for technology. Never again would the pursuit of the lesser power be allowed to tear the world in two. In this new world, the proper order would be preserved: mindpower would be first, handpower a distant second. To that end, all use of tools must be rigidly bounded, vigilantly overseen—not simply to prevent the dangerous proliferation that had led to the Split, but to place a guard upon the human imagination, upon

which the way of the hands exerted a deadly pull. Thus the
Limits were born. Rhodri, Percival's kinsman and trusted
lieutenant, spent nearly forty years in their creation: twenty
thick volumes identifying and defining the boundaries
within which tools could be safely manufactured, employed,
modified, repaired, and developed. There was a section for
every tool and trade then known to humankind; there were
sections on handpower's application to life, work, thought,
government and learning; there were sections, many of
them, on methods of oversight and punishments for transgression. So comprehensive was Rhodri's work that over the
ensuing centuries few new Limits had needed to be created,
though enormous numbers of commentaries, glosses, and
interpretations had been written on nearly every phrase and
paragraph of the original volumes. In the Guardians' Fortress an entire wing was given over to a great library of
these, maintained by the Suborder of Searchers, one of the
four branches into which the Order of Guardians was divided.

Bron reached the seniors' classroom, and took his place
on one of the benches. The shutters on the long unglazed
windows stood open to the spring sunshine, admitting both
light and chill. The room was loud with the voices of children. Amid the hubbub, Bron sat alone.

The teacher entered the classroom, clapping his hands for
quiet. The gold medal of Guardianship gleamed on his
breast; around his waist he wore the green sash of the Suborder of Journeyers. If the Fortress was the heart of the
Guardian Order, the Journeyers were its body. In addition
to overseeing the orthodoxy of the populace and teaching at
the Guardian Schools, Journeyers conducted the Novice Examinations, headed the Trade Guilds, supervised trade apprenticeships and examinations and adherence to the Trade
Limitbooks, provided counsel to governments, and often became governors themselves. The map of the earth was a
patchwork of Journeyer Dioceses, each overseen by a Journeyer Orderhouse; the Dioceses were divided into Parishes,
each with a Resident Journeyer to administer it and a varying number of Ordermen to serve as assistants and teachers.
It was said, without much exaggeration, that there was

not a task in the world that did not have a Journeyer to do it.

"Stand, class," the teacher said. The students obeyed. The teacher allowed the silence to gather a little before he began the catechism that started every schoolday.

"In the beginning was the Stone. The Stone is the fount and substance of all power, the start and finish of all knowledge. The vastness of its contemplation sustains the world. In its mighty Gift all human powers have their source."

"Blessed be the Stone," the students chorused.

"In the beginning was mindpower. Mindpower is the first power, the noblest power, the power that shapes reality. Without it there is only chaos."

"Blessed be the ways of mind."

"In the beginning was a single world, ruled by the power of the mind, with the power of the hands held in thrall. So it was meant to be."

"Blessed be the original order of the world."

"But a time came in which corrupt and foolish men sought to break that ancient order, to set the ways of tools above the ways of mind. All things Gifted wither and die under the rule of tools, for the power of hands and the power of mind are the deadliest of enemies."

"Cursed be the ways of hands."

"Nor can existence sustain such alteration. So rose the Split, the tearing of the original world in two. On one side of the Split, the ways of hands ruled absolutely. On the other, the ways of mind took refuge. There did Percival bring the Stone. There did the Guardians build their Fortress, and set themselves to soothe the frightened people with news of the Stone's release."

"Blessed be the wisdom of Percival."

"In time the chaos of the Split receded. Beneath the eye of the Stone, our half-world became whole. It is now as it was in the beginning: mind rules and hand is subject, and the Stone watches over us all. So it has been for a thousand years. So it will be for a thousand more. The Split will never come again."

"Blessed be the Order of Guardians, which guides and protects against the corruption of the hands. Blessed be the holy Limits, which preserve and defend the Gifts of mind."

"Let us pray. O Great Stone, receive our thoughts, as You receive the thoughts of every living thing upon the earth." The pupils followed raggedly along, mumbling words spoken so many times before that they were little more than noise. "For this moment we join our small minds to the vastness of Your understanding, seeking to share the harmonies of existence that You both contemplate and sustain. Help us to be good citizens of this world, to guard the precious powers that are our birthright, the powers that have their source in You. Help us to resist the foul seed of weakness that lies waiting in us all, tempting us to the pursuit of tools. Help us to walk the proper path of mind, so that we may never stray into the wilderness of the hands, so that we may be Your servants and Your defenders, and this world shall endure forever. Amen."

There was a rustling of clothing and creaking of benches as the students seated themselves.

"Today Group One will concentrate on nearspeech," the teacher said. "Group Two will continue its review of agricultural Limits. Comyn Miner!"

Bron got to his feet. Comyn was the name by which the world knew him, a shield for his dangerous ancestral name.

"You'll supervise Group Two today. The lesson will be Chapter Three of the Condensed Limitbook, Limits 125 through 222. You know the ones I mean?"

"Yes, Master," Bron said, his eyes not quite meeting the teacher's. The Condensed Limitbook, extracted from the original Twenty Volumes, was the standard text of all the Schools. Bron knew it better than the teacher did, a fact of which the teacher was well aware.

"Be sure to discuss each Limit thoroughly." Though Bron had supervised Group Two a hundred times, he was always given these same instructions. "I don't want you only to know the Limits word for word, I want you to understand their meaning as it applies to your daily life, and as it contributes to your spiritual fitness. Is that clear?"

"Yes, Master."

"I'll examine you at the end of the day. Work diligently. Remember, the eye of the Stone is upon you."

The members of Group Two shuffled to their feet, turning toward the back of the room as Group One moved toward the front. The inequity of this arrangement, in which the Gifted received the warm benches near the fire and the unGifted were banished to the cold reaches at the rear of the schoolroom, was too habitual for notice. So it was, not just in the schoolroom, but in life. The best of the Gifted became Guardians, while the rest found positions of importance within the world. Anyone who owned a business or headed a Guild or acquired a position in government was either Gifted or had a Gifted family member. For the unGifted, a good trade or a secure service position was the most that could be hoped for.

Mindskill, as classified by the Guardians, fell into five basic categories. There was mindspeech, subdivided into nearspeech, farspeech, and, rarely, heartsensing; prescience, which included both recollection, the faculty of looking into the past, and true foreseeing; divination, most often manifested as neardivining, through which an object's properties could be sensed by touch, but sometimes taking the form of fardivining, the apprehension of events occurring at a distance; making, usually some combination of creative, uncreative, and transformative abilities; and transportation, the capacity to convey objects from place to place or to project force. Though any reasonably Gifted person could master a range of basic abilities, most Talents tended to concentrate within a single area of competence, and true multiple Gifts were rare. Had he been able to reveal it, the small spark of mindpower Bron owned might perhaps have been classified as a making Gift. But for the thousand years of their exile the family had kept their power, like their heritage, hidden— not simply because of the need to protect their secret, but because the kind of barriers their power sustained, capable of eluding even Guardian mindprobes, were illegal. From earliest childhood Bron had been classified with the mass of the unGifted, relegated to Group Two. He possessed a quicker intellect than most, however, and was often called to supervise his fellows, sparing the teacher to work with the mindskilled. In this, his final year, it had become almost a daily occurrence.

Group Two finished assembling at the back of the classroom: fifty-three of them, out of a class of sixty-five.

"All right," Bron said, launching into a routine so familiar he could follow it with only a quarter of his attention. "Before we begin, I want someone to tell me what Chapter Three of the Condensed Limitbook is about. You, Erda."

"Farming tools," Erda said tonelessly. Her face was closed and sullen; already, she was numb with boredom.

"And now you tell me, Masrich, what Limits 125 through 222 deal with."

"Hoes and rakes and hand tools," Masrich singsonged.

"Right. Now, who can recite Limit 125? Johan. I know you know this, we did it just a few weeks ago."

"Uh . . . 'He who makes a hoe shall, shall take a handle no longer than, than . . . ' " Johan trailed off, his face blank.

"Than fifteen handspans," Bron prompted.

" 'Than fifteen handspans, that shall be made of good oak or ashwood, and he shall obtain, shall obtain . . . ' Oh, it's no use. I don't remember the rest. It's something about the metal part."

Bron resisted the impulse to sigh. "Avelein, you finish it."

" 'And he shall obtain a forged tongue from a blacksmith who forges according to the Limitbook of his Guild, and he shall affix the tongue to the handle with rivets of good iron, as many rivets as shall be needed to hold the tongue firm.' "

"Good. Since you did so well, you can give me the next one."

" 'He who uses the hoe shall use it according to need.' " The words slid smoothly off Avelein's tongue, memorized by rote without thought to their meaning. " 'He shall use it in order to cultivate crops, or to weed the fields and other areas of cultivation . . . ' "

And so it went for the rest of the day, Limit by Limit, through the entire range of agricultural hand tools, progressing from their proper construction through their proper use, proper storage, proper repair, and proper replacement. All of this was easy for Bron, who from the age of eight had known by heart every word of the Condensed Limitbook. It was far less easy for his classmates, who stumbled and paused and searched vainly for the correct phrasing. In their boredom, however, they were united—and in their dislike. Bron was well aware that his superior intelligence was mistrusted. The students considered it a sign of sycophancy, the teachers an indication of instability. For as long as he could remember he had moved within a shell of isolation, without friends or companions other than his brothers and sisters. It was a situation that suited him very well. What need had he, with his thousand-year heritage, of the ordinary people among whom he was forced to live?

In public, of course, he never let himself think of this, nor considered the irony in the teachers' choice of him to instruct his fellows in Guardian law. Only in the privacy of his home, in the dying firelight, when the barriers fell and the Tale was told, did he allow his hereditary hatred to take its rightful place within his soul. Only then did he passionately reject all he had been taught and taught in his turn. Only then did he feel the rage of his subjugation to Guardian rules, Guardian teaching, Guardian Limits.

The afternoon dragged to a close. The Prayer to the Stone was repeated to end the day, and the children streamed out of school, jubilant with release. Bron waited by the steps for Olesin and Elene. Like Bron, they were marked with separateness; Olesin, slight and delicate, had been bullied at first, but was left alone after it became clear that Elene would beat senseless anyone who threatened him. In this she took after Serle, who had defended Bron in a similar fashion.

The three children set off for home. Bron walked in front, his mind far away; Elene and Olesin tagged behind, arguing in short but intense bursts. Gradually it penetrated Bron's consciousness that Olesin was calling after him. He turned, impatiently.

"What is it?"

"My foot." Olesin's fine features were puckered with pain. "I have a blister. Can you carry me?"

Bron sighed. "All right. Come on."

He stooped so that his brother could climb onto his back, and set off again down the track. Elene trotted alongside.

"Why are you carrying him?" she demanded. "I get blisters too, but no one carries me. It's not fair."

Bron ignored her; she fell silent after a while, and began to dawdle, falling further and further behind. Olesin tightened his arms around Bron's neck and leaned his chin on Bron's shoulder. Bron could not see his face, but he had no doubt it wore a smug expression.

"I heard a story in school today, Brother," he said. All the family called Bron this, to avoid the possibility of speaking his true name in public.

"Did you?" Bron asked, without interest.

"A girl in our class told about her cousin, who went on pilgrimage to the Fortress to ask the Stone a question. It took him a whole year to get there, and he nearly died from getting caught in an avalanche. Then he had to come all the way back, and that took another year. I just wondered . . . why do people have to go all the way to the Fortress to ask a question? Couldn't they ask a Guardian instead?"

"Some questions can only be answered by the Stone."

"But couldn't you tell your question to a Guardian, and he could farspeak it to the Fortress, and they could find out the answer, and then they could farspeak it back?"

"No. You have to go to the Fortress. You have to stand before the Stone. Those are the rules."

"Oh." Olesin was quiet for a little while, his arms hanging loose across Bron's chest. In spite of his slightness he was heavy; Bron's back was beginning to ache.

"Brother."

"What is it now?"

"When we get the Stone back, and live in a great palace again, will people come to ask us questions?"

Bron jerked to a halt. He swung Olesin off his back and grasped him by the shoulders.

"Are your barriers down?" he demanded, glaring into his brother's startled eyes.

"I . . . I don't know," Olesin stammered.

"They *are* down." As Bron's own barriers were down; they had flashed open the moment the question was asked.

"What did Mother teach you about barriers? What did she teach you, Olesin?"

Olesin's lips had begun to tremble. "Never . . . never to let them down, unless the family is alone or the Tale is being told. But we *are* alone, Brother! There's no one here but us!"

"How do you know? How do you know there isn't a Guardian around the next bend? The only time we can be sure we're alone, absolutely sure, is when we're all together in our house. I thought you understood these things, Olesin!"

Tears overflowed. "I'm sorry."

"Outside our house, your barriers must be up, every minute of every day, for your entire life. Otherwise"—Bron looked into his brother's face with all the sternness he could muster—"otherwise the Guardians will surely find us. They'll see what's in our minds. They'll discover the secret of our ancestry. And do you know what will happen then? Do you?"

"They'll . . . they'll kill us."

"That's right. Exactly the way they killed our Ancestor. And they'll torture us first. Is that what you want?"

"No-o-o," Olesin sobbed. "Oh, Brother, I'm sorry, I didn't mean to do it! Please don't tell, please don't!"

In spite of himself, Bron was moved by his brother's distress. "Stop crying, you'll make yourself sick. I won't tell, if you swear not to do it again."

"I swear, Brother. I swear, I promise."

"Good." Bron used the hem of his shirt to wipe Olesin's cheeks. "Now put your barriers up. And keep them up this time."

Elene had dawdled her way up to them. She looked at Olesin's tearstained face and opened her mouth to make a remark; Bron shot her a look that stopped the words unspoken. He swung his brother up onto his back again, building up his own barriers once more as he walked.

When they reached the house Annis was nowhere to be seen, as Bron had expected, but at least he was in time to save the stew from burning. She returned a little while later, her face flushed and secret. It was not worthwhile to say anything. Bron accepted the smile she gave him as she began to lay the table for supper.

As he had promised, Serle did not return until late. Elene and Olesin were long asleep when he burst into the house, bearing a wrapped bundle in his arms. He carried it over to the table and set it down. Alse, Bron, and Annis gathered round the table as Serle began to pull aside layers of cloth. Jevon, in his chair by the fire, hot poultices on his knees, turned and watched.

"This is what I've been working on all these late nights," Serle said, breathlessly. "It's for you, Mother."

"I thought you were working on your Master's project." Alse's brows were creased.

"I am. But I wanted to give you something, now that spring is coming." Serle looked into his mother's face. "You never complain, but I've seen how hard it's been for you the last few years, turning over the earth for the crops. And so I thought of a way to make it easier." He pulled aside a final wrapping. "What do you think?"

It lay on the table, new metal covered with a light sheen of oil: a plow head. It was a forged plow, just like every other plow Bron had ever seen, except for one thing: it had two blades.

The heat of the fire was at his back, but Bron felt suddenly cold. Beside him, Annis had stiffened. Jevon, in his comfortable chair, was as still as if he had turned to stone.

"What is this?" Alse's voice was hushed.

"A plow." Serle's face was bright with pride. He seemed entirely oblivious to his family's reaction. "But not just any plow. The two blades will do the work in half the time— and because it's heavier it'll turn the earth deeper."

Jevon rose painfully to his feet, his compresses falling unheeded to the floor. "What about the Limits?"

Serle looked at him. "Do you think I don't know my trade? There's nothing in the Guild Limitbook that proscribes two-bladed plows."

"Do you have a Journeyer-approved plan for this plow?" Alse's eyes were steady on Serle's face.

"It can take years to get Journeyer approval, Mother. You

need this plow now, not five years from now!''

"How could he have a plan, Alse?" Jevon said. "You know as well as I do that only a licensed Modifier can submit plans for approval."

Serle made an impatient gesture. "I don't need a Modifier for this. It's not a different blade, just two approved blades forged together. People make changes like this all the time. Remember that cupboard you built, with drawers that tip out instead of sliding on runners? Or the hoe, with the carved grip to make it easier to hold?"

"My cupboard was still a cupboard when I was done, and so was my hoe. But this thing . . . this thing is no longer just a plow. It's something else, something no one has ever thought of before. I'm no Journeyer, and still I can see that."

There was a silence. Serle's gaze was locked with his father's. Between them on the table the plow gleamed dully in the firelight. Bron watched it as he might a dangerous animal, halfway between awe and horror. He sensed, instinctively, the rightness of what his father had said; yet there was a strange power to the object, a deadly fascination. He had to put his hands behind his back, so strong was the urge to touch it.

"It can never be used," Jevon declared. There was utter finality in his voice.

"What are you talking about?" cried Serle. "Do you think I made it just to sit on a shelf somewhere?"

"A shelf? You must destroy it entirely. It's an abomination. A crime."

"You're not a blacksmith." Serle's face was flushed. The muscles of his neck and shoulders were bunched with anger. "You know nothing about forging or the Limits that govern it. I tell you, this plow does not violate any specific Limits—"

"It's not just the specific Limits, it's the intent of the Limits, their spirit and their purpose, and well you know it!"

"What do I care for spirit and purpose? The letter of the law is all that counts—isn't that what we're always told? All I've done is to read between the lines—people do the same thing every day, just to survive. Who uses an ax just for chopping wood? Who uses a spade just for turning earth? Look at the world, Father. Look at the suffering in it. Can you blame me for wanting to make things better, if only just for Mother?''

"You can't say white is black and make it so!'' Jevon was shouting now. "The ways of the world don't change just because you want them to, you impulsive, thoughtless boy! All the world must live by the Limits. Especially, *we* must live by the Limits. You've jeopardized us all by your heedless actions! It is inexcusable!''

"Be silent, both of you!'' It was Alse, her voice clear and cutting. "You'll wake Elene and Olesin. I don't want to have to trust them to keep this hidden.'' She looked at Serle. "Who else knows about this thing?''

He breathed deeply, trying to calm himself. "No one. I wanted it to be a surprise.''

"Not even your Master?''

"No. I worked on it after he had left for the day.''

"No apprentices? No curious passers-by?''

"No one, I tell you! I made sure it was secret.'' Suddenly Serle's anger was gone, like water slipping through cupped fingers. Bron knew his brother. He saw that in his heart Serle had known what he was doing. Yet because he wanted so much to make this thing, he had ignored his own understanding. Bron watched the changes that passed across his brother's features as Serle faced, for the first time, the danger his actions had brought his family.

"Good,'' said Alse. "Only we five know this thing exists. We must keep it that way.''

"I can melt it down again,'' Serle said. His voice was subdued.

"No. I don't want it to leave the house, it's too dangerous.'' She was silent for a moment, thinking; the family waited, as they always did in a crisis, for Alse to find a solution. "We'll bury it in the pigpen. No one will think of digging there.'' She began to replace the cloth wrappings. "Jevon, you stay by the fire and watch Olesin and Elene. Brother and Annis and Serle, come with me. We'll all dig.''

And dig they did, under a moonless sky, not daring to

use even a candle for illumination. With the pigs snorting around them and the night air sharp against their skins, they burrowed down through the foul muck of the pen to a depth greater than Serle's height, and dropped the plow into the darkness of the earth. It thudded when it hit bottom, more a feeling than a sound, as if it were far heavier than its actual weight. For a moment they stood still, staring into the flat blackness of the hole; then they filled it in again. Exhausted, they left the pen and cleaned themselves at the well. By morning, the trampling of the pigs would have hidden the signs of their activity.

Inside the house, Serle looked at Alse. His eyes were full of tears. "Mother, I'm sorry," he said. "I'm truly sorry. It's just . . . it's just that I wanted . . ."

Alse held out her arms. Serle bowed his head onto her shoulder. She gripped him tightly. "I know. I know you meant no harm. But—" She took his head between her hands and lifted it so she could look into his eyes. "I've told you so often, you must think before you act. We all must. More than anything in this world, our safety depends on that."

She kissed his forehead, and let him go. He turned toward Jevon. "Father . . ."

Jevon had gotten to his feet again. He put his hand on Serle's arm. "It's as your mother said. We'll never speak of it again."

Bron's mother held out her hands. "We can learn from this. The dangers we face are not only outside us. We must keep the habit of vigilance as we keep the habit of breathing."

The family formed a circle before the hearth, the shadows of the dying fire moving upon their faces. Linked, they began the process of packing what had happened tonight away behind their barriers, where, with the Tale, it would reside forever in perfect secrecy.

They sought their beds. Bron's eyes remained open long after Serle had begun to snore softly beside him. He did not close them until after the moon had set, and the sky was paling in warning of the coming day.

T*wo*

SPRING CAME all at once, in a burst of warmth and rain. In Alse's herb garden, thyme and lavender and rosemary put forth new leaves; along the road to school pale primroses and dark violets bloomed. Alse plowed up her hereditary strip of land in the village's communal fields, using the plow she had always used. The family did not allow itself to think how much more easily Serle's two blades would have turned the furrows, or how much deeper they would have cut the earth.

One afternoon in School, there was the sound of harness in the village square. One of the bolder pupils looked out, ignoring the teacher's admonition. When he turned back to the classroom, his face was pale.

"The Arm of the Stone," he said.

"Roundheads!" The whisper swept the classroom. The students abandoned their benches and pressed against the windowsills, crowding each other, craning their necks to see. Even the teacher left his dais, looking out over his pupils' heads.

A group of six men on horseback had halted in the center of the square. Their robes were not the usual Guardian gray, but black; scarlet sashes bound their waists. Other Guardians let their hair grow long, but these men wore theirs in a merciless crop close to their heads, giving them a severe and ascetic look. A small area of emptiness had opened around them, an invisible barrier that no one seemed willing to cross. The villagers kept their eyes upon the ground and their heads turned away, as if the six men did not exist. A change in the activity of the square, however, could clearly be seen. People hurried to enter their houses, vanished into shops, turned abruptly down side streets.

"Who do you think they've come for?" a girl next to Bron asked, her voice hushed, as if the men outside might hear.

"Not us," her companion replied in a whisper. "We keep the Limits in our house."

Bron could hear the beating of his heart, a slow percussion like heavy footsteps. The Arm of the Stone. Enforcers of the Limits, apprehenders and punishers of those who strayed from the path of orthodoxy: Violation's grim shadow, a dark wind sweeping across the earth and scouring it clean of wrongdoing. Their authority was absolute, their judgments final, their punishments terrible. No men in the world were more hated. No men in the world were so feared.

The square was empty now except for the six riders, waiting at its center like a hole in the sunlit day. At last the door to the Guardian Residence swung open. The Resident Journeyer hurried out, accompanied by his deputies. His usual haughty manner was absent; his deputies, behind him, were pale and nervous. Even other Guardians feared those who wore the red sash.

The teacher clapped his hands. "That's enough, class," he said. "Return to your seats."

Reluctantly, still murmuring, the students obeyed.

"Is it a Raid, Master?" someone asked.

"No, I don't think so." Usually, Roundheads appeared only where there had been a complaint or accusation of Violation; but sometimes they descended without being summoned, turning an entire town or village inside out in a comprehensive and cautionary search for Violation. "There would be Soldiers with them if it were."

"Why have they come, then?" asked another voice, fearfully.

"The Arm of the Stone does not send advance notice of its intentions," said the teacher sharply. "If you've kept the Limits, you've nothing to worry about."

The rest of the afternoon passed like a lifetime. Bron forced himself to stillness, mimicking a composure he did not feel. Behind his barriers secrets stirred, like fire below the surface of the earth. When at last school let out he collected Elene and Olesin and, gripping their hands, struck off swiftly along the road for home. They complained and protested, but he did not slacken his pace. At last the house came in sight.

"Brother!" Elene pulled to a halt. "Brother, look!"

Bron felt as if he had been plunged into freezing water. It was so exactly what he had feared that it did not seem real: three horses in red Roundhead harness, tethered in front of the house.

"Brother." It was Olesin, his voice very small. "Why are they here? Brother?"

Bron did not reply. He began to walk again. Elene tried to plant her feet on the packed surface of the road.

"I don't want to go in. I'm scared. Let's go back to town."

Bron ignored her. She began to struggle; he had to drag her behind him like baggage.

The house, when they reached it, was empty. The fire burned on the stone hearth, and a fowl was spitted, ready for roasting. A heap of turnips lay on the table, some of them peeled, a knife lying beside them as if it had been dropped in haste. The Roundheads could not have taken his family away; their horses were still here. Since they were not in the front, or in the house, they must be in the back. In the back, by the pigpen.

"You're hurting me," Olesin said timidly.

With an effort, Bron relaxed his grip. He pushed his brother and sister toward the table. "Wait for me here," he told them. "Don't move. Understand?"

They nodded in unison, side by side on the bench, their eyes as round as owls'.

Bron approached the back door. Fear lay like lead along his limbs. Deeply, he wished not to face what lay outside. But it was not in him simply to wait, like Elene and Olesin, for it to come to him. There was at least a chance he was wrong, a possibility that they were here for some other reason . . .

But when he emerged from the barn, it was exactly as he

had known it would be. The three black-robed Roundheads stood ankle-deep in the muck of the pigpen. Their eyes were closed, their features set in lines of concentration. Bron knew at once that he was witnessing mindpower on a scale he had never encountered before. This was nothing like the nearspeech his teacher practiced, or the acts of making the Resident Journeyer could perform. These men knew precisely what they were looking for, exactly where it was. He could almost sense the magnitude of the force they were creating through the power of their minds; he could almost feel it as it reached into the earth, piercing the soil more strongly than any spade, more skillfully than the most practiced hand.

Alse and Annis were standing close together outside the pen. Alse's face was stark and white; Annis was weeping, her beautiful hair disheveled down her back. Bron reached them. He touched his mother's shoulder. Immediately she turned to him, taking his arm in a convulsive grip.

The ground at the Roundheads' feet began to undulate. Clods of dirt shot up, striking their clothing. Something was visible now amid the churning earth: Serle's plow. It rose slowly upward, shedding soil in a dark fountain. The dull light of the afternoon ran like liquid along the two betraying blades.

In that moment, Bron understood that the world had come to an end. He stared numbly at what the Roundheads had resurrected from the muck. Beside him, Alse and Annis were as stiff and silent as women carved from wood.

The Roundheads withdrew their power. The plow fell, landing with a thud on the now-solid ground. They turned, and faced Alse and her children.

"Who made this?" said one of them, a tall man with blunt, weathered features and gray-blond hair. He did not speak in Guardian-language, but in the local vernacular.

Annis sobbed. Alse was silent. Her grip on Bron's arm was like a vise.

"Aren't you tired of this pretense?" the Roundhead said. "Your reactions have made your complicity clear."

Still Alse did not speak.

"Your cooperation would make things easier." The

Roundhead's face was like flint. "But I can assure you that your silence won't inconvenience us. We already know everything."

Alse met his gaze. She took a breath. "Then there's nothing I need to say."

The Roundhead looked at her for a moment longer, and then shrugged. He turned to his companions.

"This is pointless," he said in Guardian language. "Let us not prolong it."

Leaving the plow where it had fallen, they left the pigpen, the muck falling from their clothing and boots as they walked. As the leader passed, Bron looked into his hard and arrogant face. A sudden, irresistible surge of hatred shook him. As if in response, the man's head turned. Their gazes met. The leader's eyes were a very pale blue, with a dark ring around the iris. There was a deep coldness in them; it reached out to Bron, an icy finger that probed and then withdrew. For a moment Bron was paralyzed, a chill immobility that did not fade till the Roundhead was well past.

Bron looked at his mother, at her white and ravaged face. "What happened? How did they find out?"

Alse shook her head. "I don't know. Serle must have been wrong about someone seeing him—they knew all about the plow. I pretended to be ignorant, but it didn't take them more than five minutes to sense it for themselves, even down so far in the earth."

"What will they do now?" whispered Annis. She was trembling, her eyes huge.

Alse did not reply. "Where are Elene and Olesin?" she asked.

"Inside."

In the house, Elene and Olesin still sat obediently on the bench. When they saw Alse they ran to her, weeping and clutching at her skirts. Alse knelt and put her arms around them.

"Mother, why are the Roundheads here?" sobbed Elene.

"Shh, darling. It'll be over soon, you'll see."

"It's my fault, it's all my fault!" Olesin wept, his face hidden against Alse's neck. "But I didn't mean to let my barriers down, I didn't mean to!"

Also took his shoulders and held him a little away from her. "What are you talking about, Olesin?"

He turned his tearstained face toward Bron. "Brother knows."

"What does he mean, Brother?" Alse's voice was brittle.

"It happened about a month ago, when we were coming home from school," Bron answered reluctantly. "No one was there but us. I'm sure it was safe."

"And you didn't tell me about it?"

"I promised him I wouldn't," said Bron, defensive now. "He swore not to do it again. Mother, it couldn't be Olesin. He didn't know about the plow."

Alse drew breath to speak, but whatever she intended to say was never uttered. They all heard it: the jingle of harness, the thud of hooves. The front door flew open, slamming against the wall. The Roundhead leader blocked the light.

"Come out, all of you," he commanded. "I want you to see this."

The family obeyed. Three Roundheads waited before the house, holding their restive horses on tight reins. Before them, a rope tied leashlike around his neck, was Serle. His face was flushed, marked with dirt and sweat; one cheek was puffy and beginning to purple into a bruise. Alse cried out as if she had been struck, pressing her hands to her mouth.

The two remaining Roundheads appeared around the corner of the house, the plow floating unsupported between them. Serle's eyes went to it. Bron could see the muscles tense in his neck and shoulders.

"Boy." It was the Roundhead leader. "In the name of the Stone, tell us the truth. Did you make this?"

Serle raised his eyes to the Roundhead's face. There was defiance in the set of his mouth. He nodded.

"Alone? Or with assistance?"

"Alone." Serle's voice was hoarse.

"Who else knows of it?"

"No one." Serle's eyes flashed towards Alse, and then away. "My family knows nothing about it. I bear all the blame."

"It is buried in your family's pigpen."

"Once I made it, I knew it was too dangerous to use. So I buried it where no one would find it. I did it in secret, in the middle of the night. No one saw. My family knows nothing. I swear it."

There was a silence. The mounted Roundheads looked on. Their cold unblinking eyes held contempt, but no interest, as if they had seen this so many times it no longer engaged their attention. Behind him, Bron felt Annis trembling. Alse stood like a statue, her hands still pressed to her mouth.

"You are liars, all of you," said the Roundhead leader. "We are the Arm of the Stone; you can hide nothing from us." He leaned forward, speaking into Serle's face. "Nothing."

Try as he would, Serle could not withstand the Roundhead's gaze. He dropped his eyes. In his brother's face, Bron saw the knowledge of defeat.

The Roundhead leader turned to the rest of the family.

"This boy will be held until we have decided on an appropriate sentence. All of you will be questioned. Unless we summon you or give you permission, you will not leave your house, neither for work nor school nor market nor any other reason. We will be watching. We will know if you violate this order."

He looked at them, his eyes passing over each in turn. Bron felt himself shaking. He refused to turn away from that harsh gaze; he alone of his family would withstand this man's regard. Deep within him the ancestral rage strained against the barriers that held it back. The Roundhead's pale eyes paused. Once again the icy finger reached out. With a supreme effort Bron made his mind blank. After a moment the Roundhead turned away.

"You will carry this thing you have made," he said to Serle.

He gestured to his companions. Serle stooped and took up the plow, his muscles straining against its weight. The Roundheads wheeled their mounts and rode off down the road, drawing Serle behind them, his neck constricted by the rope. He looked back once. His face was white, his eyes wild.

"Serle!" Alse cried out. Bron had never heard a cry like that. It sounded as if something within her were tearing apart. She fell to her knees, weeping with an abandon such as Bron had never seen. Terrified, he tried to put his arms around her, but she pulled away and stumbled into the house. Annis ran after her, followed by Elene and Olesin. Bron heard them inside the house, a dreadful chorus of weeping, Elene's howls escalating above the others. Unable to bear it, he turned and ran, plunging into the pine forest that rose at the boundary of his family's land.

He raced between the tall trunks, his feet soundless on the carpet of needles. When he could run no more he collapsed and, lying where he had fallen, gave way at last to tears. He let his barriers drop, surrendering to the hatred that waited behind them. The features of the Roundhead leader rose up inside his mind. He wanted to strike the arrogance off that face, to extinguish the light of those cold, cold eyes. He wanted to rip and claw until there was nothing left, until all trace of his brother's transgression was torn away.

At last, a long time later, he hauled himself upright and set his back against a tree. The violence of his emotion had exhausted him, leaving him drained and strangely calm. His mind turned to what lay ahead for his brother. The Roundheads would imprison him in the Town Hall; over the next few days they would question him, probably with the assistance of torture. When his confession was judged complete, a mindprobe would be used to verify the truthfulness of his declarations. Guilt ascertained, Serle would be punished: a public lashing and, if he survived, confinement to a House of Reeducation, for a term dependant upon the severity of the crime. There were terrible rumors about these Houses, in which, it was said, the Arm of the Stone washed clean the minds of Violators and refilled them with thoughts that did not offend the Limits.

Would Serle be able to withstand the probe? The family's defenses were cunningly shaped to the natural structures of the mind, designed not merely to resist Guardian power but to be invisible to it. They had met and passed this test many times over the centuries, but every individual was different. There was always a chance Serle would not be able to hold firm. If the Roundheads did find Serle's barriers, they would break them, opening Serle's mind like an oyster, from which the pearl of the family's ancestry could then be easily plucked. Exposed, they would all be arrested and put to death.

Anger shook Bron again, focused this time on his brother. Serle understood the Limits, knew the dangers, as well as any of them. How could he have lost sight, even for a moment, of what was at stake? In all the world, there were no others of their line. If they died, the Tale would end, and it would be the Guardians, not the promised One, who put the finish to it.

But the memory of Serle, his cheek bruised, his neck corded against the rope, rose in Bron's mind. His anger dropped away, leaving an aching void behind. His brother was lost; whatever came next, that much was certain. In the space of a single afternoon, the world had turned on its head—every certainty erased, every expectation shattered. Bron thought of the Roundheads, arriving only that morning, and was astonished. It felt as if a lifetime had passed since then.

He sat in the woods as the sun sank lower, as the air beneath the pines grew chill. At last, wearily, he got to his feet and returned to the house. He found the family gathered around the fire. Jevon was in his armchair, Annis huddled by the hearth. Alse sat straight-backed on a bench, with Elene and Olesin on either side. The coals had burned low; shadows slid up the walls and chased about the room.

"Brother." Alse turned her face toward him as he entered. "Where have you been?"

"In the woods," he said. He went to sit near her on the bench. She reached out and touched his hand lightly. Then she turned to the others.

"Now we're all here, we must talk about what to do."

"What can we do?" Annis's voice was dull. She sat slumped on her stool, her arms wrapped around her knees.

"We must have a credible story to tell the Roundheads when they question us."

"We must tell them the truth, Alse," said Jevon. "What

else can we do? They already know everything. What we did that night . . . who we are.''

"They know about Serle and the plow. They don't know about *us*.''

Jevon shook his head wearily. "If they don't now, they soon will.''

"No!'' Alse leaned forward. "Our barriers weren't made just so a passing Guardian will miss our secret. They're capable of withstanding probes—as long as we're strong and do not falter. That's how I was taught, and what I've taught in my turn.''

Annis looked at her mother. Her face was still puffy from weeping. "What if Serle falters?''

"He won't, Annis.''

"How do you know?'' Annis's voice scaled upwards. "He's weak. What he did is proof of that. How can you be sure he won't betray us again?''

Alse's lips tightened. "Your brother will protect us to his last breath. I know that as I know myself.''

"You should have let him melt that . . . object down. Then they wouldn't have found it.''

"A thing like that can't be unmade. They would have seen its shape even in the formless metal.''

"Oh, what's the use?'' Annis's voice was dull again. She stared into the fire. "Our lives are ruined. Who will marry the sister of a Violator? Who will take a Violator's brother as apprentice? Who will buy eggs and vegetables from a Violator's family? Even if we survive, we might as well be dead.''

Alse rose from the bench and crossed to the hearth, all in one swift motion. She gripped Annis's shoulders and shook her, hard. "Is that all you can think about, you selfish girl? Don't you know there's more at stake here than your marriage or Brother's apprenticeship or our family's social status?''

"Leave her alone, Alse.'' Bron could see the pain in his father's face. "She doesn't know what she's saying.''

Alse turned toward him, her expression fierce in the dying firelight. "If we're to survive, Jevon, we can't be so trivial-minded. That's all that matters now—surviving. No matter

what it costs, no matter what we lose. It's our duty to the
line. You know I'm right. You know it."

For a moment they stared at each other. Bron saw the
struggle in his father's face. His father was not of the line
by blood, though by being allowed to hear the Tale he had
adopted it as his own. Not every husband, not every wife,
was so honored.

"Yes, Alse, I know it," he said at last. "But it's harder
for me than it is for you."

Alse let go of Annis and went to him. She took his hands.
"I know, my dear," she said. Gently she adjusted the compresses that lay across his knees. Then she resumed her
place on the bench, putting her arms around Elene and Olesin again.

"Now." Her voice was firm. "This is what we'll do.
We'll take the plow from behind our barriers and place it
in the front of our minds. When the Roundheads question
us, we'll tell them the truth, leaving nothing out. They'll
recognize it as the truth; maybe they won't probe us. But if
they do, we'll hold our barriers—no matter how hard it is,
no matter how painful. No matter what happens to us, or
. . . or to Serle." She paused and took a breath. "I won't
pretend that we won't suffer. The Roundheads will certainly
punish us. But if we're strong, when they leave Greshing
they'll be as ignorant of our true heritage as they were when
they came." She looked slowly around the firelit faces of
her family, each in turn. "Annis. Do you understand?"

Annis nodded, still staring into the fire.

"Look at me, Annis. Answer me. Can you do it? Can
you hold firm?"

Slowly Annis turned to meet her mother's gaze. "Yes,
Mother," she said. "I can."

Alse looked down at Elene and Olesin, who were gazing
up at her. "Don't be afraid, my little ones. Just tell the truth.
If the Roundheads reach inside your minds, all they'll see
is what good children you are. Because you'll hold your
barriers, won't you?"

"I will, Mother," Elene said.

"My barriers will be the strongest," said Olesin.

Alse touched his cheek, smiling a little. Then she turned to Bron.

"You did wrong, you know, not to tell me about Olesin's mistake."

"I know, Mother." Bron dropped his eyes. "It wasn't Olesin, though. I know that for certain."

"I know it too." She sighed. "You're strong, Brother—I think you may be the strongest of us all. I have no fear for your barriers. But you have so much anger in you. For all our sakes, you must be more careful than you were today. I saw how you met that Roundhead's gaze. You mustn't do anything like that again. Never, never let them see what you really feel."

Bron looked into her face, so like his own. Of all the family, only he had inherited the long dark eyes, the aquiline features, the straight black hair. "I understand, Mother. I won't betray us. I swear it."

"Good. Everything is settled, then." Alse took a deep breath and closed her eyes for a moment. When she opened them, they were full of tears. "I will tell the Tale now," she said, her voice thick. "For Serle."

The family sat spellbound in the firelight, as Alse spoke the words that told them who they were. As the Tale took shape within their minds, they knew it as a thing greater than themselves. They knew themselves as vessels, to keep it safe, to pass it on. It was the Tale's survival, not their own, that mattered.

On his way to his hayloft bed, Bron looked back at his mother. She was on her knees at the hearth, banking the fire. She moved as she always had, looked as she always did. He could only imagine what it cost her to be so strong.

The Guardians came for Jevon first. Alse went pale when they spoke his name; she was tense and silent until they brought him back, hours later. His face was drawn; he moved slowly to his chair by the fire, where he sat staring into the flames for a long time while Alse fussed around him, putting poultices on his knees and feet, bringing him warmed ale.

"It's all right," he said at last. "They didn't harm me. My barriers held."

Alse put her hand to her eyes for a moment.

"I did what we planned—I told the truth." Jevon shuddered. "They probed me anyway. I hope I never feel anything like that again as long as I live."

"Did they say anything . . . anything about Serle?"

"Only that it was another apprentice who reported him— jealous of his Master's project, stealing back at night to spy on him. I asked about his health, whether he needed food or clothing, but they wouldn't tell me. They have no pity, Alse. None at all."

Over the next four days the Roundheads interrogated each member of the family in turn. Annis was taken next, and then Alse. They were white and shaken when they came back, but like Jevon, their barriers had held. Elene and Olesin were taken together; Alse paced about the house till they returned, unable to hide her fear. But they were not probed at all, perhaps because of their youth, only questioned.

Bron was the last to be summoned. The Roundhead who came to fetch him hauled him up behind the saddle like a sack of flour, setting off without bothering to check whether he had secured his seat. Jolting uncomfortably on the horse's flanks, Bron was grateful for the need to concentrate on keeping his balance. The image of the Roundhead leader's ice-blue eyes rose up in his mind every now and then, catching his breath.

As they rode into the village, Bron was conscious of being watched: eyes peered from chinks in shuttered windows, and a few doors opened, just a little, as they passed. The Roundheads, quartered in the Guardian Residence, had taken over the Town Hall as their headquarters. Bron was ushered into a small room furnished only by a table with a chair behind it, and told to wait. As the minutes slipped by it became harder and harder to maintain a façade of calm.

At last the key turned in the lock. The Roundhead leader entered. He seated himself in the chair and regarded Bron with his strange pale eyes.

"Comyn, isn't it?" he said.

"Yes, Master," Bron replied. He was having difficulty

getting his breath. On the way here he had held Alse's admonishment in his mind like a talisman. Now that he stood beneath the Roundhead's gaze, he could not imagine how he had ever found the strength to look at this man and feel anything but fear.

"I see here"—the Roundhead consulted a sheet of parchment—"that you are twelve years old, apprenticed to a weaver in the next town."

"Yes, Master."

The Roundhead put the parchment down on the table and leaned back in his chair. "I want you to tell me the story of your brother's Violation, just as you remember it. Start with the first time you found out about his . . . project, or suspected it. And be honest. I'll know if you're not."

Bron had to pause a moment to reorient himself. He had expected interrogation, not conversation. It was tremendously difficult to speak unprompted into the Roundhead's attentive face; questions, however harsh, would have been easier. He could not keep his voice from shaking, or his tongue from stumbling over the words.

When he finished the Roundhead sat silent for a moment, an unreadable expression upon his blunt features. One hand toyed with the medal on his chest. It hung from an intricately worked rope of gold, much heavier than the chain the Journeyers wore. The Roundhead's attire was altogether richer than that of an ordinary Guardian. His black robe, with its square neck and pleated front, was not broadcloth but fine-patterned brocade; the black shirt he wore beneath was made of some soft lustrous material, and the red belt that bound his waist was leather rather than fabric. His manicured fingers were heavily ringed, and jeweled studs were set into his earlobes.

"Your story matches the others'," he said at last. "In fact, your stories match so perfectly I would suspect collusion, if the probes had not shown the truth of what you say."

Bron was not sure whether he was expected to reply. Silence seemed safer.

"You're an interesting boy." The Roundhead's pale eyes were still fixed to Bron's face. "You take great pains to hide your hatred of us. Even so, I sensed your feelings very strongly the day we came for your brother."

Bron stared at the man, like a rabbit before a predator, afraid to move even his eyes.

"Don't worry," the Roundhead said. "If we arrested everyone who felt as you do the world would contain only the Arm of the Stone. It's not your emotions that interest me, in any case, but your ability to project them. I don't know if you know this, but projection is one sign of an untutored Gift."

Bron shook his head. "I have no mindpower ability, Master."

"So I've been told. But mistakes can be made."

"The teachers tested me, Master."

The Roundhead made an impatient gesture, his rings glittering. "Resident Ordermen are not the most highly skilled among us. Their approach can be crude. Sometimes the Gift needs a more delicate touch."

"Master, truly, I have no Gift—"

"Enough." The Roundhead got to his feet and came around the table. "I will probe you now."

Bron stepped back, unable to stop himself. The Roundhead followed, swiftly, his hands reaching out. Bron felt his head caught in a firm grip. The Roundhead bent down, his face only inches from Bron's own. His touch was not chilly, as Bron had expected, but his eyes were glacial. Bron felt a rising pressure at the outskirts of his mind. The world seemed to drop away. He was tumbling down an ice-blue tunnel, falling as if firm ground were gone forever. A freezing wind swept through his mind, shuffling his thoughts like dry leaves, careless of where they fell. . . .

Abruptly, the Roundhead's grip was gone. Bron staggered a little, the returning world flooding painfully across his senses. He was cold, as if the frigid wind were still inside him.

The Roundhead had already resumed his seat. "I was right," he said. "You do have the Gift. I saw the spark of it inside your mind just now."

Bron felt his breath stop.

"You have very strong inhibitions. That could be why it

hasn't shown itself clearly yet. But it's there. You must stand for the Novice Examinations when you finish school."

"Wh—what?"

"You're surprised." The Roundhead smiled, a motion of his lips that did little to warm his face. "You think that because of what your brother did we would not want you. Or perhaps that your feelings about us would make it impossible for you to join us. Well, that's understandable. But these are things that can be overcome. The Gift is profoundly precious, much more important than anyone's personal history. That's not to say we accept those who are unfit. But in my probe just now I saw no handpower tendencies inside your mind. I think it's very likely the Examiners would certify you. If so, there's no reason why you couldn't try for the Novitiate."

Bron felt as if he were dreaming, or going mad. The man had seen his power, the glimmer of his forbidden barriers. Why was he talking about the Novitiate?

"Think about it," the Roundhead said. His face went blank for an instant. Bron heard the sound of the lock. The door swung open. "That's all. You can go."

Bron stood, not believing it.

"Go on, boy. You're dismissed."

Bron made his way out of the Town Hall, expecting every moment to hear the sound of feet pounding after him. There was no horseman to bring him home; he walked all the long way, his head aching, turning often to search the road behind him for signs of pursuit. It was not until he reached the house that he was able to believe he had really been let free.

The family crowded round him. He did not mention the Roundhead's strange words, saying only that his barriers had not broken. Jevon gave up his chair by the fire and Alse pushed Bron into it, piling blankets around him and putting warmed stones at his feet. He accepted her ministrations silently, shivering. The feel of the Roundhead's probe was still inside him, a splinter of ice at the core of his mind.

He had told his family, confidently, that his barriers had held. And indeed, in the first few seconds after the probe he had been sure they had—he had *felt* them, resisting the arctic pressure of the Roundhead's Gift, fading backward into the structure of his thoughts, undetectable. But in the next instant, when the Roundhead spoke of seeing power in him, he had known they had not—for how was it possible to see the small spark of his power without also seeing what it hid? Yet he had been let go—he was sitting here now, free. That would not be the case if the Roundhead had detected his secret. Which meant that his barriers, after all, had held, and the Roundhead had been lying.

Why would a Roundhead lie? Did the Arm of the Stone find it amusing to raise expectations of power in those who had none? Or maybe the man thought to use the prize of Guardianship, for which any ordinary person would sacrifice everything, as some kind of inducement—for Bron to betray his family, for instance. Could it be that, despite their clean probes and matching stories, the family was still suspect?

If the stakes had not been so high Bron might have found irony in the fact that of all people in the world such an offer should have been made to him. As it was, it was just another reason to fear. Yet as he sat staring at the shadows on the hearth, he felt something stir inside him, a yearning he thought he had outgrown. What if the Roundhead had not seen his barriers, but also had not been lying? What if more than the ancestral spark hid inside his mind? What then?

Three

**WO DAYS** passed without contact from the Roundheads. Unable to leave their home, cut off from the rest of the world, the family waited. At last, early on the third morning, the summons came. Annis found it pinned to the front door, a folded square of parchment sealed with the great red seal of the Arm of the Stone. Judgment, it announced, would be proclaimed the following day at noon in the village square. The family was permitted to attend.

That night Bron slept fitfully, pursued by terrible dreams. He saw his brother bound to the lashing stake, blank-faced in a House of Reeducation, stiff in an unmarked Violator's grave. At last, abandoning sleep, he knelt in the scratchy hay of the loft, his arms on the windowsill, watching the pale flood of dawn crest the treetops. With all his soul he wished for the power to stop time, so that noon would never come. Or to spin time backward, unlinking the chain of events that bound him to this moment, banishing all errors and transgressions back to the realm of impossibility.

The family set out well before noon, walking all the way in somber silence. When they reached the village the cobbled streets were deserted, the windows empty of watching faces. But Bron could hear the sound of a crowd, rising louder as they neared the village center.

Alise, in the lead, was the first to reach the square. She halted, her back rigid. The entire village had gathered to witness Serle's punishment. The square was packed with spectators, as were the windows of the surrounding houses; a few adventurous individuals had even climbed to the roofs. Hawkers carried trays of food, and the innkeeper had constructed a stall from which he was selling ale and cider. It was more like a fair than a sentencing. A stranger coming upon this place would never suspect that a life hung in the balance here.

Bron felt rage flash through him, shaking him to his core. In that moment he had never hated anyone, even the Roundheads who had taken his brother, as he hated the villagers.

The people closest to the family caught sight of Alse. They fell quiet. The hush spread, rippling toward the edges of the square, as if silence were a stone Alse had thrown. She raised her head and stepped forward, pulling Elene and Olesin behind her. The villagers began to move aside, pressing back as if they feared contagion, forming a broad passageway that led to the center of the square. Their faces, massed as closely as bricks in a wall, were closed and watchful. Beside Bron, Annis hid her face in her hands— Jevon had to guide her, stumbling, as she walked. Bron refused the ease of such an escape. Head high, he dared the villagers' gaze. He hungered to see their faces change beneath the weight of his hatred. But their observation, though fixed, was not direct. Not one person would meet his eyes.

In the middle of the square a dais had been erected. A stake rose from its center. Beside the stake, his arms manacled in front of him, stood Scrlc, attended by two men in leather jerkins. A bruise bloomed darkly across his cheek; dried blood dappled his bound hands and bare feet, marking the places where his nails had been torn out. His set expression did not change as his family emerged from the crowd, though Bron knew by the flicker of his eyes that he had seen them. Alse stopped close to the edge of the dais, holding Olesin and Elene in a white-knuckled grip. She gazed up at her son. Bron, behind her, was glad he could not see her face.

The dais was crowded with people. Guardians occupied the right side—the six Roundheads in front, sitting in carved chairs that had been brought out from the Town Hall, the Resident Journeyer and his Ordermen behind. To the left, the mayor and his officials stood up like servants. A youth of about Serle's age fidgeted awkwardly nearby: the jealous apprentice, Serle's betrayer. Despite the gravity of the actions that had brought him here, his features reflected no emotion deeper than the discomfort of his conspicuous position.

The Roundhead leader got to his feet. In one hand he held two rolled parchments. The other he raised for quiet. He waited as the subdued murmuring that had followed the family's progress dwindled to silence.

"Over the past week," he said, in a voice which penetrated effortlessly to the furthest corners of the square, "we have conducted an investigation into the crime of Serle Miner, accused of a Violation of the Hands. We have reached a decision, and will announce our judgment momentarily. First, however, we wish to commend the young man who brought the crime to our attention."

The Roundhead beckoned. The apprentice approached, smiling uncertainly. The leader handed him a leather purse and one of the parchments, tied with a large red ribbon.

"I present you with the standard reward, and a written commendation. May your obedience and loyalty serve as an example for all."

There was applause from the crowd. The apprentice bowed awkwardly to the Roundheads and grinned at the villagers, then climbed down from the dais, clutching his reward to his chest. When silence had reasserted itself, the Roundhead unrolled the second parchment and began to read.

"In the matter of Serle Miner, the accused, son of Jevon Miner, resident of the village of Greshing in the Sixth Diocese of the Province of the Northlands, we have made the following Investigation.

"First, we find the tool constructed by the accused to be in Violation of Subsection Thirty-six of Limitbook Fifteen, entitled *Manufacture and Use of Agricultural Tools*, and also in Violation of Section Ten of Chapter Twenty-three of the *Blacksmiths' Guild Limitbook*. Nowhere in these Limits is a tool described such as Serle Miner made. Furthermore, in Limitbook Nineteen, entitled *General Principles of Modification and Development*, as well as in all Guild Limitbooks, it is clearly stated that only a licensed Modifier may alter an established tool, or make one the Limits do not explicitly describe; and that he may do so only if a Journeyer-approved plan is in place. The accused is not a licensed Modifier, nor does a plan exist. In sum, we find compelling evidence of a Violation of the Hands.

"As a Guild apprentice, the accused certainly was aware of Subsection Thirty-six of Limitbook Fifteen, of the stipulations of Limitbook Nineteen, and of the requirements of his own Guild Limitbook. It is therefore impossible to conclude that he Violated the Limits through ignorance or by accident. In this we find indisputable evidence of a Violation of the Paths of Thought.

"We have investigated the accused's Master, Gisfrid. It is our conclusion that he was unaware of the activities of his apprentice, and in no way suggested or encouraged the commission of Limit-Violating activities. However, the atmosphere of apprenticeship he created must in some intangible way have been conducive to Violation, otherwise Violation could not have occurred.

"We have also investigated the accused's family, and it is our conclusion that they too were unaware of his activities, and similarly provided no suggestions or encouragement. However, when they did become aware of the existence of the tool, they colluded with the accused in concealing it and in hiding his crime from the authorities.

"Therefore, in accordance with the stipulations of Limitbook Twenty, entitled *Violations of the Limits, their Identification and Punishment,* as well as Perrella's Commentary of 982, Novarro's Gloss of 544, and Tace-Thomas's Commentary of 631, and through the authority vested in the Arm of the Stone, we render the following judgments.

"To Gisfrid Smith: suspension of Master Smith status for a period of one year. Status to be reinstated at the end of that time, contingent upon a successful mindprobe. Gisfrid Smith did not err by commission, but he did err by omission, and his innocence of the actual Violation cannot excuse the faulty supervision which made it possible for the Violation to occur.

"To the accused's family: placement under Watch, effective immediately, for an indefinite period to be determined by the Arm of the Stone. Individual examinations of family members have shown no suspect handpower tendencies. However, the parents' collusion with the accused indicates not simply faulty judgment, but a critical lack of loyalty to the Limits and their sacred purpose. Also, the danger of exposing infants to the corruption of handpower cannot be overstated. The younger Miner children must be carefully watched, lest they pose a danger for the future.

"To Serle Miner: for Violation of the Hands, punishment of two hundred lashes, sentence to be carried out immediately. For Violation of the Paths of Thought, confinement to a House of Reeducation until rehabilitation is complete, sentence to commence once flogging has been completed.

"From this day onward, the accused will never again be named in the village of Greshing. His name will be struck from the rolls of birth, and will not be entered into the rolls of death. The Violation must be remembered, that all may learn from it. But the Violator must be forgotten, that none may follow him.

"In the name of the Stone, so ends our judgment."

The Roundhead lowered the parchment. No one moved or spoke. On the dais, Serle stared straight ahead; he gave no sign of having heard the harsh phrases of his sentence. Bron gazed up at his brother's bruised face. He was numb, the kind of numbness that precedes agonizing pain. Strangely, the physical reality of punishment—the lashing, the House of Reeducation, the harsh Watch that was the price of the family's survival—seemed less terrible than the excision of Serle's name. With a few words he had been transformed into a ghost, his existence canceled, as if he had never lived at all.

Next to Bron, Annis was sobbing into her hands. Elene and Olesin wept into their mother's skirts. Alse's fingers were pressed against her mouth.

"It's not death, Alse." Jevon placed shaking hands on her shoulders.

"I prayed for death." Her voice was dry and hard. "Death would be kinder."

One of the men in leather came forward. He unlocked the

manacles on Serle's hands and removed his shirt. He tied a
strip of cloth tightly around Serle's eyes and thrust a piece
of wood between his teeth. Turning Serle roughly about, he
bound him to the stake with rope, stretching his arms high
above his head. The second man raised a whip. It had a
short handle, and six flexible braided-leather thongs. It
would cut the skin on the first lash, and with the twentieth
lay bare the bone.

The Roundhead held up his hand. The lashman drew back
his arm. The sun, beating down from a cloudless sky,
flooded the faces of the villagers; it poured over the dais,
the officials and the Roundheads, Serle's straining arms and
broad white back. Bron felt his head swim. It was, exactly,
an image from his dreams the night before.

"One," the Roundhead said.

The whip whistled as it traveled through the air. There
was a sharp crack as it made contact with flesh. Six thin red
lines sprang up on Serle's back. He made no sound.

"Two," the Roundhead said. The lash fell again, a second set of welts neatly crossing the first.

A simmering pressure had begun to grow inside Bron's
head. Distantly, he could hear weeping—Annis, Elene, Olesin—and strange muffled noises from Alse. He saw Serle's
arms jerk with each blow, his hands clenched against the
rope that bound them to the stake. He saw the passionless
faces of the Roundheads, their duty done, the righteous
gravity of the town officials, conscious of the passage of
justice. Behind him he felt the crowd, avidly focused on his
brother's anguish, their own virtue affirmed by each crack
of the whip.

With the sixth lash Serle cried out at last, an awful ragged
sound. Bron knew what the loss of control must cost his
brother. The lash fell again; again, Serle cried out.

With that second cry, the pressure in Bron's head broke.
Deep inside him, in the darkest spaces of his secret self,
something arrowed forward. His barriers yielded like shredding cloth. The thing tore up through the layers of his consciousness, flooding his mind and body as if he were no
more than an empty vessel. Still it swelled, like an endless
breath, until he was no longer able to hold it and it exploded

outward, a cataclysmic burst that almost took his consciousness with it, a tidal wave of power sweeping irresistibly over the crowd, the square, the entire village.

Time stopped.

Beside Bron, Annis was still as a stone. On the dais the lash was arrested in midair; the counting Roundhead stood immobile, his mouth open on a number yet unspoken. The crowd was motionless, caught between one breath and another. Birds hung suspended in the sky, as if they had been painted on the clouds. Every living thing was frozen.

All but Bron. He was the center, the fulcrum of a delicate balance. Power spread out from within him, effortless, like a great net. He did not know why the power was there or where it had come from—yet he understood that whatever he wished, he had only to think of it and it would be so.

He thought of Serle's bonds, broken; and they were. He thought of Serle, released from stillness; and he was.

It took Serle a moment to realize that he was no longer bound. Slowly he lowered his hands. He turned, his face bewildered, like someone in a dream. He looked at the broken ropes about his wrists, at the motionless lash and the arrested crowd. There was a pause that seemed to last forever. Then, quick as a cat, he turned and ran across the dais. He leaped into the crowd, toppling bodies like trees, and was gone.

The power was no longer effortless. Sparks had begun to dance around the edges of Bron's vision; he could feel his mind and body straining. Grimly he held on. But determination was not enough. His strength gave out all at once. The power disappeared like a clap of thunder. Darkness rushed in to fill the void where it had been.

When Bron regained consciousness he found himself at home, wrapped in blankets in his parents' big bed. His head ached dully, as if it were bruised inside.

"You're awake." Alse bent over the bed, putting her hand to Bron's cheek. "How do you feel?"

Bron tried to sit up, but the effort made the room spin. He lay back. "Dizzy."

"I'm not surprised. You fainted dead away, the moment

that power let us go. You've been unconscious ever since."

"Power?" The effort of speech was enormous.

"What else could it have been?" Alse sat down on the edge of the bed, absently smoothing the covers with her fingers. "There was no space between the moment before and the moment after. You wouldn't know it had happened, even, except for that feeling of . . . of nothingness, lingering behind. Perhaps that's what death feels like. The moment of death. After it let go, I was surprised to find myself alive." Her pensive expression dissolved into joy. "But here I am going on, and I haven't told you the most important thing. Serle is free, Brother! The power, or whatever it was, took him. One moment he was there, the next he was gone, vanished into thin air."

She described how the Roundhead leader had flown into a terrible rage, how he had ordered all the village officials imprisoned, the regular activities of the village suspended and the villagers confined to their homes until an explanation was found. The family was once again under house arrest.

"Your father thinks it's a Roundhead trick. But if it was their doing, why would they be so angry? What I think . . . what I hope is that someone saw Serle's plight and took pity on him. There are stories of men of power who choose not to become Guardians." She smiled, with an exaltation that trembled on the edge of tears. "Whatever it was, he's beyond their reach. I know it, as surely as I know I'll never see him again. Perhaps he'll find a place to live in safety. Maybe . . . maybe he'll even marry, have children. At least now he'll have the chance."

For a moment she was silent, her eyes distant. Then, sighing, she reached out and brushed the hair from Bron's forehead.

"As for you, you gave us quite a fright. Though you weren't the only one—the villagers were falling like flies when the power let us go." She smiled again, this time with malice. "It was worth it all, to see them lying on the ground like stunned cattle. Are you feeling better?"

"A little."

"You don't have a fever, but perhaps you should stay in

bed for now. Are you hungry? Shall I bring you some broth?''

Bron shook his head.

"All right.'' Alse got to her feet. "Rest, then. I'll come back in a little while.''

Bron shut his eyes. The ache in his head kept company with his heartbeat. On the dark screen of his closed lids the events of the afternoon replayed themselves: the pressure in his mind, the uncoiling inside him, his barriers falling—and that titanic force, bursting free, holding the world as still as stone, stopping time itself.

Power. From within him, power.

Like every boy of his line who bore the name, Bron had dreamed of discovering the Gift of his Ancestor inside his mind. From the time he first heard the Tale he had searched for it, scouring his inner spaces for the great Talent he was convinced must be his. For a long time he persisted, stubbornly, but in the end he had no choice but to acknowledge the truth. He was no different from those who had come before him. The small spark of his barriers was all the power he would ever possess.

What he remembered, therefore, was impossible. He had accepted this fact for so long that even Alse's words, even his own memory, would not have been enough to convince him it was true, had it not been for one thing. The power was still there, a bright flame folded down very deep inside his mind, sheltered by his barriers yet apart from them. He recognized this with a bedrock certainty that set all impossibilities aside.

Where had it hidden all those years? Was there some deeper portion of his mind he had never reached, even when he opened himself to the firelit passages of the Tale? But the brief chill at the thought of such an unknown inside him was quickly swallowed by a flood of exultation. He had the Gift. He, Bron, dismissed by his Teachers, scorned by the Talented. . . . And what a Gift. Not timid and clumsy, like the powers of his classmates, or inflexible and circumscribed, like the abilities of his teachers, but fully formed, shatteringly strong, unfathomably huge. He was not certain how it fit the standard categories of mindskill, for it was unlike any power he had ever heard described. In its magnitude, in its achievement, it had shown itself beyond any of them.

He quieted his thoughts and let his barriers slip aside, the better to see this miracle within himself. It was like a point of light at the bottom of a well, a coruscating pulse that matched his own. The more still he made himself, the more brilliant it became. He could see, now, how to reach for it ... just there. ...

The thing inside him surged, its pinpoint presence flashing in an instant to a rising blaze. It rushed toward him, expanding at the speed of thought, breathing out the scorching breath of power. It would engulf him, consume him utterly, turn his mind to smoke and ash ... instinctively Bron pulled back, slamming his barriers closed. With all his strength he held them in place, willing his Gift back into its deep, secret abode.

After a few moments, cautiously, he looked inside himself. The power had obeyed. Once again it was no more than a tiny pulse within him, tranquil as a sleeping tiger.

Bron took a breath, shaken. For just a second, he had not been certain he could hold it. He thought of the village square, of his barriers yielding like wet straw. He had not summoned the power, nor, except for a few brief moments, controlled it. It had passed through him as if he were no more than a conduit. Now that it had made itself known, would he be able to keep it confined? It wanted to be free. He had sensed the urgency with which it sought release; even now he could feel the echo of its desire, like a second mind within him.

He shuddered. Of all the times he had imagined discovering the Gift within himself, he had never thought he might fear it. The future seemed to open out before him, a vision of a life harnessed to a Gift he lacked either the knowledge to control or the skill to use, every moment consumed by the need to contain his power, every hour stalked by the fear that its volition might overcome his own. And there was another, more immediate consideration. The Roundhead leader, who after all had not been lying, had seen the power, or some part of it, inside his mind. Might he have recognized it when he encountered it again in the village square? Bron felt himself sliding toward panic. With an effort, he pulled himself back. The Roundheads could not have recognized him; he would not be lying here now if they had. As for the power, for better or worse it was his. It had risen in response to the deepest wish of his soul; in that way at least it had done his bidding. There must be some hope of learning, some path to control. Yet if he were to learn, he must do so on his own. There was no one to teach or guide him. In this world only Guardians walked the ways of power; the renegade masters Alse had spoken of, outlaws who chose to use their Gifts outside the established order, were more a part of legend than of life. Even assuming such men actually existed, Bron had not the first idea how to go about finding them.

He turned his face into the pillow. Pain lanced through his head like a knife. The fear he had pushed away was still with him, hovering like a shadow, ready to rush in the moment he relaxed his guard. At least, he told himself, Serle was free. If he accomplished nothing else through his Gift his whole life long, at least he had accomplished that. Surely it was worth any price he might have to pay.

Bron lingered in bed for two days, dozing and waking and dozing again. His sleep was restless, disturbed by images of flight—running figures whose faces were mostly Serle's, but sometimes changed to become his own. When he woke, it was to the consciousness of his Gift, simmering gently within him. Now and then he touched it with his mind, as if he were testing an aching tooth. It flared a little in greeting, but that was all. Apparently it was content, for now, with captivity.

Confined to the house with little to do, the family occupied its time in speculation, talking about who might have freed Serle and with what intent, discussing what would become of him. Jevon was certain that he had disappeared not simply from the village but from the world. Alse's belief in his survival did not waver. For Elene and Olesin the whole thing was like a fairy tale. Only Annis pointed out that they had passed through one danger to confront a greater: the Roundheads' attention would surely be focused on them now more narrowly now than ever. Serle, she said bitterly, had betrayed them yet again. Even Alse's rebukes did not silence her.

At first Bron intended to keep the truth to himself, at least until he had come to a better understanding of it. But as he listened to his family he realized that he could not leave them ignorant, if only so that they would be prepared for the possibility of the power being traced to him. Three days after Serle's escape, he told the story to his mother. She was silent for several minutes after he finished, a strange expression on her face. It occurred to Bron, belatedly, that she might not believe him.

"Do you know what this means?" she asked at last, speaking slowly. "Do you understand what has happened?"

Bron shook his head.

"You are the One. The One Who Comes."

It was the simple, the obvious conclusion. Yet it had not once occurred to Bron. It was his childhood wish; but now, hearing it spoken aloud, he wanted only to deny it.

"No," he said. "No, Mother. That's impossible."

"Impossible?" Alse fixed him with her gaze. "You held a whole village motionless. You made time stop. Even your namesake didn't have that kind of power."

"*I* didn't do those things. It wasn't my will that did them."

"That doesn't matter. Only the power matters."

"Mother, didn't you hear what I told you? I can't control it. I don't know how to use it. I'm afraid of it!"

"Do you know why I didn't give Serle our Ancestor's name?" Alse's eyes were feverish. "Why I named him for my father and gave you the name instead?"

"Mother—"

"Just before Serle was born, I had a dream. I saw my mother, and behind her all my ancestresses. My mother spoke to me, but it was only her mouth that moved; I knew that her voice was the voice of all of them. She told me that the child who must carry the name had not yet been conceived. That I must wait; that I must give the name to my second son."

"Mother, you're wrong. I'm not the One."

"Why not? Because you're young? Because you're afraid? This feels right, Brother, righter than anything I've ever known. Oh, that I should be the one to see it!"

The intensity on her face was more frightening even than her words. She reached out and took Bron into a tight embrace, pulling his head onto her shoulder.

"I understand your fear, my son," she murmured. "It's a lot to accept, and it's come at the end of so much tragedy—how could you feel any other way? But we must put the past behind us. We must turn to the future. Serle is lost. But look what's been gained. It's a hard exchange, but perhaps it was a necessary one."

Bron pushed away from her, horrified. "You can't mean that!"

"Can't I?" Her expression was fierce. "Our line hasn't endured a thousand years by being afraid to think such thoughts. What's happened to you can't be undone, Brother. The Stone sees everything. It waits for you now. One way or another you must come to terms with that. And you don't have much time. The future is close; I can feel it."

Bron wanted to shout at her, to rage denial. Instead he turned and began to walk toward the woods. He felt her eyes on his back, a regard more pressing than words.

The forest swallowed him. He walked, moving without purpose through the light and shadow beneath the trees, not caring where he went or that he was violating the Roundheads' house arrest, wanting only to escape the prison of fear and grief his life had become.

Also was wrong. It was her bereavement that had spoken, her need to find a reason for what had happened to Serle. His power was a fluke, a freak, a strange and fearful chance. He was not, could never be, the deliverer the Tale foretold. Such a person must possess not simply power, but strength, intelligence, courage, experience. Bron was neither wise nor brave; he knew nothing of the world. Of all of the necessary characteristics, he owned only power—power that, without knowledge, was worse than useless. He sensed its fires now, banked and sullen behind his barriers: watching, waiting, wanting. Nothing in the world could make him believe that such a thing had been worth the loss of his brother.

Eventually, tired out, he sat down at the base of a pine and leaned his head against its rough bark. Shafts of late-afternoon sun sank between the trees; the air was noisy with the call of birds settling for the night. He thought of Serle, and where, if he were still alive, he might be. Three days had passed. He could have gone a considerable distance by now, even if he traveled only at night. Most likely, he would have chosen to go through the forest, which covered the land all the way to the cold fjords of the north. If he got that far, he would be able to purchase false papers and a new identity in one of the bustling port cities—if, that is, he could find the price. With papers, he could get a place on one of the trade ships that plied the waters between this country and the larger continent to the south. Once there, he could travel anywhere he wanted. A smith's skills were always needed— he would not lack for work. Perhaps he would find a new Master, a new living. Perhaps, as Alse hoped, he would marry and have children. Perhaps he would even prosper.

But though Bron yearned to believe in this hopeful vision, it did not offer the comfort of real possibility. Even if Serle traveled to the ends of the earth, his Violation would follow him. There was nowhere in the world the Arm of the Stone could not reach, no place they did not watch. No one could elude such a ubiquity of vision.

In the following days the village and its environs were meticulously searched. Though the Roundheads released no information, the nature of their activities made it clear that Serle had not yet been captured.

The family was saved for last. There were no verbal questions this time, only mindprobes. The house and barn were turned inside out, and even the soil of the animal pens was dug through, as if Serle might have buried himself in imitation of his plow. The search, of course, yielded nothing; as before, the family's barriers withstood the probes. When Bron's turn came, the Roundhead leader was brusque and rough. Nothing was said, this time, about power.

At the end of a week, the Roundheads called a convocation in the village square. The dais had never been taken down; they stood atop it, the leader in front, his men ranked behind him. The power, the leader announced, had come from inside the village. Its source, however, was still unclear. A very deep corruption was at work; until the incident had been fully explained, the village and the surrounding countryside to a distance of five leagues would be placed under Watch.

It was a sentence of unprecedented harshness. In effect, the village and its environs had been made a prison. Squadrons of Soldiers would be brought to patrol the designated perimeter. No one would be allowed to leave, even to go to market. Outsiders could enter, but because no sane person wished to risk contamination by visiting a place under Watch, no one would come. The Watch meant not simply isolation, but poverty, want, and hunger. It was a wall thrown up against the future. All plans and prospects withered in its shadow.

For a long time after the Roundheads disappeared inside the Town Hall, the villagers milled and muttered in the square. The summer wind blew warm across the rooftops; the animals were healthy in the barns, the crops green and growing in the fields. Yet it seemed that winter had suddenly drawn close, canceling the natural order of the seasons. No one knew how long the Watch might last, or what suffering it might bring. Only one thing was certain: with a few words the village had been struck off the map, and its people removed from the living world.

Four

THE SUMMER passed. The villagers did what they could to prepare and store supplies for the winter. The mayor instituted a communal storehouse, to which all the villagers contributed their harvest, and devised a rationing system. The Guardians, supplied with food and other necessities by their Orderhouse, were not part of this system. This winter, while the villagers grew thin, they would lack for nothing.

The villagers could do nothing to change their sentence; they could and did, however, express their anger toward its source. Already set apart from the life of the village, the family was now completely excised from it. No villager would speak to them. Shops would not sell them goods. The produce from Alse's strip of land was stolen, and when she tried to harvest it herself she was stoned by a group of angry women. With grim resource, she plowed up the rocky ground around the house, and planted late crops. She managed to slip through the cordon of Soldiers and, illegally removing her Badge of Watch, sold eggs and cheese in a town more than a day's travel away. With the money she bought supplies for the winter—ale, salt beef, grain—and smuggled it back through the cordon, a bag or bundle at a time.

Jevon, like the other miners in the village, was not allowed to work. He sat at home in his chair all day long, brooding over the fire, seldom speaking except to Alse. Elene and Olesin no longer fought—they played quietly together, huddling close to Alse whenever she took a few moments away from her constant labor. Amazingly, against the pressure of his family, Annis's fiancé did not break their engagement. Annis spent more and more time away from home, shirking her tasks, sending Alse into uncharacteristic rages.

All the work that would normally have been performed by Jevon and Serle fell to Bron. He toiled from dawn until well past dusk, dropping into sleep the moment his head touched the pillow. He was conscious of his power, a bright open eye inside his mind, but it did not stir or test his control, biding its time within him. Alse had told only Jevon the truth behind Serle's deliverance. For Annis, Olesin, and Elene, the knowledge was too dangerous in this time of Watch, when patrols of Soldiers walked the woods and could seize and hold any person at will.

With the rains of autumn, a sickness came to the village. It began with a cough, quickly progressing to a raging fever and a severe congestion of the lungs. The disease, highly contagious, spread rapidly among the undernourished people. Some recovered, but more died. Greshing did not have a doctor, and no physician would come to a place under Watch; there were only the village's herbalist and two midwives to care for the sick. The Guardians, whose training allowed them to turn all kinds of illness aside, owned the power to heal the villagers. But the Order's charge was teaching and orthodoxy, not health and welfare. Beyond the defense of the Stone and the preservation of the Limits, it bore no duty toward the people of the world.

Only when it became apparent that this was no ordinary sickness, but a plague of some sort, did the Guardians take action. One morning, those villagers still able to leave their homes woke to find the Residence vacant. A barrier had been raised in the night, a seamless dome of power encircling the village and the surrounding countryside. To the eye, the barrier seemed no more than a shimmering distortion of the air, like heat rising from a slate roof in the summertime. But its transparency was deceptive. Anyone who neared it found it increasingly difficult to move and breathe. Those foolish enough to persist were eventually rendered immobile and, unable to turn back, slowly suffocated. By

the end of the first day there were already corpses, frozen
upright in attitudes of desperate struggle. Still, stubbornly,
the villagers continued to try escape. The barrier became,
literally, a wall of death.

Greshing was now a place of ghosts. Half the population
was either sick or dead. In the deserted streets the rats and
dogs ran in packs; in the silent rooms bodies lay unburied.
Those who had survived, and those who had not yet sick-
ened, waited numbly for the plague to take them, or to pass.

In desperation, setting aside his fear, Bron turned toward
his Gift. He did not want to circumvent Guardian power or
halt time this time, only to protect his family against the
plague. Surely there was some way to release, not all of his
power, but just a part of it, small enough to control yet large
enough to work his will. He had no idea how to go about
this; all he could do was reach past his barriers, with varying
degrees of caution and force, toward the spark at the core
of his mind. But no matter what he tried, it never answered
with less than the whole of its strength, igniting with an
urgency that canceled any possibility of command, tearing
up through the layers of self with terrifying velocity. Always
his barriers slammed closed before it could fill his mind, a
thing he had thought at first was volition, but that he now
recognized as reflex, entirely outside his conscious will—as
if, beyond his fear, some internal censor were at work. What
good would he be to his family, after all, if his mind were
ripped apart? Yet what good was he to them now, with the
power to protect them locked up by his terror and lack of
skill?

Jevon was the first to sicken. He began coughing in the
afternoon; by nighttime he was wracked with fever, barely
able to draw breath. None of Alse's cordials or compresses
had any effect. Panic-stricken, she sent Bron to fetch help.
But the one remaining midwife turned him from her door,
making the sign against evil.

"It's you people who've brought this on us," she shouted
after him. "Half the village is dead—I won't lift a finger to
stop *you* from dying. It's the judgment of the Stone. Maybe
if you die the plague will leave us!"

Two days later, Jevon stopped breathing. Bron helped his

mother wash and prepare his father's body. Annis, huddled on her stool before the fire, refused to assist. Alse wept quietly, tears running down her face, her hands lingering over the terrible scars that marked her husband's body. Bron dug a grave in the cold ground outside the house, and he and his mother laid Jevon in it, wrapped in the coverlet from the big bed, which had been a wedding gift from Jevon's family. It had begun to rain, a chill drizzle drifting down from clouds that seemed to hover just overhead. Bron covered his father with earth, hating the sound the wet dirt made as it fell from his spade. The guilt he felt was almost as heavy as his grief. If he had been more skilled, less afraid, Jevon would still be alive.

"This is Serle's fault," Annis said from her stool as Alse and Bron entered the house.

"Annis," Alse admonished wearily. "You know that's not so."

"It is, Mother, it is! If he hadn't done what he did there'd be no Watch. We'd be free, and this plague wouldn't have come. He betrayed us. He betrayed us all." She stopped to draw a breath; instead she coughed. Her eyes widened. "No," she said, pressing her hands to her mouth. "Oh, no, no, no!"

Alse went to her. Annis clung, too frightened even to weep. Bron turned away. Inside him his power burned, a mocking flame.

Annis suffered for four days. When she died at last, Alse and Bron buried her beside Jevon. By this time, Elene and Olesin were also sick. They lay together in the big bed, coughing weakly, shivering in spite of the blankets Alse piled upon them. She nursed them fiercely; she had a theory that the plague was less deadly to children than to adults, and was convinced her care could save them.

Two nights after Annis's death, Bron roused to his mother's hands on his shoulders.

"Wake up, Brother," she whispered.

He sat up in the truckle bed, where he had been sleeping since his father died. "What?" he said, confused. The room looked unfamiliar. A flickering light gilded the parchment that covered the windows. Outside he could hear a strange roaring sound.

"You must go out the back way and hide in the woods. Here. Put on your clothes. It's cold tonight."

Bron obeyed, still slow with sleep. "Why?" he asked. The roaring had resolved itself into the clamor of many voices. "What's happening?"

"It was only a matter of time before they decided to come for us," Alse said. She was dressing Olesin and Elene as she spoke. "Hurry. They won't wait out there forever."

She put Olesin into Bron's arms. He radiated fever. Elene, unsteady on her feet, clung to Bron's hand. Seizing a pile of blankets, Alse draped them over Bron's shoulder. She pushed him toward the back of the house.

"Go now."

"What about you?"

"I'm going to face them. Maybe I can save the house."

"I'll stay with you."

"No!" Her hair hung disheveled down her back. "I want you out. I'll be all right. It's not the first time those of our line have faced something like this."

"Mother—"

"Do as I say!" She gave him a shove that nearly knocked him off his feet. When he tried to move toward her she flung herself on him, beating at him with her hands, striking his head and face with hard, painful blows. Olesin began to howl with fear. Bron fell back under his mother's assault. She drove him through the door into the barn, and slammed it closed. He heard the sound of the bolt shooting home.

For a moment he stood, uncertain. The sound of the crowd was rising. Olesin was hot and heavy in his arms, and Elene was whimpering softly beside him. He would get them to safety. Then he could return for Alse.

He seized Elene's hand and began to run, ducking out of the barn, circling the pigpen, heading up the hill toward the forest. His breath labored in his chest. The noise of the crowd followed, and torchlight reddened the air behind him. He passed through the first fringe of trees and threw the blankets on the ground; he laid Olesin among them, pushing Elene down beside him.

"Stay here," he hissed at her. "I'm going back for Mother."

Elene nodded, whimpering. Bron turned and started back. Even as he did so, the fierce light that rose from the clearing told him he was too late. The house was blazing—he saw it as he reached the crest of the hill. Fire leapfrogged up the thatch of the roof and licked from the windows of the barn. A mob of villagers roiled around the clearing. The ragged noise of their shouting drifted up like smoke.

In horror, Bron reached for his power, no longer caring what happened to him so long as he could save his mother. He felt his Gift ignite, burning up through his mind. With all the strength he owned he opened himself to its passage. But the internal censor was too powerful. His barriers wrenched from his grasp, crashing closed with an impact that shook him to his core. Clenched and immovable, they divided his mind in two. Behind them his Gift struggled, unreachable as a star. All he could touch was the hard, breath-stopping enormity of his fear.

Below, the villagers shouted, their voices filled with savage power. They fought each other over bits of furniture and scraps of cloth, setting fire to anything that would burn. They trampled through the pigpen and the chicken coop, knocking over fencing and grinding Alse's late-season crops into the mud. Reddened by the raging fire, swept by strange shadows, they looked scarcely human.

Bron's terror was a wall. But the thought of Alse forced him forward. He began to stumble down the hill, toward the heart of the riot. Two men came to meet him, grinning, their faces filthy with mud and soot. He tried to dodge away, but someone else came from behind and pinioned him so he could not escape. Fists struck his back, his head, his chest, with a force that drove both breath and consciousness away.

When Bron came back to awareness, it was morning. The fire had burned itself out. His home was a smoldering welter of blackened timbers and tumbled stone. Debris and dead animals were strewn everywhere. A thick pall of smoke laid an acrid veil across the wreckage. The air was solid with the stench of burned flesh.

Shakily, Bron got to his feet. A searing pain gripped his ribs, doubling him over for a moment until he could catch his breath. He had been badly beaten. A red mist hung before his right eye; his cheek and jaw were stiff and swollen, his mouth metallic with the taste of blood.

Slowly, painfully, he began to search for his mother. He found her at last, facedown in the mud. Fumbling, he reached for her pulse. It was faint, but there: she was still alive. She had been used much more savagely than he. Her clothing was ripped to rags; the skin that showed through the rents was bloody and black with bruising. Her arm was broken and probably her leg as well. Her face was a mass of contusions, her teeth shattered, both eyes swollen shut. There was some kind of internal damage too, for she moaned when he touched her stomach.

With a piece of canvas salvaged from the wreckage and some branches he improvised a travois. He dragged her onto it, trying not to hear her agonized cries. Doggedly, stopping every few steps to rest, he pulled her up into the woods. He made a camp for them under the tall trees, on the springy carpet of fallen pine needles. Ignoring his own pain, he fashioned the canvas into a lean-to, heaped up pine boughs and leaves for beds, built a hearth out of rocks. He tended the invalids, washing Alse's wounds, giving Elene and Olesin water to drink, heating stones and putting them at their feet, carving meat from the butchered pigs and cooking it and feeding them by hand, morsel by morsel. But the days were cold and the nights colder. He could salvage little in the way of coverings, and the canvas lean-to could keep out neither the wind nor the rain. His family grew weaker, even as he began to heal. An agony of guilt possessed him, much worse than any physical pain. They were dying, yet he was still alive. He had failed to save them, yet somehow he had been saved.

He had feared at first that the villagers would return and, finding the family helpless in the woods, complete their work of slaughter. The days passed and no one came, but his family died anyway, Elene on the fifth day, Olesin on the sixth. Grimly Bron carried them down to the ruins of the house. He dug graves for them next to Annis's, his cracked ribs protesting every stroke of the spade. He piled their coverings on Alse, and surrounded her with hot stones. Still she shivered, drifting in and out of consciousness, moaning. She burned with fever. Her stomach was ominously distended, and most of her wounds were ugly with infection.

The morning after Olesin died, Bron turned from tending the fire to find Alse awake. He went to her and took her hand. She blinked up at him through her swollen eyelids. Her face was a terrible patchwork of scabs and yellowing bruises.

"Your cheek," she whispered. "Your eyes—"

"I'm all right. It's healing."

"How long has it been?"

"Almost a week."

"Elene and Olesin?"

Bron hesitated, but only for an instant. "They're better, Mother. I think they'll get well."

"Good." She closed her eyes for a moment. "There's something I want to say to you." Her fingers tightened around his. "I think I'm going to die. No—don't say anything. I want you to promise me something."

"Anything, Mother."

"Promise me that you'll fulfill the prophecy. Promise me that you'll take the Stone, and bring the Guardians down."

"Mother—"

"Promise me!" Her voice cracked. "You're the One. I know it. Promise me."

Bron could not look at her ravaged face. He focused his eyes instead on their linked hands. Through a throat that felt like a dry riverbed, he said, "I promise."

"Good." Her fingers tightened again; he could sense the effort it cost her. "Take care of Elene and Olesin. You're their mother and father now."

Bron nodded, unable to speak.

"That's all, then," she breathed, so softly he could barely hear her. She did not speak again. He was sleeping when she died, sometime that night. By the time he woke, she was already cold.

He buried her next to Jevon. From a piece of wood he

fashioned a marker for her grave, as he had for the graves of the others, using a charred stick to write her name. Finished, he stood back. A trampled field of mud, a tangle of wrecked wood and stone, five raw mounds of earth: all that remained of his home, his family. In time, grass would cover the bare ground, and vines and saplings would grow where house and barn had been. The mounds above the graves would settle; the rain would wash away the charcoal letters written on the markers. It would all be gone then, all but memory. Only he would know that it had ever been—he, who had had the power to save his family, and had not done so.

Grief rose up in him, as his Gift had done in the village square—shattering all control, bursting all barriers, leveling all boundaries within him. He fell to his knees and bowed his forehead on the mud, his hands digging deep into the dirt. He wept, wrenching sobs that felt as if they would tear him inside out. They did not ease his pain, but compounded it, an impossible enormity of pain, more pain than he had known the world could hold.

At last he had nothing more to give. Empty now, in body and in spirit, he lay quiet on the cold ground, his knees drawn up to his chest, his eyes closed. The world was silent around him; there was not even the sound of birds to break the hush. It seemed possible that of all the living things the village's barrier had once imprisoned, only he was left.

Out of the darkness, from the depths of his vacancy, something flared. A point of light, brighter than a diamond, warmer than the sun. His power: his faithless, useless power. If he could have done so, he would have rooted it out and put it to death, as his family had been put to death. He could not do that, for it was part of him, as much as his eyes or hair. But it no longer moved him to wonder or hope or even fear. Let it watch him all his life long, staring up out of its dark well; let it sink back into whatever obscurity it had occupied before it sprang to being within him. He did not care. He was done with it, as he was done with life.

Still, it was beautiful, like a star beckoning from the other side of a black universe . . . Almost, he could hear it calling him, a voice he could not quite understand. Without knowing why, he turned toward it, shifting on his inner axis, focusing his interior eye upon the shining matrix of his Gift. Something was different. The resistance, the binding that had always accompanied his attempts to reach it were absent. In the emptiness of loss, in the absence of hope, he saw that the spaces within him were far larger than he had imagined, enough and more than enough to contain it. And suddenly, like a veil falling, he saw how he could hold against his Gift, how he could balance its release so it would not spring up fiercely and all at once, but gently, incrementally, like the sun slipping past the dawn horizon. To see it was to do it. He let his barriers fall aside. His power came to meet him, eager, calling out in welcome. His mind trembled at its approach, but this time his barriers did not close. His Gift flowed past them and out into his larger self, a swelling tide that filled him to the furthest corners of his consciousness.

For a moment Bron sat motionless, his eyes closed. He felt like someone just returned from underground. He had not known there could be such balance, such strength; he had not understood how vast a human mind could be until his power filled him. He did not know whether the change lay in his Gift or in himself. He did not know, could not bring himself to ask, why this revelation had come to him only now, when everything it could have saved was gone. With part of himself he longed to be empty again, to curl up beside his family's graves and wait for death. Yet life ran in him as strongly as his Gift. In the end, he could deny neither one.

He opened his eyes. He sat upright. He looked around him, at the graves of his family and the wreckage of his home. There was nothing for him here. But where should he go? What should he do?

It seemed to him that he was poised upon a narrow ledge, suspended between twin abysses. Behind him, his childhood lay erased. Before him gaped the rest of his life, an uncharted blankness to which he could give any shape he chose. Of all possibilities—fear, survival, the duty of his lineage, his oath to his mother, even the untapped promise of his power—only one thing seemed to offer sufficient inducement to step forward into that empty future. Vengeance. Vengeance upon the Guardians. Makers of the Watch, builders of the barrier, they had abandoned the village to its fate, and the people to their rage. It was they who had wrought the misery for which his family had been punished. It was they who owed the price his family had paid. Perhaps he was mad to imagine he could ever take so much from them. But all he had ever known or loved was gone; he was free to be mad now, if he wished. A little while ago he had longed for death. If he failed, he would only get his wish. And if he succeeded . . . if he succeeded . . .

It was his Gift that made the difference. It was his Gift that gave the chance. He knew this in the memory of what it had done. He felt it in the way it filled him now.

The way he would take opened up inside his mind, as naturally as if it had always been there. How better to work destruction than from within the thing to be destroyed? The Roundhead leader had offered him an invitation—very well, he would accept. He would become a Guardian. He would work his way to the Order's heart. He would search for some way to strike them down. And when the path was clear, when the time was right, he would act. Perhaps, in the end, he would even take the Stone.

For just a moment the vision faltered, and he saw fully the impossibility of it. A sense of unreality overwhelmed him. A few months ago he had stood face-to-face with Alse and denied the Tale. Now he found himself moving voluntarily toward its core. How was it possible for the world to change so much in so little time? The events of the past months unfolded before his inner eye, a pattern of circumstance propelling him inexorably from point to point, depositing him at last in this moment in which nothing was left to him except a task he had once rejected with all his being. Was it possible that Alse had been right—that it was the moment, not what led to it, that was important? If he had refused just now to embrace this path, would still more have been taken from him? If he had acknowledged his mother's belief in the meaning of his power, if he had given her the promise she wanted when she first asked for it, would his family be alive and his home unburned?

Bron closed his mind. He could not think such things; he would go mad if he did. Perhaps his Gift did carry a destiny with it; perhaps he really was the One. But only time could make that clear. In the meantime, he would make his own way. It was not in him to become merely a vessel for prophecy, to bend himself to a purpose he did not own. Whatever had brought him to this path, he would not set out along it except by choice. And he had chosen: to dedicate his life to revenge, to seek to bring the Guardians down. Not for the Tale—not for destiny, or even for the promise he had made to his mother. For his family. For his mother and father and sisters and brothers. And for himself.

He pressed his hands against the muddy ground and pushed himself to his feet. He gazed around him at the ruin of his home, the place he had lived all his life till now. He would never see it, or the graves of his family, again. A fierce emotion rose in him.

"I make a vow," he said aloud. "I will not rest until I have destroyed the Order of Guardians, or until I am dead. I swear it on the graves of my family. And on the Stone."

The words fell strangely upon the silence. He felt his Gift stir. A powerful sense of sealing gripped him. Now he could never turn back. From this day on, there would be nothing but the vow.

He made his way through the woods, toward the Guardians' barrier. His body was still weak with injury, patched with fading bruises; he carried nothing with him but the tattered clothing on his back. But he was filled with purpose, and he noticed neither his pain nor the coldness of the night.

When the air began to thicken, he stopped and closed his eyes. His Gift no longer filled him; it had receded, drawing back again into its deep home. Reaching for it, he felt its eagerness. For just an instant, fear brushed the edges of his mind. But this time he was able to channel the power, to command it. From its vast store he released a single line of force, flinging it out of himself like a lance. It pierced the Guardians' barrier as if it had been made of parchment. An opening appeared, dark upon the shimmering surface, shaped to the height and width of a human body.

Ten steps took him through. At his back, he sensed the

breach beginning to close, like a healing wound. Behind him lay all he knew; before him lay perils he could not guess. Trembling with cold and with the hugeness of his intent, he set out into the night.

The Fortress

Five

ILIANE AWOKE to warmth and silence, exactly as she had woken every other morning of her life. And yet it was a wakening like no other. Today was the first day of the Novice Examinations.

She sat up against her pillows. An only child, she had her bedroom to herself. It was a spacious chamber, with fine carved beams and paneled walls hung with choice tapestries. The big four-poster bed, curtained by flower-embroidered draperies, stood at the room's center, with ornamented chests for dresses and linens along the walls. On the wide-planked wooden floor, polished each morning by the servants, lay a large Eastern rug, woven in a complex design of blue and rose. The sun, just rising, stole through the glass mullions of the two small windows, tossing gold coins of light across the whitewashed ceiling.

Ordinarily Liliane spent the moments after waking in blissful communion with the silence of her sanctuary. This morning, however, her mind turned immediately inward, consumed by the prospect of the coming ordeal. Over the next two days she would be rigorously tested and mind-probed, examined on her knowledge of history and language and the Limits, and most important, judged on her inner fitness for Guardianship. At best, it would be a grueling process; at worst, it might be painful. No allowances would be made for fear. There would be no second chances.

So long had she been preparing for this that it was difficult to believe it was actually here. Had she studied ade-

quately for the written exams? Would her Gift be
acknowledged? What would the mindprobe show? She had
asked herself these questions a thousand times, but this
morning they rose before her as urgently as if she had only
just conceived them. Since the time her Gift first manifested,
at the age of three, she had dreamed only of becoming a
Guardian. For most of her life she had been entirely confident of success. But over the past few months, as the Examinations drew closer, the shadow of doubt had inserted
itself into her mind. Now, as she sat in her bed watching
the sunlight move slowly down the wall, the possibility of
failure seemed closer and more solid than it had ever been.
She did not know what she would do if she were not allowed to become a Guardian. It had never occurred to her
to imagine another future.

She would succeed, she told herself. This was her heart's
desire. In all her life she had never failed to win a thing to
which she set her will. She would pass the tests. She would
gain the Novitiate. In three days, she would begin the rest
of her life.

She pushed back the thick coverlet and climbed from the
snowy linen of her bed, the floor cold under her bare feet.
At the coffer chests she sorted through her gowns, settling
on a plainly-cut dress of deep maroon wool, with sky blue
undersleeves and skirt. She clasped a blue leather belt about
her waist and laced her blue shoes onto her feet. She loosened her hair, combed it smooth, and rebraided it, binding
the end with a blue cord.

Finished, she inspected herself in front of her mirror, a
circle of beaten metal that gave back a slightly distorted
image of her face. In all but one respect, she liked the way
she looked: the fresh, fair skin with its faint dusting of freck-
les, the sea blue eyes with their long gold lashes, the generous mouth equipped with excellent teeth. Her hair,
however, she detested. The color was good, dark gold with
lighter sparkling highlights, but the way it curled was impossible, a thousand anarchic ringlets that ruled out any possibility of wearing it unconfined, as other girls her age did.
This morning, for once, she was glad of the sober plainness
of her thick braid. Today of all days, she must be taken
seriously.

Leaving her room, Liliane walked along the upstairs gallery and descended the curving staircase to the lobby. Like all the rooms in her father's house the lobby was very fine, decorated with painted murals, filled with rugs and carvings and curious objects her father had acquired on his travels. He was a merchant who traded in skins and furs; he was absent half the year on business, journeying by land and by sea all over the known world in order to buy and sell.

In the dining hall, the sun spread a bright carpet on the flagstone floor. The family was gathered around the great mahogany table, Liliane's father presiding at the head and her mother at the foot, with the rest of the household in between: her grandmother and grandfather, her father's newly widowed sister Celinette with her four young children, her unmarried cousin Marie, her father's secretary Stefan and his assistant Guiscard, her mother's ne'er-do-well younger brother Lucien, and her mother's two ancient aunts, Telle and Helene.

Liliane slipped into her place. A servant brought her a mug of mild ale and a plate of bread and pickle. Her family's conversation, punctuated by the quarreling of the children and Celinette's halfhearted admonitions, buzzed around her like a swarm of bees; their feelings and reactions, a silent current below their words, were as audible to her as their voices. Ordinarily she was adept at screening out such distractions, but this morning she was hampered by her nervousness. She picked at her food, unable to muster her usual hearty appetite.

"You've hardly eaten a thing," her mother said. She was a tiny woman with faded, papery skin. Liliane had inherited her delicacy of stature, as well as her riotous hair, hidden now beneath a stiff headdress. "You can't go off to your Examinations on an empty stomach."

"Let her be, my dear," Liliane's father said gently. "One missed breakfast won't hurt her."

The meal over, the family followed Liliane into the lobby, all but her grandfather, who did not approve of her desire to be a Guardian. As always, she was aware that their actual emotions were in some cases at odds with their expressed feelings. Telle and Helene, not entirely sure what she was about to do, were vaguely anxious for her. Celinette, thin and pale from grieving, was too sad to care very much. Marie, beneath her warm kiss, radiated the corrosive envy that was her most characteristic emotion. Lucien, though concerned with little beyond himself, felt genuine warmth for Liliane; his good-luck wishes were sincere. By contrast, Liliane's mother radiated overpowering dread. Pulling gently away, she bent to kiss her grandmother, who touched her cheeks with dry old hands. "I will pray to the Stone for you," her grandmother whispered, and Liliane sensed her fierce pride.

She turned to her father last. He was a striking man, dressed in dark wools and velvets, his only ornament a large gold shoulder brooch. He took her hands and kissed her on the forehead.

"You know how I feel about this, Liliane," he said. "I wish you would change your mind."

Liliane returned his kiss without replying. Like her grandfather, he believed that Guardianship was not suitable for women—more than that, he did not wish to lose her. But her possession of the Gift was indisputable, and anyway, he could refuse her nothing she set her mind to.

Accompanied by a maidservant carrying her noon meal in a covered basket and a man-at-arms from her father's retinue, Liliane left her father's house. The part of the city in which she lived was a neighborhood of broad avenues and substantial dwellings, home to many of the merchants and Guild Masters and wealthy tradesmen of the city. Closer to the city's center, things grew narrower and meaner. Tall houses shut the sun away from the twisted streets; open gutters overflowed with night soil and garbage. Washing was strung from gable to gable, and people shouted conversation to each other across the gaps. Now and then the streets opened into squares, packed with the booths of vendors and peddlers, thick with shoppers and loiterers, thieves and tramps.

The Journeyer Orderhouse was a massive structure set amid a parklike area of land, a broad green break in the stone surface of the city. It was approached by a wide highway, terminating in iron-barred gates which were kept open during the day to accommodate the traffic that passed constantly in and out. Carved into the wall above the gates was the symbol of the Order of Guardians, a representation of the Fortress enclosed in a circle. Beneath was painted the emblem of the Journeyers, in the green that was their color: a quartered circle displaying a staff, a Guildsman's badge, an eye, and a book.

Followed by her maidservant and the man-at-arms, Liliane approached the gatekeeper's lodge. A bell hung by the door. The fluttering inside her chest had increased; it was hard to breathe. She closed her eyes for a moment to compose herself. Reaching out, she rang the bell.

A man dressed in Guardian habit, with a green Journeyer sash about his waist, appeared in the entrance.

"What can I do for you, young lady?" he said in vernacular.

Liliane replied in Guardian language. "I'm here for the Novice Examinations."

"Are you, then?" he said, still in vernacular, looking her up and down. "We don't get many girls for that."

Liliane needed no Gift to sense his feelings. Her nervousness vanished in a flash of anger. "Well, I am an exception. Kindly find someone to conduct me to the Examination room."

With a mental shrug, the man disappeared inside the lodge. After a moment a servant appeared and beckoned Liliane forward. She followed, her maidservant behind her, through a sizable open courtyard, along a maze of passageways and halls, and at last, into a large audience room. The servant gestured toward a Journeyer sitting at a small table, set before a door at the room's far end.

"Give him your name. He'll tell you what to do."

The Journeyer inscribed Liliane's name on a slate below a column of others, and instructed her to choose a place upon the benches that filled the room. About fifty candidates had arrived so far. Already the air was thick with apprehension, a concentrated emotion Liliane found difficult to screen away. Over the next hour candidates continued to trickle in, until nearly two hundred crowded the room. Out of them all, there was only one other girl, a starved-looking creature in shabby ill-fitting clothing.

At last the Journeyer rose from his chair and clapped his hands for attention.

"The Novice Examinations are now closed," he said. "Testing will proceed as follows. This morning we will speak to each of you individually. This afternoon the written portion of the Examination will be conducted. Tomorrow we will verify your Gifts and conduct the mindprobes. Results will be announced the following afternoon. May the Stone guide you all."

For the next four hours the candidates were interviewed, disappearing through the door at the far end of the room as their names were called. Some of the meetings took only about five minutes, others as long as fifteen. Most of the candidates returned to seat themselves again on the benches; there were a few, however, who did not come back. Because she had been one of the first to arrive, Liliane's turn came early. Beyond the door lay a long hallway. A Journeyer was waiting to escort her into one of the offices that lined it.

"I recognize your family name," he said, closing the door behind them and motioning for Liliane to sit. "You're from one of the old mindpower lineages."

"I am, Master."

"It's rare for a girl of your background to come forward." He seated himself across from her. "Are there no others of your generation with the Gift?"

"No, Master. I'm an only child. I do have cousins, but none of them are Gifted."

"Why do you wish to become a Guardian?"

He was a burly, pleasant-looking man, with long gray hair braided down his back. His brown eyes, though narrow and observant, were not unkind. Liliane could just sense his doubt of her qualifications, but no more than that. Like all Guardians, his guard was very good.

"There's been a Guardian in every generation of my family," she said, her voice a little unsteady with nervousness. "It's a long tradition that I want to carry on. I want to use my Gift to serve the Stone and the Order, to help protect the powers of the mind and guard against the evil of handpower. I want that more than anything in the world—I always have.''

''How does your family feel about it?''

Liliane dropped her eyes. ''If I had a brother, and he had mindskill, I wouldn't be sitting here.'' She looked up again. ''But if I pass the Examination, my family will support my Novitiate.''

''It's not easy, you know.'' The Journeyer's face was grave. ''It's not all nobility and the wonder of the Gift and the service of the Stone. The Novitiate is very difficult. Many of those who qualify drop out, or are eliminated in later testing.''

''I know it will be hard.'' Liliane kept her eyes steady on his face. ''I'm prepared.''

The Journeyer raised his eyebrows. ''Are you? If you're to become a Guardian, you must be willing to give up your home, your family, your friends. You must endure hunger and cold, and work until you feel you cannot move another muscle. You must strain your mind and your Gift to the breaking point. You must embrace loneliness without complaint, obedience without question. You must leave your old self behind and become someone new. Are you prepared for that? Can you even imagine it?''

His tone stung Liliane. ''No, Master, I can't,'' she replied. ''But I don't think anyone out there in that room can either.''

There was a pause. Then he smiled. ''You have a point. Tell me, what form does your Gift take?''

''I'm a heartsenser. I also have some ability for divination.''

''A heartsenser?'' The Journeyer did not react with his body or his voice, but suddenly Liliane could read his feelings. ''That's a very rare form of the Gift.''

''They tell me so.''

''How does it manifest itself?''

''I hear people's emotions and feelings and reactions, the way others can hear words and sounds. I have to be fairly close for it to work—it's weaker with distance.''

''Are you sure it's heartsensing? That Gift is closely related to nearspeech. Often those who claim it are only intruding into others' minds, without realizing it.''

Once again, Liliane was stung into a response—not just by his tone, but by the sheer number of times during her life she had had to respond to the same kind of doubt. "I've been tested, Master, many times. My Gift is vouched for not just by myself but by all my teachers. And I hope you'll vouch for it also, when I tell you that right now I can feel your surprise, because in all your career you've never encountered a heartsenser, and also your interest, because if I'm genuine discovering me might reflect very well on you."

The Journeyer looked at her, his emotions fully concealed now behind his guard. For a moment she was afraid she had overstepped. At last, however, an unwilling smile pulled at his mouth.

"How long have you had this Gift?"

"Since I was three years old."

"Don't you find it burdensome to be constantly bombarded by others' emotions?"

"When I was very small, it was sometimes hard for me to tell other people's feelings from my own. But as I've gotten older, it's become easier to . . . to screen it off, somehow. I don't know exactly how to describe it. The emotions are there, and I'm aware of them, but they don't really touch me. Like words spoken in another room—you hear the sounds, but they don't take your attention. Of course when it's like this''—she gestured toward the room where the other candidates sat waiting—''when the emotion is very concentrated and everyone is feeling something similar, it's much more difficult.''

"Very interesting." The Journeyer leaned back in his chair, steepling his fingers under his chin. "Very interesting indeed. I think I must allow you to take the Examinations after all.''

Liliane felt something turn over inside her. "Would you have sent me away if I wasn't a heartsenser?"

"I might have. You're female, and gently reared. Candidates like you aren't often strong enough to survive the journey to the Fortress, let alone the Novitiate itself. Even if you do win through, you'll face a tougher struggle than most. Heartsensers are more fragile than other Gifted. It's the nature of the Talent. Well. We'll see what the Examinations say, and what the mindprobe shows. You can go.''

Liliane returned to the bench and her bored maid. She knew now for certain what she had only suspected before, that it might not be enough for her to pass the battery of tests that comprised the Examinations, or to demonstrate the singular strength of her rare Gift—because she was female and wealthy, and therefore assumed to be weak. She had hoped the Journeyers who administered the Novice Examinations would be more enlightened than those who ran the exclusive Guardian School she had attended, but it appeared they were not. She did not try to suppress the anger she felt. The edge it gave her would offset her nervousness, and sharpen her performance.

By early afternoon, all the candidates had been interviewed. Out of the original two hundred, about one hundred and eighty remained. They were given a half hour to themselves before the start of the written tests. Some left the room, presumably in search of food or necessary rooms; others took out packed lunches. Liliane opened her basket, dividing her food with her maid. The size of her meal was embarrassing; she was tempted to share it with the other female candidate, who had brought nothing at all. But when she glanced at the girl's thin face, she was met by such a strange look, fixed and somehow knowing, that after all she did not offer.

The break ended. Slates and styluses were distributed, and for the next six hours the burly Journeyer who had conducted Liliane's interview called out questions on subjects ranging from the practical application of the Limits to details of Guardian history. The candidates were allowed five minutes to inscribe their answers on their slates, which were then examined by the Journeyers in attendance. Scores were recorded and the slates were erased, ready for the next query.

It was long after dark before the candidates were dismissed. When Liliane reached home she had barely enough energy to answer the questions with which her eager family plied her. She escaped at last to her room, with her meal on a tray. She fell asleep before she could finish it.

On the second day of the Examinations the candidates were divided into groups of ten and set to wait in antechambers. One by one, they were conducted into the room beyond, where a Journeyer tested the strength and nature of their various mindskills. For Liliane alone, two Journeyers were present. They questioned her in detail about her Gift, and then called in various individuals, some of them Guardians, some of them servants, so that she could identify the emotions of each.

Of her group, only one was rejected. The rest were given an hour-long break. The mindprobes would be conducted that afternoon.

Much of Liliane's nervousness had abated after the first morning. She was confident of her achievement on the written test, and she had sensed, even through their heavy guards, that the Journeyers were impressed by her Gift. But during the hour of rest, she found herself growing apprehensive again. Nothing could be hidden from a mindprobe. It revealed the whole of a person's thought and motivation; it detected the presence of heretical inclinations and handpower weakness; it located the guards by which the unfit often sought to conceal their wrongdoing. It was capable of finding things that were unknown even to the individual in whose mind they resided. Liliane knew of no handpower desires within herself, no aberrant thoughts or impulses. Certainly she had committed no Violations. But the fear of something hidden, some buried urge of which she was not aware, haunted her. Like all children she had learned in School the stories of the world's famous Violators, some of whom had committed no actual crime. Their corruption had lain latent within them, unsuspected until the mindprobes ferreted it out. Liliane could not imagine that she was one of these. But no doubt they had not imagined it either.

The break over, Liliane's group gathered again in the antechamber and waited silently for the resumption of testing. Liliane saw her fear mirrored on their faces; distantly, she felt their dread.

She was the first to be summoned. Waiting for her in the

small testing room was the Journeyer who had conducted her interview.

"Don't be afraid," he told her.

But she was afraid. It was all she could do not to flinch away as he placed his hands upon her temples. She sensed the approach of his mind; suddenly she was falling, tumbling down a long corridor filled with clouds. She felt the touch of power, swift and sure. A procession of disjointed images whirled past her inner vision, as if her thoughts were cards being shuffled at lightning speed. Almost before she had a chance to grasp the invasion, it was gone. The Journeyer stepped back. His expression was unreadable. She could not feel his emotions.

"You can rest for a little while in the outer room," he said. "Don't worry if you feel confused or weak—it's a common side effect. It passes quickly."

"That's . . . that's all?" Liliane said dazedly.

"Yes. Your testing is complete."

Liliane returned to the antechamber, where her maid helped her to the bench and poured her a cup of the water that had been provided. She felt dizzy, and an ache sat behind her eyes. She was conscious of a sense of surprise. She had been prepared for the mindprobe to be painful or frightening, but except for that first brief instant, it had been neither. What it had been was . . . intrusive. She had not expected the intimacy of it, the crawling sense of being touched in places that till now had been closed and secret.

She could feel the covert regard of her fellows, anxiously scanning her for some inkling of what lay ahead. Before she was really ready she rose and, leaning on her maid for support, began the journey home. She was too weary to feel anything but relief. The Examinations were over.

At noon the next day, the candidates gathered again in the long windowed room where the written tests had been administered. Their silence was overwhelmingly underscored by tension. Liliane found it hard not to fidget as she sat on the bench next to her maid. There was a quivering at her throat, as if a moth were trapped inside her chest. The other female candidate was seated a few benches to the

right. Her face was calm, her body relaxed, as if the outcome
did not matter to her.

After an interminable wait, the door at the room's far end
opened, and the Journeyers entered. In the silence each foot-
fall was clearly audible. They halted, facing the candidates.
One of them stepped forward, a little ahead of the rest.

"The time has come," he said, "to announce which of
you have been selected for the Novitiate. I know how deeply
each of you desires to be Chosen, and how hard you have
worked to prepare for the Examinations. I regret that we
cannot accept you all. But only the most Gifted and the most
fit can be eligible for the Novitiate.

"Out of the one hundred and seventy-nine candidates
tested over the past two days, we have selected ninety-two.
Stand up when you hear your name."

He began to read. Liliane leaned forward, her hands
clenched tightly in her lap, trembling with the strength of
her desire. When he actually spoke her name, there was a
moment of blankness; then, with a rush of unbelieving joy,
she pushed herself to her feet. The pressure of the past two
days, the years of preparation that had preceded them, broke
in her like a dam. She felt tears stream down her cheeks,
beyond her power to control. In all her life, she had felt no
happiness to equal this moment.

The Journeyer finished reading and lowered the parchment. Through her tears Liliane was aware of the tumult of
emotions around her: elation from those who had been Chosen, every shade and nuance of despair from those who had
not.

"Those who have been rejected," the Journeyer said,
"are now dismissed. The Chosen may remain."

The unChosen candidates got to their feet and filed from
the room. Many were weeping openly. Liliane was suddenly, acutely aware of how easily she might have been
among their ranks. Briefly, she felt their agony as more than
an observer. But her joy was too great to allow for more
than a moment of compassion.

"Be seated," the Journeyer said. The Chosen obeyed.
The other girl, Liliane saw, was still present. Unlike the rest,
she neither wept nor smiled; her grave face was as calm as

it had been before the announcement, as if she had known all along she would be Chosen.

"The past two days have been difficult," the Journeyer said. "But the time will come when you look back on them and long for something so easy.

"The Novice Examinations did not end today. What you have just experienced is only the first part of your Testing. The next, and much more arduous part, is the journey to the Fortress. If you can complete that journey, you will know you have the strength to be a Guardian. As will we.

"Starting from this day, you have one year in which to reach the Fortress, turn in your Validations, and claim your Novitiates. If you do not gain the Fortress in that time, if you are even one hour late, your place will be forfeited. For those of us who know it, the Fortress is no more than four months' journey from this city. The exact location, however, is a secret known only to Guardians and to those who have made pilgrimage. We Guardians, and all pilgrims, are sworn by the Stone to secrecy. I can tell you only that the Fortress lies to the north, in the mountain range that rises in the middle of this continent. You Chosen ones must discover the rest for yourselves.

"May the blessing of the Stone be upon you all. May its power guide you on the journey to come."

One by one, the Chosen were called up and given their Validation Certificates, rolls of parchment secured with the Journeyer Seal. Liliane received hers from the hand of the Journeyer who had conducted her mindprobe. He smiled as he held it out to her.

"You've gotten your wish," he said.

"Thank you." Liliane could not suppress the answering smile that lit her face.

"It's too soon for thanks, little heartsenser."

Liliane looked directly into his face. "I will reach the Fortress. I will claim my Novitiate. I will become a Guardian."

He met her gaze, his eyes opaque. "Perhaps you will."

Her maid in tow, Liliane left the room. Even the Journeyer's prejudice could not spoil her happiness. Whatever terrors the coming journey held, whatever rigors awaited her in the Fortress, she had achieved her heart's desire. The shape of her future was set, exactly as she had planned it.

Reaching the street, she saw the other Chosen girl just in front of her. On impulse she ran to catch up with her, leaving her maid and man-at-arms behind. She touched the girl's shoulder, and found herself fixed with the same odd look that had taken her aback two days earlier. So close, she could feel the emotion that went with it: a kind of expectancy, as of something long anticipated, now come to pass. She had the oddest feeling that the girl had been waiting for her.

"Did you want something?" the girl said. If she had not been so thin she might have seemed stocky. She had large brown eyes and straight brown hair, cut above her shoulders like a boy's. Her clothing was mismatched and patched but very clean.

"Just to congratulate you."

The girl's brown eyes were steady on Liliane's. "Why?"

"Because you're the only other girl. Because it's so much harder for girls who are Gifted."

"Yes." The girl nodded in acknowledgment. "It is."

Who was she, Liliane thought, this stranger who looked at her as if in recognition, this ragged person who held herself with a dignity equal to that of any member of Liliane's family? How would she manage to equip herself for the journey ahead? Clearly she was poor. She would not be able to afford the blankets, the tents, the food required for survival. Liliane had intended only to congratulate her on her successful candidacy, but suddenly she was moved by a different impulse.

"My family's hired a guide to take me to the Fortress," she said. "Perhaps you'd like to come with me."

Though technically it was illegal to divulge the Fortress's location, there was a loophole in the law. Successful pilgrims were sworn never to write or speak their knowledge of where the Fortress lay, but there was nothing to prevent them from leading others to it. Some pilgrims, committing a route to memory, set themselves up as guides, charging a fee to lead parties of pilgrims and candidates through the mountains. Liliane's father had hired one of these over a year ago, in anticipation of his daughter's Choosing. He did not wish her to go, but if go she must, she must have every chance of success. Those who tried the journey guideless usually died in the attempt.

The girl looked at her. Even now, she was not surprised. "Are you sure?"

"Yes," said Liliane. She had not been, when she first spoke the words, but she was now, with an absoluteness that defied analysis. "We've survived the Examinations together. It would be good if we journeyed together, too."

The girl smiled. It changed her face completely. "I think so, too. Yes. I'll come with you."

"Good." Liliane smiled back.

"There's just one thing." The girl lifted her chin. "I can't pay." Liliane could feel the humiliation the words caused her. "I can work my passage—I can be your maid, your groom, anything you like. But I can't pay."

"That's all right." Liliane was not concerned. She could talk her father into anything. "You'll be my companion. You won't have to pay."

"All right, then. It's settled."

The girl held out her hand. Liliane took it. The girl's skin was dry, rough with the calluses of hard work. Liliane was conscious of the softness of her own fingers, smooth with creams, the nails polished and unbroken. She pulled away.

"We'll be leaving one week from today, at first light. My house is in the merchant sector."

Liliane gave the girl her address. Then, followed by her scandalized maid and the imperturbable man-at-arms, she set off for home. The girl watched her as she went, all the way out of sight; Liliane could feel that steady gaze. She walked quickly. She could not quite believe what she had done.

One look at Liliane's face was all her family needed to know she had been successful. They crowded round her, embracing her with their various emotions. Marie, as usual, was envious; Telle and Helene, though they did not really understand, were happy for her. Lucien was also glad, and even Celinette set aside her sadness long enough to put her arms around Liliane and whisper congratulations. Liliane's grandmother glowed with pride. Like her granddaughter, she was a heartsenser, and in her youth had burned with ambition to be a Guardian, but her brother had been Gifted, and her father had not allowed her to take the Novice Examinations. Liliane returned her grandmother's kiss with special tenderness. She knew the heart's desire she had achieved had not been hers alone.

Liliane's mother hung back a little from the others. She had, Liliane knew, prayed her daughter would not be Chosen. As Liliane went to her she felt her mother's terrible pain. But nothing could dull her joy, not even her father's somber face when he returned later in the evening and discovered what had happened. It was not simply that he grieved to lose her. He feared terribly for her safety. He was especially tormented by the length of time that would pass before he knew whether she had survived to reach the Fortress. During the ten-year term of their training candidates were forbidden all contact with their families. The groom who would accompany Liliane, for safety's sake and for his own pilgrimage, would bring news much sooner than that, but even he might be gone as long as two years.

Over the next week, the family threw itself into preparation for Liliane's journey. The guide, though engaged well in advance, must be contacted to confirm her place in the party. A traveling kit must be assembled, following a list provided by the guide—heavy clothing, cloaks, and boots suited to journeying; tents, blankets, and other camping equipment; and a number of visas and passports, for they would be passing through several countries along the way.

Liliane had little difficulty persuading her father to pay the guide fee and assemble a traveling kit for the other Chosen girl. He was not at all dismayed by the girl's apparent poverty and inferior class. Such a girl, he pointed out, would have far more experience of hardship than Liliane. She might be a great help along the way.

As the days passed, Liliane felt her old life slipping away. The bustle of preparation, the familiar routine, seemed oddly distant, as if she had turned in a doorway to look back at a room she had already passed through. Before her, a footstep away, the journey beckoned; in the far distance, her goal of

Guardianship rose like a sunlit mountain peak. Between, shadowed in deep obscurity, lay the expanse of her training. She had only the vaguest idea of what the coming years would bring. The exact nature of the three-year Novitiate and the seven-year Apprenticeship was known only to those who had experienced them.

Brief, unpredictable instants of dread pierced her dreamy detachment. The moment of departure, in particular, held a promise of pain she had not yet found the courage to face. Invested Guardians were not prohibited communication with their relatives, but the remoteness of the Fortress, the cloistered life of Speakers and Searchers, and the farflung assignments of Journeyers and Soldiers made contact difficult. It was possible, even probable, that she would never see her family again.

The night before she was to leave, Liliane's mother came to her room, her face swollen with weeping.

"Don't go, Liliane," she begged. "You're my only child. I can't bear it that I'll never see you married. I can't bear it that I'll never hold my grandchildren."

Liliane put her arms around her mother. She said nothing, for there was nothing to be said. This was her life. This was her heart's desire. What were a husband, children, a house of her own, compared to that? At last her mother left, quietly, beyond tears now. Liliane lay in her bed, certain she would never sleep. But she did, deeply and without dreams.

She woke before dawn. She sat up in her bed, her beautiful room around her. The pain she had feared filled her now, raw and immediate. Rising, she walked about, her feet sinking into the rich pile of the carpet, running her fingers over the smooth wood of the furniture and the textured paneling of the walls, burying her face in the musty brocade of her bed curtains. She wanted to remember this place with all her senses, this room where she had first dreamed of becoming a Guardian, where she had prepared herself for what, today, she would journey forth to claim. In all her life, she had never woken anywhere but here. How could she leave it?

Outside, dawn rose slowly above the city, though in the streets it was still dark. The other Chosen girl had arrived—

she was waiting when the groom brought the horses round, curled up in the gateway as if she had been there most of the night. She had been given a horse; she sat it nervously, obviously unskilled in riding. Liliane sensed her excitement, her eagerness to be gone. It was clear that the thought of leaving brought her no pain. Her name, Liliane had learned, was Goldwine.

Liliane's family and all the servants had gathered on the porch that fronted the house. She bid the servants good-bye first, feeling their pride in her. She embraced her family: the frail aunts, Celinette and the children, all crying noisily, Lucien, even Marie, in whom she detected a real, if surprised, sadness. She put her arms around her fragile grandmother, who could not speak. Her grandfather, once again, had absented himself. She held her mother for a long time, and it was the terrible agony her mother felt that broke her control. Weeping, she threw her arms round her father's neck, clinging to him like a child.

Liliane's father embraced her tightly. He kissed her hair.

"May the Stone protect you," he murmured, his voice rough. Gently, he pushed her away. "Go now."

Liliane obeyed, stumbling a little. The groom helped her to mount her horse. They rode away, the groom in the lead, heading for the city gates, where they would meet the guide. As they rounded the corner of the street, Liliane turned to watch her father's house drop out of sight. She felt the most terrible pain she had ever known, as if her childhood home were something within her that was being ripped away. It was not too late—she could still turn her horse about, gallop wildly back to the safety of all the familiar things that lay behind . . .

But she did not. She was aware of Goldwine's wonder, of the groom's anticipation of the adventure and far places that lay ahead. She had always known that to gain what she wanted most, she must leave everything else behind. Taking a deep breath, she wiped the tears from her cheeks and set her eyes ahead.

Six

**ILIANE AWOKE** to Goldwine's hand on her shoulder. Outside the tent, dawn was a rising luster.

"I let you sleep a little late this morning," Goldwine said. "Come on—breakfast's ready, such as it is."

Liliane struggled out of her nest of blankets. For warmth, she kept on her clothes at night—getting dressed was a simple matter of pulling on boots and cloak. She pushed back the flap of the small tent she shared with Goldwine, and emerged into the morning.

The camp was pitched in a rough declivity between two soaring peaks. Raised in a city located on a level river plain, Liliane's only experience of mountains had been the sight of them—jagged irregularities marring the smooth curve of the horizon, purpled by distance, serene and unknown. From so far away she could never have conceived of their enormity, of the steep rises and vertiginous drops, the savage extremes of weather, the thinness of the air, the vegetation twisted by wind and altitude, and above the treeline, the unbroken bleakness of jutting rock and tumbled scree, interrupted only by vast expanses of virgin snow. After eight months of travel she could not shake the feeling, even in level places, that a careless step would send her tumbling to her death.

In a hollow swept clean of snow, Goldwine had built a fire, using the dried dung of their remaining horse and what bits of tough vegetation she could scavenge. The iron pot, suspended on a tripod above the flames, held their morning meal, a very small measure of gruel. Though the party's numbers were much reduced, supplies had also been depleted, and for the past month rations had been cut in half. In another pot steeped the infusion the expedition's guide had given Liliane from his medical stores to soothe her hacking cough, a lingering legacy of the serious lung fever she had contracted two months ago.

She had survived her illness. In that, she was luckier than most of her travelmates. Of the original party of thirty—the guide and his four men-at-arms, eighteen candidates, and seven servants—only seventeen remained. Two of the candidates had died early in the journey when bandits attacked the party; another had disappeared into the white vastness of a vicious blizzard. Several more succumbed, during a period of storms that forced the party to camp in an unheated barn outside one of the wretched mountain villages, to an illness similar to Liliane's. The majority of the deaths, however, including that of the groom who had accompanied Liliane and Goldwine, resulted from the treachery of the mountains, from falls and rockslides and the many other hazards of this alien territory. Liliane could still call horribly to mind the screams of the candidate who had plunged to his death in a glacial crevasse.

Liliane was no stranger to death. Her old nurse had died when she was ten, her favorite uncle not long after, and there had been a succession of stillborn brothers and sisters. Yet such passings—natural, to be expected in the course of things—were utterly unlike the random fatalities of the journey, one following another in a succession too swift for the mind to properly grasp. Except for the groom, Liliane had known none of her companions before the start of the trip, and had no reason to grieve for any of them. Even so she carried the burden of their deaths, like phantom baggage, a little heavier with each passing.

The guide, a sinewy man of undeterminable age, his face weathered and creased from a lifetime of exposure to climatic extremes, had made this mountain crossing more than fifteen times. He had warned the candidates, early in the journey, what to expect.

"It's traveling in the winter that makes things so difficult," he told them. "If the Novice Examinations were held in the spring, we could journey through the summer; there'd still be snow and ice, but the days are longer and there wouldn't be nearly as many storms. But''—he shrugged fatalistically—''the Guardians know best. Who am I to question the wisdom of the Stone?''

Often Liliane found herself remembering the Journeyer's warning to the assembled candidates on the day of Choosing. She had thought, then, that she understood what he meant when he talked of Testing. She had believed that desire and resolve were all she needed; as always before in her life, the tenacity of her will would make up for her lack of experience. But this winter crossing was a trial of strength no one who had not experienced it could grasp. Ruthlessly, it cut down the weak and the unlucky; it stripped from the survivors not only flesh but ambition and desire. No resolve was equal to the constant ordeal of cold and exhaustion and hunger, to the unending spiritual burden of loneliness and fear.

Even Liliane's Gift became her enemy. Accustomed as she was to screening the relatively mild emotions she had encountered in her sheltered life, her guard was not equal to the savage onslaught of pain, despair, and terror that accompanied every waking moment of the trip. To the burden of her own fear was added the weight of everyone else's: others' nightmares and fantasies wrapped her up like the mountain fogs, others' dreads and horrors relentlessly assailed her mind. She became less and less able to protect herself. At one point during the raging fever of her illness, she had believed she possessed no self at all, had become nothing more than a composite of the passions and phobias of those who surrounded her.

It was Goldwine who saved her. Survival was the natural parameter of Goldwine's life; with a generosity Liliane might not have expected, she shared her skills. She took on the work for both of them until Liliane learned to do her part. She nursed Liliane through her illness, forcing her to eat and drink, tying her to her horse each morning, seeing to it that they did not fall behind. She lent the strength of her person as a shelter when the emotions of others became too much to bear. She never tired, or flagged, or faltered;

there seemed to be nothing she did not know how to do, nor any adversity she could not master. Most of all, she never allowed Liliane to despair. Her Gift, it turned out, was prescience. She had seen Liliane's approach long before the Novice Examinations; the look she had turned on Liliane in the Examination room had, after all, been recognition. She had seen them traveling together. And she had seen their arrival in the Fortress. Her certainty that they would survive was unshakable.

In the end, it was debt that made friendship possible. Without Liliane, Goldwine would have been forced to undertake the journey alone; without Goldwine, Liliane might never have completed the journey at all. These parallel obligations canceled all distinctions of background and class, and made the two girls equals. In the close confines of their tent they had recounted to each other all their hopes and dreams, and shared all the moments of their lives. Liliane had heard of the abuse Goldwine had suffered at the hands of her stepmother and, later, the uncle to whom she was sent after her parents' death, a drunkard who put Goldwine out on the streets to beg a living for him. Goldwine had hung mesmerized on Liliane's accounts of her home, her wealth, her loving parents.

Liliane sat down, close to Goldwine for warmth. The wind whipped around them in sharp gusts, its chilly fingers searching for gaps in their clothing. The valley in which they were camped was a gray place, littered with gravel. Snow patched the ground, sculpted by the wind into strange shapes. Underneath, the backbone of the mountain was fractured and worn by the enormous pressure of the glaciers that periodically inched down from higher elevations, extruding themselves and retreating again in mysterious icy cycles. Small winter-killed plants clung stubbornly to notches and cracks in the stone. The sky was dark blue, like translucent enamel; from it the rising sun poured down, entirely without warmth, striking diamonds from the snow.

"Our last day," Goldwine said.

Liliane nodded. She only half-believed it. They had been traveling so long that the journey had come to seem more real than the destination.

"I can hardly remember what it feels like," Goldwine said. "Being inside, I mean. Sleeping in a bed. Not that I had that much experience of it before."

"Not being cold or hungry. Not being afraid."

"Do you think, once we've been there a while, we won't be able to remember any of this"—Goldwine gestured round her at the rock, the snow, the tattered tents—"either?"

Liliane shook her head. "I'll never forget it."

"You're right." Goldwine made a face. "Who could forget eating gruel twice a day for six months?"

"Or having your eyelashes freeze together from the cold."

"Or having the skin on your nose fall off from frostbite."

"Or not changing your underlinen for six months."

"Ugh. Or pissing in a snowdrift."

"That," said Liliane with certainty, "I hope to forget as soon as possible."

Their breakfast finished, they put out their fire and packed up their camp, a routine so familiar they no longer had to think about it. They had only one horse between them now; the other had broken a leg halfway through the journey, and the hardy packmule had been given to another member of the party whose mount had succumbed to the cold.

The party set out, strung along in single file. Slowly they passed along a ledge, into another valley, across a snowfield. The guide rode in the lead, with one of his three remaining men-at-arms placed in the middle of the procession and the other two bringing up the rear. All four men held their crossbows primed and ready, for even in these desolate regions there were bandits, bands of ragged outlaws who specialized in preying on pilgrim and candidate travel groups. The bandits feared nothing, not even the Suborder of Soldiers; over the centuries they had managed to evade most of the bindings meant to trap them, and were undeterred by the periodic campaigns mounted against them. It was rumored that they were Gifted, able to maintain a shield of invisibility to protect themselves. They struck like lightning, vanishing back into the wastes of rock and ice from which they had come, as evanescent and eternal as the snows themselves.

After several hours the party reached a large, fairly level expanse of cracked and fissured rock, bounded on one side by a sheer drop, on the other by towering peaks. Far away, the flat plain ran up against another soaring cliff wall. The guide reined in his horse.

"This is as far as I'm allowed to go," he called. "You must be alone when you claim your Novitiates. It's an easy ride from here—straight to the Pilgrim Pass. There's a guardpost at the entrance where they'll take your Validations. May the Stone protect you all."

He wheeled his horse around, and with his men-at-arms rode back the way they had come. Eight months coming, eight months returning. The candidates, at least, had only a little more traveling before them.

The group remaining—four servants and nine candidates—plodded toward the cliffs, high and dark against the sky. The Pilgrim Pass was a slash of blackness piercing the gray of the rock. It took a little over an hour to reach the guardpost, a large building made of roughly-dressed stone. A man in Guardian habit was waiting outside it. His head was shaved, his waist tied with the golden sash of the Suborder of Soldiers. About his hips was a swordbelt, from which hung a variety of daggers and a single large broadsword.

"Declare yourselves," he said in Guardian-language.

One of the boys spoke, his voice cracked and hoarse. "We are Chosen candidates, here to claim our Novitiates."

"Validations."

The candidates presented their Validations. The Soldier took them and disappeared into the building, where he remained for some time. The candidates waited in nervous silence, huddled against the omnipresent wind. At last the Soldier emerged.

"In the name of the Stone, your Novitiates have been accepted," he said. "You may proceed through the Pilgrim Pass. Beyond it is the Fortress. Ride up to the gates, and wait. The servants may not accompany you. They will be allowed to pursue their pilgrimages later."

Two by two, the candidates rode into the narrow defile. The cliffs rose straight and smooth, bracketing the pass as precisely as the sides of a box, so high the sun could not reach more than halfway down the gap between them. Mind, not nature, must have created this, Liliane thought, awed by the magnitude of such a force. There was no wind, but a cold deeper than any gale breathed from the rock.

Abruptly the cliffs fell away, and the candidates found themselves at the edge of a broad alpine meadow. Peaks soared around its perimeter, rank upon rank of them, marching away into unguessed distances. It was almost warm in this place, the wind gentled to a breeze. The snow, which still blanketed the trail behind, had already melted here, exposing coarse grass, sere and brown with winter. A road of hard-packed gravel stretched away across the meadow, toward a great black wall that spanned more than half the valley.

It was, at last, the Fortress.

Liliane stared toward this fabled place: the heart of the world, the abode of the Stone. So long had she been approaching it that arriving carried a sense of unreality, as if the inky ramparts might turn out to be a mirage. With amazement, she understood that the journey was over. She had crossed the hostile mountains, survived the savage winter, transcended herself and her own limitations. She had passed the final Test. She was a Novice now. The joy of it seemed too large for her body to contain. She felt tears overflow her eyes and run down her cold cheeks. In that instant, it was all worth it—the journey, the suffering, the loss, everything.

She felt her companions' emotions, variants of her own. They were pale and skeletal from the journey, some with bandages or slings, some hoarse with congestion of the lungs, all of them visibly marked by the hardship of the last eight months. For a moment she was profoundly aware of the bond that existed between them, the bond of their ordeal; but she also felt the distance. For all they had shared and lost, she hardly knew them, these other candidates. Survival had taken all their strength. There had been nothing left for friendship.

Of them all, only Goldwine shed no tears. She sat behind Liliane on their horse, staring silently toward the dark mass of the Fortress. Liliane could feel her tension, and another emotion, so uncharacteristic that it was a moment before she identified it as uncertainty. For the first time since embarking on the journey, Goldwine was not confident of what lay ahead.

The Novices set out along the road. Straight and sharp-edged and perfectly symmetrical, the Fortress seemed oddly artificial against the irregular shapes of the mountains. As they neared it, its gargantuan scale became apparent, as large as any worldly city. Its shadow extended far across the valley, swallowing the candidates while they were still some distance away.

They reached the gates and halted. The gates were constructed of colossal weather-scarred timbers, massively barred with iron and studded with rivets the size of shields, rising at least three times the height of a man. The walls, twice again as tall, were composed of great mortared blocks of black stone. From this perspective, stretching away to either side, unbroken by other entrances or openings, they seemed nearly endless. There was no bellrope or other way for the candidates to announce their presence. They waited, in a silence unbroken by any sound or sign of life.

At last, without any perceptible signal, the gates began to swing ponderously inward, parting just enough to admit a single horseman. One by one, the Novices passed through the opening.

Beyond lay another world.

The candidates found themselves at the entrance to a vast courtyard, a flagged expanse broad enough to fit an entire village. It was bounded on the left by a long line of stables and workshops, and on the right by a massive keep, with several levels of narrow windows and great double doors at its center. At the far end rose a second keep, more elaborate, with turrets and balconies and porches. Four fountains marked the center of the court, water pouring from dozens of spigots. Around them seethed a hive of activity. Carts rattled across the cobbles, grooms and stableboys ran to and fro, servants carried trays and baskets and bundles of laundry, gray-garbed Guardians moved about their business, the sashes of the four Suborders bright about their waists. The air was thick with the smells of smoke, animals, and food. The noise of voices, hammers, cartwheels, feet, and a million miscellaneous activities was deafening.

The impact upon the mountain-bound senses of the candidates was overwhelming. They clustered together like stunned birds, staring dumbly at the chaos in front of them. For a long time no one paid them any heed. At last two Guardians, a man and a woman, emerged from the hubbub. They wore the blue sashes of the Searcher Suborder.

"Dismount," the man said, curtly.

The candidates obeyed. Stableboys appeared to lead the horses away.

"Your belongings will be held for distribution to pilgrims," the man said. "From this moment, you own nothing. Boys, follow me. Girls, go with my companion."

They turned and, without looking back, began to move toward the edifice on the right. The candidates hurried in their wake. The huge double doors had smaller doors cut into them; the candidates followed their guides through these, plunging into the darkness of the interior.

The female Searcher led Liliane and Goldwine deep into the building, through corridors and lobbies and atriums and courtyards, past schoolrooms and refectories and other chambers whose purpose could not be guessed. She moved so quickly that there was no time to grasp orientation or direction, only a flow of disjointed images, bewildering not simply in the swiftness of their passage but in the impression of utter uniformity they produced. Everywhere was the same irregularly mortared stone, the same splintery iron-barred doors, the same torches with the same smoke plumes above them, a denser blackness on the dusky masonry. The torches were set at distant intervals; shadows congregated everywhere, obscuring entranceways, swallowing corners, shifting in the recesses of the arched ceiling. Oddly, it seemed colder within this place than it had been outside, in the court.

They came at last to a flight of stairs. At its top lay a broad corridor lined with narrow galleries. The Searcher ushered the two girls into one of these. Unshuttered windows ran its full length. Wooden pallets with straw mattresses were ranged along the walls, each with a small chest beside it and two wooden pegs above. The Searcher stopped halfway down the room and pointed at two pallets, side by side.

"These will be yours," she said. Her face held no expression; her blue eyes were as chilly as the flagstone floor. "In the chest you will find the proper garments for a Novice. Put them on, fold the garments you are wearing, and place them at the end of the bed. You may use your own boots until you can be fitted for shoes. You may dress as I speak."

Obediently Liliane and Goldwine pulled garments from the chests: undershirt and hose, tunic and leather belt, cross-tied leggings and a short cloak. The undergarments were made of coarse linen, the rest from rough-spun wool. Everything was a uniform dull gray. The Searcher addressed them as they removed their own clothing, her voice clear and cold.

"A Novice has no possessions. From now on, what you need will be lent to you by the Order of Guardians: two sets of clothing, one pair of boots, two blankets, one pillow, one mattress, one slate, and one stylus. You are responsible for these items. Any you lose you will have to earn back. You go to bed when it is dark, and rise with the dawn. There are three meals a day in the refectories downstairs. The necessary room is beyond that door. You are required to bathe weekly, and you will be examined once a year by our physicians. Any illness must be verified by your Group Leader before you are given sick leave. You may also request a day of seclusion in the infirmary when your monthly time is on you. Be careful of such requests, however. We do not encourage malingering. Do you understand me thus far?"

The two girls nodded.

"The building in which we stand is known as the Novice Wing. It is the only place where Novices are allowed to be. If you enter any other part of the Fortress without explicit permission or direction, you will be severely punished. It will be some time before your training begins. Until then, you will do as you are told, without question or protest. A Proctor has been assigned to your group from the Third-Year Novice Girls' Class. She will come to you presently and give you further instructions. Do you have any questions before I go?''

Bemused, their senses still stunned by the abrupt transition from the small world of the journey to this huge community, Liliane and Goldwine shook their heads. Without another word the Searcher turned, and walked swiftly from the room.

Shivering with the intense cold of the unheated gallery, the two girls finished dressing. Their new clothes were heavy and stiff, much too loose on their emaciated frames. They sat down side by side on one of the lumpy pallets.

"I'm so cold," Liliane said, her teeth chattering.

"So much for a real bed and a fire," Goldwine replied. She could not quite manage the matter-of-fact tone she attempted. "Maybe the classrooms are warmer."

"What do you think she meant about our training not beginning right away?"

"I don't know." Then, with something like panic: "Liliane, I don't know anything anymore. I never saw past this moment. I saw us standing before the Fortress, but I never saw inside. I don't know what comes next."

Liliane put her arms around her friend. Goldwine huddled against her, shivering. Liliane gazed at the spartan rows of pallets, the rough stone of the walls, the thin blankets and flat pillows, the shades of gray and dun and black. It was not at all what she had anticipated. She had not been foolish enough to think she would find in the Fortress any echo of the luxury of her home, but she had expected at least warmth and some degree of comfort. She reached for the euphoria she had felt such a little time ago, but in the strangeness of this place she could not find it.

After what seemed a long time, a tall girl of about fifteen entered the room. She was dressed in the Novices' coarse gray garments, her long red hair neatly braided down her back. A silver medallion hung around her neck. She looked Liliane and Goldwine over, as the female Searcher had done, her eyes appraising.

"I'm Raisa, your Third-Year Proctor," she said in a brisk voice. "I'll be responsible for your Study Group for the next few months. Once your schooling starts, a Group Leader will be chosen from among you. For now, if you have any questions or problems, come to me. Don't go to the others in your group, don't go to your teachers. I'm the one you see. Are you with me?"

"Yes," Liliane and Goldwine chorused.

"Good. I'll show you around now, and then you can join the rest of your group for supper. Don't worry if you're confused at first—everyone is. You'll catch on quicker than you think."

She led the way out of the sleeping gallery. The Novice Wing, Liliane and Goldwine learned, was composed of five floors and several basement levels. The basements housed the servants' quarters and were also used for storage. The first floor contained the kitchens, the refectories, the assembly halls, the infirmary, a number of courtyards where Novices practiced various skills, the classrooms, and the apartments of the teachers, all of whom were Searchers. This was known as the Learning Level. The other floors, known as Living Levels, housed the Novice Classes; First-, Second-, and Third-Year boys on the top three floors, girls of all years on the second. The whole of the wing was strictly segregated according to class year—each class was forbidden the areas assigned to classes senior to theirs, though they were allowed unlimited access to areas assigned to junior classes—and also by gender. Males and females mixed only on the Learning Level.

Classes were divided into cohorts called Study Groups, each containing approximately one hundred Novices, each assigned to one of the cold stone galleries. Groups ate, slept, worked, and studied together. First-Year training began in the autumn. It was May now; this meant that Liliane and Goldwine must wait four months before they could start to learn. Until then, they would be known as Unclassed Novices, without status, tasks, or duties beyond those their teachers gave them.

"But don't worry," said Raisa with a laugh. "You'll be kept busy."

Raisa's explanations were crisp and clear. She stopped often so Liliane and Goldwine could ask questions; she pointed out landmarks, and gave them memory tricks to help them recall places and things. She explained the meaning of the small symbols set into the stones, indicating the nature of the floor, the purpose of the rooms, the preserves of the various classes. Even so, after only a little while Liliane was hopelessly confused. The Novice Wing was like a vast labyrinth. The pervasive sameness of the rooms and halls made it hard to tell one floor from another, let alone one section from the next; the explanatory symbols were numerous and complicated, difficult to make out in the dimness of the halls. It seemed dauntingly possible to lose one's way and wander into forbidden territory. Without providing details, Raisa hinted at the awful punishments exacted for trespass, not by the teachers but by the Novices themselves.

While the Living Levels had been largely empty, the Learning Levels were crowded. Servants ran errands, swept and scrubbed floors, carried baskets of washing. Teachers conducted classes. Novices sat at desks and inscribed their slates, gathered in a circle to learn some sort of mindskill, performed manual tasks, lined up for physical training, passed quietly in the corridors. According to Raisa, there were more than two thousand people in the wing—approximately fifteen hundred Novices, and several hundred teachers and servants.

"But this—the Novice Wing—is only the smallest part of the Fortress. You saw the keep at the end of the courtyard? That's the Apprentice College. It's much larger than our wing. Beyond that are the wings where the Guardians live. Each Suborder has a wing to itself. The wings make a square, and at the center is the Garden of the Stone. They say it's beautiful there, with trees and grass and flowers. No matter what the season is in the rest of the world, in the Garden it's always spring."

For just a moment Liliane felt Raisa's yearning, quickly suppressed. Though the pride Raisa felt in the Fortress and her knowledge of it was clear, Liliane could read little feeling from the other girl. She gave an impression of guardedness, as if heavy emotional dampers were in place. Everyone here, in fact, seemed more than normally opaque—a welcome change from the claustrophobic, unchecked fog of emotion of the journey.

A bell sounded. Bells, Raisa had told them, marked every hour and every activity. It was necessary to keep careful track of their sequence, for there was nothing in their ringing to differentiate them.

"It's suppertime," Raisa said. "I'll take you to the First-Year refectory now and introduce you to your Study Group."

In the refectory the Novices sat at long tables, monitored by blue-sashed Searchers. Raisa conducted Liliane and Goldwine to a table on the left side of the room, briefly announced their names to the girls sitting there, and departed without a backward glance. At a gesture from the presiding Guardian, the other Novices edged over, providing a little space at the end of one of the benches for Liliane and Goldwine to seat themselves.

The refectory was a cavernous room, with a vaulted ceiling from which hung chandeliers full of smoky candles. A frieze of some sort ran around the walls, but the light was too dim to make out details. Like everywhere else, it was very cold. The rough wooden tables and benches were set so closely it was barely possible to move between the orderly lines of seated Novices. Girls occupied perhaps ten tables, all on the same side of the room.

A Searcher mounted the dais at the far end of the room, and, standing before a lectern, intoned the Prayer to the Stone. As servants brought dishes to the tables, he opened a heavy leatherbound book and began to read selections from commentaries on the Limits. The Novices ate in silence; there was not even whispered conversation. The food was plentiful and good—a meat stew with vegetables, mashed turnips, and dense brown bread—but despite the starvation diet of the past few months, neither Goldwine nor Liliane managed to eat very much. Liliane was exhausted, her senses painfully overloaded, and her cough was bothering her again. She longed for sleep.

The meal closed with another invocation to the Stone. The Novices rose silently from the benches. Liliane and Goldwine followed the girls at their table as, in single file, they threaded their way along the corridors.

In the sleeping gallery torches had been kindled along the

walls, their smoke rising to further darken the plume marks on the ceiling. The fading light of evening crept through the windows, accompanied by a chilly breeze. The girls sat on their beds or moved about; some pored over their slates, some practiced minor feats of mindskill, a few played a game with homemade cards, and the rest sat in groups or by twos, talking in quiet voices. As different as the mood was from the regimented atmosphere of the meal, it was still subdued, with the same strong sense of emotional restraint.

Liliane and Goldwine found their beds. The clothing they had left folded had been removed. Liliane felt a sense of loss. Now there was nothing familiar, not even her shift. Of all the people and things she had ever known, only Goldwine remained.

The girl on the bed next to Goldwine's was darning a pair of hose. She looked up, with the appraising stare common to everyone here. She was slender, with olive skin, coarse black hair, and almond-shaped brown eyes. She was less guarded than most of the others; Liliane could feel her curiosity.

"You're the new ones," she said, her Guardian-language heavily accented. "My name's Verain. What are you called?"

Goldwine and Liliane spoke their names.

"This is free time," Verain told them. "We can do as we like for the next hour, as long as we don't leave the room. A bell will tell us when to go to bed. There's bells for everything here."

Liliane shivered in the draft from the windows. She wanted nothing more than to lie down, but no one else was doing this, and she was determined not to call attention to her weakness. "Is it always this cold?" she asked.

"As long as I've been here. They say in summer it can get hot. I hope so. Where I come from it's hot all the time." She looked at Goldwine. "What's your Gift?"

"Prescience. What's yours?"

"I'm a firestarter. A maker." Verain's tilted eyes shifted to Liliane. "How about you?"

"I'm . . ." Liliane caught herself. Her Validation, unlike Goldwine's, contained a special stricture, forbidding her to admit publicly to the true nature of her Gift. "I'm a near-diviner."

Verain had finished with the hose. She put them aside and took a tunic from the large pile of garments beside her. She turned it over to search for holes; she found none, but began to sew anyway, pushing her needle through the unblemished sleeve.

"Why are you darning that tunic when there's nothing wrong with it?" Goldwine asked.

"I'm under Obedience. I have to mend one garment belonging to every girl in the Study Group. I suppose now you're here I'll have to do it for you too."

"I don't understand."

"Didn't Raisa tell you about Obediences?" Goldwine shook her head. "Obediences are . . . well, they're tasks. The teachers assign them. Obediences teach us the habit of full and unquestioning submission to the will of our Masters." She sounded as if she were quoting verbatim from some memorized lesson. "Sometimes they're given to punish us, but mostly it's not for any reason, really."

"They make you do things like that?" Goldwine sounded disbelieving. Despite her visionary Gift, she was a supremely practical person; wasted time, wasted energy, were anathema to her. "Pointless things?"

Verain's eyes flicked up to Goldwine's face. "It's not pointless. I just explained." She focused again on the tunic. "Usually Obediences are simple. Like not speaking to a certain person, or not eating certain foods, or not wearing your underlinen. But sometimes they're more involved. I heard of one girl who had to sleep under her bed for a month. And there was another who had to cut off all her hair and make a necklace out of it, and wear it for an entire *year*." There was awe in her voice. "But mostly two weeks is as long as you get."

Liliane was caught by a sudden wave of dizziness. She closed her eyes.

"Is your friend all right?" she heard Verain ask.

"She just needs a good night's sleep," Goldwine replied.

"Don't count on that."

"Why not?"

There was a pause. Liliane sensed something new. Verain was afraid. But it was a dread bounded by very strong inhibitions, as if she had been forbidden to admit what she feared—and anyway it was just a flash, quickly suppressed. Liliane opened her eyes. Verain's face showed nothing.

"I only meant it's cold," she said. "Too cold to sleep well."

She bent her head over the tunic, apparently engrossed. She did not speak again.

Goldwine came to sit beside Liliane on the bed and wrapped a blanket around her shoulders. Goldwine's capable hands were steady: she was the comforter again, the coper, the role she had worn so well along the way of the journey. But Liliane could feel her friend's exhaustion and bewilderment, as consuming as her own, and recognized the brittleness of this façade of calm. Throughout the journey she had relied on Goldwine's imperturbable certitude—first for comfort, then for survival. It was fearful to reach out and not to find it.

They sat side by side, silent, until the sleep-bell rang. At once the girls stopped whatever they were doing and got into their beds, taking off their boots and cloaks but keeping the rest of their clothing on. Five minutes later the torches extinguished themselves, and the room was plunged into darkness.

In spite of her weariness, Liliane lay open-eyed for a time, listening to the breathing and shifting of the others. Her coverings were not quite enough to dispel the chill, and the straw mattress beneath her was lumpy and uncomfortable. In the long window across the room she could see the moon, drifting pale among pinpoint stars. I'm in the Fortress, she thought. Soon I'll start the process of becoming a Guardian. This is what I gave up my family for, what I've been journeying toward for nearly a year. This is my heart's desire.

But the strangeness of the Novice Wing was all she could feel, heavy and silent, comfortless and cold. Her family, her desire, even the journey, seemed impossibly distant, as if she had only dreamed another life, lying here in the frigid dark.

At the deepest point of her illness, the level from which

she might have chosen never to return, Liliane had found herself at a black, still place inside her mind. It was small and yet boundless, a blissful void of silence. The din of others' emotions could not penetrate it, nor others' power touch it. When she emerged from delirium, she carried with her the memory of this place. Though she never again sank so deep, she found that she could return at will to the shadowy reaches of this part of herself and, for a time, find peace.

For comfort now, she sought those quiet depths. She felt calm reach up to her. The cold unease of her surroundings receded. As she sank toward sleep she felt, briefly, the pulse of power. It was a power her Gift recognized, though she herself did not. For just the instant of her sensing, it seemed to reach inside all her empty spaces and make them full.

Liliane dreamed that she was buried under an avalanche, smothering to death beneath cold white snow. She struggled to draw breath, her lungs straining, and as she did she realized that she was not dreaming: her mouth and nose and eyes really were covered. But not by snow: by hands, clamped so that she could neither see nor cry out.

"Are you awake?" a voice hissed in her ear.

Liliane nodded, as best she could under the pressure of the hands.

"Don't scream. If you scream you'll be punished. Understand?"

Liliane nodded again. The hands removed themselves. Gasping for breath, she opened her eyes, and for a moment felt herself catapulted back into dreams. Bending over her was a figure clad in flowing white robes, with a raised hood and a completely flat, white face. Nose and mouth were no more than straight black slits; the eyes were two inky holes. Somewhere within the blackness, she could see the glitter of the creature's gaze.

"Get up," the thing whispered. It reached up a gloved hand to touch its face, pulling at it, and Liliane realized that she was looking at a mask.

Trembling with shock and chill, she obeyed. Other white figures moved from bed to bed, rousing all the sleepers. At a gesture from the robed ones, the girls began to remove their clothes.

"Strip, you two," the figure hissed. It was standing between her bed and Goldwine's. "Down to your undershirt and leggings. Quick."

Liliane obeyed, her teeth chattering. The night air was like metal against her bare skin. Fear filled the room as tangibly as the cold, overspilling the bounds of the girls' guards. Was this what Verain had meant about not expecting a good night's sleep? What was going to happen? Was it part of Novice training?

When all the girls stood shivering in their shirts and leggings, the robed ones gestured again. Two by two, the girls filed out of the gallery, silent on their bare feet.

"Follow the line," the robe hissed at Liliane and Goldwine. "Don't make a sound."

The column of girls padded down the stairs and along the corridors, shepherded by the robes. Five out of every six torches had been extinguished for the night, and at the midpoint the icy passages were nearly pitch-black. The entire Novice Wing was gripped in a thick silence, as if no other living thing were abroad. The cloud of fear accompanied their progress; from the robed escorts Liliane could sense no emotion whatsoever.

They reached the first level and began to descend yet another flight of stairs, into the basements beneath the main structure. Down and down they went. Oddly, it grew warmer, a damp warmth musty with the smell of unused places and ripe with mold, undercut from time to time by a whiff of sulfur. There were no torches here; the robes held up their hands, in which glowed pale spheres of mindlight. The flagged floors were damp beneath Liliane's bare feet, and occasionally something dripped on her from the low, arched ceiling.

They halted at last before a small wooden door. One of the robes produced a heavy key and unlocked the padlock. The door groaned slowly open, revealing pitchy blackness. The robe tossed a light-sphere through the entrance; it arced away, trailing spectral shadows. At the robe's gesture, the girls filed inside. Liliane heard splashing; when she reached the threshold she saw that the room, its floor deeper than that of the passages, was flooded. Stepping down, she found herself nearly knee-deep in water. The air was touched by an unpleasant vegetable smell, and the submerged stones of the floor felt slippery and soft, as if they had been overlaid with muck or algae. The light-sphere, hovering just below the ceiling, illuminated ancient masonry and, here and there, a slender supporting column. Nowhere could Liliane see walls.

The girl in front of her stopped, and she halted too, her bare toes curling against the nastiness of the slick floor. She was seized with the idea that there might be creatures swimming in this stagnant underground lake, or some horrible fungus growing up between the flags. . . . She glanced around for Goldwine, and realized with a surge of terror that she could not see her friend. All around her stood the strangers of her Study Group, staring straight ahead, their faces set. The fog of fear had become stronger, in some cases approaching panic. It was very quiet, though somewhere, faintly, Liliane could hear sobbing.

"What's going to happen?" she whispered to the girl who had been ahead of her. The girl turned her pale face to Liliane's.

"They're going to put out the light and leave us here."

"Why?"

"They call it hazing. They throw illusions at us, as horrible as they can make them—it's different every time. We can't run or fight back. If we fall down they make us get up. If we cry they make it worse. It goes on until they think we've had enough, and then they bring us out again."

"But . . . why?" Liliane stared at the girl. "Is it part of our training?"

The girl's face was hard. "It's tradition. Thirders always do it to Firsters. We'll get to do it too, when we're Third-Year Novices."

"Why would we want to—"

"Shut up, new girl. You'll get me in trouble."

The light, when it went, did not dwindle or fade; it simply vanished, plunging the room into a darkness so complete that it seemed not simply a lack of illumination, but an actual substance pressing against Liliane's eyes. She heard several of the girls gasp. Her heart beat fast against her throat. She was gripped alternately by the sense that she was confined within a dwindling space hardly larger than her own body, and the feeling that she was poised at the edge of unimaginable vastness, which would swallow her up if she lost her balance or moved even a step.

For a moment there was only the darkness. Then, with shocking suddenness, came the onslaught. Hideous forms rushed out of the blackness, twisted into nightmare shapes that both mocked and imitated the forms of living creatures, glowing with their own pallid light. They whirled and lunged at the helpless girls, claws and tentacles outstretched, dripping jaws agape. Liliane cowered away, raising her arms to shield herself. The desire to flee was overwhelming; she struggled to remember that she was not supposed to move. These things are illusions, she told herself frantically. There's nothing in this room except stinking water and the girls in my Study Group. It isn't real. It isn't real.

With an effort, she lowered her arms. She forced herself to stand straight again. As if it had been her belief and fear that gave them substance, the creatures grew filmy and insubstantial. Suddenly it was bearable. She was even able to think, fleetingly, that it was all rather childish.

Abruptly the illusions were gone. Unbroken darkness returned. At first it seemed nothing was happening, but then Liliane became aware that the air was growing warmer—stifling, in fact, a clammy, foggy heat. She felt sweat break out on her body. The water too seemed to have become warmer, thicker, viscous as blood. She was possessed by the overpowering certainty that something inhabited it, something huge and blind and ancient as the stones themselves, something that was, even now, swimming toward her through the sticky liquid.

She told herself again that this was illusion, that the water was just water and contained nothing living. But this time she could not convince herself. She knew, she was absolutely certain, that the liquid was moving . . . any minute now something would touch her feet . . . She was filled with a repulsion so powerful she felt she would die if she could not escape. All around her, roiling like smoke, battering at a guard the journey had made strained and fragile, was the unleashed panic of her helpless Study Group. She felt herself stretching toward a breaking point.

Instinctively, she sought the safety of the still place at the center of her mind. She burrowed toward it through the disordered layers of her consciousness, struggling against the pressure of the fear that tried to turn her back. Gathering herself, she punched through the final wall, and fell downward, into silence.

A long time later she became aware that the illusion was gone. The light-sphere had rekindled itself, and the door had opened. At a signal from one of the robes, the exhausted girls began to file from the room, their heads hanging, some of them staggering as they walked. Their ordeal had wrung all emotion from them; they were blank and empty. The guard of the robes was more relaxed now. Liliane could feel their fatigue, their contempt for their bedraggled victims. In one case, there was a kind of satiation, as if some deep inner need had been met.

As Liliane passed the group of robes, a gloved hand shot out and gripped her arm.

"You," the robe whispered. "It was you."

In the holes of its mask, Liliane could see its glittering eyes. Here, she realized, was the source of the satiety she had sensed.

"Don't play innocent with me," the robe hissed. "I know what you did. I'll be watching you from now on, little Unclassed girl."

The glove tightened on her arm. Liliane felt bones and muscles grinding together. In spite of herself, she let out a small cry of pain. A strange satisfaction flashed out from behind the robe's guard. Released, she stumbled after the others.

When they regained the gallery most of the girls collapsed onto their beds without bothering to remove their soaked leggings and undershirts. For Liliane the memory of the viscous water-illusion was too strong. She removed these articles of clothing and placed them on the chest to dry. In the bed beside hers, Goldwine lay rigid, her blankets pulled to her chin. In the half-light of the gallery her face seemed very pale; her eyes were huge, as if with shock.

"Are you all right?" Liliane whispered.

"I suppose so." Then, in a fierce whisper: "This is a terrible place. I hate it here."

"Goldwine, you don't mean—"

"Leave me alone, Liliane. Just leave me alone."

She turned her back, pulling the coverings over her head. Liliane could feel her baffled fury, a helpless turmoil of emotion utterly unlike the stubborn determination with which she had met the hardships of the journey. She knelt and laid her hand on her friend's stiff shoulder, but Goldwine did not emerge from her blanket cocoon. At last, wearily, Liliane returned to her bed.

She had reached a place beyond exhaustion. Her body seemed to drift on a great sea of weariness, attenuated and weightless. Goldwine's words echoed in her mind. She thought of the reasonless cruelty of what she had just experienced. Why should Third-Year Novices be allowed to haze First-Year Novices? Why should everything be so cold, so gray? How could she learn in such an atmosphere? How could she spend ten years in such a place?

It came to her then, with the solidity of revelation. This afternoon, standing at the edge of the meadow, she had thought the Novice Examinations behind her. But she had been wrong. She was still being Tested. The cheerless corridors, the discomfort, the strange Obediences, the torment of the hazing—all of it was a Test, an enormous, living sequel to the Examinations.

It explained everything. There was even a kind of comfort in knowing that what she had just experienced was part of a larger pattern that was neither capricious nor unnecessary. Yet, contemplating her understanding, Liliane felt her soul tremble. She had believed the Testing over. It was hard, very hard, to know she must endure more. How long would it continue? Until the autumn, when the real training began? Until the close of the Novitiate? Until the finish of the Apprenticeship? How would she know when it had ended? How would she know if she had succeeded, or whether she had failed?

The urge for tears was strong. But weeping did no good, the journey had taught her that. It had taught her, too, the importance of fixing her gaze upon the end point of her goal, rather than on the road she must take to reach it. Within the understanding of the Test lay the strength she needed to survive it. Eventually, Testing must end. Eventually she would become a Guardian.

For a moment Liliane felt the pulse of her purpose, as strong as it had been at the edge of the meadow. But almost at once it was swallowed by the overwhelming need for rest. Dropping down into the darkness of her deepest self, she felt again the touch of that vast, benign presence. This time she recognized it, an understanding that stemmed from the nameless place toward which she was descending. It was the Stone. As she drifted into sleep, it wrapped her in its power, rocking her gently in a deep ocean of silence.

Seven

HEN THE rising-bell rang, Liliane had already been awake for half an hour. Outside, the summer dawn was rising. Above the tide of light the sky was still nighttime indigo, and the crescent moon was visible, a curl of silver amid glinting stars. As usual, a current of air stole through the unglazed windows, but in the last two months, as the brief alpine summer settled upon the Fortress, the breath of the wind had lost its sharpness and could sometimes feel almost pleasant.

Liliane had trained herself to wake like this most mornings, ahead of the bell. With the Fortress still wrapped in dreaming stillness, the emotions of its thousands of occupants quieted by slumber, she was able to drift for a while amid blissful near-silence. It was the closest she was able to come in this place to the precious moments of morning peace in her room at home.

Around her the girls of her Study Group huddled beneath their blankets, breathing and turning and coughing and sighing. Over the past two months new arrivals had swelled their number to nearly ninety. Yet, though Liliane ate and slept and worked with these girls, though she could attach a name and a scrap of history to every face, she did not feel as if she were part of a group, or knew her fellows with more than a surface familiarity. At first she had assumed this distance stemmed from herself, or rather from her family's social standing. While many male Novices were descended from influential mindpower lineages like her own, most female Novices came from modest backgrounds, or even, like Goldwine, from wretched poverty. As time passed, however, she reached a different understanding. Distance was the custom here. Personal information was shielded like buried treasure; conversations skimmed the surface of experience, changing course abruptly at the first sign of dipping too deep. Friendships like Liliane and Goldwine's were nowhere in evidence.

Liliane turned her head toward Goldwine's bed, forgetting for an instant that the other girl was no longer there. She closed her eyes, cursing the stubborn habit of expectation that would not allow her to stop looking for her friend.

She had first noticed Goldwine's absence six weeks ago, at the evening meal. Her whispered inquiries to her tablemates brought only blank looks. It was not uncommon for Novices to disappear; between Validation and Apprenticeship a Novice class might be reduced by as much as a third, through illness, judgments of unfitness or failure, escape, and suicide. Liliane could not believe that any of these things had happened to Goldwine. But when she returned to the sleeping gallery, she found a new arrival sitting on Goldwine's bed. For the first time since she had gained the Fortress, she panicked. She grabbed the stranger by the shoulders, shouting questions into her face: Where was Goldwine? Had the girl seen her, heard anything? Was Goldwine sick? Was she injured? The girl, starvation-thin from her terrible journey, her face blank with bewilderment and exhaustion, stared at Liliane with frightened eyes. Timidly, she whispered that the bed had been empty when it was assigned to her. She knew nothing about a previous occupant. She knew nothing about anything. Her eyes filled with tears.

With an effort, Liliane got control of herself. She forced herself to sit down on her bed, where she remained, stiff as a block of wood, until lights-out. She was too consumed with fear to spare even a shadow of sympathy for the pathetic newcomer. She was aware that she was being watched, covertly. She had the sense that the other Novices knew the answers to her questions and took pleasure in not telling her.

The next morning Liliane approached Raisa. To her immense relief she learned that Goldwine was not ill, nor injured, nor expelled. She had been transferred to another Study Group.

"Is she being punished?" Liliane asked.

"People are moved a lot their first year. Almost no one winds up with the Study Group they start out with." Raisa shrugged. "It's not punishment, it's just the way things are."

"But why?" Liliane could not hold back the tears that filled her eyes.

"It's the way things are," Raisa repeated. "Your friend will be all right."

"But—"

"Let it go, Liliane. If you want to survive this place, you have to learn to accept the things that happen here. Questions only get you noticed, and being noticed always gets you in trouble. Go to breakfast now. Remember, an obedient Novice is never late."

Liliane understood that Goldwine's reassignment was yet another aspect of the Testing. But understanding, which made it possible to bear the drudgery that filled the days and the hazing that broke the nights, could not blunt the ache of Goldwine's absence. No vestige of her former life remained now. She felt rootless, pastless, as if she had never had any existence but here. She found herself drawing inward, like the other girls, seeking the safety of a strong emotional guard. The less she showed of herself, the less there would be to take away.

Often, in later years, Liliane thought that this was the one point when she might have yielded to the despair that ceaselessly prowled the periphery of Novice life. It was the Stone that saved her. The vast continuum of its power underlay the Fortress as solidly as the bedrock of the mountain; it became Liliane's refuge, a safe haven to which she could flee. She had only to quiet her thoughts and drift toward the dark place at her core. There, somehow, she was able to touch the edges of the Stone's contemplation, to apprehend the glittering vistas of its vision, opening out before her in transcendent and infinite progression. The harmony of its song never failed to bring her some measure of peace. It was possible, upon returning, to feel the full strength of the purpose that often, in the dim corridors of the Novice Wing, seemed frighteningly distant.

Liliane sought that refuge now. She closed her eyes and allowed herself to fall away from the cheerless room, the breathing of her companions, the scratchy blankets, the knowledge of the coming day. The Novice Wing, the Fortress, the world itself shrank to insignificance. There was only the measureless and mysterious flow of power, and her own small Gift cradled gently within it.

Dawn became morning. The clouds turned from gold to rose. The sun eased above the horizon, leaching the last trace of indigo from the sky. Down in the courtyard, cocks began to crow.

The rising-bell, harsh and sudden, wrenched Liliane from contemplation. She sat bolt upright in bed. Around her, the rest of her Study Group was rising. The room filled with morning sounds: the rustling of covers, coughing, whispered words, the creak of clothing chests.

Under Raisa's watchful eye, the girls dressed—quickly, for the sleeping gallery was cold no matter what the season—and made up their beds in the prescribed fashion, blankets tightly tucked in and pillows neatly at the top. Finished, they lined up down the center of the room, waiting for Raisa to give the signal for the necessary room. The necessary room was a rectangular stone chamber with twenty wooden seats, ten on each side; beneath the seats, stone channels snaked their way to the basement cesspit where all the Wing's drains and necessaries emptied. Daily scouring could not eradicate the smell of waste that centuries of use had imprinted upon the stones. The lack of privacy was even worse than the stink. Liliane had not yet grown used to the embarrassment of relieving herself in company with nineteen others, and she suspected she never would.

The next signal marched the girls out of the sleeping gallery, down the central hallway, and into the Novice Girls' Washroom, a huge windowless chamber that took up the entire width of the building. The floor was deeply cut with channels, and sloped on all four sides toward a central drain that breathed out the sulfur stench of its basement terminus.

Twenty round tubs, in which the weekly baths were taken, were crowded together at one end of the room; the rest of the space was occupied by rows of narrow wooden tables. The girls entered the washroom one Study Group at a time, taking metal basins from the shelves beside the door. They received a dipperful of hot water from the servants who manned the steaming coppers, and carried their basins to the tables, where they washed their faces, hands, ears, and necks. Proctors and Group Leaders monitored the process, reprimanding those who did not do a thorough enough job, calling out sharply to halt whispered conversations. Finished, the girls dried their faces and hands on the hems of their shirts, emptied their basins into the drain, and lined up yet again, ready for the descent to the First Level and the morning meal.

In the refectory Liliane took her assigned place, glancing around in search of Goldwine. Often Goldwine did not come down to breakfast, being under some Obedience or other, but today Liliane glimpsed her friend several tables away. There was a full plate of food before her, but she was not eating. Within the past few days her brown hair had been shorn close to her scalp. Vermin? Liliane wondered. Punishment, more likely.

Breakfast over, the Novices bowed their heads for the Prayer to the Stone. Twenty minutes were allowed between the meal and the first class or worksite of the day. Liliane and Goldwine sometimes met during these brief between-activity periods, each waiting at a mutually agreed-upon site whenever she could, on the chance the other could slip away also.

Liliane reached their meeting place: a flight of stairs tucked behind an odd angle of wall. The hollow beneath it was filled with shadows, and anyone who huddled close against the stones was invisible to passersby. Goldwine was already there. The two girls embraced. It was over a week since they had seen each other.

"How is it with you?" Liliane whispered.

Goldwine shrugged, a wordless answer. "You?"

"I'm fine. Goldwine, what happened to your hair?"

Goldwine's face tightened. "It's a penance. I'm under a

food Obedience. The table monitor caught me trying to
sneak bread out of the refectory a couple of days ago. First
she took it away, then she gave me a lecture. Then she asked
me what a Novice's greatest desire should be. She wanted
me to say obedience, of course. But I said, a full meal and
a good night's sleep. So they cut off my hair, and told me
that for the rest of the week I could look at food but not eat
it."

"Oh, Goldwine."

"It's not so bad. I've been hungry before."

"You bring these punishments on yourself. Why can't
you just accept the Testing?"

"It's not Testing, it's cruelty."

"Goldwine—"

"No, Liliane. You know how I feel. Look at the hazing.
What does it Test, except how well the older Novices can
think up horrible things to do to underclassmen, or how
much suffering we can endure before we go crazy? A few
nights ago they took me to a room by myself and locked
me in. They made something happen—a sound, a feeling,
I'm not sure what. It was like it was in my bones, like it
was inside my head and wouldn't ever leave. They never
said it, but I knew, I *knew*, if I just broke down and begged
they'd make it stop. Tell me, Liliane, what's the point of a
Test like that?"

Liliane felt her friend's bitter anger. From the beginning,
Goldwine had been unable to accept the necessity, which
Liliane saw so clearly, of surrendering her own will to the
larger will that guided the Novitiate. She was capable of
submission to things she understood—superior strength,
physical limitation, the power of nature—but the strictures
and Obediences to which Novices were subjected made no
sense to her, and though Liliane had tried again and again
to explain, she either could not or would not understand.
She responded as she had responded to every other hardship
of her life: with resistance. This instinct to struggle had enabled her to survive her terrible childhood and had served
her well along the journey, where will was often the dividing line between life and death; but in the Fortress, where
the full weight of Guardian authority was set against will,

as well as anger, greed, vanity, pride, and desire, it was a profound liability. She was punished, and punished again, and punished still more. The more she suffered, the more angry she grew. The more angry she became, the more she resisted. The more she resisted, the more she was disciplined, an escalating cycle Liliane could not bear to contemplate too closely, for fear of where it might lead.

"You're missing the point, Goldwine," she said, though she knew it would make no difference. "I know the hazing seems cruel. But it's not the cruelty that's the Test. The Test is acceptance. Not knowing the purpose of what you suffer, not knowing the meaning of your suffering, but accepting it even so."

"I can't do that." Goldwine shook her head. "I can't, Liliane."

"You didn't beg, did you."

"Of course not." There was a shadow of pride in Goldwine's voice. "They had to stop in the end because they got tired."

Liliane sighed. "It's going to be worse for you now."

"That's exactly my point." Goldwine leaned forward, intent. "They make us suffer deliberately. They *want* us to be miserable. It's not just the hazing. It's everything—the stupid work assignments, the cold, the uncomfortable beds, the constant humiliation. And the isolation. You know how often they change bed and Study Group assignments—it seems random, but it's not. They do it to interrupt friendships and separate girls who might be getting close. Look at you and me. They saw we were friends, and so they pulled us apart."

"But that's the Test, Goldwine. To survive alone. To endure loneliness."

Goldwine shook her head. Her face was grim. "No. They want us separate because we're more vulnerable that way. They strip us of everything we know and care about, and then they humiliate us in the ways that touch us most deeply. They're trying to change us, Liliane. Even you, who are so good and so obedient, and believe with all your heart in what they do to you." She reached out a hand toward Liliane's curls, cascading loose across her shoulders. "I see they've finally gotten round to your hair."

Liliane pulled back, defensively. "I'm not the only one with a hair Obedience. There are at least four other girls in my Study Group alone."

"But not just any girls. Only the ones with beautiful hair."

"My hair isn't beautiful, Goldwine. I've always hated my hair."

"Oh, really? How will you feel at the end of two weeks, or whatever it is, when it's a filthy rats' nest and you have to shave it off just to get rid of the lice?"

Liliane felt her cheeks reddening. The impulse to raise her hands to the knots and tangles that already, after two days of Obedience, had begun to mat her curls, was very strong. But for the next three weeks touching, as well as braiding or washing or combing, was forbidden to her.

"All right, Goldwine. I admit it—I'm vain of my hair, though I never knew it till now. But that's the point, don't you see? Vanity has no place in a Guardian's life, any more than pride does, or possessiveness. If things are taken away from us, it's only so we can gain something greater. Yes, there's suffering and loneliness, yes, there's deprivation and humiliation. But how can the teachers trust our vocation unless it's tried as fully as possible? How can they know, really know I mean, that when the time comes for us to be Guardians we'll have the strength, if they don't Test us now? We have to prove ourselves. We have to be proven."

Goldwine shook her head again. Liliane could feel her resistance, like something hard and immovable at the end of a long fall.

"Do you know why I wanted to become a Guardian, Liliane?"

"Of course. You want to serve the Stone. As I do."

"No." Goldwine's eyes were hard. "Oh, I told myself that. To serve the Stone, to protect the world from Violation. But the truth is, I just wanted to be comfortable. To live in a fine Orderhouse and have three meals every day and a warm cloak to wear and shoes even in summertime. To be respected. Never to be beaten or humiliated again." She laughed softly. It was a strange sound, issuing from a face that seemed, for a moment, almost as strange. "You know, I never really admitted that before. Not even to myself."

Liliane stared at her friend, wordless. For a long moment there was silence.

"Goldwine," she said at last. "Goldwine, even if you really feel the way you say—"

"No." Goldwine reached out and placed her hand on Liliane's lips. There was challenge in her face. "Don't tell me I'm just imagining things, or under stress, or angry. That's not the way it is. I'm sorry if what I've said shocks you. But I can't take it back. It's the truth."

Liliane tossed her head to dislodge Goldwine's fingers. "Of course I'm shocked. But that's not what I was going to say. What I was going to say was that you *did* believe in the purpose of Guardianship when I met you, and on the journey. Even if those other things were underneath, you did believe. I felt it, and I'm never wrong about things like that."

"Yes, I believed then," Goldwine said reluctantly. "But it was a false belief, Liliane. It was a mask for those other things."

"So maybe that's why this has happened to you. Maybe the Fortress has stripped you of your old belief because it wasn't good enough. Belief doesn't just vanish, Goldwine. If you believed once, you can believe again. You just have to find a better way, that's all."

"You make it sound so easy."

"It's not easy. But it is possible." Liliane projected into her voice all the certainty of which she was capable. "It *is,* Goldwine."

Goldwine dropped her eyes. For a moment she did not speak.

"My Gift doesn't talk to me anymore," she said at last. "All my life I've known exactly what was in front of me. Now . . . now I don't know what will happen in the next few minutes, let alone the next few months or years. It frightens me, Liliane. I've never not known what to do."

"I'm frightened too, Goldwine. But that's the way of things. You can't always know what's coming. Sometimes you just have to have faith. Please try to have faith. If you can't do it for yourself, do it for me. I want us to be Guardians together, the way we planned. I want that to come true, even if you haven't seen it. You can't let me down.''

Goldwine smiled a little. ''All right,'' she said. ''I'll try. For you.''

She leaned forward and put her arms around Liliane. Liliane gripped her friend, as if to anchor her in place.

''I love you, Goldwine.''

''I love you too, Liliane. You're the only person I ever have loved.'' Goldwine tightened her grip, and then pulled away. ''I have to go, or I'll be late for Guard Class. I may not be humble, but I am punctual.''

''Oh, Goldwine.'' But Liliane could not help laughing.

Despite the possibility of her own lateness, Liliane waited for a few moments after Goldwine had gone, so that anyone watching would not see them together. The brief moment of lightness that had closed their meeting had vanished. Goldwine's bitter words hung in her mind. From the time of their arrival she had sensed her friend's disillusionment. Never, however, had she suspected it ran so deep.

For perhaps the hundredth time she wondered how what was so clear to her could be so inaccessible to Goldwine. She had felt love in Goldwine's parting embrace, and at least some hope; but those things had only floated above the deeper ocean of her doubt, and her agreement had sprung as much out of a wish not to hurt her friend as from any real sense of possibility. What would it take to break down the wall of her resistance, to resurrect her misplaced belief? What if she was not able to reach deep enough within herself to find the transformation she needed? For the first time Liliane allowed herself to look fully down the line of Goldwine's actions, to follow to the end the path traced by her doubting words. For the first time, she faced the possibility that Goldwine might not survive the Fortress.

She clenched her fists and dug her nails into her palms. She closed her eyes against her treacherous vision. It was impossible. It could not happen. If Goldwine were gone, she would be alone in this place. She did not know if she had the strength to bear that Test.

*   *   *

Liliane slipped into the room where her Study Group's Guard Class was conducted. Like most other rooms in the Novice Wing, it was a featureless cube of dark stone, its ceiling stained with the smoke of uncounted centuries of torches. Narrow windows ran down one side, left open in summer, covered in winter by tanned hides. Wooden benches were lined up in neat rows. The air was murmurous with the voices of the Study Group.

Training in the maintenance of a personal guard began the day after a Novice's arrival, and continued, three times weekly, for the whole of the First Year. Nearly all the fledgling Novices had at least rudimentary practice in this skill, but the emphasis in the Fortress was very different from that of the Guardian Schools. There, the guard was just another technique to be mastered; in the Fortress, it was a requirement. Mental privacy was one of the most precious possessions of any Gifted individual, and breaching it, whether deliberately or by accident, was prohibited. The uniformity with which personal guard was maintained in the Fortress muted even the rawest emotions to a bearable level; for the first time in eight months, Liliane was nearly free of the pressure of others' feelings. The techniques she learned worked also to strengthen her own fragile defenses. She had never thought, before coming here, that she might eventually become able to screen herself completely, or learn to use her Gift at will rather than involuntarily. Already, however, she could see that one day it would be so.

The teacher, a blue-sashed Searcher, entered the classroom. She gave a short lecture, conducted a practice session, and then tested her students' guards by throwing random thoughts. She employed no more than a moderate degree of force—personal guard was expected to hold only against accidental or casual intrusion, and must always remain permeable to a mindprobe. Anything stronger was classified as a barrier, and was strictly illegal. The class ended, as all classes did, with a recitation of the Novice's Pledge.

"I pledge myself to the Stone, to the Order of Guardians, to the Fortress, and to my teachers. In unquestioning obedience I serve them, to the utmost of my skill, to the last of my strength. There is no will but theirs. There is no world but this.''

Class was dismissed, and Liliane headed for her work assignment for the day: a huge courtyard where, together with a group of Novices from a number of other Study Groups, she would spend the next few hours sweeping, washing, and polishing the flagstones. All Unclassed and First-Year Novices regularly performed a variety of menial tasks: scrubbing stairs and floors, cleaning hallways, tending gardens, swabbing necessary rooms, laundering clothing. Frequently, these chores were redundant or even pointless. Once Liliane and another girl had been required to strip every bed in every sleeping gallery of the girls' floor, and then go round and make them up again with the same linen.

Liliane arrived at the designated courtyard and began to work. By noon the flagstones and the chinks between them were thoroughly swept, and half of them scrubbed. There was an hour's break for the midday meal, and then the Novices returned to their task. The sun, moving across the sky, fell full upon the courtyard. Some of the Novices removed their outer tunics and worked in their shirts. Liliane allowed her mind to drift, away from the scrub brush in her hands, the ache in her shoulders. Her tangled hair fell across her face, its ends trailing in the dirty scrub water.

Her eye was caught by movement to her left, and she turned her head to see a teacher escorting another Novice into the courtyard. Wordlessly, he gestured at the work in progress. The Novice took up a brush, knelt, and began to scrub.

Through the screen of her hair, Liliane watched him. He was tall and slim, with long arms and legs. He had straight black hair in a braid down his back, and eyes almost as dark, surmounted by level black brows. By the symbol on the breast of his tunic he was in the third year of his Novitiate, though he looked older than most Thirders. Third-Year Novices were rarely assigned menial labor, and never made to work with Unclassed Novices. This young man must have committed some really terrible infraction.

Abruptly, a group of Thirders entered the courtyard. Thirders had much more free time than Firsters or Seconders;

they often used it, with the approval of the teachers, to roam the Novice Wing and harass lowerclassmen. One of the Thirders, a muscular boy with fair hair and bad skin, clapped his hands.

"Stand up, all you Unclassed worms!"

They obeyed, including the tall dark-haired Thirder. The three harassers wandered around, pretending to inspect the courtyard, finding a smudge here and some dust there, tweaking noses, upsetting a bucket or two. They ostentatiously ignored their classmate, walking around him as if he did not exist.

"You," said the fair-haired Thirder. He jabbed his finger into the chest of a timid-looking boy. "Let's see how good your Guardian-Lore is. Recite the Suborders."

The history of the Order, the hierarchy within the Suborders, the names of the Founders, and other details of Guardian organization was collectively known as Guardian-Lore. Every Novice was required to memorize it verbatim. Calling for recitations was a favorite form of Third-Year harassment.

"Recitation of the Suborders," the boy said, in a rapid monotone. "Speakers, those who link with the Stone. Journeyers, those who bring the Limits to the world. Searchers, those who study the Limits. Soldiers, those who defend the Stone."

"Now you." The Thirder pointed at the only other girl, an Unclassed Novice from Liliane's Study Group named Jeneret. "Recite the Order of Command."

"Recitation of the Order of Command," Jeneret said, breathlessly, her brown eyes very wide. "The leader of a Suborder is the Staff-Holder. Below him is the Council of Six. The Council is made up of the Treasurer, who oversees finances, the Castellan, who oversees staffing and provisioning, the Apprentice-Master, who oversees the Apprentices and their education, the Limit-Master, who oversees doctrine, and the Second, who is assistant to the Staff-Holder and becomes Staff-Holder if the current Staff-Holder can no longer fulfill his duty. Below the Council are the Ordermen—"

"Just a minute." It was the second Thirder, a girl with

sharp, narrow features and thin blond hair. "You forgot something."

Jeneret, interrupted in midsentence, visibly tried to collect herself. "I . . . I did?"

"Something important." The Thirder leaned forward, her face thrust toward Jeneret's. "Think. *Think.*"

Jeneret's eyes darted back and forth. Her mouth was slightly open. The silence grew. At last the fair-haired Thirder cuffed her lightly on the cheek.

"I worry about worms like you, by the Stone I do." He shook his head with mock concern. "How will you get through your Novitiate if you can't even remember Guardian-Lore? Go stand against the wall—right up against it, with your nose pressed against the stones. You can stay there for the rest of the day. Don't even think about moving till the evening bell rings."

Jeneret obeyed. Liliane caught an echo of her relief at not having received a worse punishment.

"You." The Third-Year girl pointed at a robust-looking boy with a large cheerful face. "What did that one forget?"

"The sixth member of the Council of Six," the boy said at once, virtuous in his correctness.

"Go on."

"The sixth position is different for each Suborder. For the Speakers, it is the Stone-Watcher, who oversees linking with the Stone. For the Journeyers, it is the Journey-Master, who oversees Journeyer activities within the world. For the Searchers it is the Book-Master, who oversees the library and the education of the Novices. And for the Soldiers it is the General, who oversees military training and warfare."

"Acceptable," said the Thirder. "But I don't like your attitude. Go stand with the other one."

The boy's face fell visibly. He turned to obey. The fair-haired Thirder gave him a push, and he stumbled and slipped in a puddle of water where a bucket had been overturned. Whatever guard he had was unequal to the humiliation he felt.

The last Thirder had moved to stand before the Third-Year Novice so inexplicably assigned to work the courtyard. He was a slight young man, with loose reddish hair and pale skin. He had a beaklike nose, heavy eyes, and a straight, serious mouth. His features conveyed an odd distant serenity, as if his mind were far away.

"Hello, Selwyn," he said. His voice, reedy and spiteful, provided a startling contrast to his dreamy face. "Fancy finding you here, working among the idiots. Oh, sorry, I forgot. It happens quite a lot, doesn't it?"

Selwyn, the punished Novice, did not reply. He gazed over the other's head to a point somewhere on the wall opposite. Liliane was quite close to him, yet she could feel nothing from behind his personal guard, though a subtle defiance could be read in the straightness of his back and the apparent relaxation of his body.

"Especially these days." The spiteful Thirder shook his head in mock concern. "But then, some of us aren't very careful who we choose as friends. By the way, how *is* your good friend Kenlin? Or should I say your *witless* friend Kenlin? They say he didn't manage the removal of his barriers very well."

"I haven't seen Kenlin recently," Selwyn replied. His voice was polite and distant.

"That's not really surprising, since he's in prison. But you'll see him soon. We all will." He stepped forward and stuck his forefinger in Selwyn's chest. "Now. I'm in the mood for a Recitation. The History of the Founding, I think. Yes, that'll do nicely."

Selwyn took a breath. His hands were linked behind his back; Liliane saw them clench, and then relax. She could only imagine how he must feel, a Thirder being harassed as if he were a Firster. But when he spoke, his voice was smooth and clear, completely emotionless.

"Long before the worlds split, the Stone was held by an evil sorcerer. For centuries he and his descendants used mindskill to keep it hidden, greedily hoarding all its power for themselves. Many sought to free the Stone from bondage, but not until the worlds began to pull apart did one come who could fulfill the quest: a great and noble man named Percival.

"Percival scoured the world from one corner to the other in search of the Stone, tireless in his quest. Eventually he reached the lands of the sorcerer's heirs and found what he had sought so long. He mustered a mighty army, and in a great battle defeated the sorcerer's descendant and won the Stone. In revenge for its long exile, he caused the descendant to be executed, together with every member of his family. He cursed the name of this man and all his forbears, back to the beginning of time itself.

"Percival and his companions brought the Stone into the world of mindpower. Never again, they vowed, would the Stone lie hidden, withheld from the peoples of the earth. They swore to devote their lives and their Gifts to preserving the precious skills of mind against the consuming evil of handpower. From this vow sprang our name: we became the Order of Guardians.

"Four of Percival's most trusted lieutenants set themselves to fulfill the task they had sworn to achieve. To Dafydd fell the duty of bringing news of the Stone's restoration to the people of the new world. He was the first Journeyer. To Rhodri came the work of making Limits. He was the first Searcher. Maris learned to link with the Stone and receive the gift of its knowledge; he was the first Speaker. And Gilbert, whose Gift was fighting and strategy, was the first Soldier. It was he who ensured the protection of the Order in the great work it had begun.

"The Suborders that sprang from these four men—"

"All right, we've heard enough." The fair-haired Thirder was plainly bored. "You can stop now, Selwyn."

The spiteful Thirder turned, a quick motion, like a bird. "*I* haven't heard enough."

"It's not really a Test, Jolyon," said the girl. "Not for him."

"I want him to finish, Catlin."

"You know he never makes mistakes," the fair-haired Thirder said. "If you want to punish him, just do it. Why use the Recitation as an excuse?"

Jolyon had turned to Selwyn again, and was looking right into his eyes. "Because he hates it," he said, softly.

"You're dreaming," said Catlin. "You know how he loves to show off. Nothing could suit him better than to do a Recitation without a mistake. Spare us, please."

There was a pause. Liliane could feel guard-muted impatience from the fair-haired Thirder and Catlin, varying degrees of unfocused discomfort from the Unclassed Novices, and nothing whatsoever from Selwyn. From Jolyon, however, she received a very strong sense. She was suddenly, crawlingly certain that he was the robe who had singled her out the first night of hazing. She had felt his mind at every session since then, reaching toward her through the torment, probing and prying around the edges of her dark sanctuary like someone trying to pick open a latchless door. His mental touch was repellant. Even from the distance of her refuge she could feel his malice, the way the Novices' pain and fear aroused him. But though she feared him, though his spite had some time ago turned to anger, she did not let him in. He had no right to the secrets of her inmost self.

What she felt now, reaching out for dark-haired Selwyn— the malevolence, the anger, the painful, cramped excitement—transported her for a moment out of the courtyard and turned afternoon to midnight. Unable to stop herself, she shuddered.

Jolyon saw the motion. He turned his head in the swift, avian manner that seemed characteristic of him. "What are you staring at?" he demanded.

Liliane could feel his mind, nudging at the edges of her Gift; it was loathsome. "I . . . I'm sorry," she stammered. "I didn't mean to stare."

"Didn't mean to," he mimicked. "Well, drop your eyes. All the way down, that's right. Look at your knees. No— don't bend your neck. Just your eyes."

Liliane obeyed, looking down so hard her eyes crossed. She felt his attention leave her.

"All right, Selwyn, you don't have to go on with the Recitation. But don't think you're getting off lightly. You can do the rest of the scrubbing and polishing that these Unclassed fools were meant to do. And then you can do it a second time. And you'll stay here till you're finished, even if it takes all night. Understand?"

"I understand." Selwyn's voice was composed. Liliane still felt nothing from him. He must have an incredible guard.

"You heard him, Selwyn," the fair-haired Thirder said, bored. "Get to work. The rest of you, stand back."

The Unclassed Novices, with the exception of the two against the wall, stepped away toward the edges of the courtyard. Liliane began to do the same, her eyes still painfully lowered.

"Where do you think you're going?"

Liliane froze. "With . . . with the others."

Jolyon's gaze moved from her head to her feet and then up again. It was the same regard she felt when she passed by him after the hazing, reaching out to her as she approached, pressing against her back as she moved away.

"You can help him," Jolyon said. "But don't look at him, understand? And don't speak. Don't say a word. Selwyn—the same goes for you."

Calmly, Selwyn had gathered up the extra buckets and brushes and placed them neatly by the wall. He had begun to scrub again, quickly and efficiently. Liliane got a bucket for herself and began to work on the other side of the court, as far from Jolyon as she could get. For a while the Thirders watched. It seemed they might stay all afternoon. But eventually, urged by Catlin and the other Thirder, Jolyon consented to depart.

Selwyn and Liliane finished scrubbing and began to polish. Since the Thirders were no longer there, Liliane did not bother to keep her gaze lowered. Now and then she straightened up to rest her back, or shifted to ease the pressure of the hard stone against her knees. She was aware of the impassive regard of the other Unclassed Novices, standing about the periphery of the courtyard like lumps of rock, and, now and then, the swift flash of Selwyn's gaze.

"I'm sorry you got caught up in this."

They had begun scrubbing at opposite sides of the courtyard, working their way inward, and now were side by side in the middle. Liliane was startled: a Thirder rarely spoke to an Unclassed Novice in any context other than hazing or harassing. Since Jolyon was gone, it seemed safe to disregard his prohibition. She turned her head to look at Selwyn, tossing back the hair that had fallen across her face. His eyes met hers directly. They were long and very dark, with whites so clear they seemed translucent. His level black brows were knitted in a small, habitual frown.

"It might have happened anyway," she said in a low voice. "He hates me."

"Hates *you*?" He sounded faintly mocking.

Liliane felt herself flush. "I'm only an Unclassed Novice, I know. But it's true. It's—" She stopped herself. The only other person who knew about the dark place within her was Goldwine. "It's been that way from the beginning."

"Be careful, then." Selwyn's whisper sounded serious now. "He can make a lot of trouble for you. Whatever he wants, give it to him. Don't resist him—he hates that more than anything. Believe me, I know what I'm talking about."

"Is that what you did? Resist him?"

His face did not change, but abruptly Liliane caught a flash of emotion, the first she had felt from him. She could not quite identify it—it hinted of some much larger, discordant feeling. It was quickly gone, however, and she wondered if she had imagined it.

"Maybe." He shrugged. "It doesn't matter."

"I never saw a Thirder harass another Thirder before. Making you do Recitation like that—I thought only Firsters were treated that way . . ."

Liliane trailed off. Selwyn's face had regained the stony quality with which he had confronted Jolyon. She received no sense of emotion, yet overwhelmingly, she felt rebuffed.

"It happens," Selwyn said. He got to his feet to exchange his cloth for a broom, his turned back like a finished sentence. Liliane wished she could retract her words.

The evening bell rang, and the other Unclassed Novices straggled off toward the refectory. Liliane and Selwyn remained, sweeping as the twilight deepened, scrubbing and buffing beneath the rising moon. Selwyn maintained an impenetrable wall of silence. It was well past midnight when they finished. Liliane hoped Selwyn would speak in parting, but he did not.

Moving along the dusky passages, Liliane imagined she could feel the weight of the Fortress bearing down upon the earth, as if it were heavier at night than during the day. As she reached the girls' floor she sensed fear, wafting toward her like smoke. Its source was a group of Novices, herded by white-garbed robes to a hazing session. She pulled back into a dim corner to let them pass, drawing up her own guard. The Novices' bare feet made a soft slapping sound, and their faces looked pinched and dull in the dim light. They disappeared around a bend in the corridor, leaving only shadows behind.

She felt motion in the air nearby. A hand came out of nowhere and closed round her mouth.

"Don't make a sound," a voice hissed in her ear.

Liliane froze. The hand removed itself. A viselike grip fastened on her arm. She felt herself pulled round, to confront the face she knew she would see.

"You spoke to him," Jolyon hissed. His eyes glittered strangely in the uncertain light. "You looked at him. I told you not to. Did you think I wouldn't wait? Did you think I wouldn't watch?"

"I . . . I . . ." Liliane stammered. "I'm sorry . . . I didn't think . . ."

"You Firsters never do." He shook her, like a cat with a bird. "Disobedience is forbidden in the Novice Wing. Don't you know that?"

"I . . . I didn't mean to be disobedient."

" 'Didn't mean to.' That's what you said this afternoon. But disobedience seems to be a pattern with you, little Unclassed girl. Look at the hazing. The whole point is endurance. But you—you don't endure. You hide."

Liliane trembled. Her heart faltered with terror. "I don't know what you mean," she whispered.

"Oh, yes you do." He shook her again. "You know who I am—I saw it in your face this afternoon. So tell me—and tell the truth. What is it you do when the hazing starts? Where is it you go? Why aren't you afraid of us?"

She could feel him—his cruelty, his eagerness, leaking like acid through a personal guard that seemed as ineffectual as the greenest Novice's. I'm afraid of *you,* she wanted to say, but her throat had closed, and when she opened her mouth nothing came out. Abruptly, Jolyon abandoned words. She felt his power flashing toward her; it did not stop when he struck her guard, but punched right through, careless of the rule of privacy. Reflexively she arrowed back within herself, diving down into her inner darkness, like a small animal fleeing a predator. From a distance she felt him rummaging through her mind, foraging clumsily from point to point like an engine of war. But he could not touch the place where she hid, nor even get close enough to see it. No one could.

At last she sensed that he had withdrawn. Cautiously, she allowed herself to flow back into the familiar channels of her consciousness. Her mind felt bruised and beaten. Jolyon was breathing harshly, as if he had run a marathon. She could feel his arousal, his frustration, his rage.

"You're holding out on me, you little bitch," he panted. "I know you're doing something. I know it."

"No." She cowered in his grip. Without meaning to, she had begun to weep. "Please, I'm not doing anything."

"It's a mistake to fight me." He was shaking her again, back and forth. The pain in her head ignited with each jerk. "You saw what happened today. I can do more than that, a lot more. I can make your life more miserable than you can possibly imagine. That isn't just an empty threat, little Unclassed girl. I have the power. Do you believe me?"

"Yes! Yes, I believe you!" She babbled, hardly knowing what she was saying. "Please, you won't have to do anything. I'll be obedient, I swear I will. You won't have to punish me again. I'll do whatever you say. I promise, I promise."

Her words dissolved into weeping, great sobs that shook her body. He held her, relishing her fear, drinking in her surrender. At last, with a final shake, he released her.

"All right," he said. "I think you've learned your lesson."

"I have learned it," she wept. "I have."

"Remember it the next time I come for you during the hazing. Obedience, little Unclassed girl—that's the key."

"Obedience. Yes. Obedience."

"You can go, then. Go on—get out of my sight."

Liliane did not need to be told again. She turned and stumbled down the corridor. Jolyon's eyes followed her all the way. Not until she passed through the door of her sleeping gallery did the pressure of his gaze leave her.

She crossed the floor, moving through the strips of moonlight that fell through the windows. Fumbling off her boots and tunic, she crawled beneath her blankets. Fear was an icy knot within her; she shivered as if it were the dead of winter rather than a mild summer night. Her bruised mind ached, a dull throbbing that kept time with her heartbeat. She kept her eyes fixed on the door, half-expecting to see Jolyon materialize within its frame.

After a while, however, she grew calmer. Perspective returned. Jolyon was malicious and cruel, but he was only a Novice. Obedience was what she owed her Masters; she owed nothing to him. He could threaten, he could promise, but what could he really do to her besides punish her physically? Her Gift was more than equal to his; he could not break her if she did not allow it. Selwyn had warned her not to resist him, but how could she do otherwise? What Jolyon sought was the inviolate center of her self, as precious within her as the Stone within the Fortress. It could not be given, or opened, to anyone. She knew this as clearly as she knew her own name.

Jolyon was a Thirder. In a little over a month he would graduate to the Apprentice College. If she could endure the next few weeks, she would be free of him forever.

One week later, the Fortress was summoned to witness an Expulsion. The Violator was a Third-Year Novice on the verge of Apprenticeship named Kenlin—evidently the same Kenlin whom Jolyon had identified as Selwyn's friend.

As the Study Groups gathered in their assembly rooms after the noon meal, even the admonishments of the teachers could not still the whispering as they traded hearsay about the ceremony and speculated on the nature of the Violation Kenlin had committed. Kenlin, it was rumored, had been discovered to be harboring illegal barriers of blocking, behind which he had hidden the fact that he was a heretic: a Christian. Christianity was a cult that had flourished in the world before the Split; most of its adherents had remained in the world of handpower, but a few had entered the mindpower world, where they set themselves to challenge the authority of the Guardians. They were not successful, and by the second century Post Split the cult had ceased to be a threat, hunted almost to extinction by the Soldiers. Only a few small groups remained, hidden in deep forest or inhospitable desert, surviving into modern times by maintaining an isolated and spartan existence and rarely revealing themselves to the outside world. From one of these, presumably, Kenlin had come. But why he had chosen to enter the Fortress, whether he was an apostate or a spy, no one knew.

The summons came at last. Marshaled by their teachers, the Novices left the wing, passing through the double doors into the noise and light of the court. From the Apprentice College came a similar column of Apprentices. The two groups converged at the wide archway that rose just past the string of artisans' workshops on the left side of the court, and marched side by side into the corridor beyond. The low-ceilinged passage was faced with cream-colored stone, embedded with flecks of some glittering material. Torches cast a yellow glow; at the far end showed a different light, cool and pale. Liliane could hear the sound of voices, ebbing and flowing like the sea.

Emerging from the corridor was a little like falling, so vast was the space that lay beyond. The walls formed an immense circle, capped by a pointed ceiling so high that its stonework could barely be made out. Tiers of benches girdled the circumference of the building, rising steeply to nearly half its height. Above the benches glowed windows of dark stained glass, depicting scenes from Guardian history. The pale illumination came from six enormous globes of mindlight, fixed upon the air at equidistant points high above the central circle; their glow was caught and reflected by the sparkling flecks in the stone, so that tides of light appeared to slide across the walls. The tiers of benches were packed with Guardians, thousands of them, their robes bound with the sashes of all the Suborders: white for Speakers, green for Journeyers, blue for Searchers, gold for Soldiers. A roar of talk rose up toward the distant ceiling. Below it lay the great flux of emotion that was, for Liliane, as tangible as the voice of the crowd.

The teachers chivvied the Novices upward. Liliane found

herself in the next-to-last tier, a dizzying distance above the floor. She cast her eyes across the crowd below her, searching for Goldwine; instead she saw Selwyn, several tiers below and almost directly in line with her own seat. Even from the back there was no mistaking that smooth dark head, those straight shoulders. Liliane watched him, wondering what it was about him that fascinated her so. His extraordinary impenetrability? The fact that sadistic Jolyon hated him? How must he feel, sitting among the other Novices, waiting to witness the expulsion of his friend?

A great trumpet blast ripped the air, discordant and strange. Utter silence fell. Out of the corridor marched four groups of men, their waists bound with sashes in the colors of the Suborders, cloths of the same hues tied diagonally across their breasts. These were the Councils of Six, responsible for the governance of the Suborders and the fulfillment of the Guardian mission within the Fortress and in the world. After them came the four Staff-Holders. Magnificent surplices covered their dull Guardian robes, and the mindlight flashed from the long staves they carried: ivory for Speakers, malachite for Journeyers, lapis lazuli for Searchers, tigereye for Soldiers. A lone man brought up the rear, his hair cropped short, his waist wrapped with scarlet. This was the leader of the Arm of the Stone. Though the Arm was technically part of the Suborder of Journeyers, it functioned as a separate entity, with its own Council of Six and its own chain of command.

In a circular space at the center of the amphitheater four ornate chairs had been arranged in a semicircle, with a larger chair beyond them on a dais. The procession marched once around the circumference of the central area, and then seated itself: the Councils and the leader of the Arm on the lowest tier of benches, the Staff-Holders in the four lesser chairs.

Another trumpet blast sounded. A single man moved alone into the circle: the Prior, leader of the Order of Guardians, the most holy and powerful man on earth. Alone of all Guardians, the Prior did not wear Guardian clothing, but was clad in a robe of some fabulous changeable fabric, shot through with all the colors of the Suborders—now green, now gold, now blue, now white. In his left hand he held a thick staff made of twisted strands of ivory and tigereye, malachite and lapis. A finial of garnet capped it, flashing blood-red in the pale mindlight.

The Prior seated himself on the dais, his polychromatic robe swirling about him. He gestured. From the corridor advanced a little group of Soldiers. Two of them supported a boy in Novice clothing. A man with the red sash and cropped hair of a Roundhead walked behind.

The group halted. The Soldiers pushed the Novice to his knees. The Roundhead stepped forward, unrolling a scroll.

"We have gathered here to witness the Expulsion of Kenlin, a Third-Year Novice of the Order of Guardians." The Roundhead's voice rang out across the immense space. "In accordance with the Limits and with Guardian rule and custom, Kenlin has been found guilty of the following Violations of Paths of Thought:

"Undermining the dignity of the Order through inappropriate words and acts, namely, the creation of scurrilous cartoons and caricatures of his superiors, discovery of which led to the arrest and mindprobe that uncovered his larger crimes.

"Presenting falsehood to the Order of Guardians, through an untrue history designed to conceal his origins among the heretical sect of Christianity. Christians do not acknowledge the authority of the Guardians, the primacy of the Limits, or the sacredness of the Stone. Though Kenlin abandoned these beliefs while still a child, the stain of heresy can never be erased—a fact he himself acknowledged by his concealment of the truth.

"Maintaining illegal blocking barriers, behind which the foregoing Violation was hidden.

"For these crimes, Kenlin has been sentenced to the strictest punishment the Order of Guardians can exact. His power will be taken from him. His medal of Novitiate will be destroyed. His forehead will be marked with the Sign of Violation. He will be expelled from the Fortress and thrown upon the mercy of the mountains.

"Thus does the Order of Guardians deal with those who Violate the sacred Limits from within, and flout the rule of

Guardian law. In the name of the Stone, so ends this judgment."

The Roundhead lowered the scroll, rolling it up and placing it in his sash. He stepped forward and grasped the silver medal on the Novice's chest, pulling it roughly over Kenlin's head, laying it on the ground before the Staff-Holders. As one, the Staff-Holders bent their gaze upon the small silver disc. A tremor of power shook the air. The spheres of mindlight dimmed a little. There was a flash, brighter than the sun, briefer than a breath. The silver lay transformed, a blackened lump.

The Roundhead took up the ruined medallion, wrapped it in a cloth, and placed it in the breast of his robe.

The Prior rose from his chair and descended from the dais. The Soldiers hoisted Kenlin to his feet, grasping his hair to pull back his head. The Prior stretched out his hand and placed his palm upon the Novice's forehead. He spoke, his voice rolling out above the assembled crowd.

"I, Percival, Prior of the Order of Guardians, call the Stone to witness. I call it, that it may know how we defend it against those who would do it harm. I call it, that it may see the face of its enemy."

The silence that gripped the gathering was so intense it was a pressure upon Liliane's ears. Somewhere, something stirred—the Stone, responding to the Prior's summons. Its presence spilled into the great space, like molten rock pushing its way through the dense layers of the earth—a colossal force constrained somehow by the medium through which it flowed. The air around the Prior trembled with power, a shimmering aura shot through with all the colors of his robe.

"In the name of the Stone, I kill your Gift." Percival's voice was no longer a sound, but an element in the titanic sea of power. "In the name of the Stone, I mark you with the Sign of Violation. In the name of the Stone, I banish you from the Order of Guardians, and from the Fortress, and from the company of humankind, forever."

There was a flash—of light, of power. Kenlin's head snapped back. A livid four-quartered circle now marked his forehead. He hung in the grip of the Soldiers, his eyes closed, unconscious.

The presence of the Stone was overwhelming. Liliane's head felt as if it might burst. She was almost blinded by the opalescent play of light that enclosed the Prior and the disgraced Novice. Just as it seemed she could not bear an instant more, the power began to sink away, slowly at first, and then more rapidly, like a river draining through fissures in its bed. It left a resonance in its wake, some discordant sense Liliane could not immediately identify. Without thinking, she reached out, realizing even as she did so that what she sensed was not the Stone, but the unguarded emotion of someone within the crowd.

Before her gaze fell upon the dark head many tiers below, she had identified the source: Selwyn. He was no longer impenetrable, no longer even opaque. What she felt from him was the darkest emotion she had ever felt from a single person—a corrosive tide of rage, hate, loss, and hunger, flooding out of him as if he were yielding up his entire soul. She pulled back, shocked. Her mind felt raw, as if it had been burned. After a moment she reached forward again, cautiously. But there was nothing now, only the shifting stew of feelings that was the crowd.

The Soldiers carried Kenlin, limp as a doll, out of the circle. The Prior followed, the Staff-Holders and the Councils of Six behind him. The teachers rose, and began to organize their charges for the return march. As Liliane descended the stairs, she pondered what she had sensed from Selwyn. It had been unlike anything she had ever felt—in its power, in its pain. The ceremony might have been its trigger, but not, she was certain, its genesis. There had been an oldness to what she had perceived, as if it ran in channels carved very deep in Selwyn's soul. Nor had the release been chosen. Surely Selwyn would never voluntarily free such a thing. It was not like the small lapses of demeanor and attitude for which the Novices were routinely punished, not even like Goldwine's stubbornness and anger. If the Masters ever saw what she had seen, she had no doubt Selwyn would find himself where his friend Kenlin had just been.

She could not understand how she had sensed him so strongly from such a distance. Usually it was necessary for her to be close in order to receive with such intensity. She shivered. Deeply, she wished she had never been vouchsafed this vision of Selwyn's inner self. His face, calm under Jolyon's harassment, hung in her mind. She thought of the clear, dark eyes that had met her own. Nothing in their regard had suggested such bitter depths.

The column of Novices marched across the courtyard and through the double doors of the Novice Wing. Liliane was one of the last to enter. She heard the doors close behind her, thudding solidly against their jambs, shutting away the air and space of the court. The darkness of the Novice Wing descended like a familiar ache, and she prepared herself to take up once more the burden of duty.

The

Roundhead

Eight

ORNE ON a tide of Novices, Bron moved along the central corridor of the Fifth Level. Behind the impassive mask of his face, his heart was racing. Moments ago, ending an agonizing week of waiting, the results of the Apprentice Examinations had been released. All Third-Year Novices had immediately dropped whatever they were doing and stampeded for the Fifth Level, where parchments listing the standings were posted outside each sleeping gallery.

Reaching his own sleeping gallery, Bron jostled with the other members of his Study Group, trying to get close enough to read the lines of crabbed script:

> *Anton, passed with Second Honors—Journeyer.*
> *Artur, passed with Third Honors—Journeyer.*
> *Brand, passed without Honors—Soldier.*
> *Callion, passed without Honors—Searcher.*
> *Cristefor, passed with First Honors—Speaker.*

And so on through the alphabet, until, almost at the end, his own name appeared:

> *Selwyn, passed without Honors—Journeyer.*

Amid the shifting press of bodies, Bron stood immobile. He felt as if someone had struck him a tremendous blow.

He closed his eyes for a moment. But when he opened them the inscription was still there, in uncompromising black letters: Selwyn. Without Honors. Journeyer.

He felt pressure building inside his chest, battering at his barriers, straining his careful mask of calm. Blindly he pushed away from the knot of his Study Group. He moved swiftly down the corridors of the Fifth Level, heading for the Third-Year Boys' Washroom. Half-hidden in the shadows of the back wall was a small wood-planked door. He passed through it, mounting the curving stairs that lay beyond it two at a time. At their top was a trapdoor. He flung it open and, in a convulsion of muscles, hoisted himself through the opening, onto the roof of the Novice Wing.

An enormity of light and air enclosed him. High above, the sky spread out forever, blue and pure as glass. The sun poured from it like honey from a spoon, and the wind moved softly against his skin. Nothing here spoke of walls or corridors, of the rules and constrictions of the Novice Wing. His body, responding without conscious thought, propelled him forward. He ran at top speed across the smooth flagstones, each taller than a man and twice as wide. Briefly, the joy of motion possessed him. He forgot what had sent him up here and what waited below, and for a moment became simply a body in transit.

Too quickly, he reached the limit of the great space, where the Novice Wing merged with the outer walls of the Fortress. He came to a stop against the rough black stones, warm with the accumulated sun of the day. He leaned the length of his body against them. High above his head, they cut the bowl of the sky in half.

He had discovered the roof early in his Second Year. As one of his many punishments he had been assigned to scrape away the spongy fungus that flourished in the chinks between the washroom floorstones, a task that brought him to the back wall and the narrow door set into it. No one else was about; he yielded to curiosity. He was awed by the roof's tremendous scale and, more than that, captivated by its silence. The cacophony of the great court did not rise this high, and the heavy stones of the Novice Wing held fast all noise within. The only sounds here were nature-sounds: the rushing of the wind, the patter of rain, the call of birds.

The roof became his refuge. Here he could escape the claustrophobia of the dark corridors and the confinement of discipline. Here he could let his disguise slip a little and touch his real, hidden self. He knew very well the danger of doing so, even in this place where there was never any sign of another living soul. Yet, though maintaining barriers was as natural to him as breathing, in the Novice Wing much more must be hidden. The strain of constant vigilance was sometimes almost beyond bearing. Without these moments of solitude, he was certain he would have betrayed himself long ago.

A waist-high balustrade ran along the side of the roof that overlooked the court. About halfway to the trapdoor, a chunk of stone had come loose and fallen. Bron settled himself upon it, leaning back against the balustrade. The breeze moved on his face, smelling of the grass and flowers that carpeted the alpine meadow outside the Fortress. Yet it carried a chilly edge, and the angle of the sun was lower than it had been a week ago. Beneath this perfect afternoon the voice of autumn could be heard, a promise of dying light and lowering chill and the long descent toward the dark heart of winter.

Bron closed his eyes and yielded to emotion. It overpowered him, a disappointment so terrible it was like physical sickness. In the few seconds it had taken to read the black letters beside his name, all his plans had crumbled into ruin. Before him lay the necessity of beginning anew, of building again from nothing. So overwhelming was this prospect that he could not, as yet, allow himself to face it.

When he first reached the Fortress, it had not taken him long to realize that his best hope of fulfilling his vow lay in Speakerhood. Journeyers were too much in the world, their assignments often taking them away from the Fortress for years at a time. Searchers, cloistered in the Library or patrolling the cheerless corridors of the Novice Wing, were low in the hierarchy of power. Soldiers, the Guardians least endowed with mindskill, were a group apart, sharing their quarters with the infamous prison annex, where Violators and other criminals, both Guardian and unGifted, were confined. They had their own customs and traditions, and the other Suborders considered them only a small step above the unGifted.

Only Speakers possessed real power. Of all Guardians, they owned the highest learning, the greatest intellects, the strongest Gifts. It was they who charted the course of the Order; for as many centuries as anyone could remember, the Prior had been chosen from among their ranks. It was they who controlled access to the Stone. Maris, the Suborder's Founder, creator of the doorless prison-room in which the Stone resided, had taught the trick of entry only to his followers. From that day to this, only Speakers had ever seen the Stone. Even the Garden could not be entered without their consent.

And so Bron set himself to become a Speaker. He excelled in academics, became proficient in the use of a variety of weapons, performed manual labor with a will and energy few could match, and shone in the practice of mindskill. By the time he reached the Fortress he had grown adept in the use of his Gift, and in the controlling and channeling necessary to disguise its magnitude. He had never again been able to match the enormity of power he had released that first time, when he freed Serle; even so, in its strength and flexibility his Gift was far beyond any other he had encountered, either in life or in learning. He was aware that the Guardians would view so much power not as a thing of value, but as a threat; more than that, he did not want them to know until the end what stood against them. And so, though he made sure to outshine his peers, he never allowed more than a fraction of his Talent to touch the outside world. His teachers never knew that he had already, on his own, gone far beyond the basic techniques in which they daily instructed him.

Yet there was one area of mindskill he was stubbornly unable to master. Despite the most strenuous effort, near-speech eluded him. It had never been difficult for him to reach inside others' minds; he had done it now and then in his pre-Fortress travels, when he wanted people to forget him or think of him in a different way. But he found it almost impossible to open his mind to others' sendings.

Nearspeech was the least demanding manifestation of mind-power, easily learned by even the weakest of the Novices; the failure of his immense Talent to encompass such a minor skill was both mystifying and humiliating. Worse, it posed a danger to his plan. Alone of all the Suborders, Speakers required proven capability in four of the five classifications of mindskill, excepting only prescience. The number of times this rule had been waived could be counted on the fingers of one hand.

Bron knew himself, in all respects but nearspeech, to more than satisfy Speaker requirements of excellence. Surely, he told himself, so many talents must outweigh a single failing. Surely, in their desire for his multiple strengths, the Speakers would overlook his single weakness. But during the grueling course of the Apprentice Examinations this belief, upon which he had staked his future, began to falter. He was only barely able to communicate mind to mind with the Guardians who examined him. As they persisted, relentlessly, his ability faded until he could not pick out a single thought. In the stern faces of his Masters he read, for the first time, the possibility of failure.

Failure loomed above him now like the walls themselves, no longer fear but fact. Bron clenched his fists, grinding his nails against the stone on which he sat. Hatred rose in him, like an old sickness. He knew the cause of his rejection, yet he could not accept it, could not concede a philosophy that placed all his abilities in the context of a single deficiency and pronounced the whole worthless. To pass him without honors, he who had been first in his class almost since his arrival ... to make Cristefor, whose focus so often fragmented under pressure, a Speaker, and reject him, stronger than any of his fellows. ... How blind, how stupid they were. How narrow-minded and inflexible, tradition-bound, capricious, ignorant, contemptible. ... There were not enough epithets in the world, nor any that were not stale and threadbare from constant use.

Yet even through his rage, Bron could not deny the presence of a deeper understanding. As accomplished as he was in the ways of disguising his power, when he first entered the Fortress he had still possessed his old failing, his ina-

bility to conceal his anger. Not the deep ancestral rage—
that lay safe, with the Tale and his vow and the truth of his
Gift, behind his barriers—but rather the smaller furies, unpredictable as the winter storms that battered the mountains,
rising up every day in response to the injustice of the teachers, the stupidity of the Obediences, the privation of the
surroundings, the meaninglessness of the daily routine. His
Masters saw his rage, just as the Roundhead leader had seen
it four years earlier. They set themselves to root it out. The
severity and frequency of Bron's punishments and Obediences soon became a matter of awe among the other Novices.

Bron understood that his anger, a liability in the outside
world, was in the Novice Wing a deadly danger. He worked,
as he had never worked in his life before, to build a wall
around it. He constructed an edifice of control that concealed
all inner trace of emotion. He achieved a discipline of face
and body that masked all outward hint of feeling. Still the
persecution continued. No matter how thoroughly he hid
himself, no matter how outstandingly he performed, he was
unendingly, relentlessly punished. In the Novice Wing, the
punishments seemed to say, the past was never left behind.
Faults and flaws might be overcome, but the teachers never
forgot they had once been there.

Bron's friend Kenlin had offered a different explanation.
"Your problem is you've taken it too far," he told Bron.
"You look them in the face when they punish you. When
they beat you, you act as if you feel nothing. Before, they
only wanted to know they'd gotten through. Now they want
to break you."

"They'll never break me," Bron replied.

"You could pretend, couldn't you? Slump a little. Act
fearful. Flinch."

"No!" Bron shook his head. "No. I won't do it."

Kenlin had looked at him with his intelligent hazel eyes.
"There's no dishonor in pretending to be something you're
not, if it serves a larger purpose."

Kenlin, Bron thought. He saw him as he had been—his
sharp features, his straight fair hair, his characteristic, quiz-
zical expression—and as he had become, blank and imbe-

cilic, his mind destroyed by the undoing of his barriers. They had been friends throughout their Novitiates, in the circumspect way of the Novice Wing. Bron had sensed in Kenlin a core of isolation as intractable as his own, and it was this unspoken sharing, more than anything else, that drew them together. In the manner of Novices, however, as well as by mutual inclination, they had shared little personal information. When Kenlin's secret was revealed, Bron was as shocked as anyone—not by the heresy, which meant little to him, but by the discovery that someone else had maintained a subterfuge as complex as his own. Yet Kenlin's barriers had been built to hide a past he had rejected, while Bron's hid the only things in the world that were of value to him. They had not, after all, been very much alike.

Above the roof of the Novice Wing, the sky was darkening toward evening. Bron's hatred had subsided, his rage had drained away. He contemplated the bleak light of understanding that remained. The gap in his Talent might well have put Speakerhood out of reach, but the real determinant had been himself. It did not matter if his fault were failing to conceal his anger, or concealing it too well. He had attracted the Guardians' ire, and it was this that had cost him his dream. The true measure of his failure was not lack of ability, but lack of control.

He buried his face in his hands. An agony of self-loathing possessed him. All the punishments, all the Obediences— why had it never occurred to him that they would influence the outcome of the Examinations? Now the terrible years since his family's death counted for nothing. The hunger and cold and pain he had suffered in the corridors of the Novice Wing had been wasted. The faces of his parents and siblings rose in his mind, drifting like smoke behind the screen of his barriers. He saw them as they had been in life, and as they had become in death. What would they feel if they could see him now? What would they say to him if they knew he had failed?

He raised his head. The sun had sunk below the top of the walls. Their shadow stretched long upon the stones, its chill swallowing the day's accumulated warmth. It was time to quit the roof and seek the perpetual twilight of the floors below.

Bron pushed himself to his feet, his hands against the cooling balustrade. He felt perspective returning. The remembered faces of his family had held reproach, but also the reflection of his vow. His emotion was a costly indulgence. He had come too far, borne too much, to yield now. He had lost one path; for his family's sake, and for his own, he must seek another. Somewhere in Journeyerhood there was a way. There had to be.

It could have been worse, he told himself. Journeyers at least possessed influence and prestige—not as much as Speakers, certainly, but a good deal more than the other two Suborders. Perhaps if he sought a career in administration he could avoid the postings to farflung lands that were a feature of Journeyer life. Administration . . . perhaps eventually the Council of Six . . . and another possibility, brushing the outer fringes of likelihood, but worth considering even so: the Arm of the Stone. Roundheads were set apart from other Guardians, mistrusted even by their fellows, but unquestionably they formed a powerful elite. Yes, Bron thought. He must set himself to watch, when he reached the Apprentice College, to see if perhaps the path he sought lay there.

He made his way across the flagstones. He paused before lowering himself through the trapdoor, testing his barriers, inventorying his features, settling his mask in place. He felt the habit of purpose, momentarily interrupted by the shock of the afternoon, reasserting itself within him. It was not yet possible to see the shape of the new way upon which he had set his feet. He knew, however, that the way was there. For now, that must be enough.

The following day the Third-Year Novice Class was dismissed. There were no ceremonies, no speeches, no congratulations or farewells. Apprentices-to-be left the Novice Wing as they had entered it, with nothing but the clothing on their backs.

Uncharacteristically, Bron found himself dawdling as he made his way to the designated departure point. He sought to fix the details of this hated place indelibly in his mind, so he would never forget what he had suffered here. At the same time, as he gazed into rooms, paused at the turns of hallways, and lingered in courtyards, he understood that he was watching for a face, for the Novice with curly golden hair who had shared one of his punishments.

Though celibacy was a matter of choice for fully Invested Guardians, for Novices and Apprentices it was not. Contact between the sexes for any purpose other than academics was strictly forbidden. Of course this did not stop the Novices. Bron had had his share of furtive trysts, in the cold shadows beneath stairways or in the corners of damp, mold-smelling cellars. He had never been with the same girl twice, nor did he allow himself to think about them afterward—in the bleak corridors of the Novice Wing, infatuation was a weakness capable of undercutting the foundation of every discipline.

Perhaps it was only because he knew he was soon to leave the Novice Wing that his usual strictness had failed him, although he could not think what it was about this Novice that had lodged her so firmly in his mind. He had not touched her, after all; she was not even the kind of girl he had wanted, when it had been possible to want a particular girl rather than the release any girl could give. Yet there had been something in her sea-blue eyes as they rose to his, half-hidden behind the riot of her beautiful hair; and she had claimed his enemy as her own. Jolyon hated principally those who defied him. There must be strength in this girl, beneath her soft and submissive manner. What could she possibly have that Jolyon wished to take?

Bron reached the gathering place, an open court on the First Level. More than five hundred Apprentices-to-be packed the courtyard. The Journeyer Suborder was the largest of the four, and most graduating Novices found themselves in its ranks. Apprehension was evident on every face. Almost from the moment they entered the Novice Wing, Novices dreamed of leaving it. Yet the Apprentice College and what went on there was a mystery. They would be Apprentices for seven years—a fearful amount of time, especially if the Apprenticeship were as terrible as the Novitiate.

Across the court Bron glimpsed the features of his enemy. As if in response, Jolyon raised his eyes, fixing his hooded gaze on Bron's face. Bron turned away, moving within the crowd until Jolyon was lost to view. Even so he fancied he could feel Jolyon's stare, as if the restless heat of it could penetrate flesh and blood.

He had hoped that Apprenticeship would send them to different Suborders, freeing him of Jolyon's spite, but it seemed this was not to be. From the time of their first meeting, in the Study Group to which both had been assigned after their arrival in the Fortress, they had been enemies. There was an instinctive antipathy between them: Bron perceived Jolyon's cruelty, his unhealthy need for others' pain, while Jolyon, who possessed an unerring instinct for the things people most wished to keep hidden, somehow guessed the hatred that burned at the heart of Bron's deception. Since he had become a Thirder, with license to harass those under punishment or Obedience, he had consistently singled Bron out for persecution. Again and again, through mockery and humiliation, he tried to breach Bron's self-control, to trick him into revealing what lay beneath. Each time he fetched up against the wall of Bron's composure his fury and frustration grew. What Jolyon loved most in the world was to break people down; what he hated most in the world were those who did not yield. Over the past months his malice had transformed itself into something much deeper. It looked out of his eyes whenever their gazes met, a loathing as hot as the earth's core, as cold as the spaces between the stars.

There was a commotion in the corridor outside. Ten Apprentices strode into the court: nine young men and one young woman. Like sheep the gathered Novices turned toward them, their nervous muttering stilling to silence.

"Good morning, Novices. We're your official escort." One of the Apprentices, a young man of about twenty, stepped forward. There was none of the furtiveness of a Novice about him; he wore his dull-colored clothing and shining silver medals with casual assurance. "We'll start by dividing you into groups. When you hear one of us call your name, come and stand before us.''

Chaos and confusion ensued, but eventually the crowd ordered itself into nine clusters of approximately fifty Novices each. The girls made up a small tenth group, headed by the female Apprentice. Jolyon, Bron was pleased to see, had been assigned to a group other than his own.

"Quiet!" The Apprentice leader clapped his hands for attention. "Line up now—each group in double columns, ready to march. For the next few hours we'll be showing you over the Apprentice College. We'll also be telling you some of the things you need to know about Apprenticeship. Pay attention—there's a lot to learn, and you may not hear it twice." He surveyed the huddled crowd with genial contempt. "By the Stone, you're a pathetic lot." He turned to the Apprentice beside him. "Did we look this miserable when we passed over?"

"Worse," the other replied, and laughed. The rest joined in. To the Novices, it was as startling as a thunderclap.

"Don't look so grim," the leader called. "This is the day you've all been waiting for. All right—move out!"

The Apprentices set a swift pace, charting a self-assured course through the busy corridors of the Novice Wing. Novices, servants, even teachers pressed back against the walls to make way. On the faces of the watching Novices, desire was as transparent as glass. For just these few moments, Bron and the others were invested, like dim satellites, with an echo of the Apprentices' mythic brilliance: the embodiment of every Novice's most fevered dream.

The great double doors of the Novice Wing stood open. As Bron's group, last of the ten, passed into the sunlight of the court, their leader called out to them.

"Look back, Novices. No Guardian ever forgets this moment."

Bron turned his head. Around him, the others did the same. The huge portals, banded and studded with iron, scarred by age and weather, were swinging ponderously inward. The blackness of the Novice Wing's interior narrowed, like an eye vanishing behind closing lids—a rectangle, a column, a sliver, then gone. Since his arrival in the fortress, Bron had seen the doors daily from within, but from this perspective only twice. From this moment, he would never see them otherwise.

The Apprentices herded their charges across the busy court. Ahead, the doors of the Apprentice College stood wide. Four shallow stairs brought them into a vast, light-filled lobby. Large windows opened onto the sunlit court; torches blazed in brackets, and chandeliers crammed with candles depended from the ceiling. The walls were made of pale gray blocks, bare of adornment, though the doors and windows were framed in elaborate carving. The whole of the huge space was filled with people—Guardians with belts of every hue, Apprentices, servants—moving singly or in groups, pausing to exchange greetings or gathering in little conclaves to converse. The sound of voices rose toward the ceiling, not the stentorian tones of admonishing teachers or the monotonous chanting of Novices at their lessons, but the textured hum of real conversation, punctuated now and then by the ripple of laughter. To the Novices, fresh from the dark discipline of the Novice Wing, it seemed stunningly alien, as if they had been set down in a foreign land whose language and customs they did not know.

The Apprentice guides deftly negotiated the crowd, steering their charges toward the flight of stairs that vaulted upward at the far end of the lobby.

"These are the Stairs of Learning," the Apprentice in charge of Bron's group said over his shoulder. "We're on the first floor now. All the assembly rooms and courtyards and laundries and storage rooms and infirmaries are here. The second floor belongs to the Soldier Suborder, the third to the Searchers, the fourth to we Journeyers, and the fifth to Speakers. Apprentices of the Arm of the Stone are on the sixth floor. You can go anywhere you want in the Apprentice College, but not there. It's forbidden to all but Roundheads."

The Stairs of Learning were numerous and shallow, and appeared to rise up forever. A steady stream of traffic moved up and down them; here and there Apprentices sat in little groups, usually close to the balustrade but sometimes right in the middle of the steps, taking no notice of the crowd, which moved around them without protest. On each floor a broad passage led away on either side of the landing. The same torches that lit the Novice Wing burned here, with the same black smoke-plumes above them, but because there were more of them, or perhaps because of the lighter stone of which the Apprentice College was built, the impression of murky dimness that gripped the Novice Wing was completely absent.

Reaching the fourth floor at last, the guides turned their charges smartly to the right. Seven smaller corridors led off the main hallway, one for each of the seven Apprentice years. The nine groups of boys were guided down the last of these. The party of girls had already gone off on its own—as in the Novice Wing, girls of all years were housed together.

The corridor gave onto a small self-contained world. There was a refectory, a large washroom, several necessary rooms, a number of common rooms, and twelve fifty-bed dormitories. Every chamber had at least one fireplace; the dormitories and the refectory each had two. The guides allowed barely a chance for the Novices to grasp the luxury of their new living quarters, however, whisking them off almost at once on an exhaustive tour of the fourth floor. There seemed no end to its multitude of classrooms, practice rooms, tutorial rooms, conference rooms, Masters' studies, workshops, and auditoriums. The Apprentices flung explanations over their shoulders as if they were skipping pebbles across the surface of a pond; the Novices, most of whom had long since ceased to grasp more than a fraction of what they heard, trailed wearily behind.

At last, without any idea how they had got there, they found themselves in their living quarters once more.

"That's all for now," the guide said. "The evening meal will be served at the eighteenth bell. Tomorrow your Mentors will be assigned. You'll get your medals next week, and after that you'll begin classes. Get a good night's sleep—you'll need it!"

He turned, and was gone. It occurred to Bron that he had never told them his name.

Like sleepwalkers, the Novices dispersed themselves

around the dormitories. When the bell sounded they straggled into the refectory. Servants brought food, hearty and plentiful. Without the anchoring presence of teachers at the tables or a reader at the dais the meal felt strange and unreal. Afterward, exhausted beyond words, Bron lay down on his bed. He pulled the two blankets up to his chin. Warmth surrounded him: the warmth of the roaring fires, the warmth of thick wool. It seemed the most luxurious thing he had ever felt.

"Selwyn Forester."

Bron burrowed into his blankets, not wanting to wake. A hand gripped his shoulder and shook him, insistently. He opened his eyes, pushing himself up on one elbow, opening his mouth to say something angry to his disturber—Semyon, the Novice who had chosen the bed next to his. But the expression on Semyon's face held him silent.

"Selwyn Forester."

Slowly Bron turned his head. They stood at the foot of his pallet: two men with cropped hair, their black robes bound with scarlet sashes. The warmth of the blanket-cocoon turned suddenly to ice.

"Selwyn Forester," the Roundhead repeated for the third time. His voice was neutral, his face expressionless. "Get up off your bed. The Arm of the Stone summons you."

Bron stumbled from the pallet. Panic was rising in him, curdling the heavy meal inside his stomach. Silence gripped the room; the fearful faces of his fellow Novices were like a painted frieze around the walls. The Roundheads took his arms, the firmness of their grip just short of painful, and pushed him out of the dormitory and into the corridor beyond.

Behind his frozen face Bron's mind ran in desperate circles. They had found him out. But how? He had been certain the stringent mindprobes of the Apprentice Examinations had not located his barriers. He had *felt* his barriers hold; examining them afterward, he had found no crack or crevice. Had he betrayed himself somehow? Had he been followed to the roof, perhaps? Or had it been that moment during Kenlin's Expulsion when rage overwhelmed him and he lost control, so that for a moment his entire mind went dark? He had felt a presence then, a contact so brief he was persuaded, when no repercussions followed, that he must have imagined it.

It did not matter. Whatever the cause, the result was the same. He would be questioned, probed, branded, and cast out. The moments he was living now were among the last he would ever experience with a whole mind. The fear was so terrible that after a little while it passed into something else—a kind of unearthly distance, as if his mind had risen out of his body, floating up toward the ceiling and hovering there like a shadow. He could no longer feel his legs; the grip on his arms was only the most distant pressure.

The Roundheads bore him up the Stairs of Learning, past the fifth floor and toward the sixth: the forbidden floor, the domain of the Arm of the Stone. Here the stairs terminated, not in a passageway, but on a broad rectangular landing closed by a red-painted door. The Roundheads stood before it, sending out some sort of mindsignal. Bron heard the sound of bolts. The door swung open, revealing a wide empty hallway, running straight as a rule toward an end too far to see.

The Roundheads resumed their swift pace. They urged Bron past rank upon rank of tightly closed red doors, past the right angles of other corridors and large arches giving onto shadowy open spaces, through big circular areas from which four, five, or even six hallways sprang out like the spokes of a wheel. There was a strange featurelessness to this place—every door identical, every arch the same as every other, every stone cut to precisely the same size and shape. The walls were faced, not with the pale-gray blocks that composed the rest of the Apprentice College, but with large panels of sand-colored stone, striated with russet markings and smoothed to a satiny sheen. The many torches burned with a pale clean light, without the sooty plumes that marred the ceilings everywhere else. Though the other floors had seemed crowded, the sixth was nearly empty. They encountered only four other people: two Roundhead Apprentices staring with frank curiosity, a servant with downcast eyes, and a black-robed Roundhead Master, who gazed through Bron as if he were invisible. Briefly, as he passed, Bron felt the chill of mindtouch.

At last they halted before an entrance no different, to all appearances, from the others. The Roundheads closed their eyes: the mindsignal again. The door began to open. This time a human hand was responsible. In the entrance stood a tall man, with black robes and close-cropped hair. His scarlet sash was like a wound across his narrow middle. The gold medal of Guardianship shone dully on his breast. He gestured, silently. Bron's guards propelled him forward, pressing him into a chair set before a long wooden table. Without a word, they departed.

The Roundhead closed the door and crossed to the table, seating himself behind it. Clasping his hands beneath his chin, he regarded Bron with a level and emotionless stare. Bron forced himself to return the gaze, though his fear was like a live thing within him; he refused to give this Roundhead the satisfaction of seeing him break.

The silence lengthened, an endless note played on an invisible instrument. Bron's gaze was locked to that of the man before him. The rest of the room, the rest of the Fortress, dropped away. It was hypnotic, like a dream.

"Well," said the man at last. His voice was pleasant; it seemed to slide along the chords of quiet rather than to break them. "Welcome to the Apprentice College, Selwyn Forester. You must be feeling somewhat overwhelmed. I can remember, from my own Apprentice days."

Bron felt sick. This man was preparing to destroy his mind. What was the point of this banal greeting?

"Let me introduce myself," the Roundhead continued. "I am Marhalt, Apprentice-Master of the Arm of the Stone. I apologize for bringing you here without explanation, but I thought it best not to announce my purpose in front of your classmates. I want to talk with you about your Apprenticeship, about your plans for the future."

Was this some strange Roundhead game? Why should a member of the Council of Six wish to discuss his Apprenticeship, or anything else to do with him?

"I quite understand if you feel confused or fearful." Marhalt's voice was soothing, without threat. "After all, there's usually only one reason for a summons from the Arm of the Stone. But you have no cause to fear. You've done nothing wrong. I haven't brought you here for Interrogation, only for conversation—I give you my word. And the word of the Arm is not given lightly.''

So certain had Interrogation seemed, as Bron stumbled along the passages of the sixth floor, that it was almost impossible to grasp the meaning of any other future. Yet surely a Roundhead would not be forsworn. Faintly, like an awakening candle flame, he felt the stirring of hope.

For the first time he took in his surroundings. The large chamber was sparsely furnished, with only the carved chairs in which he and Marhalt sat, the long oak table between them, and a number of document cases and coffer chests near the door. There were two mullioned windows at Marhalt's back, and a small hearth framed by a carved mantel, within which the yellow-blue flames of a coal fire leaped and cracked. Thick ivory-colored candles were set in holders around the walls and on the table. They neither smoked nor dripped, consuming themselves entirely as they burned. The light they cast was softer than the ruddy glow of torches. It picked out the rich patterns of the thick carpet that softened the stone flags, and pulled flashes of color from the folds of the tapestries that hid the walls.

It was the most luxurious room in which Bron had ever found himself. Yet the dark colors, the muted designs, the preponderance of empty space, spoke of a degree of reserve, and of a certain austerity. These things showed also in the face of the man across the table. He looked to be somewhere in middle age, though with Roundheads it was impossible to tell. He had dark hair, a patrician nose, and finely shaped, mobile lips. His eyes, when the light caught them, flashed an unusual shade of amber. He was very thin, the bones of his face clearly sculpted beneath the smooth-stretched skin; his hands were long and slender, with big joints and neat oval nails, the index and middle fingers stained with ink. Unlike other Roundheads Bron had seen, he wore no jewelry beyond his Guardian medal on its thick chain.

Bron's mind was working more normally now. Reason told him that while the Roundhead would not swear falsely, his assurances could not be trusted. This might not be the last night of his life, yet he could not believe such a man wanted simply to talk to him. Behind his mask, invisibly, he collected himself, gathering strength for whatever was to come.

"What is it you wish to know from me, Master?"

"I assume you've given consideration to your future as a Journeyer," Marhalt said. "Your ambitions, your hopes for a posting. Perhaps you'd tell me some of your thoughts on that subject."

"My only ambition is to serve the Stone, to uphold the Limits throughout the world, and to defend against the evil of handpower."

Marhalt's lips quirked, very slightly. "Commendable. But I was hoping for something a little more specific."

Evidently this man would not be satisfied by the formulaic platitudes that had served in the Novice Wing. Bron tried again.

"I'd thought to find a place in the Fortress. I want to specialize in administration. The preservation of the Order is as important as anything to be done within the world. The Fortress is the heart of the world, after all. It's where I think I can be of most use."

Marhalt raised his eyebrows. "Don't you think you might find that a bit limiting?"

"Limiting?"

"You are a young man of obvious ability. Surely you don't really want to become one small component of an army of clerks and bureaucrats." He leaned forward a little, his eyes fixed on Bron's face. "Let there be no subterfuge between us, Selwyn Forester. I know you wanted to be a Speaker. Have you given any thought to why you were not allowed to become one?"

It was a moment before Bron trusted himself to speak. "I'm not good at nearspeech."

"Come, come." Marhalt's face was suddenly hard. "You're too intelligent to believe it was only that. Let me say it for you—you are willful. You are arrogant. You find it difficult to obey. You find it irksome to conform. *That* is why you did not become a Speaker." He smiled, a very small curving of his lips. "Oh, yes, Selwyn Forester. I've been watching, these past three years and more. I know quite a lot about you."

Only by the most extreme effort of will was Bron able to keep his mask intact. Marhalt's amber eyes pinned him like an insect; he could feel the Roundhead's Gift, the barest touch of a power greater than any he had felt from a Guardian before. The faint smile Marhalt still wore conveyed, not amusement or mockery, but knowledge, as if Bron's barriers were no more than parchment, upon which the core of his deception cast a visible stain.

"Do you want to know why I watched?" Marhalt said.

"Yes," Bron whispered.

"It was your application for the Novice Examinations that first caught the eye of the Arm of the Stone. You were, as you yourself must know, an unusual candidate—fifteen, rather than twelve or thirteen as is customary, born to a language different from the one in which you took the Examinations. Not to mention the gap in your history between your twelfth and thirteenth year."

"I explained all that when I applied," Bron said. His voice sounded scarcely louder than the crackling of the flames on the hearth.

"Yes, you did. You had planned to take the Examinations when you were twelve, but that was the year in which they were canceled because of the great plague that swept the northlands. All your family died but you. You crossed the sea, fleeing the sickness, looking for work and a place to live. Once you settled it was necessary to satisfy the two-year residency requirement before you could apply to take the Examinations."

"My employer will vouch for me."

"He has already done so. You may be interested to know that he went to the trouble of investigating you himself—he showed us the records of his research. He found nothing to contradict your story. Of course, most of the town of Rosburg, where you say you were born, was destroyed in the plague riots, including the Journeyer Residence with all its records."

"I didn't know that," Bron said faintly. "I've told the truth, Master. I swear it."

What chance was there that any of his secrets remained intact? They had been watching when his story and his name had still been new, his guard less rigorous and his mask far from perfect. He might have betrayed himself a thousand times and never known it. Over the past three years, he had reveled in his contempt for his Novice Masters—so arrogant in their power, so easily deceived. Yet all the while he had been guilty of the same failing, for never once had he suspected Roundhead scrutiny.

The silence drew out. The room was filled with sliding light and drifting shadow. He could see the candle flames reflected, like pinpoints, in the amber depths of Marhalt's eyes. Unmask me, he thought. Unmask me, and be done with it.

"I tell you these things, Selwyn Forester, only so that you may know how our attention first fell on you." Marhalt's voice was quiet. His face held neither condemnation nor anger, nor any of the implacable hardness Bron had seen in the Roundheads who had taken his brother. "It's our policy, you see, to keep watch over candidates who have shown themselves to be unusual, no matter how well-explained they may be. And so we set ourselves to observe your Novitiate. The Novitiate is never easy, but for you it was more difficult than for most. In your time in the Novice Wing, you were punished more than any Novice in recent memory. You were given a name by your fellows, were you not?"

"I was called the Obedient," Bron said woodenly.

"The Obedient." Marhalt seemed to linger over the syllables. "Your conduct was without blemish, your academic achievements of the highest order, your mindskill ability beyond any of your fellows. Yet your Novitiate is one long record of Obedience, one long stretch of penance and humiliation."

"I brought my punishments on myself, Master," Bron said. "I know that. I do know why I was made a Journeyer."

"Ah, but you do not know. It was the Arm of the Stone that made you a Journeyer."

Bron stared at the Roundhead, not certain he had heard correctly. Marhalt raised his hands, steepling his fingers beneath his chin.

"If the decision had been left to your Novice Masters, the qualities that unfitted you for Speakerhood would probably have unfitted you for any area of Guardianship. You might well have found yourself outside the gates with the badge of failure sewn to your clothing. But we of the Arm see things differently. We have to. We follow a different mission, and we require different standards of thought and action. In the very qualities your Novice Masters detested, the voice of promise spoke to us. Nor did it escape us how thoroughly you managed to defy your Masters, while never showing yourself to be less than thoroughly compliant. We find such . . . subtlety very attractive."

A strange suspicion was growing in Bron. He felt as if he were dreaming, or going mad.

"Which brings me to the purpose of this conversation." Marhalt lowered his hands, clasping them on the table in front of him. His amber gaze was steady on Bron's face. "I am offering you an Apprenticeship in the Arm of the Stone."

The words seemed to dance on the air. Bron could almost see them, written in fire. He felt his throat close up. He could not speak.

"Unfortunately, I cannot allow you time for consideration. I must have your answer now—that is the condition my colleagues have imposed on your acceptance. Well? What do you say, Selwyn Forester? Will you become one of us?"

Bron's mind spun. A few moments ago unmasking had seemed inevitable; now the world had turned on its head and all possibilities had been transformed into their opposites. Surely the Arm of the Stone would not make such an offer unless his secrets were, after all, safe. Unless the offer were not genuine—unless it were some kind of trick, a trap for self-betrayal . . . though why should the Arm of the Stone bother with traps and tricks when they could probe him and know everything in an instant? But such questions did not matter. The rest might be uncertainty, but there was one thing he knew: what Marhalt held out to him, clothed in the trappings of choice, was no choice at all. One did not refuse the Arm of the Stone. He drew a deep breath, and met Marhalt's eyes.

"Yes," he said. "I will join you."

Marhalt smiled, his lips lifting in their slight curve, for all the world as if he had not been certain of Bron's reply. "I am pleased," he said.

"You do me great honor, Master." Bron heard his voice, clear in the quiet room. For the first time since he had arrived on the sixth floor, he felt a kind of balance. If indeed a game were being played, at least now he could play in return. "I'm deeply grateful for this opportunity."

Marhalt smiled again, privately. "Come to me in seven years," he said, "and tell me then. There's no need for you to return to the fourth floor. Your Apprenticeship can begin at once. But before I call my colleagues to escort you to your new quarters there's something I want to tell you. It's important that you understand certain things about the Arm of the Stone, as well as the circumstances under which this offer comes to you.

"I've told you that we of the Arm are different from other Guardians. This is necessary, by the nature of our task. To us fall the most terrible duties any Guardian is called upon to perform. Our work brings us face to face with Violations and Violators so profoundly evil that our souls are placed at constant risk. Yet no matter what monstrosity challenges us, we must be capable of confronting it without being stained. We carry the twin burdens of judgment and purity. Our decisions must possess the wisdom of the Stone itself, our actions echo its perfection. Where Violation is concerned, there is no margin for error.

"We of the Arm must own strong Gifts and high intelligence, as do all Speakers, and some Journeyers. But for us, other abilities not common to most Guardians are equally essential. We must be quick-witted and decisive, able to confer judgments swiftly and without hesitation. We must be capable of acting independently, with no guidance but our mission and our knowledge, for where we go there is no one to tell us what to do. We must honor tradition as we honor the Stone, but we cannot follow it blindly—it is not for us, as it is for others, to rely on precedent and established practice alone. No Violation is like any other. No standard set by past Investigations will ever fit a new situation precisely. We must not simply know tradition, we must be able to shape it, to fit it to the circumstance in which we find ourselves.

"There is another thing. If Violation is to be found and judged, it must be known. Knowing Violation is not simply holding acquaintance from without—that is, through history—though of course we must know this as intimately as we know ourselves. It is, it must be, understanding from within. We must know the Violator's mind. We must walk in his footsteps. We must apprehend his thoughts. We must comprehend his actions."

Marhalt leaned forward. His face was focused and intent.

"There is a final characteristic, an attribute more important than all the others. Devotion. The service of the Stone through the preservation of orthodoxy must be our most profound and consuming passion. It must rest at the core of our beings—white-hot, free of doubt or stain. Only devotion can make us proof against the perils of confronting Violation, over and over, for the whole of our lives. Only devotion can forge our abilities into a weapon that strikes for, and not against, our cause. Without it, all our qualities are nothing, and worse than nothing. The line between the mind that Violates and the mind that judges Violation is very narrow. It is devotion, and devotion alone, that draws that line."

Marhalt sat back in his chair. He clasped his fingers beneath his chin. The light of the candles cast the angles of his face into sharp relief.

"Unfortunately, it is in this area that danger presents itself. The capacity for devotion cannot be easily assessed in advance. Every new Apprentice presents a risk. We are not often wrong, but when we are, great evil can result. There have been more than a few betrayals of our cause over the centuries."

"I would never betray the Arm of the Stone, Master," Bron said. "I swear it."

"You needn't swear to me," Marhalt replied. "It's my colleagues who are unconvinced. There are some who feel you are too intractable, too stubborn, too willful even for the Arm of the Stone. They point not only to the opinion of your Novice Masters, but to your friendship with the Novice Kenlin—proof, at the very least, of a serious deficiency in judgment."

Bron shook his head. "I knew nothing of Kenlin's Violation. Kenlin told me nothing about himself. I was probed—it was certified that I was telling the truth."

"I'm not one of those who questioned your veracity, Selwyn. You are far too intelligent to take such a stupid risk. I tell you this only to make a point. There are those among us who are certain you will fail. Know that it is doubt, and not promise, which prompted us to break with tradition and recruit you immediately after your Novitiate, rather than waiting until your Second Year of Apprenticeship, as is customary. Most of us feel that difficult metal simply needs longer shaping. But there are those who fear that certain flaws may never be hammered into virtues. You will be Tested many times in the coming years."

"I understand, Master."

"No, you don't. But I am not asking you to understand just yet. Only to remember."

"Then I'll remember, Master."

"See that you do."

Behind Bron, the door swung open. The two Roundheads who had brought him stood at the threshold.

"My colleagues will take you to your quarters now."

Bron got to his feet. Exhaustion rolled over him in a great wave. Not until that moment had he realized how drained he was.

"Selwyn."

Nearly to the door, Bron turned.

"Tonight you begin a new life. You've already seen how different the Apprentice College is from the Novice Wing. The sixth floor is more different even than that. The freedoms here are beyond any you have ever known. Our association is like nothing else within the Fortress. You must put aside your old ways. Your new Masters will not tolerate them.''

To Bron's weary gaze the glow of the candles upon the oaken table formed a spreading nimbus, blurring Marhalt's spare features, pale against the dark setting of his robe. His words carried a sense of warning, but not of admonition. It was more as if the Roundhead sought to communicate some important truth.

Bron's guides bore him away. Once more the red-streaked halls enclosed him. He had the sense that he was not walking, but falling, as if he had been tipped over the lip of a well. The light of the world he knew receded above him. It would be a long time before he stood on solid ground again.

Nine

"AND SO we conclude," the teacher said, "our study of handpower's rise to ascendancy in the world before the Split."

Bron shifted his position on the hard stone bench. The classroom in which he sat was semi-circular, with walls and ceiling of russet-streaked stone. Like most spaces on the sixth floor, it was windowless: illumination came from a large globe of mindlight that hovered just below the ceiling, its pale glow caressing the stone and lending the floors and benches a misleading semblance of softness. The young men who crowded the room were all Apprentices in their first year of Roundhead education, known as First Arm. They occupied the tiers of seats as uniformly as blocks of masonry: two hundred and fifty black tunics, tied with two hundred and fifty red sashes, topped by two hundred and fifty pale faces.

The Roundhead teacher stood in the flat half-circle between the bottom rank of benches and the back wall. His cropped hair was white, his face like a leather garment gone soft with use. Even men of power could not cheat time forever, but it was the custom among Roundheads to do so for as long as they could. Most maintained the appearance of youth well into their sixties and even seventies. The signs of age this man presented marked him as well over a century.

"It is no exaggeration to say that this study forms the foundation of all your future education." The teacher's voice carried effortlessly to the highest tier of benches. He paced as he spoke, disdaining the carved wooden lectern. "As your training on the sixth floor progresses, you will find yourself calling, again and again, upon the basic principles you have learned over the past six months.

"For example, much of your Second-Year study of the pathology of Violation will be based on what I have taught you about what leads men to stray into the errors of the hands." The teacher halted, his gaze singling out an Apprentice high in the upper rank of benches. "Reimund."

"We are all of us born with a stain of weakness." Reimund rose to his feet. "A fatal susceptibility to the fascination of tools. Within each handpower device lies the germ of a hundred more. One thought, one idea, one device is enough to set a man's feet irretrievably upon the path of handpower."

"Correct. Similarly, when you reach your Third Year and begin to examine the world of handpower more closely, you will find you already know the truth that underlies its horror." This time he pointed. "Piers."

Piers stood. "In the handpower world, every man is mad. Every hand wields madness. The lust for technology is all there is, a consuming sickness that can never be cured."

"Very good. And in your final years of Apprenticeship, in which you will learn how to carry the mission of the Arm of the Stone to the world, you will discover that beneath every well-conducted Investigation lies the first thing I ever taught you: the Rule of the Three Differences." Once more he pointed. "Rafer."

An Apprentice toward the bottom of the classroom rose swiftly to his feet. "Difference the First is the Difference of Guarding. The handpower adept believes that the power of the hands must never be constrained. But we understand that in the hands of the unworthy, any power can be a danger. The proper use of power can be ensured only by placing a guard upon its practice. To guard is the First Charge of the Arm of the Stone, and from this springs our First Power: to watch."

"Excellent," the teacher said. "Sabaion, the Second Difference."

"Difference the Second is the Difference of Stability. The

handpower adept marches a road mapped by constant
change, moving blindly toward unguessed destinations. But
we value stability. The Limits are our solid foundation, a
mountain peak from which we can see all the world. Stability can be guaranteed only through the diligent preservation of the rule of mindpower. Preservation is the Second
Charge of the Arm of the Stone, and from it stems our
Second Power: to Investigate.''

"Reimund, the Third Difference.''

Reimund was already standing. He was one of the most
frequent contributors to class discussions, and something of
a favorite. "Difference the Third is the Difference of Balance. To the follower of handpower, balance means nothing—all must be handpower, nothing else must exist. For
us, balance is all. Unless the proper equilibrium is maintained between the powers of mind and hand, our world
cannot endure. Balance is assured only through the Limits
and their stern enforcement. Enforcement is the Third
Charge of the Arm of the Stone, and from it stems our Third
Power: to punish.''

"Thank you, Reimund.'' The teacher clasped his hands
behind his back, and began to pace once more. "To guard,
to preserve, to enforce: of all men on earth, only we bear
these Charges. To watch, to Investigate, to punish: only we
wield these Powers. It is we who hold back the tide of dissolution from the world. It is our orthodoxy that illuminates
the darkness of the world's Violation. The unGifted are safe
to live and breed and die only because we protect them. The
Order of Guardians itself can teach, administer, and study
only because we walk the earth. Remember this. It is your
creed.''

The teacher halted before the lectern. Resting both hands
on its carved surface, he surveyed the assembled Apprentices. Like all Roundheads, he was strongly Gifted; the passage of his gaze was like a blast of heat across Bron's face.
The mindlight throbbed softly in the silence, a visible echo
of the Apprentices' beating hearts.

"During the next six months we will focus on the process
by which our world came to be. I have told you how, in its
rush to ascendancy, handpower pushed the ways of mind

and those who clung to them so far aside that they fell out of the old world entirely—people, houses, forests, whole villages, entire tracts of land, all transported to some strange other-place. I leave you today with a question. Was the new world a preexisting place, to which the followers of mind-power were conveyed like objects moved from one room to another? Or was it something they became, something entirely new, a world growing like a plant from the scattered seeds of the Split? Consider this question carefully. I will call upon you during our next class to hear what you have concluded.

"Very well, Apprentices. You are dismissed."

The silence that had held throughout the lecture broke, an explosive eruption of coughing, rustling garments, murmuring voices. The Apprentices began to move toward the central stairway that bisected the tiers of benches. In their black clothing they resembled a flow of ink emptying from an inkstone, except that they left no stain. Each Apprentice bowed his head as he passed before the teacher. The teacher received these salutations without expression. When Bron's turn came he felt the heat of the man's Gift, slipping like skillful fingers across the contours of his mind. He was aware of his barriers, tensing invisibly against the force brought to bear against them, relaxing again as the teacher's attention left him.

The students lingered in little groups outside the classroom, already beginning to follow the discussion the teacher had ordered. Bron, alone, headed for his room. He moved through the corridors with a confidence he had once despaired of ever achieving, past russet-streaked walls and ranks of doors and hallway intersections as apparently undifferentiated as blades of grass. Though the sixth floor seemed featureless, it was only so to the untutored eye. For those who knew, it was replete with signs and symbols, messages of direction and purpose contained in every surface: certain juxtapositions of the rust-red striations on the walls, oddly shaped flagstones inlaid beneath archways, the color of mortar in the masonry above the doors.

Bron reached the Apprentice Quarters, and opened the door to the room he shared with five of his classmates. Entry-sensitive torches flared to life, revealing a spacious chamber, with roughweave hangings on the walls and straw matting on the floor. Immediately beyond the entrance was a common area; at the back were six curtained bed-cubicles. A large fireplace occupied much of one wall. As Bron had hoped, the room was empty. Relishing the rare privilege of privacy, he took a heel of bread from the provision cabinet beside the door and went to sit in his cubicle.

He was used, now, to the comfort of this room and its appointments. The first time he had seen it, however, hanging exhausted in the grip of his Roundhead guards, its opulence had seemed impossible, dreamlike. His roommates, five young men with the black tunics, red belts, and cropped heads of Roundhead Apprentices, had pointed him silently toward the single empty bed. Their faces were closed, their eyes suspicious. To Bron, they seemed as unreal as the room itself.

He was to discover that the lavish appointments, as well as the luxury of sharing space with only five others, were just the beginning of the distinctions and privileges Apprentices of the Arm of the Stone enjoyed. As the Arm was an elite within the Order of Guardians, so its Apprentices were within the Apprentice College. The linen and wool of Bron's clothing was nearly as fine as the Masters' own, the food in the refectory was the best he had ever eaten, the beds were real feather beds. There were servants to keep the rooms clean and the provision cabinet stocked; nearly everything else, from the ever-burning torches to the never-dying fires, was power-automated. When Roundhead Apprentices descended to the fourth floor to take the classes they shared with ordinary Journeyers, they moved within little shells of separation, as if their evident disdain for lesser mortals formed a physical space around them. Even Apprentices in their Seventh Year deferred to them.

Such understandings were far away on that first night, and for many weeks thereafter. The whole of Bron's initial time on the sixth floor possessed, in memory, the sense of a fevered dream, a fragmented chaos of strange faces, labyrinthine spaces, and incomprehensible customs. A few images separated themselves from the confusion, like boulders on a plain: the sight of his black hair falling to the floor as a servant sheared his head in the Roundhead crop. Putting on the red sash for the first time, half-expecting it to burn his skin through his clothes. Losing his bearings in the blank corridors and wandering for hours before he found his way again. Clearest of all, however, was the memory of waking that first morning, to a room he did not recognize, to the knowledge that his presence here was not, after all, a dream. In Marhalt's chambers, presented with the necessity of acceptance, Bron had not had time to examine the implications of his forced choice. Now, as if a curtain had been swept aside, the full measure of his predicament confronted him. Even if his secrets were still safe, how could he hope to keep them hidden in the domain of the Roundheads, among men whose greatest skill, whose deepest passion, was the penetration of deception?

Fear became his shadow, darkening every waking moment, spilling over into sleep. He expected discovery hourly, daily. Every task seemed a Test. Every word held the possibility of betrayal. Now and then he thought of himself, on the roof of the Novice Wing, evaluating the Arm of the Stone as if it were merely another choice that might serve his purpose. From his new perspective, the arrogance of this seemed pathetic. Yet how could he have known, then, that the Arm of the Stone could not be chosen? How could he have known that on the sixth floor there was no room for any purpose but survival?

But even such desperate emotion could not resist the passage of time. As Bron's barriers continued to withstand the Masters' probes, discovery began to seem less inevitable. Gradually he became conversant with the customs of the mysterious organization of which he was now a part; slowly he learned to read its signs and symbols. One day, he looked within himself and realized the fear was gone. He had come to understand not just his environment, but how to survive within it.

The door swung open, crashing against the wall. Bron jumped, jerked from his reverie. Two of his five roommates entered, deep in conversation.

"... because Gates are the only conclusion that makes

sense," Derain was saying. "After handpower pushed mindpower out of the old world, there were just a lot of little pieces of mindpower floating around in limbo. But they still had to be connected to the handpower world in some way, or how could Dafydd have journeyed to all the mindpower places with news of the Stone?"

"But that would mean hundreds of Gates," Nils objected. "Today there are only twelve. What happened to the rest?"

The two crossed the room, seizing food from the cupboard as they went. They seated themselves at the table in the common area, preparing, with their customary relish, to follow the Roundhead teacher's end-of-class directive.

Bron had never imagined, before he reached the sixth floor, that anyone could talk the way his roommates—and all other Roundhead Apprentices—did. Day and night, in their cubicles or in the washrooms, after class or during meals, at the behest of their teachers or on their own initiative, they conversed freely about matters which, in the outside world or in the Novice Wing, would have led at the very least to punishment for Violations of Paths of Thought. They debated the handpower personality, thinking up examples of traits and actions that might push a person into Violation. They dissected the methods by which famous Violators had expressed their depravity, theorizing on how it might be possible for a Violator of the most dreadful magnitude to hide his perversion completely and never be caught at all. They criticized the lectures, mocked the teachers' mannerisms, complained about the workload, and altogether demonstrated an astounding absence of both inhibition and reverence.

In the very brief time Bron had spent on the fourth floor, he had sensed the existence of a degree of latitude greater than any he had known before. Had he spent his first year there, like the other Roundhead Apprentices, or been provided with the initial orientation period they received on recruitment to the Arm of the Stone, the correspondingly greater freedoms of the sixth floor might not have seemed so shocking. Marhalt had warned him; but, fresh from the strictures of the Novice Wing, Bron had no context in which to place that warning. The first time he heard his roommates engage in one of their freewheeling discussions, he was convinced that he shared a room with Violators of the deepest hue. He had wondered, panicked, whether he would be tainted by his involuntary association with them.

But such freedoms were as integral to the strange new world in which he found himself as the russet-marked stone that faced the walls. In a sense, his thoughts had always followed forbidden channels; the adjustment was easier for him than it might have been for someone else. But old taboos were not easily lifted. Even after six months it took an effort of will to speak up in class. He was still capable of being shocked by some of the things he heard. And he could not stop himself, when he listened to his roommates mocking the Masters or trading scurrilous gossip about the Interrogators, from thinking of Kenlin, who had been condemned by a drawing.

"Maybe the number of Gates decreased as the Split progressed and the connections between the worlds dropped away," Derain said. "Maybe in a thousand years there won't be any Gates at all."

"All right." Nils was a muscular young man with the fair hair and blue eyes of a Northerner; he affected a slow deliberation of speech that Bron had at first mistaken for dullness, though in reality, like all Roundhead Apprentices, he was piercingly intelligent. "Suppose I accept your theory. How do you explain how the separate realities joined up to become a single world?"

"Maybe the process that worked for handpower worked for mindpower, in reverse. If the exclusive pursuit of handpower had the effect of pushing away pieces of the world, why shouldn't the opposite occur when people exclusively pursued mindpower?"

"But the original mindpower places couldn't have added up to anything like the size of the world we live in now."

"Maybe the boundaries of the mindpower places expanded," Derain said irritably. He was a thin, twitchy boy, with a sour disposition and a face as pale as curdled milk. "There was both a drawing together *and* an expansion."

"But what was the process, Derain? What was the actual means by which the boundaries spread?"

"How should I know?" Derain hissed with exasperation. "Why must you be so literal, Nils? Can't you just think about things for the interest of thinking them, instead of proving everything down to the smallest fact?"

"A fact is a fact, but an assumption is just a theory," Nils said with unruffled calm. "If you want something to be taken seriously, you have to prove it."

Derain was angry now. "They're not just assumptions. I've thought them through. And if you could spare a second to listen instead of talk, you'd agree."

Bron, who had been following the theoretical portion of the conversation with interest, ceased to pay attention. He disliked his roommates, with their affectations and their egotism and their way of allowing every discourse to degenerate into personal confrontation. The feeling was mutual. In part, this sprang from his class status—though he was First Arm like the others, he was only a First-Year Apprentice, while all of them were in their Second Year—but also, oddly, from the fact of Marhalt's patronage. No one could remember the last time Marhalt had selected an Apprentice in his First Year of Arm training to Mentor. Should Bron be respected for his brilliance, or suspected for his uniqueness? Bron's roommates seemed to have settled on the latter. Within the rigid conventions of Apprentice society, they avoided him as much as they could, ignoring him when he was with them and speaking to him directly only when there was no alternative. It was one of the only boons of his association with them.

The rest of the group—Godard, Gavin, and Medrano—arrived just in time to give fresh life to the discussion, and the conversation continued unabated until the bell rang for supper. It was the custom for roommates, known as Living Groups, to follow activities as a unit; Bron tagged behind the others as they made their way to the refectory that served First Arm Apprentices. They continued to argue as they shoveled food into their mouths, tripping over the ends of each others' sentences, raising their voices as if correctness could be determined by loudness alone. As he often did to escape their bickering, Bron turned his mind inward. Rarely able to find silence on the sixth floor, as yet unsuccessful in locating any place where he could be alone, he had become skilled at creating a kind of solitude inside his head.

Supper over, he set out for Marhalt's chambers, where he would spend the next two hours. As his Mentor, Marhalt required these meetings twice a week. Most Apprentices visited their Mentors only half as often.

Marhalt, Bron had discovered, had begun his career as the Primary of an Investigation Team. He quickly became known for the brilliance, speed, and meticulousness of his work; his cases were studied by senior Apprentices in the special classes of the Fourth, Fifth and Sixth Years as textbook examples of procedure. During his tenure he had handled a larger workload than any other Primary active at the time, specializing in complex cases involving multiple and mass Violations. He was responsible for the apprehension of several of the more famous Violators of recent history, as well as the discovery and destruction of no less than four handpower rings. In a world of Limits, beneath the eye of the Arm of the Stone, experimentation with tools and technology was not common, yet it was not unknown either. Individuals engaged in such pursuits generally worked alone; now and then, however, they banded into rings or networks, pooling their skills and their appetite for corruption, venturing far past the boundaries the Limits set on the practices of the hand. Though these groups placed themselves at greater risk of discovery through their intense activity, because of their greater resources they were better able to conceal themselves. Even if they were caught, they usually managed to destroy much of what they had created. Marhalt was one of only five Investigators in history who had ever apprehended more than a single handpower ring; he was the only one who had ever apprehended a ring with its oeuvre intact.

After twenty years of service, Marhalt was recalled to the Fortress to receive a posting high in the Arm of the Stone's hierarchy. Four years before, he had been named Apprentice-Master, the youngest member of the Council of Six in the Arm's history. Now, at the age of fifty-seven, Marhalt was as close to a legend as a living man could be, able to command the full power and privilege afforded to the Arm of the Stone. Yet though his rank reserved for him a splendid suite in the Roundhead section of the Journeyer Wing, he preferred instead to occupy relatively modest rooms in the Apprentice College. Though he was entitled to the services of a veritable army of clerks and assistants, he employed no staff, performing all his paperwork himself. While most Roundhead Investigators amassed considerable fortunes through confiscation of Violators' assets, Marhalt had never taken for himself any of Violation's forfeits; he owned nothing beyond the furnishings of his rooms. And though the Council of Six were exempt from the requirement of Mentorship, Marhalt chose to Mentor even so. He was responsible for a small, handpicked group of students, all of them extraordinarily Gifted.

Bron often puzzled, uneasily, over why Marhalt had placed him among this number. He did not question his intellect or the strength of his Gift, for even on the sixth floor he knew himself to be more than the equal of any of his peers. Yet he lacked nearspeech, the mindskill most essential to those who would become mindprobers. And the catalogue of faults Marhalt had enumerated at their first meeting was much on his mind. Why was it, he wondered, that Marhalt did not share the suspicion of the nameless colleagues he had invoked—or, if he did, was able to look beyond it to something else? What, exactly, did he see?

The architrave above Marhalt's door was mortared in a unique design, indicating his rank within the Arm of the Stone. Bron paused for a moment before the red-painted panels, smoothing his face, drawing up his mask. A certain apprehension always preceded these sessions, but tonight what he felt was closer to fear. Two days ago he had endured the first of an Arm Apprentice's required mindprobes, and in a few moments he would discover how he had fared. In the domain of the Arm, there was no condition that did not invoke its opposite; the unusual license the Apprentices enjoyed in speech and thought was matched to a very precise degree by the closeness with which they were monitored. Other Apprentices were probed annually, but

Roundhead Apprentices must face the probe three times a year.

Bron knocked. Marhalt opened the door himself, as he always did—he never wasted power on acts that could be performed by hand. They seated themselves in their usual places, Marhalt behind his oaken table, Bron in the chair facing it.

Marhalt preferred to begin their sessions with an interval of silence. He sat with a stillness that conveyed both attentiveness and repose, his long fingers clasped beneath his chin, his eyes resting gently on Bron's face. Even after many months, Bron found these initial moments difficult to bear. Marhalt's clear gaze conveyed neither judgment nor censure, nor any other emotion Bron could identify. But there was tremendous power in his regard. The full weight of his attention was not easy to sustain.

In the chaotic days that followed his arrival on the sixth floor, Bron had truly feared his Mentor. Never had he encountered a Guardian of such subtlety and perception, or one so powerfully Gifted. He had dreaded the evening sessions, the hours spent pinned like an insect to the beam of Marhalt's observation. It had taken all the strength he had to hold his own beneath that amber gaze. Yet at the same time, the senior Roundhead provided the only point of constancy amid the bewildering flux of new experience. It had been Marhalt who imparted the details of Roundhead rules and customs, who mapped the endless corridors, who revealed the meaning of the signs hidden in wall and floor. It had been Marhalt who provided instruction in the strange conventions of Apprentice life, and offered coaching in the unfamiliar ways of Roundhead classrooms. Unlike the harsh Searchers of the Novice Wing, he seemed genuinely to desire to convey learning. He prized discourse above recitation, and greeted mistakes not with punishment, but with explanation. He never, as the Mentors of Bron's roommates did, utilized caprice as an element of his teaching: he did not levy penalties in the absence of fault, or set Tests designed mainly to humiliate, or dispense cryptic utterances that resulted in discipline if they were not interpreted correctly.

In the multilayered world of the Arm, Marhalt was a man of rare directness. Though every phrase he uttered might leave a hundred unspoken, what he did say could be relied on absolutely. As day followed day, Bron's dread began to ease. He found himself less driven to search his Mentor's words for hidden meanings, his teachings for secret misdirection. Marhalt's scrutiny might never become easy to bear, but after six months Bron was as certain as it was possible to be that he was equal to it. The evening sessions were more now than just a test of strength—not anticipated, but no longer feared.

When Marhalt judged they had been silent long enough, he lowered his hands and clasped them before him on the table. "Well, Selwyn," he said. "Tell me what you have learned these last two days."

With a fluency that once had been pretense and now was habit, Bron began to relay a synopsis of his studies. Apprentices of the Arm of the Stone followed a curriculum nearly identical to that of ordinary Journeyers, studying the basics of the fifty-five recognized Trades and their Limitbooks, receiving tutoring in advanced mindskills, and pursuing a host of academic subjects. In place of the Trade Apprenticeship followed by other Journeyers, however, Roundhead Apprentices attended a special class each year, pertaining to the mission of the Arm of the Stone. The first of these, in which Bron was now enrolled, examined the causes and process of the Split. The second provided a detailed study of the handpower-prone personality. The third taught of the handpower world itself. The fourth, fifth, and sixth addressed the skills all Roundheads must possess—Investigation, Interrogation, judgment, sentencing, and punishment.

"Very good," Marhalt said when Bron was done. "I'm pleased with your academic progress, Selwyn."

"Thank you, Master."

"As to your probe, the Interrogators report nothing amiss. Your mind seems well in order."

It was the moment Bron had dreaded, come and gone so swiftly he had not even had time to anticipate it. It required some concentration to keep his face from showing the relief he felt. He had been fairly certain his barriers had held, but it was never possible to be completely sure.

"Thank you, Master," he said again.

Marhalt raised his eyebrows. "You don't seem especially moved. Were you so positive of your own perfection?"

"No, Master." Even after six months, Bron was not always successful in gauging his Mentor's expectations. "But I know the Arm of the Stone can see me more clearly than I see myself. I've been preparing myself to accept either judgment."

Marhalt regarded him for a moment without speaking. He was frowning, as if the answer had not quite pleased him.

"There's a matter I must discuss with you, Selwyn," he said. "I thought it best to wait until after the mindprobe, in case it revealed some deeper problem. It does not. Yet still my colleagues and I find ourselves concerned."

The sinking dread Bron felt was like traveling back in time to his first weeks on the floor. "Have I done something wrong, Master?"

"I wish it were that simple. It is not what you have done, but rather what you have not done. You've been six months on the sixth floor. Academically, you have more than fulfilled your promise. Yet in almost every other sense you seem unable to find your place here."

"I'm . . . not sure I understand."

"No?" Marhalt's eyes bored into Bron's. "You participate in our life here, yet too often you seem only to be going through the motions. You would rather observe your fellows than mingle with them. You prefer to watch activities than to contribute to them. I'm not saying you don't do everything that is required of you. Even my colleagues cannot fault your mastery of our conventions. Yet it seems to us that your heart is not in what you do. You follow, but you do not truly join."

Bron was cold, cold to the bone. He could think of no safe reply.

"We're not unaware that adjustment has been difficult for you, Selwyn. You lack your first Year of Apprentice training, as well as the three-month initiation other Arm Apprentices receive before they begin instruction on the sixth floor. Yet you are intelligent and Gifted, more than most, and I've spent much more time with you than the average Mentor spends with his pupil. These things should have been sufficient to overcome your initial disadvantage. Clearly, however, disadvantage remains. I must tell you that some of my colleagues have begun to wonder whether you are truly committed to our way of life."

"Master, I'm fully pledged to the Arm of the Stone." The quiet of the room seemed to swallow the words. "I swear it. Have my actions ever given you cause to think otherwise?"

"No." Marhalt's steady regard did not flicker. "But mine is not the only voice on the sixth floor. Do you remember what I told you on your first night among us, about the Tests you would face?"

"I remember, Master."

"You are no longer in the Novice Wing, where every pupil stands alone. Our standards are different. Freedom we encourage, individuality we allow, intelligence we prize— separateness, however, we cannot tolerate. We of the Arm must be one, in word and thought, in duty and in deed, conjoined like the parts of a body, which are many yet together compose a singular entity. You must surrender your solitude, Selwyn. You must join us in your heart and mind, not just with your lips and through your physical presence among us. You must be ours completely, or you cannot be ours at all."

Marhalt's eyes, clear as topaz, were locked to Bron's. The force of that gaze was elemental. Bron sensed his Mentor's power, like the whisper of a rising storm. He felt his Mentor's will, pressing against the boundaries of his own.

"You have one month in which to address the difficulties I have spoken of. One month. No more."

Bron swallowed. "Yes, Master. I understand."

"You know I cannot help you pass this Test. But there is a warning I can give you. The task before you does not begin and end with yourself. It is not only your acceptance of us that is at issue, but ours of you. Think about that. Be very sure you understand it. And take care before you choose which path to follow. There are many ways to joining. The one you take must be the best of them.''

''I won't fail, Master. I swear it.''

''See that you don't. You're here mainly because of my faith in you. It would be well if that were justified.'' For a moment Marhalt looked at him. Outside in the black night, a storm had begun. Sleet clattered against the windows like handfuls of sand. ''That's all, then. You may go.''

Bron got to his feet. He felt as he had in the beginning, when every session with his Mentor had been a terrible trial of strength. On unsteady legs he made his way toward the door. Halfway, Marhalt's voice reached after him.

''Selwyn. One more thing.'' Bron turned. Marhalt often added a postscript to an apparently finished session; he imparted a good deal of crucial information this way. ''Your question has been approved. You'll be summoned for pilgrimage tomorrow.''

This news, which an hour ago would have produced a powerful combination of elation and dread, now evoked barely a flicker of feeling. ''I'll be ready, Master.''

When he reached his room he found his roommates seated at the table in the common area, working on language exercises. As usual, they ignored him. He crossed to his cubicle and, pulling the curtain, lay down upon his bed.

From his first moments on the sixth floor it had been clear to Bron that, like discourse and conduct, personal interaction was governed by rules very different from those that had shaped his life till now. The carefully guarded distance of the Novice Wing was entirely absent. Roundhead Apprentices associated easily and extensively, and friendships and cliques flourished undisturbed. Of course, like everything else on the sixth floor, this was both more and less than it seemed. Fiercely competitive as they were, arrogant and intolerant as they were trained to be, Roundhead Apprentices could not fraternize without friction. Nils and Derain, for example, frequently appeared to hate one another; it often seemed to Bron that they were held together solely by their need to disagree, like two extremes endlessly struggling for a middle ground.

Determined not to make the mistakes he had made in the Novice Wing, Bron had fitted himself to this new mode of being as seamlessly as he could, learning what was expected of him and discharging it as perfectly as possible. He followed his roommates from classroom to assembly hall to refectory, sat patiently through their group meetings, endured their endless debates, even speaking up now and then for form's sake. Yet even if he had not disliked his roommates, he would have had little desire for intimacy with those he was sworn to destroy. And though his attention was held by the academic aspects of Apprentice life, the social activities of the sixth floor—the fraternities and gaming clubs and debating clubs and power competitions—bored him. As Marhalt had correctly perceived, his conformance was entirely outward.

Fresh from the Novice Wing, where hypocrisy and obedience were interchangeable, it had never occurred to Bron that the Masters here would notice the difference, or care if they did. He cursed himself now for his lack of acuity. In this, as in everything else, the Arm of the Stone was more subtle than any ordinary group of Guardians. He should have seen it for himself before Marhalt was forced to point it out to him, before it ceased to be an expectation and became a Test. He knew himself, at this moment, to be as close to failure as he had ever been.

Beyond the curtain he heard his roommates, murmuring at their language exercises, their voices rising occasionally in a burst of conversation. Marhalt had made it clear that merely changing his own behavior would not be sufficient; he must somehow contrive to make his participation welcome. If he broke the shell of his indifference, if he feigned enthusiasm for his roommates' dull social routines and peevish bickering, if he pretended to hang on their words and seek their wisdom, would their suspicion and dislike become acceptance? He did not think so, at least not in the bare month he had been given. The gulf between them was not just his choice, but theirs. The patterns of their interaction, established early, had never varied over the past six months. It seemed more likely that such a radical shift of behavior would only cause them to distrust him more.

Bron turned over on his bed, pulling the pillow across his head. He felt the familiar pressure, the rise and spread of trapped, bitter anger. No matter how many pitfalls he avoided, there was always another waiting just beyond; no matter how many mountains he climbed, he never came to level ground. The need to be alone ran through him like a fever, powerful and futile. He thought of the empty air and spreading light of his rooftop refuge, willing his mind to return to that place, to grant him at least the illusion of solitude. But though he pressed the pillow down until he could barely breathe, though he thrust his fingers into his ears and clenched his eyelids until constellations of light burst behind them, he could not shut away the voices of his roommates—five hostile strangers, upon whose favor his future as a Roundhead might well depend.

Bron fell asleep that night without ever turning his thoughts to his promised pilgrimage. It was on his mind when he awoke, however, and as the hours passed he found himself shifting like the needle of a compass between poles of anticipation and fear.

Annual pilgrimage to the Garden of the Stone was the right of every Guardian and Apprentice, a privilege available to no other citizen of the world. Ordinary men and women might approach the Stone once in a lifetime, if at all. Pilgrimage was an event around which whole lives were planned, a climactic moment forever dividing and defining the plane of existence. Successful questioners found themselves transfigured, not only inwardly but in an outer sense as well, for the world gave great honor to those who returned from pilgrimage. Yet for every pilgrim who survived, a hundred more did not. The mountain journey was long and arduous, even in the company of a trained guide. Only the Guardians knew the true number of those who perished in pursuit of their dream, often without ever glimpsing the high black walls they sought.

In the thousand years since their defeat, no member of Bron's family had ever stood before the Stone. This was not simply because the goal of pilgrimage lay within the stronghold of the enemy, but because no barrier or disguise could elude the Stone's omniscience. Inevitably, it would recognize who stood before it. What would happen then could not be known. In deference to the ancient bond, the Stone might keep its knowledge secret. But there was at least a chance that the Speaker with whom it communicated would absorb its recognition, shattering a disguise that for ten centuries had endured intact.

From the moment he had made the decision to seek the Fortress Bron had faced this risk, as profound as the many others he had taken in his struggle to fulfill his vow, but infinitely more significant. He feared it as he had once feared the mindprobes of the Apprentice Examinations, as he had once feared Marhalt's gaze. Yet beneath fear lay desire, a thousand years deep. To come into the presence of the Stone as his ancient namesake had . . . to feel its recognition . . . to confront, after a millennium of separation, the power that but for Percival would have been his birthright . . . he knew it might mean his death. Yet he wanted it more than he had ever wanted anything, except the fulfillment of his vow.

The summons came after the noon meal, in the form of a tall white-sashed Speaker. He was all gray but for the sash: robes, beard, and hair. He stood stock-still in the Apprentice-crowded corridor, like a pale rock at the center of a black river. His gaze was as strong as any spoken call. Bron approached him like someone hypnotized. The Speaker took Bron's shoulder, a grip whose very looseness implied enormous strength, and they set off along the corridors of the sixth floor.

The Speaker set a swift pace, traversing passages and doubling back along them, making random turns, crossing and recrossing his own footsteps until, intimately as Bron had come to know these hallways, he had completely lost his bearings. They came at last to a corridor that seemed to offer no exit, and halted before the blank end wall of striated stone. Bron felt the Speaker's grip tighten slightly.

"Close your eyes, Apprentice," the Speaker said. His voice was not much more than a whisper. Among themselves, Speakers rarely used spoken words. "For a little while you will sense things that will puzzle and frighten you, but on no account must you open your eyes until I tell you to do so. Do you understand?"

"Yes, Master," said Bron. He heard the beating of his heart, louder than a thousand marching feet.

Abruptly, the ground disappeared. He seemed to hurtle forward at tremendous speed. He went rigid, expecting the impact of solid stone. But there was only the briefest impression of a barrier, resisting for an instant and then yielding. Open air rushed past his face. They had, he realized, passed through the wall itself, and were now on its other side.

At that moment, the journey ceased to be a journey in real time, and became a dream. Locked behind the darkness of his closed lids, Bron was bombarded by rapidly changing sensations: constriction, as of narrow hallways; expansion, as of vast open spaces; the stuffy warmth of indoors, overlaid by the biting cold of outside, replaced by warmth again. Beside him, his Speaker guide was as still as a sleeper; the light pressure of the man's hand never changed. At last the velocity seemed to lessen. The air altered yet again, becoming soft and cool, suggestive of the wetness of growing things. There was ground beneath his feet once more, springy and yielding. A surge of memory overwhelmed him. For just an instant, he was beside his mother in her herb garden, his boots sinking into the dark soil.

"Open your eyes," said the ghostly voice of his companion.

Bron obeyed, blinking against the light. Around him spread a broad sweep of turf, broken here and there by graveled walkways, punctuated by trees and shrubs. Spring flowers glowed amid the green, yellow and lavender and white. The air stirred with soft currents, bearing a thousand changing scents, rippling with the call of birds and the faint sound of running water. Sunlight slid between the branches, casting trembling shadows beneath the trees and pooling upon the grass.

Instinctively Bron raised his face, responding to a warmth he had not felt since the last time he sought the roof of the Novice Wing. High above hung a circle of pellucid sky, as neat as the lid of a box. Black storm clouds heaved and roiled all around its perimeter, as if trying to overcome the force that held them back. Beyond the treetops the crenellations and roofs of the Fortress could be seen, humped and rounded with half a winter's burden of snow. A blizzard raged above them, a white tide battered by winds whose savage force, unheard and unfelt in this quiet place, seemed unreal as a dream. Against the darkness of its setting, the light pouring from sky to garden was a cylinder of gold, as if walls of glass pierced the heavens to link earth and sun together.

Bron felt awe. The power that held this place, setting winter constantly and permanently aside, was beyond anything he had ever imagined.

The Speaker's hand urged him forward. Directly ahead lay an open space. At its center rose a domed white building, the smooth curves of its surface unbroken by either opening or ornament. Bron felt his breath catch. This was the Room of the Stone, the famous doorless chamber Maris had built. No more than twenty paces away, the heart of the world lay beating.

The pressure of the Speaker's fingers signaled a halt. They stood motionless in the soft green grass. All Bron's fear had gone. He felt weightless, suspended like a swimmer in a strangely timeless waiting. The glowing air was as heavy as amber. Beneath it nothing stirred—no tremor of awareness, no breath of force, no sense of the Stone at all.

The building's snowy surface rippled. Bron felt the brush of power against his skin, warmer than the breeze—but human power, not the power of the Stone. A hand emerged, scarcely less white than the building itself. Slowly, as if he were rising to the surface of a pool of milk, an entire man took shape, his gray Guardian robes belted with the white sash of a Speaker. Complete, he halted. Behind him the wall shuddered, and once more assumed solidity.

"You are Selwyn Forester, Apprentice of the Arm of the Stone," the Speaker said. His voice was as soft and whispery as that of Bron's guide.

"Yes, Master," Bron replied.

"Your question is an inquiry as to the health and well-being of Catarina Lorulla, of the Third Diocese of the Province of Italia."

"Yes, Master." Catarina was the wife of his employer,

in the city in which he had finally settled after the plague; as part of his official history, she was a safe subject for inquiry.

Without speaking, the Speaker turned. The wall trembled; he reentered, disappearing as he had appeared, piecemeal.

It was beginning. Bron felt the Garden all around him, hushed and expectant. Each detail of flower and leaf was as clear as if it had been drawn upon his eye. The breeze brought a thousand different scents, each intoxicatingly distinct. For caution's sake, he closed his eyes to the verdant season, retreating into the darkness of his inner self. He patrolled his barriers, alert for crack or breach. He was aware of the banked fires of his Gift, glowing gently beneath their layers of concealment.

Abruptly, his perspective broadened. He still stood in twilight in the narrow no-man's land of his Apprentice self, the hidden city of his true being at his back. But now, across a strip of green grass, he could see the tumult of a great sunlit river. It was composed not of corporeal waters but of power; it reached out to girdle the world. It was the Stone. Not an abstraction, as in the Tale or the mouths of men, but real— real, and unimaginably huge.

Bron felt his Gift again, stirring, pushing against the boundaries of its disguise. He reached automatically to contain it, realizing even as he did so that, for the first time since he had freed Serle, its will outstripped his own. He struggled to hold it, but he could not. It twisted out of his control, igniting into full presence. It punched through his barriers, peeling away disguise; it arrowed forward, and plunged itself into the torrent of the Stone's power.

Bron was pulled after, willy-nilly, his mind a helpless prisoner of his Gift. The waters of the Stone closed around him. It was not a river at all but an ocean, larger than the world, reaching out to fill every crevice and corner of existence. Within it, crossing and intersecting in endless profusion, a fiery network of being linked everything that *was*— sentient and inanimate, plant and animal, living and dead and yet to come. Currents heaved and roiled, in constant change and endless motion, as people and things came ceaselessly into the world, ceaselessly lived, and ceaselessly were destroyed.

Harnessed to his Gift, Bron slid through the currents like a salamander. A single thread enlarged, became a highway of fire. With the certainty of purpose, his Gift followed it. Faces and places rushed past Bron's inner eye: men and women, buildings and fields, rocks and roads, all tied to the cord of the same current—until at last the humming velocity slowed and halted, alighting upon a single point of vision.

Bron saw a man, stripped to the waist, bent over a black-smith's forge. Sparks flew from the steady impact of his hammer. His sweat took on the color of the forge-fire as it glistened on the great muscles of his back. Raised and livid, the marks of a lash cut twisted paths across his shoulders.

The man dropped his hammer, raising his arm to wipe his brow, and Bron saw his brother Serle.

Serle paused a moment, his chest heaving with effort. He was no longer the boy Bron remembered, his adult face both familiar and unknown beneath the sweat that glossed it. He looked older than his twenty-eight years, and tired. But his body was sturdy and well-nourished; the forge around him was spacious, with well-maintained equipment and piles of finished ironwork.

He bent again to his labor. Sparks spat and the iron glowed orange. The sound of the hammer was like the distant tolling of a bell.

Bron was conscious that the brief stability that held him in place was eroding. Each instant brought clearer awareness of the riptides of force about him. The current to which he was attached whipped and swayed, dancing to the endless cycle of change. A thousand voices filled his head, each articulating something particular to itself. A thousand possibilities sprang from every breath, as each passing instant brought transformation to the world. Bron saw himself, a blazing network of force-lines, a tiny mirror-image of the Stone, clinging precariously to coherence; he saw his being pulse and strain and knew it was only a matter of seconds before he was pulled apart, and all his personal fire merged once more with the universal fires of being.

Somehow, he found the strength to let go. He felt himself

pulled away at tremendous speed. Images flashed by, too swiftly to grasp. He burst all at once from the surface of the ocean, and found himself standing again, in the dark, on solid ground. At his back, his barriers rose unbreached. Before him, the sunlit waters sighed and heaved and breathed the breath of power. His Gift had dwindled to its usual spark, quiescent and docile within him.

He opened his eyes. He could not tell whether seconds or hours had passed. Beside him, his guide was like a statue, his hand still lightly in place on Bron's shoulder. The Garden, the light, the gleaming building—all were unchanged. Yet Bron felt that the self he had regained was not quite the one he had left. No human consciousness could touch that web of power and return unaltered.

The wall stirred and rippled and disgorged the other Speaker. His hands were loosely clasped before him, his stance relaxed. Instinct, unexplained but certain, told Bron that the two Guardians had not noticed his incursion, nor followed the power-road that led to the truth of his lineage.

"The Stone, in its wisdom, has answered your question," the Speaker said in his shadowy voice. "Catarina Lorulla has been dead these two years of a fever of the lungs. Her husband and children survive."

Bron, too elated to spare much thought for poor Catarina, arranged his features into a semblance of regret. "Thank you, Master," he said softly.

The hand of Bron's guide tightened upon his shoulder. "Close your eyes," the Speaker whispered.

No sooner had Bron done so than they were on their way. Cold, warmth, constriction, expansion; all the sensations of the journey out, but reversed, until Bron felt the barrier, like a web across his face, and his feet rested again on hard stone. The Speaker's hand left his shoulder. Bron opened his eyes and turned. He stood a little distance from the wall. His guide was just passing through it, melting into the stone like a drop of water falling onto porous fabric. The polished masonry seemed to glow even after he had disappeared, a lingering afterimage in the shape of a man.

Bron made his way through the quiet corridors, so transported that he barely felt the floor beneath his feet. He had known, when he faced the Stone, that he would feel its power, but he had never dreamed he might actually enter the tides of its contemplation. Like his ancient namesake, he had ridden the Stone's fiery currents, plumbed its great consciousness with his own. After a thousand years of separation, he had reclaimed his ancient birthright. And within the experience, like a gift, he had found his brother.

Joy shook him, and triumph, and exultation, a storm of feeling almost too fierce to contain. If he had not stopped and held himself motionless, his eyes closed and all his concentration focused inward, he might have lost hold of his barriers as he had at Kenlin's ceremony, and opened his deepest self upon the watchful hallways of the sixth floor.

At last, calmer, he moved onward. The image of Serle, his face glazed with the sweat of the forge fire, hung in his mind. In all the years he had grieved for his family, he had never allowed himself to hope his brother might have survived. To know he was still in the world was like opening a long-healed wound, as close to pain as it was to happiness. Where had Serle settled? Was he married, had he children? Had his time as a fugitive changed him; was he wiser now than he had been as a boy? Was he happy? It seemed unbearable to Bron that he did not know these things. And yet he would not be forced to remain ignorant for long. In a year he would make pilgrimage again. What he had done once, he could surely do a second time.

Contempt rose up in him, rich and biting. How could they call themselves men of power, these Speakers who had not sensed the presence of his mind beside their own, who had not recognized his Gift even in the fullness of its flight, who trained seven years to do what he had done as instinctively as if he had been born to it? But then, he had always known himself to be stronger than they. Or could it be, perhaps, that some hereditary connection to the Stone survived within him, some primal recognition that was a function of his Gift?

Perhaps that was why, after so many years of obedience, it had acted of itself. The feel of it, as it twisted out of his control, matched his recollection of the long-ago release that had freed Serle. Yet the memory of that defection carried no sense of connection, no feeling of recognition—nor the experience itself, vast and strange and shatteringly powerful as it had been. Of the thousands of words and phrases he had heard in his life, describing the Stone, reverencing it, calling upon it, not even the Tale came close to expressing the sheer inhuman hugeness of its vision. There had been no particularity at all in the flow of the Stone's awareness— people, hillsides, animals, rocks, trees, all encompassed equally in the orbit of its observation. If it had picked him out from all that spinning multiplicity—he, Bron, separate from any other being in the world—he had not felt it. For a long time he had not been certain which was greater, his fear of the Stone's recognition, or his desire for it. The fact of recognition itself, however, had never been in doubt. Now, looking back, he found he could not say with certainty whether the Stone had noticed him at all.

He felt the aftermath of euphoria, settling within him like ash. His mind, briefly opened to a profundity far beyond its scope, was closing; already the clarity of the experience was slipping away. The insistent messages of his overtaxed mind and body pushed themselves to the forefront of his consciousness. Pain blossomed behind his eyes, and his arms and legs felt heavy as lead.

Reaching his room, he threw himself on his bed. Behind the darkness of his closed lids he sought to reconstruct the planes of Serle's face. But that too was fading. His memory could conjure up only a form in the firelight, an arm that rose and fell, the marks of a lash snaking across a muscled back. And, beyond it, an enormity touched but not comprehended, larger than the world, more alien than a star.

Ten

AFTER HIS pilgrimage, Bron never again feared discovery upon the sixth floor. If he were invisible to Speakers in the Garden of the Stone, surely there was nowhere he could not hide.

He turned his mind to the Test he had been set. The rules of social engagement on the sixth floor, while different from those of the Novitiate, were just as highly codified. The Living Groups formed the foundation of the social structure: roommates were assigned to one another for the duration of their Apprenticeship, and were expected to eat, study, attend class, and socialize as a unit. From these basic groups, many larger associations sprang. Hundreds of clubs, societies, fraternities, and leagues flourished on the sixth floor, based on every conceivable criterion, from mindskills to philosophy to sports. It was the custom for each Living Group to belong to several such societies. Bron's roommates were members of a sporting league, a debating club, and a loose association of Apprentices who organized an annual floorwide nearspeaking contest.

These were the practices of centuries. The pressure to follow them, as Bron had discovered, was enormous. Even so, there were a few who stepped beyond tradition, among them the Apprentices Marhalt Mentored. In defiance of the conventions that confined personal loyalty to Living Groups and prohibited close association between members of different classes, these eight young men, extending in class affiliation from Third to Sixth Arm, formed a close-knit and exclusive clique. Bron was not certain whether it was their connection with Marhalt, or their piercing intellects and flawless Gifts, that lay behind the Masters' tolerance of their unconventional association; whatever the reason, they were not interfered with. Among their peers they were viewed with respect, mixed with a good deal of envy and a certain amount of mistrust.

Bron had wondered, early in his time on the sixth floor, whether the bond that drew the disparate members of the group so closely together was capable of binding him also. But though it was clear they knew who he was—all of them, at one time or another, had nodded to him as they passed in the hallways—they never attempted to approach him. Perhaps, like his roommates, they were suspicious of the favor that had brought him Marhalt's patronage while he was still in his first year of training. Perhaps they were waiting for him to prove himself in some way. In truth, Bron did not care very much. He was no more interested in the company of Marhalt's pupils than he was in that of any Roundhead Apprentice. If they did not wish to include him, he would not seek to change their minds.

His Testing, however, caused him to reconsider this determination. Further thought had only deepened his sense of the futility of approaching his roommates. With Marhalt's pupils, on the other hand, though they had never shown the slightest interest in him, there was no entrenched history of dislike, no preconstructed walls of hostility. More than that, mindful of Marhalt's admonition that the path he chose must be the best, Bron was aware that his roommates occupied a place somewhere in the lower middle of the social scale. Despite their unconventionality, Marhalt's pupils formed a clearly marked elite.

Late one afternoon, he made his way to the common room where Marhalt's pupils gathered to study. Two, both Fourth Arm, sat in armchairs discussing some academic issue; a third, a year behind them, hung silent on their words. A fourth, an Apprentice in his third year of Roundhead training, sat alone at one of the tables, hunched intently over a scroll. Bron approached him.

"Excuse me," he said to the young man's bowed head.

"I have a question about Oromar's Gloss. I thought perhaps you could help me."

The Apprentice looked up. He was stocky, with red hair and milky skin, his brows and lashes so pale they were almost invisible. He met Bron's eyes without hostility or surprise, apparently unannoyed at the interruption.

"Oromar's Gloss," he said. "It's been a long time since I read that. Have a seat."

Bron did not really have a question about the Gloss. The Apprentice seemed to sense this; by tacit agreement they abandoned Oromar after only a cursory discussion, moving on to related issues. The Apprentice, whose name was Gilles, was an engaging conversationalist, extremely intelligent even by the high standards of the sixth floor. He manifested a partisanship of opinion as ardent as that of any Arm Apprentice, yet he listened as intensely as he spoke, allowing Bron to finish his statements before rushing in with a reply.

The bell rang for the evening meal. Bron, more involved in the conversation than he had realized, found himself astonished at the passage of time. The other Apprentices rose and approached the table. Their faces bore none of the suspicion Bron was so used to seeing in his roommates; these three looked pleasant, even friendly.

"You're Selwyn," one of them said.

"Yes."

"You wish to join us?"

Bron stared at the young man. Surely it could not be so easy. "Yes," he said cautiously.

The Apprentice smiled. "Then welcome."

The little group surrounded him, and swept him out into the corridor. They neither invited nor questioned; they seemed to assume he would wish to accompany them. In the refectory, the others who comprised the group were already seated at the table Marhalt's pupils claimed for their exclusive use. They nodded a greeting as Bron approached, apparently as unsurprised by his sudden presence as their fellows had been. Matter-of-factly they shifted their chairs to make room for him; servants were already approaching, carrying an additional place setting. Bron found himself between Gilles and one of the Fourth Arm Apprentices who had been in the common room earlier. They passed him the salt dish and reached across him for the ale pitcher as familiarly as if they had known him for years. Bemused, he sat silent, allowing the tide of their talk, bantering and serious by turns, to wash over him. Like all Arm Apprentices they were boisterous, raising their voices and competing to be heard, yet there was no rancor in their discussion, and the simmering tension that marred the conversations of his roommates was completely absent.

The next morning Gilles appeared at the door of Bron's room, ready to conduct him to breakfast. He was waiting again, after classes ended, to escort him to the common room. He had, it seemed, appointed himself Bron's guide. So it went, hour by hour, day by day—an assimilation so swift, so complete, as to seem dreamlike. Within a week, Bron's life had entirely changed. He had acquired eight new companions, a host of unfamiliar activities, and an apparently established place on the sixth floor.

It was not until much later that he understood this assimilation was not quite as miraculous as it appeared. From the moment he set foot on the sixth floor, Marhalt's pupils had waited for his approach. The patronage of their Mentor did indeed provide a bond that canceled differences and made them one, but it was a tie that needed acknowledgment to become binding. If he had not come to them, they would never have reached out to him. Each member of the group had undergone this rite of passage, although none had delayed as long as he.

Marhalt, doubtless aware of what was going on, withheld comment until just before the end of the allotted month.

"It would seem," he remarked, steepling his fingers beneath his chin, "that you have passed the Test you were set."

"I'm relieved to hear it, Master."

"You've done well, Selwyn. But then, I expected no less."

"I'm grateful for your confidence, Master."

For a moment Marhalt was silent. A storm was blowing in the darkness outside. The wind howled as it flung itself against the walls, and fugitive drafts stirred the fire-fed warmth of the room.

"Do you miss your solitude, Selwyn?"

Bron knew better than to lie. "Sometimes, Master."

"But you've found good companionship. The association you have made will serve you well during your Apprenticeship, and after it, too." He smiled, a very slight lifting of his lips. "If I'd been able to advise you, I would have told you to do exactly this."

The fire crackled, the wind screamed; and Bron understood that he had met not one Test but two. Behind his mask, rage vaulted into being, fierce as the storm. Yet even as it shook him he saw the absurdity of his reaction. Why should he be angry? Such private Testing was the subtext of all Roundhead education. There was not a Master on the sixth floor who did not secretly try his pupils.

Bron and Marhalt never spoke again about this Test, nor indeed any of those that followed. Yet Bron never forgot it. Even at the time, without benefit of hindsight, he could sense the profundity of the change it had wrought, a fault line across his personal history, heaving his future into as-yet-unknown shapes. The path he walked now was not simply one he would never have chosen, but one he would never have imagined. He could not begin to tell where it might lead.

In initiating change for himself, Bron had also worked change in others. In his classes the teachers spoke to him more approvingly; in the halls and refectories Apprentices who had never glanced at him before acknowledged him by name. Even his roommates were less hostile. It seemed that it was not only Marhalt's pupils who had been waiting for him to discover his proper place, and not only Marhalt who was pleased he had found it.

Nearly every moment not occupied by classes or sleep was spent with his new companions. Initially, he found this constant company a strain—not because of the physical proximity, which was nothing new, but because of the full and unceasing engagement they demanded. Goading, questioning, teasing, they forced him into participation. "Selwyn is pursuing silence again," they would say when he tried to take refuge in his old technique of allowing his mind to wander behind a façade of attentive listening. "You'll lose your voice if you don't use it, Selwyn. Perhaps you should have been a Speaker instead of a Roundhead." It was not a joke Bron appreciated. Yet though their insistence was unyielding, it was never less than good-natured, and after a while he found he no longer resented their interference. Cautiously, he began to take pleasure in their discussions and debates, which never took the twists and turns his roommates' did. He began to perceive that there might be value in the open exercise of an intellect till now held mostly within himself.

Marhalt's pupils were nearly as ardent about recreation as they were about learning. Like all Apprentices, they maintained membership in a number of clubs, among them a sporting fraternity called the Green League, whose specialty was a raucous ball game played against a similar group called the Yellow Alliance, and a prestigious speaking society called the Confederation of the Hand, which mounted a yearly series of formal debates based on historical questions of Violation. They also had a passion for card and board games, which they undertook with a fierce competitiveness completely absent from their other pursuits.

"Where have you been all your life?" they asked him, when they finally understood that it was ignorance, not affectation, that caused him to hold back from play. "Everyone plays cards. Or at least dice."

"My father was a laborer," Bron told them stiffly. "We had to work. There wasn't time for entertainment."

In this way, Bron discovered that he had joined a company of aristocrats. Every one of his companions came from wealth, the kind of riches only the most ancient mindpower lineages could claim. The fact that he had not suspected it earlier said a great deal about them. The fact that their treatment of him did not change, once they learned his peasant origin, said more.

In this, as in most things, Marhalt's pupils demonstrated a cooperation and tolerance that, in its grace and consistency, was unlike anything Bran had encountered in the Fortress. The group represented many Class years and a wide variety of Gifts and interests, yet differences were minimized rather than dwelled upon. Lesser abilities were addressed by coaching rather than ridicule; superior talents and higher learning were freely shared. The Sixth Arm Apprentice was perfectly willing to read his texts to the underclassmen, and to pass on the advanced mindpower techniques he was perfecting.

"There's a code we keep," Gilles told Bron early in their association. "We acknowledge our variances, but we don't allow them to divide us. If one of us is weak, the others assist. If one of us is strong, he owes his strength to all. We're more than just a collection of individuals. Our unity is larger than any of us alone. We never allow ourselves to lose sight of that."

It was common knowledge on the sixth floor that Marhalt's pupils were not quite like other Apprentices. Almost from the moment he joined them, however, Bron saw how feebly this perception reflected the truth. Like all Arm Apprentices they were devoted to the Roundhead mission, burningly eager to finish their education and take up the fight against Violation. But there the similarity ended. Taking their unconventional Mentor as their template, they strove to emulate Marhalt's straightforward discourse, his toleration of dissent, his rejection of pettiness, his indifference to the outward trappings of power. They maintained a judicious distance from the fevered fanaticism that claimed so many upon the sixth floor: they never fought power duels to prove the superiority of a point of view, or held mock trials to judge and sentence, and subsequently ostracize, Apprentices they deemed unfit. They did not express open longing, as Bron's roommates did, for the rule of punishment Investment would bring them, nor spend hours imagining in grisly detail the penalties they would visit upon the guilty. The upperclassmen refused to engage in the physical and sexual abuse of younger Apprentices that was common among their fellows; they were known, in fact, for their habit of interfering. It was the only open confrontation they allowed themselves. In other matters, they expressed their disagreements through withdrawal rather than declaration.

More than anything else, it was this habit of reticence that made it possible for outsiders to perceive their deep difference as little more than snobbery or affectation. Skillfully, they drew about themselves the mantle of their Mentor's eccentricity: an unconventional Master, producing unconventional pupils, another of Marhalt's famous peccadilloes, tolerated for the sake of his titanic reputation.

Tolerant Roundheads, Roundheads without viciousness. Once Bron would have thought these mutually exclusive terms. But that was what his companions were; it was what Marhalt himself was teaching them to be. It was not lost on him that, having joined at last, he had become part of a group that was in many ways as distant from the mainstream as he himself had been. He could not help wondering what use they would have for their tolerance upon Investment, when they must take up the task of inflicting the Roundhead mission on the world. How would their moderation serve the implacable requirements of Roundhead judgment? How could their mercy survive the absoluteness of Roundhead punishment?

Roundheads though they were, he could not hate them. If his guard relaxed even a little, he found in himself a kind of surprised warmth—particularly for Gilles, who had first befriended him, and for Aleynn, a Fourth Arm Apprentice whose body was as frail as his mind was strong. These were people with whom he might have chosen to associate, had he not been divided from them by the gulf of his heritage and his vow. It was a strange knowledge to find in himself. But the ways of joining, once so alien, had in the space of a few months become the shape of his life. His perspective had changed in ways he could not yet fully identify. He suspected that if he were to return to his former situation, he might not be so content with it as he once had been.

Bron's First Year drew to a close, and his Second began. In the special Roundhead class he embarked upon the study of the pathology of Violation, a precise catalogue of the human weaknesses through which the love of tools imprinted itself upon the soul. He learned the Five Signs of the potential Violator: impulsiveness, impatience, intransigence, intellect, and invention. He learned of the ways in which the people of the world were measured against this scale.

"Upon entry into Guardian School," the teacher told the class, "children are categorized by two standards. The first is the degree to which they manifest the Five Signs. The second is the degree to which they are Gifted. In every Orderhouse there is a Catalogue, known only to Guardians, kept by the Arm of the Stone, containing the name of every man or woman who has ever lived in that Diocese and their ranking on the two scales of fitness. Because of the Catalogue, there is no person in the world the Arm of the Stone does not know. It is one of the most powerful tools of our orthodoxy."

Bron could not prevent himself from thinking of Serle, who had embodied every one of the Five Signs. Certainly his name would have carried the red symbol that identified those at highest risk for Violation. Serle had needed no betrayer. The eyes of Arm had been upon him all along.

Bron's second pilgrimage took place almost exactly a year after the first. Once again, guided by a firm-handed Speaker, he stood in the Garden of the Stone and let his power work its will. His incursion, longer this time and more distinct, showed him that Serle continued to prosper. Two apprentices worked beside him in the forge; a red-haired wife passed to and fro, accompanied by a small sturdy daughter who reminded Bron piercingly of Elene.

But beyond the joy and pain the sight of his brother brought, this second journey carried little of the euphoria of the first. Emerging from the alien reaches of the Stone's vision, Bron felt understanding, half-formed a year earlier, solidifying within him like lead. The Stone of his direct experience and the Stone of the Tale were two entirely different entities. The second Stone, in which he had believed all his life—powerful, awe-inspiring, yet not beyond the reach of a human mind or the comprehension of human feeling—did not exist. The truth of the first Stone, a power so vast even its enormity could not be comprehended, made that clear. Only the second Stone, the illusory Stone, could have recognized him; the real Stone was utterly indifferent to his identity. Its vision was a vision of inclusion, of simultaneity, of entirety. It did not see single things; it saw everything.

It had been vengeance and not prophecy that had brought Bron to the Fortress. He had set aside the destiny his mother invoked and replaced the purpose of the Tale with his own. Even so, he had never thought to question the Tale itself. It was the touchstone of his inner being, as deep within him as his blood or breath. But he had sensed, a year ago, that his journey within the Stone had changed him; he sensed it even more clearly now. Lying wakeful in the dark, his roommates' breathing loud around him, he found his thoughts flowing in strange channels, pursuing questions that a year ago he would not have been able to conceive. It was almost more than a man could do to ride the maelstrom of the Stone's power and emerge intact; to communicate with it, let alone constrain it to human expectation, seemed impossible. How then could his ancient Ancestor have made the bargain that stood at the center of the Tale? The Stone did not perceive or weigh one spark of being above another, or perceive these sparks as separate in the way humans did. Why, then, should it care where it was or with whom? The Stone's power encompassed the entire world of life and death, unconstrained by time, without reference to space. How could any human being lay claim to such a power, let alone assert a claim more binding than another's? Could a tree claim ownership of the forest in which it stood? Could a grain of sand boast possession of the beach that cradled it?

Often Bron reached through the heavy darkness of the Fortress night, searching for the beat of the Stone's awareness. Now and then he found it, though from so far away he could do no more than eavesdrop. There were no answers in those pulsing rhythms, only the circling of his own uncomfortable thoughts. Listening, he could not help but ask one more question. If it did not matter to the Stone who he was, then who was he?

Bron's Second Year came to an end. Two of his companions received their Investments, and the group was smaller for a while, until Marhalt selected two Third Arm

Apprentices to take their place. The group absorbed them as seamlessly as it once had absorbed Bron. Within a few weeks of their approach, it was as if they had always been part of it.

The Third Year of Arm training brought new study, of the world of handpower. Like physicians monitoring the progression of a disease, heavily-barriered Roundheads periodically journeyed through one or another of the twelve Gates that offered entry into that other place. They could remain only for a short time, for the forces of handpower were capable of breaching even the strongest barrier, weakening and ultimately destroying the mindpower that was its opposite. Much of the information these agents brought back was taught in the Third Arm class, so that Apprentices might understand the true nature of the enemy they faced.

The handpower world, Bron learned, was not truly a world at all, in the sense that the mindpower world was a world. Devoid of the unifying forces of mindpower, it was little more than a collection of linked fragments, possessing neither uniformity nor coherence. Here the tools of the Split had become things called machines—devices that possessed no soul, yet somehow lived and acted of their own power. They ate and voided, like living beings, but unlike living beings were capable neither of limiting their appetites nor controlling their waste. The hills and plains of the handpower world were littered with the excreta of machines, fouling the air and water, sickening the people. Cities the size of countries pressed upon the earth, with great keeps and fortresses that rose miles into the air. Metal engines roamed the land on pathways of stone; huge metal monsters took to the air, belching fire and smoke. There were mechanical weapons that hurled tiny objects with such force that they passed completely through a man's body, and others that could obliterate entire cities in a flash of light, or poison populations through the air they breathed, or burn their skins with invisible fire.

The men and women of this world were soft and weak, unable to perform even the simplest acts without the assistance of machines. Machines grew their food and prepared it. Machines fabricated their possessions, built their buildings, addressed their most basic bodily functions. Their houses were filled with machines; sometimes machines were placed inside them by the physicians of the handpower world, who reveled in performing such hideous experiments upon their living patients.

Like his fellows, Bron found these revelations so perverse, the world they described so alien, as to be almost beyond comprehension. The Roundhead Master, at the start of the class, had warned of this.

"The things you will hear from me," he told the gathered Apprentices, "will tax your belief as much as your understanding. In the context of our ordered and balanced world, it is nearly impossible to imagine a place so corrupt, so aberrant, so abandoned to chaos as the world of handpower. Yet the eyewitness accounts of generations of Roundhead agents confirm the truth of it. As you stand appalled before their testimony, there is one thing you must never allow yourselves to forget. The world of handpower sprang from a world that once was very much like this one. Containing the same tools, populated by the same people prone to the same weakness, can our world be any more immune from transformation than that old world was?"

As a child, sitting numb with boredom through sessions of Guardian School or leading plodding classmates through recitation, Bron had possessed the same unformed perception of the Limits' purpose as any other citizen. Not knowing what handpower could become, the evil the Limits held away seemed vague, as fearful and yet unlikely as the ogres and banshees of folk tales. More than that, all truth had been subordinate to the cadences of the Tale: as the product of the order of Guardians, the Limits were to be detested equally. Serle's heretical plow had brought the ghost of a larger perception, the faintest breath of chill through a door just cracking open; but the door had slammed shut almost at once, and in the horror of the events that followed Bron had forgotten it ever existed.

In his Third Year, however, that door began to open once again. He was fully aware that he learned within a closed system, where the teaching both sprang from and perpetuated a particular point of view. And yet the echo of truth was clear even through the flow of Roundhead speech. The machines the Roundhead Master described, the ways of life they engendered and the perversion of the world they shaped, defied invention or misdirection. Slowly, in the horrors unfolding before him, Bron found himself forced to confront a less personal understanding of the Limits, a more immediate apprehension of the purpose they had been created to fulfill. Detest their makers as he might, the need for protection Rhodri the Limit-Maker had tried to answer seemed real. Nor was it possible to dispute the fact that, for the thousand years of the Guardians' rule, the world had never again succumbed to the madness of the hands.

These perceptions did not sit easily beside Bron's heritage and his vow. But he felt no need for reconciliation. His purpose lay inviolate within the walled city of his true self; it bore no relationship to what occurred outside, in the growing structure of his Apprentice persona. What he learned, what he did, what he was in that place was as irrelevant to his inner being as a mask to the features of its wearer. When the time came, he would shed that mask like a second skin. He would tear down the edifice of Guardianhood he had built. He would smash its walls and level its buildings, and fill its streets with the rubble of his disguise.

It was not until late in his Third Year that Bron undertook his third pilgrimage. His Gift, plunging into the now-familiar currents of the Stone, found and followed his brother's path. Once again, Serle was at his anvil. The forge door was open; night streamed in, black and windy. In the shadows, Bron could see the watching faces of his brother's apprentices. Serle's arm moved, delicately shaping the glowing iron. Finished, he plunged his work into a barrel of water. Clouds of steam rose hissing toward the sooty ceiling. He held up what he had made. It was a tool head of some sort, but not like any Bron had seen before.

Bron remembered a different night, a different place, the sheen of firelight on a different piece of metal. Yet the coldness he felt now was the same. The thing his brother held, still smoking slightly with the heat of creation, was Violation.

Bron yielded to the tides of power that tore at him, flying backward toward his waiting body. Returning, the shock of what he had witnessed made him stagger. He was certain some terrible knowledge must be written on his face. As usual, however, the Speakers noticed nothing.

Back in his room, Bron drew the curtains of his cubicle and gave himself up to horror. It had never occurred to him that his brother, who had nearly died for his transgression, would do other than forswear Violation forever. Serle was not like the Violators of history, who abandoned themselves to their pursuit. His had been an isolated mistake, the misjudgment of an impulsive boy. Yet with his own eyes Bron had seen his brother perfecting, with quick expert touches, a forbidden device. The words of the Roundhead Master of his Second Year pronounced themselves inside his head: *A Violator unmanifest may be saved. A Violator manifest is lost. Once the power of the hands expresses itself in action, the lust for it overruns the soul like leprosy. He who languishes in that grip can only yield, again and again, until he is found and stopped.*

How many forbidden tools had Serle created in the years since his escape? How many would he yet create? He was older now, more skilled in concealment, ensconced in a place where no one, presumably, knew his history. He might be able to avoid detection for a long time. But Violation could not be hidden forever. Its products might be kept secret, but ultimately their nature disturbed the order of things in a way that could be clearly sensed by those who had been trained to do so.

Bron felt fury rising within him. Serle had not changed at all. A grown man, he was still as full of thoughtless impulse and selfish desire as he had been in boyhood. What rationale could he have constructed this time, what invented imperative, to allow him to ignore the danger of his actions? What story could he have conjured up to justify drawing his apprentices into his pursuits, perhaps even his wife and child, spreading the pattern of Violation not simply in his own soul, but in the souls of those around him?

Bron was aware, suddenly, of the strangeness of his thoughts. His brother, his feet set again on the disastrous path that had nearly killed him a decade before, was in mortal danger. Why was he thinking of Violation rather than of Serle? Why was he thinking of the need to rescue his brother's wife and apprentices, rather than of the fact that, this time, there would be no one to rescue Serle himself?

It came to him that he was thinking as a Roundhead might.

The understanding was like a blow. It seemed to catapult him outside his body to a small, still place he did not know. Until this moment, he had thought himself the person he had always been. Pursuing activities he had never imagined, absorbing learning he had never dreamed of, he had believed he was simply wearing one more mask. But the mechanics of outer change had slowly worked an inner alchemy. Without realizing it, he had become someone else.

For the first time, he consciously understood that he had come to accept the necessity of Serle's judgment. Serle had meant no evil when he made his plow, nor did he mean evil now; Bron knew this as clearly as he knew his own name. Yet the learning he had received told him that motives could not be weighed. Intentions meant nothing. Love for the Violator could not mitigate the ugliness of his act. There was only the fact of Violation, raw and unadorned.

Bron felt structures crumbling in his mind, edifices crashing to the ground. From what seemed a great distance he looked upon himself, a person to whom the fact of Violation had become as significant as the person who Violated. Somehow, the sixth floor had breached the barriers that guarded his inner self. How had it happened? How had he failed to see it until now?

Assuming the long habit of discipline, he forced himself to rise from his bed. He joined his companions, telling them a false story of his pilgrimage, making false answers to their questions. He accompanied them to the evening meal. Afterward he studied, then played a round of cards. The others saw nothing amiss. They did not perceive that it was an automaton who did these things, a body playing proxy for a mind far removed.

In the days that followed, Bron assessed the changes within himself. It was a long time since he had taken detailed stock of his inner landscape. Beguiled among the corridors of his Apprentice-self, he had neglected the pathways of his truer being. He could find almost nothing within him that was not stained by transformation. The Stone was not as he had believed it, nor the Tale. The Limits were more than he had thought them, and he no longer understood the Order he was vowed to destroy as he once had. The wall of his hatred, so carefully constructed, had been breached: he had come to respect, even to like, members of the group that had destroyed his family and his childhood. Once, like a heartbeat, his vow had formed the foundation of every breath. He could not remember when it had become possible to pass whole days without giving it a thought.

Even his rage was not what it had been. The cruel Watch that had killed his family was repeated daily throughout the world, a pall of injustice reaching back across the centuries, a thousand years of terror and pain. In the light of those millions of catastrophes, his personal tragedy seemed to dwindle, like his own consciousness caught within the contemplation of the Stone. His family had suffered, but so had others. Not one of them had been avenged.

What did all of this mean for his purpose, for his vow? He did not know.

He dreamed of his family now, more often than he had in years. Sometimes he saw their faces ravaged as they had been in death; sometimes he walked the forests of his childhood and heard their voices calling, in words he could not understand. Sometimes he stood again beside the wreckage of his home, looking down upon the raw graves of his father and mother and sisters and brother. He was seized suddenly with the conviction that they were not dead. He threw himself to the ground, scratching at the dirt with his fingers. He thought he could hear their cries for help, their anguished struggle for breath. But though he dug and dug, deep into the earth, through soil, through rock, through the fire at the earth's heart, he could not find their bodies. Time and decay had taken them. There was nothing left.

Eleven

N A warm autumn day early in his fourth year of Arm Apprenticeship, his classes at an end for the afternoon, Bron headed for the common room to join his companions. On the way two of them, Aleynn and Barach, caught him up. Barach, on one side, drew him into discussion. Aleynn, on the other, walked silently, abstracted.

"Hold on a minute." Aleynn halted in the middle of the corridor. "There's something odd here."

For the first time Bron realized that, somehow, they had gone off course. They were not in the portion of the floor where the common rooms were located, but in the area reserved for mindskill class and practice rooms.

"What is it?" Barach said.

Aleynn shook his head. He was a Sixth Arm Apprentice with a peerless Gift of neardivining, a frail young man whose blue-tinged skin attested to the frequent lung fevers no health-preserving techniques or bindings could forestall. "I'm not sure. I got a strange sense just now . . ." His voice trailed off. His face wore an intent listening expression.

"I can't feel anything," Barach said. A Fourther who had joined the group only a year before, he was a farspeaker of rare ability, with a smaller but well-developed talent for projection. "Anyway, these are practice rooms. They're heavily shielded. I don't see how you could sense anything from them."

"There was something. I know there was." Aleynn

stepped forward and pushed open one of the doors. Torches, sensitive to entry, flared to life, disclosing a vacant chamber.

"You see?" Barach said.

But something in Aleynn's face had changed. He moved back, pulling the door closed.

"That room has been covered by a semblance," he said urgently. "It's a baiting. I'm sure of it."

Roundhead training, though thorough, was entirely academic. Even Invested members of the Arm were not allowed to mindprobe unsupervised until the two-year internship that followed their graduation from the Apprentice College had been completed. Sometimes, unwilling to wait, eager Apprentices kidnapped servants or, less often, Apprentices from other floors, and subjected them to mock-Interrogations. The custom was known as worm-baiting. Officially, baiting was illegal; mindprobing could do damage even in the hands of experienced practitioners, and torture was prescribed only where a crime was suspected. Unofficially, however, it was widely tolerated. Many Masters felt it formed a valuable hands-on adjunct to the theoretical studies of the Fourth, Fifth, and Sixth Years.

"A baiting?" said Barach. "Are you sure?"

"As sure as I can be without actually seeing it."

"What do you want to do?"

"Stop it, of course."

"That semblance is a good one, Aleynn. It won't be easy to break."

"Selwyn can break it, if we assist him."

"Well." Barach looked at Bron. "If Selwyn's willing, so am I."

"Selwyn?" Aleynn's gaze was steady. "It's your choice, of course. No one will think less of you if you don't do this."

Bron was not foolish enough to believe that—nor, indeed, to imagine that choice came into it at all. The situation bore all the marks of engineering; clearly it was a Test of some sort. He was tempted to refuse simply out of his recognition of this. But he loathed baiting. Test or not, he was glad for the chance to interfere.

"I'll help you."

"Good." Aleynn nodded. "Now, this is what we'll do.

Selwyn will gather his strength. I'll lend mine to bolster it.
When we're ready, Barach will take our combined power
and throw it at the door. We'll enter immediately. Hopefully
surprise will be on our side. And then . . .'' He paused, tension apparent in the set of his jaw. ''And then we'll do
whatever has to be done.''

They joined hands. From the part of his Gift he allowed
the world to see, Bron extracted as much power as he judged
to be necessary, and a little more, gathering it in the air
before the three of them, creating a tight ball of force. He
sensed Aleynn's power flowing to join his own. The pressure built, causing the air to tremble. The door groaned
slightly on its hinges. He squeezed Barach's hand. There
was a pause; then, abruptly, the pressure disappeared, like
the snap of a slingshot. The door flew open, crashing against
the wall.

Where a few moments before there had seemed to be only
empty space, there now appeared an unpleasant tableau.
Five Roundhead Apprentices were grouped around a chair
to which another Apprentice had been bound—a Journeyer,
by his green belt. He slumped bonelessly in his restraints,
apparently unconscious. Two servants lay on the floor at the
edge of the room, trussed like chickens, their eyes terrified
but sensible. The baiters had frozen at the opening of the
door. Their faces, turned toward it, wore identical expres-
sions of shock.

Aleynn strode forward. ''Stay where you are, all of you,''
he said in his husky voice. ''Don't even think of moving.''

He bent over the bound Apprentice, gesturing Bron and
Barach in the direction of the servants. Four of the baiters—
two Fourth Arm, two Fifth Arm—stood like statues as Aleynn began to work at the Journeyer's ropes. But the fifth
moved, stepping around another whose tall form had partially concealed him. He fixed his eyes not on Aleynn but
on Bron. With a leaden sense of recognition, Bron saw that
it was Jolyon.

Jolyon had been selected for the Arm of the Stone nearly
two years ago. He had already acquired a small but significant reputation for zealotry, and a group of like-minded
Apprentices had begun to gather around him. It was unheard-of for Apprentices who had not yet begun Interroga-

tion classes to participate in a baiting, yet Bron was not surprised to find his enemy here. Jolyon's face was as set and expressionless as a piece of statuary, the otherworldly quality of his features emphasized by the severity of the Roundhead crop, but the hot malevolence Bron remembered so well boiled undimmed in his regard.

The baiters watched in silence as Bron and Barach worked at the ropes that bound the servants. The knots had been tied by power, and were hard to undo by hand, but like their Mentor, Marhalt's pupils did not waste their Talents on small acts. When they were finished, Bron and Barach helped the servants to stand, supporting them until they were able to remain upright on their own. Approaching the unconscious Journeyer, they heaved him to his feet, draping his limp arms over their shoulders. They started for the door, their burden sagging between them, the servants stumbling behind.

In the doorway, Aleynn turned and faced the baiters.

"What you've done here is loathsome," he said. His voice was rough with outrage and the congestion of his lungs. "It's bad enough for you Fourth and Fifth Arm Apprentices, but don't you know better than to involve one who is only Third Arm? Don't you know you can kill people this way?" He paused a moment to get his breath. Behind Jolyon, the others stood watching. Bron would have bet money that it was not they who had involved Jolyon, but the other way around. "I won't report you this time. But I'm familiar with your signature now. If you repeat this little experiment, I'll know. And I won't be so gentle, or so discreet, when I find you again."

"The Masters don't try to stop us." It was Jolyon, his thin voice as spiteful as ever. "Why should you be able to?"

No lowerclassman spoke this way to an Apprentice in his final year. Bron could see Aleynn's shock. "How dare you?" he said, each word a separate breath.

"We aren't afraid of you." Jolyon's insolent gaze did not falter. "You'll be graduating in a few months anyway. You won't be able to do anything after you're gone."

"There'll be others to watch. I'll see to it."

"What if you do?" Jolyon took a step forward. His hot eyes were fixed on Aleynn's face. "You interrupted us today. Maybe your friends will interrupt us tomorrow. But however many of you there are, there will always be more of us. You know it. You know it as well as I do."

There was a pause. In the silence, Bron could hear Aleynn's labored breathing. Then, slowly, the senior Apprentice shook his head.

"You're a disgrace to the Arm of the Stone."

"Do you think so?" Jolyon's voice was very soft. "But I'm here, aren't I?"

Aleynn did not reply. He turned, his face set, and stepped into the corridor. The door, untouched, swung slowly closed.

In silence, Aleynn leading now, they made their way to the red door that marked the limit of the Roundhead domain. They ushered the two servants outside onto the landing. Barach and Bron lowered their still-unconscious burden to the ground.

"Take him to the physicians at once," Aleynn told the servants. "Say you found him lying on the stairs. Not a word of the baiting. Not a word of what we did. Do you understand?"

The servants nodded, silent. Baiting was a fact of a servant's life; they knew the rules. They did not wish to tempt for real what they had just escaped in imitation, by revealing their knowledge of this illegal activity.

Closing the door behind them, Bron, Barach, and Aleynn moved down the empty corridor.

"Did you get any sense of how badly they hurt that Journeyer?" Bron asked, glancing at Aleynn.

"Not really." Aleynn was exhausted. His lips were blue, and Bron could hear the rattling in his chest as he struggled for breath. "He was hurt, though. When I touched his ropes, I sensed . . ." He shuddered. "There was definitely a mind-probe, and whoever did it wasn't especially skilled. He slammed into that boy's mind like an anvil falling on a nut. And . . . he enjoyed it."

"It was the one who spoke," Barach said with certainty. "What's his name?"

"Jolyon," Bron said.

"I saw the way he looked at you, Selwyn. Is there something between you two?"

"There's something between him and a lot of people." Bron shrugged. "It goes back to our Novice days."

"He's dangerous. You can feel it."

"He's everything the Arm of the Stone should not be," Aleynn said. "Which is to say, everything it too often is."

So astonishing was this remark that Bron was not certain he had heard correctly. Roundhead Apprentices freely criticized one another, the Masters, the workload—but never did they breathe the smallest breath of censure toward the Arm itself. To do so was a punishable act of disrespect. He glanced at the senior Apprentice, just in time to catch the look he and Barach exchanged, briefer than words, eloquent of some secret meaning.

They were silent all the way to the common room. Just before they reached it Aleynn paused, placing a hand on Bron's shoulder.

"Not many Apprentices would be willing to do what you did today, Selwyn. I'm grateful."

Bron looked him in the eye. "So I passed?"

"Passed?"

"The Test. It was a Test, wasn't it?"

To his credit, Aleynn did not drop his gaze. "No one doubts your belief, Selwyn, or your committment to our way of thinking. But we needed to know whether you were capable of acting on it."

"Couldn't you have asked me? Couldn't you have come to me and said, We need your help, will you help us? Did it have to be a Test?"

Aleynn only looked at him. "Don't be angry, Selwyn," he said. "All of us are Tested, one way or another."

But Bron was angry. He hid it, entering the common room with the others, joining in the general discussion for a while and then sitting down at a table alone to study. Distracted by the press of feeling within him, he could not concentrate. He looked at Aleynn, bent over a scroll, his lips still pale with fatigue, and at Barach, deep in conversation. A long time ago, he had passed irrevocably across the threshhold of his own reticence and into friendship with the older Apprentice; with the younger he felt something of a bond, for he came from a background of poverty not unlike Bron's own. But the Test, and the secret glance they had exchanged, seemed to hold a different truth. For the first time since he had joined the ranks of Marhalt's pupils, he felt excluded. He would not have believed, a few hours ago, how strongly such a thing would affect him.

After supper, he made his way to Marhalt's chambers. The hour was late, but the candles had not yet been lit. The open casements framed a sky heavy with the colors of sunset. The air moved through them, carrying the scent of wildflowers from the meadow outside the walls, a final breath of summer.

"I'm going to dispense with our usual routine tonight," Marhalt told Bron. He was seated at his desk, the fiery sky behind him. "There's something I want to discuss with you."

Bron had expected this. He waited.

"Aleynn tells me you assisted him this afternoon in halting a baiting."

"Yes, Master."

"I understand he gave you the option of refusing."

"Yes, he did."

"But you did not refuse."

"No, Master."

"I know how these things can be, Selwyn. Perhaps the pressure of your senior classmate's expectation pushed you to take an action you might not otherwise have thought to follow."

"No." Bron chose his words carefully. "I acted of my own will. I would have done the same, no matter what the situation. I detest baiting—as you did, Master, when you were an Apprentice. I was glad to stop it. I'll do so again, freely, if I'm given the chance."

Marhalt got to his feet. Taking a reed from a porcelain jar on the hearth, he ignited it at the grate and set about lighting the candles. One by one they flared to life, washing the room in a rising tide of gold. The rectangle of sunset, by contrast, sank further toward darkness, its oranges and vermilions yielding to the approaching night. Finished, Marhalt did not seat himself again but stood, uncharacteristically, by the hearth. Shadow moved on the spare planes of his face.

"Those of us who oppose the practice of baiting are very much in the minority," he said, his eyes on the flames. "Those who act on their opposition, even more so. You've marked yourself by what you did today."

"I know that, Master."

Marhalt still held the reed. He turned it around and around in his fingers. "Aleynn tells me that one of the Apprentices you surprised today is known to you."

"Jolyon. Yes."

"An old enemy?"

"I suppose you could call him that."

"What is the origin of his hostility?"

"I don't really know. Jolyon . . . Jolyon is a person who enjoys hatred for its own sake."

"I understand that he made you a frequent focus of his attention during the Third Year of your Novitiate."

Bron pressed his lips together. "Myself, and others. Jolyon is . . . very zealous."

"Zealous. That's an interesting word to choose. It can convey more than one meaning, don't you agree?"

"Zeal is an expression of devotion, Master," Bron said formally.

"Would you say that of Jolyon? That he is devoted?"

"I don't feel comfortable passing judgment on Jolyon, Master." Bron could not see where Marhalt was heading with this strange line of questioning, though without doubt he was heading somewhere. "He has his own style of loyalty to the Arm. It isn't what I would choose, but everyone is different. I don't doubt he's as eager to be of use to the Order of Guardians as I am."

Marhalt tossed the reed into the fire. He turned to look directly at Bron. "Let me put my question another way. What happened today, what you and Aleynn and Barach stopped from happening—as you rightly point out, such activities embody a particular style of loyalty. Yet is it the Arm that is served by such devotion, or the person who practices it? Tell me, Selwyn, do you believe that men like Jolyon bring honor to the Arm? That they bring glory to the Stone?''

In the grate, the fire spat as a chunk of coal collapsed. A fountain of sparks shot up, pushing the shadows back; for a moment the objects in the room were plucked, bright and distinct, from the pervading dimness. The events of the afternoon unfolded rapidly in Bron's mind. He heard again Aleynn's remark, and saw the glance Aleynn and Barach had shared. The Test, after all, had not been of his companions' making.

''No,'' he said. He had the feeling of opening a door into the dark. ''I don't believe they do.''

Marhalt stepped away from the hearth and around the table. He seated himself once more in his chair and fixed his eyes on Bron. Behind him, night had fallen completely. The sky was velvet black, and thick with stars.

''The words I'm about to speak,'' Marhalt said, ''are perhaps the most important I will ever say to you. When I am done, I will offer you a choice. You must make that choice tonight, in this room. Your decision will be irrevocable. If you refuse what I offer, you will never again have the chance to choose it.

''I know you're conscious of the difference between my point of view and the views of other Masters. You don't know, however, the depth of that difference, or the road it has led me to follow. That is what I will tell you now.

''To put it plainly, I believe that the Arm of the Stone has become corrupt. In the old days, the Arm served the world and the Stone equally. Today the Arm serves itself first, the world second, and the Stone last of all. We have lost sight of the pure and original purpose for which we were founded nine centuries ago—to discover Violation, to eradicate it, and to ensure it does not occur again.

''Those who govern the Arm of the Stone have come to believe that the world's adherence to the Limits is best achieved not through education and example but through terror. Over the centuries they have made the Arm of the Stone the most feared and hated group in all the world. Like a plague wind we sweep across the earth, taking vengeance, ravaging minds, planting over and over the seeds of bitterness and loathing. The purpose of Investigation, which should be the revelation of truth and the destruction of Violation, has become, too often, the demonstration of our own righteousness. Every Investigation must display to an awestruck world our infallible knowledge, our implacable will, our omniscience, our ubiquity. The establishment of guilt has become more important than guilt itself. Though history teaches that not all improprieties are actual Violations, that accusations are often falsely put forward, it has become axiomatic that every Investigation must yield a Violator. Hundreds of innocents—hundreds, Selwyn—have been judged to fulfill this purpose.

"Power has made us venal and greedy. The authority of the Arm is routinely abused to gain temporal power and wealth. What citizen dares to protest when the Arm seizes the property of a Violator, property that by law should revert to the community? Power has twisted us—we have come to love pain for its own sake, to take nourishment from the terror in the eyes of those we Interrogate, to relish the sensation of a mind helpless beneath the weight of the probe. Our cruelty is a plague, a sickness rotting the body of the Arm from within.

"Worst of all, our corruption has eroded our effectiveness. The incidence of Violation is greater now than at any time in recorded history, and the magnitude of individual Violations grows a little worse with every passing year. If we continue thus, we will eventually lose the ability to discharge our mission in any form. The line of balance between hand- and mindpower will be undrawn. Another Split will take place. And this time, there will be no Percival to save the Stone."

Marhalt had leaned forward as he spoke. His voice was charged with passion; his thin face burned with the intensity of his belief. Never had Bron seen him display such open feeling. He seemed, almost, a different person: a secret Marhalt, briefly freed from a more rigid shell of himself.

"I have taken it as my life's mission to restore the original purity of the Arm of the Stone. For the past seven years,

I have been training Apprentices to share my vision. There are also Masters who have adopted my cause. Eventually, with care and patience, there will be enough of us to force the change we seek. When that day comes the old guard will fall from power. The work of renewal will begin. And the Arm of the Stone will become again as it was in the days of its founder.

"Now it's your turn, Selwyn. You must choose, either to join us or to reject us. I won't lie to you about the danger. If you join us, you will live with that danger every moment of your life. If you refuse . . . if you refuse, I give you my word you will not suffer. However, I will be forced to remove your memory of this night, and also to withdraw as your Mentor. I cannot allow you to retain this knowledge unless you make it your own. I cannot allow you to remain at my side unless you are one of us."

He stopped speaking. Silence flowed in to fill the spaces where speech had been. Slowly he resumed his normal pose, elbows on the arms of his chair, fingers tented beneath his chin. Above them, his eyes were steady on Bron's face.

Bron stared back, speechless with shock. For once he made no attempt to hide what he felt. Surely Marhalt would not expect him to receive such revelations with equanimity: a Roundhead, condemning his own kind, seeking their overthrow. Until this moment he would not have believed it possible. Marhalt's eccentricity, his iconoclastic teachings, his pupils' virtues, admirable in a human being but nearly useless in a Roundhead—he had perceived these things, he had wondered at them. Even so, he had not imagined that they might represent more than a difference of degree. Stunned, he saw them now for what they were: the outward signs of a divergence almost as profound as his own.

The atmosphere of Marhalt's chambers wrapped around him, warm and tranquil. The fire flashed on the hearth; shadows moved in the folds of the tapestries. Familiar as they were, these things seemed suddenly veiled with difference, as if he had passed through a mirror and come out its other side. Across the table Marhalt waited, his eyes lit to topaz by the golden candlelight. Bron could feel the pressure of his Mentor's expectation, as he had felt it just over three years ago, when he had come to this room for the first time.

"My companions," he said. His voice was rough; he had to clear his throat to soften it. "They're all part of this?"

Marhalt nodded. "When I take an Apprentice to Mentor there's usually a period of about a year before I offer the choice I just offered you. The ground must be prepared; inhibitions and entrenched judgments must be peeled away. It is also necessary to Test. I cannot reveal myself to anyone who is not fully tried."

"I've been with you much longer than a year."

"You lacked experience. The least of my pupils is Third Arm. I felt it best to wait until you had gone at least that far."

"And today? That was the final Test?"

"Yes. I demand it of all my pupils. I must know they are capable of taking action when it is required."

"What if I hadn't acted?"

"I would have Tested you until you did."

"What if I never had?"

"That would not have happened, Selwyn. I'm seldom wrong in those I choose, and I know I am not wrong in you. I'm more certain of you, in fact, than I have ever been of any of my pupils. Have you never wondered why I took you to Mentor, when you have no nearspeech and can never become an Investigator? For a Roundhead, as you must know, that's a very significant lack. Oh, you have intellect in abundance; you have power you have only begun to tap. But those qualities, persuasive as they are, would not have been enough to make me choose you, had it not been for one thing." His eyes were as sharp as glass. "It was for your anger that I chose you, Selwyn Forester. Your anger, and all it implies."

The air in the room seemed suddenly to have become too thick to breathe. "My anger?" Bron said, faintly.

"Are you surprised? You should be. It was your anger that made my colleagues want to reject you. To them, it seemed a dangerous weakness, a crack in the armor of fitness, an invitation to corruption. But I—I saw something else. I saw that your fury was not wholly selfish—you raged not simply for your own humiliation but for the fact of humiliation itself, not just for your own injustices but for the injustices all Novices are made to suffer. It was I who kept you in the Novice Wing against your Masters' wishes. It was I who brought you to the sixth floor against my colleagues' fears.'' He leaned forward. ''I did those things because I believe that you have already, on your own, come to conclusions very similar to mine. I think I do not need to open your eyes to the corruption that surrounds you, nor enter your mind to help you shed your resistance to change—you alone of all my pupils.''

The amber gaze was like a hand around Bron's throat. Not since his first days upon the sixth floor had he felt such fear. How much did Marhalt know? How much had he guessed?

''Answer me, Selwyn Forester. Will you join us?''

The world seemed to have become a box. Everything in Bron shouted refusal. He had his own cause. He did not want another. What if Marhalt's design led him into ruin? What if, swallowed up by Marhalt's intent, he became unable to fulfill his own? Yet this thing, offered to him as a choice, was not a choice at all. He did not fear for his memory; his barriers were equal to any attempt upon his mind. But he saw the falsity of Marhalt's assurance of safety. Whatever Marhalt had perceived or guessed, he owned at least a part of Bron's secret now. If he left his Mentor's side, he would never be safe again.

Bron felt dizzy. He had already lived this moment of false decision. He had already experienced this forced plunge into a situation whose implications he neither grasped nor had the time to consider. He had already opened his mouth to say these words, dropping them one by one upon the quiet air—

''I will join you.''

There was a pause, and then Marhalt smiled. It was a real smile, strange upon his ascetic features. Looking over Bron's shoulder, he clapped his hands, twice. The door swung open. His pupils spilled into the room.

''They've been waiting,'' Marhalt said to Bron, ''to welcome you.''

They crowded around Bron's chair, clapping him on the back, uttering words of congratulation. They were smiling; their voices made their pleasure plain. Gilles clasped Bron's shoulder. Aleynn took his hands in both his own. "You understand now, don't you?" he said.

Barach laughed. "Of course he does. Look at his face."

Bron was overwhelmed. He could not speak. The others, after a little while, tactfully withdrew. Seating themselves on the floor, perching on the edge of Marhalt's table, propping themselves against the wall, they began to talk of changing the face of the Arm of the Stone.

In a sense, Marhalt's plan was a simple one. He aimed to replace every member of the Council of Six, thereby assuring the accession to Staff-Holder either of himself or one of his protégés. He had already used his influence to gain prestigious positions for many of his students. Bron was surprised at some of the names he heard.

The new Arm Marhalt planned to build would be founded on men like his pupils: men who brought no hidden bias to their search for Violation, who valued the detachment of reason above the fire of zealotry, who took no personal pleasure in the delivery of their duty. They would be loyal to the Stone first, to the Order second, to themselves third and last. They would rely as much on their intellect as upon their Gifts. Questioning would be the first avenue of approach, with the mindprobe used only as an adjunct. Torture would not be used at all. Judgment would be rendered fairly, for judgment's sake alone. There would be no abuses—no innocents sentenced to provide an example, no theft of goods or property, no terrorizing of communities, no unnecessary pain. The only fear this new Arm would invoke would be the fear of Violation; the only hatred, the hatred of Violators. As for the infamous Houses of Reeducation, they would be entirely abolished. Better a quick execution than the living death of the thought-clean.

The group talked on, eagerly. At last Marhalt held up a hand.

"It's late. We must attend to necessities." He looked at Bron. "If our cause is to remain hidden, it must rest behind

barriers even the most potent mindprobe will not detect.''
He smiled faintly. ''Actually, the very illegal barriers others
are punished for maintaining. Necessity is a strange parent.
I will teach you these barriers now. You must raise them at
once. Your companions will help you perfect them, and lend
you their guard until you are fully proficient.''

He rose to his feet and came round the table, positioning
himself in front of Bron's chair. He placed his hands upon
Bron's temples, his touch light and cool. Beyond him the
others watched. Bron sensed something passing through his
Mentor's fingers, from Marhalt's mind into his own.

Marhalt stepped back, withdrawing his hands.

''Now. I've given you the means. Show me that you can
build the barrier.''

Tentatively, Bron looked within himself. What Marhalt
had placed inside his head was a body of knowledge, a
schematic for barriers unlike any he had ever encountered—
but, he sensed, no less effective than his own. Carefully he
followed the guidelines he saw inside his mind, laying the
foundations of this second wall a safe distance beyond the
first. He felt it taking shape, rising stone by stone till it stood
complete, its shape hidden below the ordinary contours of
his thoughts.

''Good,'' said Marhalt, who had been following the process. ''By the time of your next mindprobe, this will be
second nature. These barriers are very strong; they will defeat even the most extreme application of Roundhead power.
But make no mistake.'' His gaze was stern now. ''I designed
these barriers, and I can break them. Don't think to use them
to deceive me, or to hide any secret purpose of your own.
To make certain of your faithfulness, I will ask you to open
them, twice a year, to my mindprobe.''

The others watched, their faces grave. Bron nodded. ''I
understand,'' he said.

The session was over. The group was released into the
russet corridors. They moved swiftly, not speaking. They
saw no one—they might have been the only living beings
upon the sixth floor. Bron walked at their center. Their bodies made a shield around him, as did their guarding minds.

Bron had heard them talk. It was impossible to doubt the purity of their devotion to Marhalt's cause of renewal. They truly abhorred the corruptness of the Arm of the Stone, truly desired redress of the cruel oppression the Arm had visited for so long upon the world. This was the true measure of the difference he had sensed in them. In a strange way it made the change in him, the attenuation of his hatred and the shifting of his anger, less terrible. Those who had wrought that change were no more Roundheads, in the traditional sense, than he. It was not the thing he hated that had breached his barriers, but something else.

Despite his reluctance for their perilous purpose, Bron could not help but feel within himself the resonance of their impassioned statements. In a sense, their goal was not unlike his own. What was change, after all, but a form of destruction? Yet as much as they desired the ending of the old order, they wished also to build a new structure to replace it. Bron's vow allowed only for obliteration. In his midnight musings, as the distant tumult of the Stone's power turned about the edge of his senses, he had begun to grasp the difficulty the changes within him posed for this goal. Accepting the evil of Violation and the threat of handpower, he must also grant the necessity of protection. If the Guardians were gone, who would ensure the Split did not come again?

Roundheads that they were, to Bron's companions the answer could only be the Arm of the Stone—cleansed, renewed, purged of evil. Bron was not certain he could accept this. Did the evil lie in what the Arm of the Stone did, or in the organization itself? Even if Marhalt and his coconspirators did succeed, could practices so entrenched ever really be abolished? Might not the old ways, gradually, reassert themselves, so that three centuries from now all would be as it had been?

Bron was aware that his situation contained not simply peril but irony. He, who had maintained a barrier since childhood, had tonight been taught to build another. He, who concealed a deadly secret, had tonight received a second, nearly as dangerous as the first. He, whose anger had made him solitary all his life, had by that very anger drawn to himself a man who had forced him into joining. Joining once, he had unwrought nearly everything he had believed. Tonight, unwilling, he had joined again. What would this new joining unmake?

The

Spy

Twelve

OR THE second time that day Liliane dressed her hair, drawing the comb through the resisting curly mass of it till it lay smooth and obedient on her shoulders. She rebraided it down her back, binding the ends with a green cord. She inspected her reflection in the mirror that hung on the wall of her small room in the nonresident section of the Journeyer Wing, turning this way and that to make sure her gray gown fell in proper folds, her green Journeyer sash was even about her waist, and her gold Guardian medallion lay square upon the center of her breast. Finished, she seated herself on her bed, her ankles neatly crossed and her hands decorously folded in her lap.

Her room in the nonresident portion of the Women's Section of the Journeyer Wing was well-furnished and comfortable. Though it was equipped for four, she occupied it alone. She had been a Journeyer for more than ten years, but this was only the second time she had been in the Journeyer Wing; the first had been just after her Investment, when she had waited with other new-made Journeyers to receive her first assignment. Then, she had had roommates—eager, determined young women about whom she now remembered nothing. At the time, the only thing about them that had seemed important was that they were not Goldwine—Goldwine, who should have been the one to share this hard-won moment, but who instead had abandoned the Fortress late in the First Year of her Novitiate, vanishing without trace into the summer night.

There was nothing to do now but wait. Sometime in the next hour, a knock would come at the door. Outside, a black-robed man would be waiting: a messenger from the Arm of the Stone. He would guide her deep into Arm territory. There, from a Roundhead whose identity she did not yet know, she would receive a mission—a mission whose nature was, at the moment, a mystery.

"As you see, there are no details," the Journey-Master had told her, earlier in the day. "Your summons was not even signed. But that is the way of the Arm. They feel no need to explain themselves to lesser folk."

They were sitting in his spacious chambers, a small table of refreshments between them. An ordinary Journeyer would not have merited a personal interview of this kind, but Liliane was no ordinary Journeyer. The rarity of the heartsensing Gift and the demand for the unique services it could provide placed her and those like her among the Suborder's most valuable assets. Heartsenser identities were a closely guarded secret; for each assignment they adopted a different name, a different history, so that who and what they were might always remain concealed. Those they served directly were aware of the truth of their natures, but nothing more; even the Council of Six knew them only by the numerical codes they received upon Investment. Only the Journey-Master could pair the numbers with names and faces.

Liliane looked at the square of parchment she held. At its top was a pool of dark red wax, larger than her palm, imprinted with the symbol of the Arm of the Stone, a circle surrounding an open eye. The massive seal weighted the document, dwarfing the spidery lines of writing below it:

Heartsenser 10779 is to be recalled at once to the Fortress, for the purpose of undertaking a confidential mission for the Arm of the Stone.

"Do you know, Master," she said, "why they requested me in particular?"

"Surely you are aware that you are regarded as one of

our most promising young heartsensers. They are the Arm of the Stone; what would they ask for but the best?''

''I'm grateful for such praise, Master. Yet . . . I fear the Arm may overestimate my skills. I haven't been long in the world, as you know. Would they not be better served by someone with more experience?''

''Are you questioning your summons?'' He looked at her keenly. ''Such postings are the cornerstones on which illustrious careers are built. I had thought you to be a young woman of some ambition.''

''I would never presume to question an assignment, Master.'' Liliane looked down at her clasped hands. ''My only concern is that the Stone be best served.''

''Of course.'' He seemed to relent a little. ''It's my understanding that mind-mapping is required for this mission, as well as skill in the detection of barriers and semblances. Expert scrivening is also necessary—there is, I believe, some question of forgery. There's also need for a good deal of . . . initiative, for lack of a better word. I understand this is a very complex mission, and some ingenuity will be needed to accomplish it fully. All these are qualities you possess in abundance.''

''Thank you, Master, for telling me.''

He looked at her, an ancient man whose watchful face and sharp, clever eyes spoke of a lifetime of successful intrigue. ''It's rare for the Arm to seek the services of someone who is not of their number. You've been greatly honored by this choosing. Be mindful of that. Remember that your success or failure will not reflect only on you but on the Suborder of Journeyers as a whole. Never allow the wider implications of your performance to fall from sight.''

''I won't fail you, Master. I swear it.''

Now, as Liliane sat on her bed, those brave words haunted her. She fully understood the honor of her summons; without hubris, she knew that what the Journey-Master had said about her Gift was true. Nevertheless, she could not banish the part of herself that wished the Arm of the Stone had never looked her way. The Arm gave rich rewards to outsiders who served them successfully, but they were stringent in their judgment of those who failed. She might gain a great deal by this mission. She might lose everything she had.

Traditionally, those with heartsensing abilities specialized in statecraft, serving as secretaries and assistants to governors, kings, and ministers. During her Apprenticeship Liliane had dreamed of the treaties she would create, the wars she would avert, the intrigue she would unravel. Like the guides who brought pilgrims through the mountains, she would spend her life charting clear paths across the peaks and valleys of politics.

Her Mentor, a Journeyer who was not a heartsenser herself, but who specialized in the training of that Talent, offered a somewhat different perspective.

"Once you're Invested, you'll be worth a king's ransom," she told Liliane. "If you become one of the best, you'll be allowed to choose your postings, a thing permitted to no other Journeyer. Yet all your life, you will never be more than a servant. You will never wield temporal power, only assist those who already possess it. The credit for the work you do will go to those you serve, for you can serve them only in secret."

Liliane already knew these things. From the beginning, she had understood that her profession would bring her little personal honor, that the shroud of deception in which she was required to cloak her Gift, so that her fellow Apprentices might believe her nothing more than a talented diviner with an aptitude for nearspeech, must become the habit of a lifetime. "Such things aren't important to me, Mistress. I only want to serve the Stone."

"And you will. Yet you may find yourself, at certain points in your life, uncertain of how what you do accomplishes that goal. The orders you'll be given won't always be honorable. Your missions won't usually be straightforward. The fact is, the most common employment for those of your Talent is espionage."

"But I'm to be a diplomat," Liliane protested. "And I've chosen scrivening as my Trade."

Her Mentor shook her head. "There's some advice I give all my heartsensers, Liliane. Though your lot in life is to serve others, never neglect to serve yourself as well. You possess something of surpassing value. Remember that. Learn to use your Masters' need of your Gift to your advantage. If you can't do this—and believe me, there are

many who cannot—you won't survive long outside the Fortress.''

At the time, Liliane found such cynicism shocking. But
in the years that followed she was often to remember her
Mentor's words and, in time, to come fully to understand
their wisdom.

Her first assignment was as a clerk to the Abbot of an
eastern Orderhouse. After slightly more than a year she was
promoted to Secretary, and transferred to the Supervisor of
the neighboring Diocese's Guardian Schools. These dull
postings, in service to men who did not merit her abilities
and were unaware of her Gift, were far beneath her true
capacities; she recognized them, however, as Tests. She was
careful never to yield diligence to the weight of boredom
she often felt, discharging her mundane duties as if they
were of paramount importance. Eventually her patience was
rewarded. She received her first real political placement:
Secretary to Pietra, the Journeyer First Minister of the largest of the island kingdoms of the Midland Sea.

Though she did perform clerical tasks for Pietra—taking
notes, writing reports, managing expenses, organizing records—she soon found that her chief duty was to act as a
kind of eavesdropper. Recording minutes at certain meetings, concealed behind a screen or a false wall at others,
standing behind Pietra at audiences or sitting to his left at
state dinners, she worked constantly to penetrate the disguise
of words and manner and sometimes Gift that concealed the
true intent of those with whom he dealt. All Guardians, and
many of the people of the world with minor or proto-Gifts,
knew how to sequester their thoughts so that even a nearspeaker could not hear them; few, however, were capable
of setting a similar guard upon their feelings. What the mind
and the mouth did not betray, emotion often did. In the
Fortress Liliane had proved particularly adept at this sort of
detection, with a special affinity for the sparking traces of
feeling that betrayed the presence of illegal barriers or
stronger-than-allowable personal guards.

Liliane had never expected that her lot as a heartsenser
would be easy. She fully understood that she must exercise
her Gift professionally as she had never allowed herself to

use it personally, reversing the habits of a lifetime spent guarding the secrets involuntarily entrusted to her by others. But the ways in which Pietra employed her went beyond anything she had anticipated. He ordered her to scan not only those with whom he had official contact, but the other Guardians of the court, the tradesmen and commoners who came daily to do business, even the servants. He required her to include in her reports not just details relevant to his governance of the realm, but the most minute nuances of personal feeling. It did not take her long to grasp that this had less to do with politics than with his desire to know such things about others, his need to coerce and manipulate and humiliate those around him. Increasingly, her duties came to seem burdensome. The faces of those whose privacy she breached haunted her as she lay in bed at night. As she placed her too-revealing reports in Pietra's hands, she was often troubled by a sense of treachery.

The worst was yet to come. Six months after her arrival, Pietra summoned her to his workroom.

"I want to sleep with you," he told her, without preamble.

Liliane was stunned. "But Master, I'm a heartsenser," she said when she could speak.

"What's that got to do with it?"

"Master, I follow the Celibate Rule. Surely you've heard of the dangers relationships of . . . of that kind hold for heartsensers—"

"Ah, but it's my understanding that the danger arises only if the heartsenser is willing. And unless I very much miss my guess, that's not the case here, is it?"

"Such a thing would be completely improper." Liliane could not keep the fear from her voice. "Our superiors would never tolerate it. It could mean the wreck of both our careers—"

"Not mine." He leaned forward, his face predatory. "Understand this. I've been First Minister here for a very long time. Those you call superiors are my friends and colleagues. If you attempt to speak of this to anyone, I will let it be known that you've become unbalanced by your duties, to the point of entertaining fantasies and making accusations against all the Journeyers of my court. Heartsensers are known to be unstable, and this is your first major assignment. No one will question my assessment.''

''I can appeal for protection. I can demand a probe—''

''I can also see to it that you're put away where they keep the heartsensers who have gone incurably mad. Believe me, if you go there, no one will ever listen to you again.''

Liliane stared at him. She could not speak.

''Here's your choice. Obey me and prosper—if you do, your superiors will have only the best reports of you. Or refuse me and suffer. Bad reports are as easy to write as good ones. You can have the afternoon to think about it.''

Later, when she had gained more experience, Liliane understood that Pietra's threat was not as potent as it seemed. Her value as a heartsenser might well have carried her word over his. But she was young and uncertain, still a neophyte in the politics of position, not entirely sure of her own worth—and very much afraid of Pietra. It seemed to her that she had no choice. She knew she would most likely survive the experience, for it was true that the heartsenser's own feelings were the key. The cautionary tales her Mentor had told her, of the ones who went mad, had all been stories of love or lust, of minds forced too far open by desire, of Gifts unable to support the double weight of reciprocated emotion. Any intensely shared feeling held similar peril. The necessity that brought most heartsensers to the Celibate Rule caused them also to hold aloof from most forms of human closeness.

And so Liliane went to the small, distant chamber Pietra had chosen for their tryst, and suffered mutely through the experience. She was unable to hide her shame and disgust; the pleasure Pietra took in that was even greater than his enjoyment of her unwilling body. Afterward she returned to her bedroom. The pain of the things he had done to her would not let her sleep. She lay staring up at the carved beams of the ceiling, longing with despairing intensity to peel off her skin and free herself of her soiled and violated body. How would she bear the burdens of the day now, knowing the night held horrors even worse? The prospect of failure rose up before her, as close as the mattress beneath her back. And she knew beyond doubt that whatever terrible things Pietra forced her to, failure would be worse than any of them.

In that knowledge, somehow, she found the strength she needed. Day by day she survived; night by night she endured. She discovered within herself a talent for dissimulation she would never have suspected. She became an automaton, harvesting the feelings of others, burying her own in the dark place inside her mind. Pietra, who treated her badly in almost every other respect, was as good as his word in one regard. She was aware that he sent excellent reports to her superiors.

After three long years, she received transfer orders to the Osman Empire, where she was to take up the post of Secretary to the Regent, a Journeyer named Costares. It was a promotion, a reward for dutiful service. The sense of release Liliane felt as she left Pietra's court was like rebirth. She was aware that her new duties might be little different from her old: she understood now that this was the sacrifice she must make to the way of service she had chosen, a kind of life-Test. But during her time with Pietra, she had come fully to understand her Mentor's advice. She was required to serve others; she could choose, however, to serve herself as well. Never again would she allow herself to be used as Pietra had used her. If it ruined her, so be it.

Costares was a ruler of wisdom and ability, revered by his staff, beloved by the populace. He treated Liliane fairly and with respect. His use of her Gift was straightforward and without duplicity: when she sat beside him during negotiations, judgments, sessions with ambassadors and emissaries, meetings with traders and merchants, her task was to monitor whether words and motives coincided, and nothing more. After a year and a half Costares rewarded her with the title of Assistant and the use of his seal. He handed over to her many of his routine duties, and entrusted her with diplomatic and information-gathering missions of an increasingly difficult and confidential nature.

Liliane would have been content to remain in the Osman Empire indefinitely. She liked and respected Costares; her work for him seemed more consistent with her vision of service to the Stone. But after five years she received a summons, sealed with the seal of the Journey-Master himself, recalling her to the Fortress. Costares was sorry to lose her. On the morning of her departure he presented her with an exquisite woolen traveling cloak in Guardian gray, lined with Journeyer green. She had worn it every day of her journey and slept beneath it every night. It lay beside her now as she sat on her bed, ready to travel with her into the unknown future. She reached out her hand, closing it round the heavy material, feeling her heart beating against her throat.

There was a single tap at the door. She sprang to her feet, the cloak slipping from her fingers. Outside the Arm of the Stone stood waiting, a stocky man in sooty black, with cropped hair and a cold closed face. His eyes looked, not at Liliane or even through her, but beyond her, to a point just past her shoulder. He raised his hand, motioning her to follow.

He led her out of the nonresident section of the Journeyer Wing, and up two flights of stairs to the top floor, where the Staff-Holder, the Council of Six, and the Arm of the Stone had their quarters. A pair of ornate iron gates across the central corridor marked the entrance to Arm territory. They swung apart as Liliane and her guide approached, closing soundlessly at their backs.

They crossed a large open area, a kind of foyer. Next came a series of vacant chambers whose purpose Liliane could not guess, and after that a huge assembly hall, with beams and panels of carved wood. Everywhere, against a background of pale gray stone, was the color red. Scarlet tapestries hung on the walls, crimson banners fluttered from the ceilings, vermilion-dyed rushes swathed the floors, rich garnet-red glass filled the lancet windows that ran down one side of the assembly hall. The sun fell through the panes, throwing bloody shadows on the floor; as Liliane passed, each casement flashed a ruddy beam across her eyes.

Another flight of stairs brought them to a mazelike region of halls, lined with red-painted doors. Liliane's guide halted before one of these, indistinguishable from the others, even to the odd spiky symbols cut into the architrave. There was a pause, and then the door swung open. The guide motioned her through.

"Wait," he said, the only sound he had made since coming to fetch her. He turned about, and was gone.

Like everyone else, Liliane had heard tales about the luxury with which the Arm of the Stone surrounded itself. The riches they possessed, it was whispered, surpassed those of kings. Now she saw for herself the truth of it. The room in which she found herself was an office, but so opulent it hardly seemed designed for working. Jewel-toned rugs were thickly strewn across the floor. Exquisitely worked tapestries completely concealed the walls and ceiling, giving the room more the feeling of a tent than the cube of stone it was. Ornamented chairs were set randomly about, and a gilded divan, covered with cushions of multihued silk, was carelessly pushed against one wall. Beside the divan, standing slightly askew on a heap of carpets, rose a large screen of filigreed silver, detailed in enamel and set with precious stones. An enormous desk, with an equally imposing chair behind it, occupied the middle of the space. Beyond were ranks of chests, and a parchment case that stopped just short of the ceiling, each of its cubbyholes filled to overflowing with scrolls and papers.

The room was brilliantly illuminated by six multibranched standing candelabra. They were crammed with candles— not the dripless kind one most often saw in the Fortress, but tapers which, over time, had deposited upon their holders such an encrustation of wax that the supporting form was no longer visible. The wax had precipitated itself also onto the carpets below, spoiling the exquisite designs, a slowly accreting range of miniature mountains rising upward toward their source. Soot made black streaks across the tapestries that covered the ceiling; the heat of the flames had singed the fabric behind them, opening holes through which the stone walls could be glimpsed. This indifferent desecration of beauty, as well as the odd disarray that gripped the room, had a deliberate feel. It was as if whoever owned the room were saying to the observer: Look at the luxuries with which my life is filled. Look how little I value them.

Liliane did not dare seat herself. The dancing candle flames, a hundred different tiny motions, made her dizzy. The room, though without visible source of heat, felt airless and close.

One moment the space was empty but for herself. The next moment he was there, materializing soundlessly against the heavy folds of tapestry. Liliane was impressed, as she was meant to be. But awe was immediately supplanted by recognition. The man before her was Jolyon.

Nearly twenty years had passed, but Liliane had not forgotten him, nor the intensity with which, in the first months of her Novitiate, he had tried to make her yield to him the secrets of her inner self. Again and again he had assaulted her mind during the hazing sessions; twice more he had waylaid her in the hallways and tried to terrorize her into surrender. He had enlisted his fellow Thirders to persecute her, so that for a little while she was punished almost as much as Goldwine. If he had had a year to work on her, he might have gotten what he wanted. But after only four months, graduation to the Apprentice College removed him from Liliane's life. She thanked the Stone for her deliverance, and assumed he would forget her.

But when she herself graduated, and encountered him face-to-face in the hallways of the Apprentice College, she saw by the way he looked at her that he had not forgotten her, nor her defiance of him. Early in her First Year she and two female classmates were kidnapped by a baiting ring. Blindfolded, she waited as first one, and then the other of her companions was subjected to a brutal mock-Interrogation. Inexplicably, the baiters let her go unharmed. Before they left, one of them pulled her into a close embrace. "Jolyon sends his remembrances," he whispered, his wet mouth against her ear. "He says to tell you he often thinks of you."

After that, she lived in dread. Even her sleep was not free of it. She was well aware that Jolyon nursed grudges the way others hoarded gold; she was not the only Apprentice marked by his attention. But knowing did not make the fear easier to bear. Many times more she was kidnapped during her Apprenticeship. On each occasion, though she was forced to listen to the torture of others, she herself was never harmed. She attributed this to a refinement of sadism, in that he wanted to inflict on her a suffering that lasted not for an hour or two but for years; it was only later that it occurred to her to wonder whether he had somehow discovered she was a heartsenser, whose ruin would not, like the others', be ignored. Not until she was Invested, a full-fledged heart-senser shielded by the authority of the Suborder of Journeyers, was she able to feel safe again.

His strange dreamy face seemed little altered by passing time. He was surely close to forty now, but he looked no more than twenty-five. He wore a Roundhead's black robes and red sash, and also red boots, a sign of rank. In the manner of most members of the Arm, he was decked with jewelry, his fingers heavy with rings, his Guardian medallion strung on an intricately-worked gold chain, jeweled pendants glinting at his earlobes. He watched her like a man not fully awake, his heavy lids half-closed. Between them showed the hot regard she recalled so well.

He knew her, despite the years that had passed since last they met. She could feel it. In the close air of the room, she felt her heart beating like a runner's. Was the assignment only a pretext? Had he brought her here to try once more to take what she had long ago refused him? The secrecy of heartsensers was supposedly proof against all intrusion; theoretically, he should not have known who she was before he summoned her here. Yet in all the world, what was there the Arm of the Stone did not know?

He stirred at last, moving to the desk and seating himself behind it. He gestured to one of the chairs.

"Sit down."

His voice too was just as she recalled, reedy and sharp. Fear made her body icy, but her years with Pietra had given her practice. She reached into her reserves of control for the demeanor of a good Secretary: back straight, face smooth, hands neatly clasped upon her knees. As was the custom, she kept her eyes lowered, fixing her regard on Jolyon's hands, toying with the small precious objects that littered the surface of his desk.

"As you know, you've been called here to receive a posting,'' he said. "You're to go to the Britannic Isles, to the Northern Orderhouse there. The Arm-Master's Secretary is recently deceased. You'll be taking his place.''

"I'm honored to serve the Arm of the Stone, Master.'' Liliane kept her voice low; it was easier to control that way. "What is my charge?''

Jolyon tossed aside the silver filigree bird he had been playing with, and picked up an ivory egg. The gems of his rings caught the candle flames. His nails were blunt and distorted, bitten to the quick.

"There's a Violator in the Northern Orderhouse. Your task is to gather information for the Investigation we plan to conduct.''

"May I know the Violator's identity, Master?''

"He is the Arm-Master.''

In her astonishment Liliane forgot herself and looked up, meeting Jolyon's brooding gaze. Hastily she lowered her eyes.

"I see you appreciate the unusual nature of the situation,'' he said.

"I hadn't realized there could be Violation among the Arm of the Stone, Master.''

"There's Violation everywhere.'' Jolyon's voice was cold. "What kind of Guardian are you, not to know that?''

"Forgive me, Master. I meant no disrespect.''

"Your charge will be twofold. First, you will search for forgery and deception. Among other things, the Arm-Master is a heretic. He's been using the Northern Diocese as a testing ground for Zosterian philosophy.''

The Arm of the Stone was known for the number of its secret societies, clustered throughout its ranks like clots in a bowl of cream. The Zosterians, however, were not secret at all. Named for Zoster, the founder of the Arm of the Stone, they were reformers who advocated change in practices of Investigation and governance that had endured unaltered for centuries. In an unheard-of breach of tradition, they had undertaken the expansion of the movement beyond the Arm of the Stone. It had proved surprisingly popular. Though less than ten years old, Zosterianism already numbered thousands of non-Roundheads among its supporters.

"I wasn't aware that Zosterianism had been designated a heresy, Master."

"It hasn't. But if one of the movement's founders is exposed as a forger and a liar, that will change. The Arm-Master has put many unorthodox methods into place in the Northern Diocese. His reports indicate a drop in Violation, ostensibly as a result of these changes. But I have it on reliable authority that this is a fiction, concocted to support his political agenda. Your task is to search the records, including the Catalogue, for alteration of numbers, deletion of information, spurious reports, or other signs of tampering. We've arranged for your assignment to coincide with the Progress he undertakes every year, which will make it possible for you to examine the local records and to interview the Resident Journeyers. You are also to question the Journeyers of the Orderhouse and the Arm's clerical staff. We must know how many Guardians this man has drawn into his orbit, and how they are helping him. Am I clear so far?"

His hands traveled about his desk as he spoke, picking up and discarding tiny objects one after another. Trained as she was to interpret the language of the body, Liliane recognized in his restless motion an intensity of feeling not reflected in his voice. "Yes, Master," she said.

"The second portion of your charge is more difficult. You are to thoroughly scan the Arm-Master's mind. I understand you're something of a prodigy in barrier detection. We're certain he harbors illegal barriers, though the probes have never found them. Also, we have definite knowledge that he is a Violator, of the Paths of Thought at the very least. But as an Arm-Master he is exempt from probing, and so we have been unable to get into his mind to find precisely where his Violation lies. If you can, you must discover this also."

Liliane hesitated. She was fearful of challenging him. Honesty, however, compelled her to speak. "Master, I'm confident I can fulfill your requirements. I'm a skilled scrivener; if there's forgery, I'll find it. I have years of experience in mind-mapping; I'm certain I can locate and analyze whatever barriers he has. But . . . I feel I'd be serving you badly if I didn't point out that I'm not an expert in the assessment of Violation."

"We aren't asking you to classify his Violation, only to locate it. You're capable of recognizing Violation when you encounter it, surely?"

"I'm sure I am, Master. I just thought that perhaps it might be more appropriate for the Investigation Team to—"

"No." His hands came down hard among his glittering toys. "There will be no Team, not until all the evidence is in our hands. This man is more cunning than you can imagine, more powerful than you can dream. He has influential supporters and sponsors, who will do everything they can to protect him. If we arouse his suspicion before the case against him is fully proved, he will escape us. That cannot be allowed to happen. He is a canker, a sore upon the body of the Arm of the Stone. Every breath he takes is an evil, every day he lives is a blight. The mask of rectitude behind which he hides his rotten soul must be shattered. He must be paraded naked before the world so that all may see him for the foul Violator we have always known him to be."

All at once his guard was gone. A choking cloud of hatred rolled out from behind it—ancient, complicated, profoundly personal. It moved too quickly for Liliane to fully shield herself. Mercifully, it was peaking even as it struck her, already draining back into the strange ocean of self so imperfectly restrained by the sea-wall of Jolyon's personal guard. She let out her breath, slowly. Why, knowing she was a heartsenser, had he revealed himself in this way? Could it be that the release had been involuntary? Was his control as poor as that?

"So." Across from her, Jolyon was calm again. "Are we clear on the scope of your charge?"

"We are, Master."

"The task before you is very difficult. The man you go to face is clever and powerful, with long experience of deception, and a guard strong enough to defeat the most accomplished nearspeaker. If you stint or husband your efforts in any way, you will not succeed. All your talents must be brought to bear against this man—all of them, not just those you were trained for, do you understand me?"

"I'm . . . not sure I do, Master."

"I'll be clearer, then. The reports I have of you specifically indicate your ability to achieve your goals by means of . . . private as well as public methods."

For the first time, Liliane felt her composure slip. Her eyes flew upward, colliding with his. "What?" she whispered.

He smiled. His face was as ineffable as a stone idol's. "Surely you didn't think such a thing could be kept secret from the Arm of the Stone."

Liliane could not speak.

"Don't worry. Our interest isn't discipline. We fully recognize the value of a heartsenser who is capable of doing what you can do. Your actions demonstrate initiative and ambition, both of which are qualities we appreciate, as well as the ability to, shall we say, throw yourself fully into the pursuit of a purpose." He picked up a tiny onyx dagger; with its point he began to score parallel lines on the surface of his desk. "That, as much as anything else, is why you were chosen for this mission. We need an agent to whom no avenue of endeavor is closed. An agent who will not hesitate to employ the full range of her abilities to achieve her goal. If mindscan and scrivening can get you what need, well and good. But if those things are not enough, then you must look to other methods." With a sudden violent motion he thrust the little dagger point-down into the wood, where it rested, quivering. "Do we understand each other?"

Liliane was not certain whether his earlier release of feeling had been voluntary. This time, however, there could be no doubt. Not since Pietra had she been so close to something so unclean. Revulsion clutched at her, and shame, hot as molten metal. But she would die before she allowed him to see these things. That was what he wanted: to see them. She could sense his desire to pierce her control, as urgent as it had been twenty years ago.

"We do, Master," she murmured.

For a moment he watched her. She thought he would say more, but he did not. Instead he sat back in his chair, folding his hands upon the ruin he had made of the surface of his desk.

"Your contact in the Orderhouse is called Amias. He'll

expect to receive regular reports from you. He's a farspeaker by Gift, and can relay the information directly to me. Our suspect doesn't trust him, however, so be careful.''

"Yes, Master," Liliane murmured.

"You'll leave tonight at the twelfth bell. I'm giving you an escort from among my men. At the moment, there's a travel advisory in force for the Fortress Passage. There's been an upsurge in bandit activity, as I'm sure you've heard.''

"Yes, Master." Liliane nodded. "Security was very tight on the journey in.''

"It may slow you down. Even so, you should be in Britannia by May.'' He turned slightly and lifted his hand. From one of the cubbyholes behind him a soft leather document pouch emerged, drifting through the air to fall lightly on his palm. "I've created an identity for you. You will be Madelaine Lenoit, a commissioned Secretary to the Arm of the Stone. With your experience as a covert operative it shouldn't be difficult for you to maintain the deception. I've also compiled some information for you. There's background on the Arm-Master and his career, a synopsis of the recent history of the Northern Diocese, and something to acquaint you with the details of Zosterian heresy. There's also a travel itinerary and a validation document for you to present when you arrive.''

He tossed the pouch toward her, not bothering with mind-power this time. Liliane reached out and picked it up. It was heavy, thick with papers.

"Take this also." Jolyon cupped his palms together; a brief pulse of light flashed between his fingers. He held out his right hand. It contained a ring, a thick band of gold set with garnets. "My symbol is on it. It will identify you to Amias.''

Liliane took the ring from his palm. It was warm, either from his flesh or from the power that had created it. She resisted the impulse to shudder.

"Do you have any questions?''

"I do, Master. How quickly should I complete my investigation?''

"Six months ought to be sufficient. Eight at the outside.

If you need more time than that, you'll need to clear it through Amias.''

"Can I count on quick withdrawal, if it becomes necessary?''

"Amias has a transfer document already prepared.''

"One last question, Master. What is the Arm-Master's name?''

"His name is Selwyn Forester.''

Once again, forgetting herself, Liliane looked up. "But I met him,'' she said, careful to keep any feeling from her voice. "In the first months of my Novitiate. He might . . . it's possible he might recognize me.''

Jolyon raised his eyebrows. "You were only a child then. How could he recognize you?''

He was right, of course. Liliane lowered her gaze.

"He has no way, in any case, of knowing what you are. Even the Arm of the Stone can't break the secrecy with which you heartsensers are surrounded.''

But you did, she thought. Code or not, he had known who she was before she ever set foot in his chambers. She knew it, as surely as she was sitting here. "Yes, Master.''

"Are all your questions answered?''

"They are, Master.''

"I'm sure I don't need to emphasize how confidential this mission is. Only the men who escort you, and Amias, have been told what you will be in Britannia to do.''

"I understand, Master.''

"We of the Arm rarely reveal our affairs to others.'' On the desk a small golden sphere began to move, describing a slowly narrowing spiral. "You have been extraordinarily honored tonight, in the things you've learned, in the service you are being given a chance to do. No doubt you're aware of this. Perhaps you've already begun to count up the rewards success will bring you.''

"No reward could be greater than the service itself.''

"Very nicely said.'' The little sphere had reached the central point of its revolutions; it hovered there, vibrating, as if it still wished to move. "I urge you, however, to think just as fully about the ways in which failure could cripple your

career. As for betrayal . . . well, I'm sure I don't need to say
any more about that."

"I would die first, Master."

"You would certainly die after." The sphere's vibration
reached a pitch its metal could not withstand. Abruptly its
sides collapsed. It lay still, a crumpled clot of gold. Jolyon
looked at it for a moment; then he snapped his fingers, and
it was gone.

"That's all, then. You may go."

Liliane rose to her feet and bowed formally. Turning, she
advanced over the heavy carpets. Would he open the door
for her? It did not seem so. She reached for the handle. As
she did the door began to swing toward her, a little too
quickly, forcing her to take an awkward step back. From
behind her, she felt his sour malice.

She passed into the hallway. The door closed solidly after
her. She leaned against the wall, her legs suddenly weak.
She felt as if she had walked through fire and come out the
other side.

In her room again, she sat on her bed, drawing Costares's
cloak around her. Opening the pouch Jolyon had given her,
she scanned the papers inside. The travel itinerary revealed
a journey of approximately three months. The validation of
her commission, sealed with the red seal of the Arm of the
Stone, was terse and to the point. A thick sheaf of papers
held the details of her new identity; a thinner packet dealt
with Selwyn Forester. There was also a new sash for her to
wear, Journeyer green like her own, but bordered and tas-
seled in red to mark her service to the Arm of the Stone,
and a red symbol to be pinned upon her left shoulder.

Putting back into the pouch everything except the papers
pertaining to Selwyn, Liliane began to read.

Selwyn's Apprenticeship was marked with honors and
distinctions. He had achieved Investment in six years, the
only person in the history of the Order ever to do so. Once
Invested, he received a position as assistant to his former
Mentor, Marhalt. After only a year he was promoted to Deputy Apprentice-Master, an extraordinary honor for one so
young. The expectation had been that he would remain in
this position indefinitely, succeeding eventually to Marhalt's

position on the Council of Six. Three years later, however, Selwyn surprised everyone by applying for the post of Investigation Field Monitor. His request was granted—another mark of unusual favor, for such a position was ordinarily held only by Roundheads with substantial Investigation experience. As Field Monitor, Selwyn traveled from Orderhouse to Orderhouse, reviewing Investigation Teams, overseeing performance and procedure, verifying records and examining methods, reporting his findings directly to the Council of Six. Early in this period, he and a group of like-minded colleagues founded the Zosterian movement.

After five years as Field Monitor, Selwyn applied for transfer to the Britannic Isles. Again, his request was granted. He was named Arm-Master of the Northern Orderhouse. Though the position of Arm-Master was an important one, Britannia was a stagnant backwater, known as a final destination for those whose lack of talent or favor shut them out of more desirable appointments. The Northern Diocese in particular owned a reputation as a rock-bottom posting. It seemed an odd destination for a Roundhead of such evident Gift and ability. In the context of Selwyn's Zosterianism, however, it made more sense. Zosterianism was vigorously opposed by much of the Arm's governance; it was only because certain powerful moderates, such as Selwyn's Mentor, Marhalt, were known to be sympathetic to it that it had survived long enough to achieve the popularity it currently owned. The opportunity to bury one of the movement's main proponents in Britannia must have seemed providential to Selwyn's masters, a fair trade for the post of Arm-Master, which under other circumstances his relative youth and lack of direct Investigation experience would have made unavailable to him. In exchange, Selwyn gained a perfect field for the experimentation upon which he was clearly bent: a sparsely populated and historically difficult Diocese, where administrative indifference ensured that he could do as he pleased with a minimum of interference.

Selwyn had been Master seven years now, his task the monitoring of the Diocese's orthodoxy, the supervision and deployment of teams of Investigators, and the maintenance of the Orderhouse Catalogue and records. He had put in place a number of radical new procedures, most significant of which was the replacement of the traditional Roundhead Raids with a kind of monitoring journey, the Progress Jolyon had mentioned. According to Selwyn's reports, his experiments were already bearing fruit. The Violation statistics quoted for the most recent year were considerably lower than when he had first taken charge. The restless people, throughout the centuries given to spontaneous uprisings and acts of sabotage, seemed to have entered a period of unprecedented calm.

If Jolyon were right, it was all a tissue of lies.

Liliane put the papers aside. She drew her knees up to her chin, pulling Costares's cloak around her. Selwyn Forester, she thought. She remembered him clearly, in spite of the years that had passed since their single meeting. Though it had seemed quite natural for Jolyon to ascend to the sixth floor, she had always found it surprising that Selwyn had done so. She had never forgotten the flood of emotion she had sensed from him during the Expulsion ceremony. Such wild power, such alien force, did not seem to fit the reality of the Arm of the Stone. Oddly, it was easier to imagine him a Violator than a Roundhead.

She reached out and picked up Jolyon's ring, which she had dropped on the bed beside her as she entered her room. Its face was deeply carved with an ornate ''J''; small garnets were set around its circumference, reminding her of the bloody windows of the assembly hall. She shuddered. She could still see Jolyon's bitten fingers foraging among the small treasures on his desk. She could feel the heat of his repellent emotions, like a sticky glaze on her skin. She could hear the tone of his voice as he revealed his knowledge of what she had been certain no one but Pietra and herself knew. Had the Arm of the Stone penetrated their secret, misinterpreting the meaning of what they found? Or had Pietra deliberately revealed his own version of the story—a final act of assault on her person, a punishment for escaping him? Was this how she would be known from now on—as a heartsenser who employed her body to leverage advantage her Gift could not gain? She thought of the Journey-Master and the watchful look he had turned on her today. The shame of it, the anger, made her feel sick. The duty she owed her masters extended to the furthest reaches of her intellect, training, skill, and Gift. But she had determined years ago that it did not encompass her body. There was no one in the world who had the right to require such a thing of a heartsenser.

Even if she had been the person Jolyon thought her, it did not seem to her that it would have made much difference. Selwyn Forester was clearly an individual of extraordinary power and ability; nothing she owned seemed much of a weapon to bring against such a man, her body least of all. Why had she been given this mission? If it was really as important as Jolyon said, should he not have chosen a heartsenser with more experience, more cunning, more knowledge of Violation? She had felt his malice earlier, sitting before him in his sumptuous, disheveled office; perhaps he sought to ruin her through this mission. Perhaps, by sending her against this man who was her superior in everything but inner fitness, he had deliberately given her a charge he believed she would fail.

No, she thought. He himself had shown her, whether voluntarily or not, how vital Selwyn's downfall was to him. Surely he would not sacrifice so much hatred to some smaller spite. More than that, whatever personal satisfactions Jolyon might seek through this mission, neither the mission itself nor the choice of her as its agent belonged to him. Authority for such a charge could only have come from the Council of Six. Jolyon was their representative, nothing more; that he knew her was coincidence, that he hated her was irrelevant to anyone but himself. If, out of all the heartsensers available to them, her superiors had chosen her for this mission, who was she to question their judgment? Was she not, as the Journey-Master had said, among the most Gifted of her generation? Selwyn Forester might be a Roundhead, but she was a heartsenser. Without assistance, even the Arm of the Stone could not know the things her Gift told her.

She closed her eyes, beginning the meditation with which she preceded every assignment. In the coming months, the mission must be all there was. Such submission to purpose was the best way to success she knew, the only certain path of survival. When she was finished she would pack—it would go quickly, for she had few belongings. Once that was done, she would seek communion with the Stone. She had missed this contact, deeply, while she had been away. She would bathe in it now for as long as she could, to give her strength for what lay ahead. The Stone's voice would enclose her, a vast chorus of being in which, faintly, the echo of her own selfhood might be heard. Her Gift would stir; power would course along her limbs, weaving a web across her body, mimicking, distantly, the colossal net of the Stone's contemplation.

$\mathbf{T}$hirteen

ITH AN escort of two Roundheads Liliane left the Fortress, traveling out of the mountains along the Fortress Passage. The Passage was a broad and well-maintained highway reserved solely for Guardian use, with comfortable post-houses at regular intervals and a strong weather-binding to keep the worst of the storms away. Even when the wind howled and the rest of the world was a wall of snow, the Passage ran clear and straight, a ribbon of calm threading the tempest.

They traveled incognito. The Roundheads put off their black robes for the gray of ordinary Guardian clothing, and kept their cloak hoods drawn to conceal their cropped hair. They set aside the Roundhead privilege of comfortable cushion-heaped equipages and rode muleback like common Ordermen. To all outward eyes they were a party of Journeyers, headed for assignments in Britannia; their papers confirmed this fiction. Liliane was aware, however, that her companions would leave her before they reached the Northern Orderhouse. The Arm of the Stone knew its own. It would not do for her to arrive accompanied by Jolyon's men.

Liliane was aware that her companions were not with her only for the sake of protection but also to serve as an extension of Jolyon's eyes and ears. She often felt them watching her; they made unobtrusively certain that she was within sight of at least one of them at all times. They were never less than courteous when they addressed her, but beneath their courtesy she perceived their contempt, not so much for her in particular as for all who were not Arm of the Stone. The language of their bodies made evident their resentment of the Journeyer clothing they were forced to wear, the Journeyer status they were obliged to assume. Each time they halted at one of the Soldier checkpoints, she sensed their outrage at the indignity of their disguise.

The checkpoints, set across the Passage every fifty leagues or so, were often crowded; it was sometimes necessary to wait a day or more for traveling papers to be examined and Guardian medals to be authenticated. There had been no need for such security ten years ago, when Liliane had left the Fortress to travel to her first assignment, but during her absence the mountain bandits, who for all the centuries of their existence had never been known to expand their attacks beyond pilgrims and Novices, had begun to prey on Guardians as well. Any Guardian venturing off the Fortress Passage became fair game; the post-house barns were regularly raided, and groups of marauders had even managed to break through the bindings themselves to harass and rob travelers on the Passage. More disturbing, a bandit band had recently been caught attempting to pass itself off as a party of Journeyers. The interlopers had all been equipped with poison of some kind, and had killed themselves before they could be Interrogated—an action almost as troubling, in the level of organization it suggested, as the incursion itself.

Advancing through the checkpoints, passing patrols of edgy Soldiers, Liliane found herself thinking, as she had on the journey in, of Goldwine. She had often wondered whether her friend, when she left the Fortress, might have been intending to seek refuge among the bandits. Logic indicated that Goldwine was dead, as all who abandoned the safety of the Fortress for the wilderness outside it must surely be, yet Liliane had never been able to bring herself to believe this, just as she could not believe that Goldwine had simply wandered away, as others did, propelled by a misery that made a clean death in the snows preferable to continued life as a Novice. Certainly Goldwine had been miserable. But she was a fighter. There had been intent in her departure, and planning. She had waited until summer to leave, when the snows receded and storms were not so common, taking with her not only all her clothing and bedding, but a spare pair of boots stolen from another girl. And, though Liliane had not understood it until afterward, she had said good-bye.

"My Gift spoke to me again," she had told Liliane, at what was to be their last meeting in the hollow under the stairs. She radiated confidence, the focused purposefulness that, when Liliane first knew her, had been so characteristic of her. "I'd begun to think maybe it never would."

"Oh, Goldwine, I'm glad for you. When did this happen?"

"A little while ago. I didn't want to tell you until I was sure. I finally know why I came here, Liliane. It isn't anything like what I believed when we were traveling to the Fortress, but at least now I know what comes next. Remember that, no matter what happens. I've seen what lies ahead for me."

"Oh, Goldwine," said Liliane joyfully. "We really will be Guardians together. That's what you've seen, isn't it?"

"We'll be together." Goldwine looked at her, an expression on her face Liliane could not interpret. "I've seen that."

Even that odd look could not dull Liliane's joy. Yet somewhere within herself she must have understood, for the next day, when rumor of a vanishing swept the Study Groups, she realized immediately who it must be. The puzzle of those final words had stayed with her over the years. Goldwine's Gift had been pure and strong, but even she had admitted that she did not always read it correctly. Clearly what she predicted could not come true. Even if she still lived, by abandoning the Fortress she had also abandoned their friendship. They could never be together now.

Leaving the mountains behind, Liliane and her escort traveled north across the great continent, following the Guardian Roads. The Guardian Roads ran throughout the known world, linking city to city and Orderhouse to Orderhouse, laid with permanent power-matrices to hold their stones in place and to prevent water from pooling, snow from drifting, weeds from growing, and underbrush from encroaching on either side. There were fewer checkpoints here, and their Guardian mules were specially bred and laid about with power to give them endurance and speed other animals could not match, but even so the pace was slow. There were quicker modes of travel—distance-walking, which folded space so that leagues could be crossed in a single step, or body-translation, which took a person from one spot to another in an instant—but they were forbidden to ordinary Ordermen such as they pretended to be, reserved for Orderhouse leaders and the Arm of the Stone.

Though her taciturn companions chafed at the delay, for Liliane the monotony of the journey was a boon. There was a great deal she must learn before she would be ready to assume the false persona of her mission. Roundheads, elite as they were, did not perform their own clerical work, but maintained a special cadre of personnel to do it for them, Journeyers trained to the methods of the Arm and bound to secrecy through a type of power-conditioning that made them physically unable to speak about their work to anyone but their masters. Jolyon had provided Liliane with an exhaustive false curriculum vita establishing the necessary background of Arm service, complete with references from the Masters she had supposedly served. He had even taken the trouble to place her fictional assignments close to her real ones, so that she would not be caught out by reference to places and cities she did not know. He had also provided a description of the customs and etiquette of the Arm-trained, and a guide to methods by which she could duplicate the telltale signs of Arm conditioning.

Swaying on the back of her mule during the day, crouching over a candle at night, she committed it all to memory, embellishing it with her own experience so it would seem less rote. It was a complex deception, but she had many times assumed fictitious identities for Costares, and Pietra's court had taught her all the ways of dissembling. The confidentiality of her work as a heartsenser was not so different from the forced secrecy of the Arm-trained, and the state matters with which she had dealt carried no less weight than the mysteries of Investigation. In addition, this persona offered an advantage her other masquerades had not possessed: the trust of the Arm of the Stone. Roundheads regarded their conditioned servants as incorruptible. Her disguise would ensure she was subjected to far less scrutiny than any ordinary Journeyer.

After more than two months of travel, Liliane and her guard reached the Britannic Crossing, and took ship in a Guardian vessel. On shore again, a week of riding brought them to the Southern Orderhouse. They rested for two days and then, in the company of a small group of Journeyers, set out on the final leg of their trip.

In the Southern Orderhouse, for the first time, Liliane had put on the red-tasseled sash and red badge of the Arm-trained. Now she put on also the demeanor of her new identity. Absorbing by association a measure of Roundhead eliteness, the Arm-trained also assimilated the typical Roundhead contempt for other Guardians. Liliane made sure to ride a little apart from her fellow travelers, to pitch her tent a small distance from their encampment, to eat from her own store of provisions rather than share the general rations. Her assumed disdain, she noted with interest, was returned in kind, though only a heartsenser would have been able to perceive the distaste that hid beneath the other Journeyers' blank deference.

The night before their arrival, while the others slept, Liliane destroyed the papers Jolyon had given her. Creating a phantasmal mind-fire, she fed the parchment sheets to it one by one. When she had finished she sat for a long time in the darkness, meditating on tomorrow, on her first step into the dangerous world of her mission. She knew herself to be ready, as ready as it was possible to be. She felt no fear, only the resolute clarity of purpose.

The next morning her Roundhead escort and their mules were gone. There was some consternation among the members of the group as they searched in vain for tracks or traces. At last, finding nothing, they rode on.

Liliane's first sight of the Northern Orderhouse was through a veil of rain. It was a large square building of typical Guardian design, built of speckled granite and roofed with slate. It lay within a wild area of hills and valleys, where streams came tumbling down rocky slopes and mists rose strangely from declivities. At its feet huddled a small village. To the south, where the hills allowed, were areas of cultivation and grazing pastures; the north was moorland, rolling flat and unbroken toward distant purple mountains. Over it all the sky pressed down, heavy with cloud, diffusing a pearly light that kindled the green of grass and field, the brown of trunk and branch, to an almost unnatural vividness.

The party passed through the Orderhouse gates and into the central courtyard where visitors, Guardians and unGifted alike, were received. The gatekeeper and his staff directed the members of the party to their various destinations; Liliane, presenting her commission, was told to wait. Eventually a female Journeyer arrived to conduct her to the women's quarters. When she saw that she was to have a chamber entirely to herself, she nearly uttered a protest; amid the obviously crowded conditions, such use of space seemed unduly extravagant. But she caught herself in time. The Arm-Master's Secretary would not expect to share a room, even with other Arm-trained women.

"I hope it's satisfactory," the woman murmured. "You can see the Journey-Mistress if you wish any change."

"No," Liliane said, making her voice remote and cold. "It will be adequate."

The room had been meant for four. Narrow pallets were set at precise intervals against the wall across from the door, a chest at the foot of each and little tables in between. The walls were of dressed granite, covered with roughweave hangings to keep out the chill; rush matting hid the flagstones of the floor. A fire leaped on a wide hearth, and torches provided a ruddy light. Liliane was strongly reminded of the Apprentice College—though here, no doubt, fires needed to be replenished, torches redipped in pitch, mats swept with brooms, dust removed with cloths. There would be little power to spare, as in the Fortress, for the luxury of automation.

When the bell rang for the evening meal, Liliane followed the small group of female Journeyers to the refectory, a huge windowless room with a high arched ceiling where all the Orderhouse except for the Arm of the Stone gathered to eat. The tables were arranged in a series of concentric, three-sided squares, the open ends facing the great double doors by which the room was entered. The signs of power absent in other parts of the building were present here: a sheet of rippling mindlight hung just below the ceiling, and the air was artificially warm.

The Abbot and his retinue occupied the central tables. Less-exalted Journeyers, male Arm-trained personnel among them, were placed among the middle ranks. Clerks, teachers, trainees, and women, including the female Arm-trained, occupied the outermost rank. Liliane seated herself beside the other Arm-trained women: three of them, all clerks. They greeted Liliane with the deference of their low status. Conventions of staffing dictated that an Orderhouse's cadre of Arm-trained must include a commissioned Secretary for the Arm-Master, a certified scrivener for each Investigation Team, a small army of clerks to handle routine clerical tasks, and a Chief Scrivener, who oversaw and coordinated these diverse efforts. In the regimented hierarchy of the Arm-trained, the Chief Scrivener was prime. The Arm-Master's Secretary came next, then the scriveners, and, very much last, the clerks.

"We were concerned for you," said one of the clerks. Her name was Marya; she was tall and fair, with a square jaw and a long nose, down which her close-set blue eyes seemed perpetually to be looking. "You were due in the Orderhouse at least three weeks ago. We'd begun to wonder if you'd been lost at sea or fallen to bandits."

"The crossing was calm, and we saw no bandits," Liliane replied. "But the journey did take longer than expected. There are a great many Soldier checkpoints these days."

"What's the world coming to, when Journeyers aren't safe along the Fortress Passage?" said the second woman, Lithhilde. "Thank the Stone you've arrived. The work has been piling up—we've had to do some of yours, in addition to all our own."

"It's a busy Orderhouse," said the third woman, Chloe, in the soothing tones of a practiced peacemaker. She was the oldest of them, with the stooped posture and ink-stained fingers of someone who had spent much of her life bending over a copy-desk. "We all work hard."

"I was in Orderhouse Six in the Gallician region before I came here," said Marya to Liliane. "The workload there was much greater. We needed twelve clerks to keep up with it."

"We ought to have twelve," Lithhilde said. "Maybe if we did Master Tobias would be in a better temper."

"Don't exaggerate, Lithhilde," reproved Chloe. "You'll give the Secretary the impression that we aren't happy here. Did you have a fair journey from the Southern Orderhouse, Secretary? The weather can be unpleasant this time of year."

They chatted inconsequentially for the rest of the meal. Discreetly, Liliane scanned them, but among the jumble of their emotions she found nothing of interest. When the meal was over, she accompanied them back to the women's quarters. They bid her good night at the entrance to their chamber. As the door closed behind them Liliane caught the faint smell of mulled cider. She felt a sudden longing to sit in company, with her feet close to the hearth and her hands cupped around a hot drink. Since Goldwine, she had had no close friends. The nature of her work, and of her Gift, discouraged it. For the most part, she was content alone; but sometimes, reminded of the comfort of friendship, she found herself envying the easy companionship available to those who were not heartsensers, who did not follow the ways of secrecy and disguise that had become the shape of her life.

In her room, chilly and full of shadows, someone had left a folded slip of parchment on her pillow.

"The Cloister Court at midnight bell," it said. A small map was drawn below the words. There was no signature, but the note's author could only be Amias, Jolyon's contact. Memorizing the map, Liliane fed it to the fire.

At the sound of the midnight bell she wrapped herself in Costares's cloak and left her chamber. She moved through silent corridors darkened for the night, the cold biting deep into her bones. The Cloister Court was open to the air, with a little garden at its center. The daytime clouds had pulled aside; their remnants spread across the black sky like tattered fabric, with stars set among the rents. The moon drifted, now obscured, now clear, shedding a cold radiance.

In the dimness of the cloister, Liliane made out an indistinct figure.

"Master Amias?" she said, uncertainly.

<I am Amias,> the figure replied, in nearspeech. <Who are you?>

<I am Liliane, Master Jolyon's agent.>

<Prove yourself.>

Liliane approached him. She drew Jolyon's ring from the wallet at her belt and held it out to him. Instead of taking it, he lifted his hands. Between his cupped palms a small globe of mindlight began to grow, an echo of the chilly moon. He set it on the air between them. For a moment he regarded the ring, then he raised his gaze to her face. She could feel him assessing her, a close attention that made her want to fidget. For politeness' sake she kept her eyes lowered, fixed on a point just below his chin. She had already taken in his features in the initial glow of the mindlight: a short man somewhere in middle age, with a flat face and protuberant light-colored eyes.

<You're not what I expected,> he thought at last.

<Master?>

<So pale. So small. So young.>

<I'm thirty-three, Master.>

<I know how old you are. I know your entire resumé.> His mindvoice carried a sour quality that probably reflected his speaking voice. <I advised Jolyon against appointing you to this mission. I don't suppose he told you that.>

<Master, I'm confident I'm equal to the task—>

<That's what Jolyon said.> He waved away her explanations. <Well, it can't be helped. I accept you. You can put away the ring.>

<Thank you, Master,> Liliane replied, obeying.

<I want you to report to me here every three days, always at the midnight bell. Take no action unless you clear it with me first. Do nothing on your own recognizance. Your orders may come from Jolyon, but here you answer to me. Do you understand?>

<Yes, Master.>

<The faster you can fulfill your charge the better it will be. Unfortunately the absence of a Secretary has created

quite a backlog—there's a lot of work waiting for you. And be warned. The Arm-Master is suspicious of your predecessor's death. We took pains to make it seem natural, but he's a clever man, hard to fool. He won't trust you easily.>

Liliane felt a cold deeper than that of the air, as if the moon had reached inside her. Jolyon had made it sound as if it had been an ordinary death.

<What's your plan of action?>

<I thought I'd start by searching the Catalogue and the Arm-Master's records for signs of alteration. I'll also be looking for discrepancies between local and Orderhouse records.>

He shook his head; she could feel his impatience. <I already told Jolyon that's a waste of time. Selwyn and his men are far too clever to leave such traces. The real issue is Violation. That's what you must turn your efforts to. To Selwyn Forester himself.>

<Master, I'm trained to use my Talent in ways that are undetectable to other Gifted. But those of the Arm are more powerful than other Guardians, and if the Arm-Master suspects me, as you say, he'll be watching me closely. I'd prefer to spend some time observing him before making an attempt on his mind.>

<You don't have to worry about that kind of detection. You could scan him all day long and he'd never know it.>

<I don't understand, Master.>

<Didn't Jolyon tell you? Our esteemed Arm-Master is not highly endowed with nearspeech.>

Liliane looked at him doubtfully. In her reading she had noted that Selwyn had little Investigation experience beyond the in-house Investigations over which he had presided when he was Deputy Apprentice-Master; she had assumed, however, this was a matter of preference. It was an item of general knowledge that Roundheads were uniquely powerful nearspeakers.

<Oh, yes.> Amias's mind-voice conveyed the same feeling a sharp bark of laughter would have produced. <Have you ever heard of an Arm-Master who's never conducted an Interrogation? Almost inconceivable, isn't it? Yet that is what we have, right here in the Northern Orderhouse—a

man who has never himself Interrogated anyone, not once in his entire career. It's a scandal. In the old days such a thing would never have been allowed. It just goes to show where patronage can get you, if it's patronage of the right sort.>

<Patronage, Master?>

<Marhalt, of course. Marhalt, who protected him while he was in the Fortress. Marhalt, who protects him still.>

<I see.>

<No you don't.> She felt his contempt. <But you don't need to, to do what must be done here.>

Liliane took a deep breath. Already she disliked Amias. She could feel his sour self-importance, his churning resentment of those more favored than he. He was the kind of man who hung back when action must be taken, stepping forward only to filch the honor of others' achievements. His desire to seize control of this mission was plain. If she were not careful, he would rob her of all the credit for it.

<You're wiser than I, Master,> she thought, bowing her head submissively. <I'll do as you say, and set myself immediately to search for the Arm-Master's Violation. But I must also look for forgery, as I find time in the course of my other duties. I have no doubt of your assessment of the records, but Master Jolyon did give me orders.>

<Yes, well.> Her deference had pleased him. <Just be sure you don't neglect your primary duty.>

<The use of my Gift will come first, Master. You can depend on it.>

<I'll expect a report in three days.>

<Of course. Master—a question, if I may. It's my understanding that the exact nature of Selwyn Forester's Violation isn't known. Is there anything you can tell me that would help me begin my search?>

<His Violation lies in the Paths of Thought.> He replied quickly, as if this were something he had thoroughly considered. <I believe Selwyn Forester to be a handpower sympathizer, who works to abet the spread of Violation by laxity in Investigation and insufficient sternness in enforcement. He is also undermining the Arm through persuading its

members to the pursuit of heresy. There's hardly a Round-head here who isn't Zosterian.>

<And those who aren't? Are there any I could safely speak to?>

<Try Colm. Or Radlein. They're the only ones I trust. But Selwyn regards them as enemies, so take care.>

<I'll be discreet, Master.>

<You had better be. Selwyn Forester may not have near-speech, but he's powerful in other ways, and very clever. He knows how to read people's secrets; he knows how to bend them to his will. Be on your guard.> He looked her up and down. <He might think it worth his while to try his hand on you.>

<Try his hand, Master?>

<Zosterians don't keep the Celibate Rule, as proper Roundheads do. The Arm-Master in particular follows the pleasures of the flesh. He might not be able to resist the temptation of a female Secretary. I understand he can be quite persuasive, when he sets his mind to it.>

<You needn't be concerned, Master. I've encountered many powerful men in the course of my work. I know very well how to resist that sort of pressure.>

<Ah. But you've never met a man like Selwyn Fores-ter.> Again he looked her over, his gaze more lingering this time. <Don't make the mistake of thinking you can manip-ulate him. You are not his equal. Whatever your . . . expe-rience.>

He knew about her. She could feel his knowledge, like a greasy finger on her skin. The blood rushed to her face. She was glad of the dimness of the mindlight, which made such changes impossible to see.

<Thank you for your warning, Master,> she thought when she could trust herself to reply. <I'll take care.>

<See that you do.>

<With your permission, Master, I'll return to my room now.>

<Don't forget. Three days, at the midnight bell.>

<I won't forget, Master.>

Passing through the cloister, Liliane could feel him watching her. The itchy heat of his gaze lingered even after she gained the cold reaches of the corridors. She walked quickly. Her body was stiff with humiliation and anger; her shame burned in her face, like a brand any passerby could see. She bowed her head, gathered Costares's cloak more closely around her shoulders, and hurried through the shadows toward her empty room.

The following morning Liliane breakfasted in the refectory with the female clerks. In their company she made her way to the central courtyard. Directly opposite the gates was a narrow entryway, closed by a red-painted door. Upon it, outlined in black, was the circular symbol of the Arm of the Stone. Marya, in the lead, placed her palm flat upon the center of the symbol. There was a pause, and then the door swung open upon a wide corridor.

"Tobias will see it's set to your hand also," Marya said over her shoulder.

They passed through the door, which shut itself silently behind them. The corridor opened onto a sizeable foyer, lit by glowing globes of mindlight and hung with gorgeous tapestries depicting the history of Zoster, founder of the Arm of the Stone. Red-painted doors were set into the walls; one of them stood open upon a long hallway that terminated in an arched double portal. These doors too were automated, swinging smoothly inward as the group approached. Beyond them, a flood of natural daylight illuminated an exquisite formal garden, with clipped boxwood hedges enclosing ovals of grass centered by standard roses, heavy with dusky blooms. A small fountain whispered quietly at the garden's midpoint, surrounded by a graceful walkway of patterned stone. Despite the earliness of the season the grass was green, the flowers blooming, the air warm and moist. Obviously the Arm of the Stone maintained itself in luxury, but could even they spare the power for a weather-binding? Looking upward to the sky, Liliane found her answer, more astonishing in its way than power would have been. The courtyard was entirely roofed in glass. More powerfully than anything she had seen, even Jolyon's sumptuous neglected rooms, this glittering artifice spoke of the wealth and might of the Arm of the Stone, greater than that of kings.

"It was made by a craftsman from the Fortress," said Chloe, following Liliane's gaze. "They brought it here in pieces. The Arm of the Stone assembled it by power, one segment at a time."

"It's exquisite," Liliane said.

"In the Roundhead quarters in Orderhouse Six in Gallicia there's a column of water at the center of the Hall of Assembly," Marya sniffed. "It flows constantly upward, from the floor to the ceiling. There are fish in it, and plants, and strange creatures."

"And of course the Secretary has seen the Ring of Unchanging Fire in the Osman Orderhouse," Chloe said. "Beside such things our little glass ceiling must seem quite unremarkable."

Liliane looked at Chloe. "I've seen things that are wondrous, and very beautiful. But I've never seen the like of this ceiling."

Chloe smiled. Unlike the others, she had been in Britannia for most of her professional life, and was proud of the Northern Orderhouse and its works.

The ubiquitous red doors led off the courtyard, opening onto the workrooms and meeting chambers and offices of the Arm of the Stone. By contrast, the main record room, which took up one entire side of the court, was open all along the length that faced the garden. It was furnished in utilitarian style, with tables and benches, high desks and stools for copying, and ranks of floor-to-ceiling shelves filled with great leather-bound volumes. Mindlight obscured the ceiling like radiant smoke.

The record room was the preserve of the clerks. Marya, Chloe, and Lithhilde sought their copying desks. The two male clerks were already at work. They glanced up briefly as Liliane passed, returning almost at once to their parchments, as if their duties precluded curiosity.

Liliane moved toward the offices that opened off the main space. She avoided the two smallest, which would belong to the certified scriveners, Guilarmo and Anselm. A more sizeable office, empty, she assumed to be hers. The largest belonged to Tobias, the Chief Scrivener. He sat behind his desk, a massive man with skin so black it looked polished, absorbed in a scroll. He did not raise his eyes as Liliane approached, though she could feel his awareness of her presence. Taking her commission from her wallet, she laid it before him.

"I am Madelaine Lenoit, commissioned Secretary to the Arm-Master of the Northern Orderhouse, reporting for duty."

He looked up. His eyes were like circles of jet set in old ivory. Putting down his scroll, he took up her commission and began to scan it. His personal guard was excellent; even so, Liliane could clearly sense his mistrust. The ranks of the Arm-trained included women, but they generally did not rise higher than Scrivener. Though it was not unheard-of for a woman to achieve the rank of Secretary, it was decidedly unusual.

"Everything seems to be in order," Tobias said at last. His voice was the most profound bass Liliane had ever heard, each perfectly articulated word touched with an accent she could not place. "On behalf of my colleagues and myself, you are welcome in the Northern Orderhouse."

"Thank you, Chief Scrivener," Liliane replied.

"The vacancy in your position has created a substantial backlog. You may have today to familiarize yourself with our procedures and files, but you must begin your work tomorrow."

"I'm eager to take up my duties, Chief Scrivener."

Tobias reached into the open chest that stood beside his desk and produced a ring of keys.

"These are yours." With slow dignity he rose to his feet. "Follow me."

Each Orderhouse maintained its own system of record-keeping, no two quite the same. Here, Liliane learned, the leather folios were grouped by subject: Investigation Team reports, formal accounts of Investigations, records of Violation, records of punishment, and the dossiers of Violators and those under Watch. The files were kept chronologically, subdivided by Parish. A master volume provided keys, references, and cross-references. In addition to the general records, the scriveners for the respective Investigation Teams maintained the folios in which the Investigation transcripts were kept. The Arm-Master's Secretary was responsible for the Arm-Master's reports and other files.

For several hours Tobias conducted Liliane about. His manner, while never less than perfectly courteous, was formal to the point of coldness; the distrust she had sensed initially never modulated. He left her at midday, when the noon meal arrived, taking his food into his office and closing the door. Though the Arm of the Stone maintained its own refectory, its cooks did not serve the Arm-trained; their midday meal was prepared in the Orderhouse kitchens and fetched on trays by the clerks. The clerks ate in the main room, conversing softly among themselves. The scriveners sat together in one of their offices. Liliane, like Tobias, dined alone.

Liliane's office was lit by torches rather than mindlight. Deep-red hangings muffled the walls, and red rushes were strewn across the floor. There was a long open document case behind the desk, and a locked chest in which work in progress could be placed. On the wall opposite, four locked cabinets contained the Arm-Master's records—correspondence, reports, minutes of internal and other meetings, accounts of the annual Orderhouse probes, and personnel files.

High on the wall to the left of the desk, the hangings were cut out to accommodate an ornately fashioned iron grille. This was where the Catalogue was kept. Liliane found, on her ring of keys, the one that unlocked the grille. She pulled it open, silent on oiled hinges, to reveal a large wooden box, standing on its narrow end amid a welter of wine-colored velvet. With difficulty, for the box was very heavy, she removed it from its place. She laid it upon her desk and, with another of the keys on her ring, opened it. Inside lay the Catalogue, long and narrow and as thick as three fists. Its cover was of wood, painted a rich ruby color. The Roundhead symbol was carved upon it in heavy relief. Cabochon garnets were set at each of the four corners.

With reverent hands Liliane lifted the Catalogue from its box. She opened it to the first page. The sheet, tissue-thin, was divided by a thick line ruled in red ink. Each half of the page contained a column of names, written in archaic ancient script. The names were entered alphabetically, by

Parish. Each name was followed by a series of symbols. In most cases the notations were made in black, indicating fitness, but there were several names that carried the red sign of the handpower-prone. At the top of the sheet was written: "Year of the Stone 353 (Post Split)."

Liliane stood gazing at the neat ranks of names and symbols, their ink only slightly faded by the passage of so many years. She felt a sense of awe she could scarcely comprehend—not simply for the Catalogue, and its testament to the centuries of Guardian rule, but for the impossible circumstance that had brought her to stand here, gazing upon a thing none but the Arm of the Stone, and those they trained, were ever privileged to see. In the coming days she must examine its pages, not with reverence, but with the eye of a scrivener seeking forgery. She felt herself tremble. It seemed close to blasphemy.

Yet it was not blasphemy. She was here by order of the Arm of the Stone. She was, as Amias had reminded her the night before, its instrument.

Carefully she closed the Catalogue; gently she returned it to its box. She stood the box in place again and locked the iron grille. She turned her mind to more mundane matters. But she never quite lost awareness of the stone niche and what it held. That night, as she fell toward sleep, she seemed to see the garnets behind her eyes, like drops of old blood struck at their hearts with inner light.

Selwyn Forester did not call Liliane to his office that day, nor the next. A week passed, and still she had not met with him. He sent her work, mountains of it—minutes to be transcribed, letter- and report-drafts to be copied fair, expenses to be added and reconciled with receipts—but always by messenger. She locked the finished papers into her chest at night; in the morning they were gone, replaced by new ones, with detailed instructions in Selwyn's slashing, irregular hand. So overwhelming was the workload that she had not yet been able to spare time to begin her examination of the records.

As the days passed Liliane began to grow concerned. Was he so distrustful of her presence that he had determined to avoid her entirely? Often she saw him from a distance, moving swiftly through the garden or across the periphery of the main record room, a tall, slender figure, his back very straight. Whether alone or accompanied by others, he projected an aura of focused purpose, a sense of urgent destinations and vital tasks. The work she received showed him to be a man who focused with equal meticulousness upon a dizzying variety of issues—from the planning of the annual Progress to suspicious words overheard in the Orderhouse stables, there was nothing he seemed to consider beneath his attention.

Each morning, carefully, Liliane ran her hands over the papers he sent her. Her skill in divination made it possible for her to sense the echoes of emotion, if whoever had written the words had felt strongly enough when they were set down. But Selwyn's papers were entirely devoid of feeling— paper and ink, nothing more.

Eight days after her arrival, she unlocked her chest to take out the morning's work and found a note. It directed her to report to Selwyn's office at the tenth bell, so that she might record the minutes of the monthly meeting between the Arm-Master and the Abbot of the Orderhouse.

At the appointed time she rose from her desk, taking with her a set of wax-coated tablets and her stylus. She passed through the main record room and into the garden. Selwyn's office was immediately to the right; the architrave above his door was marked with the strange spiky symbols of the Arm of the Stone, a code only the Arm and their workers could read. She stood for a moment, gathering her resources. She was, she realized, extremely nervous.

Taking a deep breath, she lifted her hand and knocked.

''Come in,'' a voice called from within.

The chamber beyond was large. Abundant natural daylight poured through the two glass-paned windows that faced the garden, supplemented in the darker recesses of the room by standing torches. The furnishings were rich: a fine oak desk, a number of document cases crammed with scrolls and folios, an ornate standing bookshelf filled with leatherbound books, several chairs with tapestry cushions to soften their seats, choice hangings on the walls, and two sizeable woven rugs across the floor. Every object was of the highest quality, beautifully wrought, harmoniously combined; yet the whole was entirely utilitarian. There was no luxury beyond what was needed. Clearly this was a room not for show but for business.

Selwyn Forester sat behind the desk. The boy of memory had become a man; a neatly sculpted beard outlined his mouth and chin. But the dark eyes, the level brows, the strong and pleasing features, were just as Liliane recalled. His black robe, unadorned except for the gold chain from which his Guardian medal hung, emphasized the pallor of his skin. He did not wear the Roundhead crop, but kept his black hair long, pulled back and braided into a club at his neck. It was an affectation of Zosterians, a reflection of the traditional images of Zoster himself. Most Roundheads in the Orderhouse maintained this style; Amias and a few others were conspicuous by their exception.

Selwyn gestured to a chair. His fingers were long and well-kept. He wore no rings.

"Sit down," he said. His tone was cool and uninflected, the words utterly devoid of feeling. His steady gaze gave no hint of recognition. "It was remiss of me not to meet with you sooner. I apologize for that."

"I know you have many matters to occupy you, Master."

"Yes. This is a busy time for us. The annual Orderhouse probes will take place in a few weeks. And this year's Progress is only four months away; we've only just begun to plan. Have you had a chance yet to familiarize yourself with the Progress?"

"I've been looking through last year's reports, Master."

Selwyn nodded. "No doubt you've been told that the Progress is a substitute for the Raids. In fact it's a replacement of them, both in practice and in philosophy. The terror of the Raids breeds only hatred, and history shows that Violation is as likely to come from hatred as from inner unfitness or outer corruption. If you know anything about Zosterianism, you'll know that is a principle central to our philosophy."

As he spoke, very gently, Liliane reached out with her Gift. She sensed nothing; he was as opaque as his voice would indicate. It was very rare that she could not glean at least something from those she scanned. Perhaps more force would yield better results, but in spite of what Amias had told her she dared not try that yet. His body, she was interested to note, was as closed as his mind. He sat behind his desk with the precise degree of straightness, his hands clasped before him with the exact degree of looseness, as to convey absolutely nothing beyond the correctness of his posture.

"But you'll discover these things for yourself," he said. "In the coming months much of your work will relate to the Progress."

"Yes, Master."

There was a pause. He regarded her steadily with his long dark eyes. She waited, her gaze fixed on a point just below his chin.

"I think it's only fair to inform you that I've contacted my superiors to request you be removed from this position."

Liliane felt her heart leap into her throat. "Is my work not to your satisfaction, Master?" she managed to say.

"It's not your work. A few criticisms, as you saw in my notes, but otherwise very competent. No, it's simply that I'd already chosen someone for the position. I submitted an application after Linorio died. It wasn't until a few weeks ago that I learned you'd been appointed instead."

"I . . . was not aware, Master."

"I want someone familiar with this region, you see. Someone already trained in the methods and philosophy we follow here."

"Master, I have experience in many settings. Every Orderhouse is different—in each of them I've had to learn new ways of doing things. I'm completely confident I can become skilled in the methods you refer to. As to philosophy, I made it a point to thoroughly study Zosterianism before I came here. You'll find I have a full command of its principles."

"I'm not trying to cast aspersions on you or your abilities, Madelaine. You're obviously highly skilled. But we're trying something radically new here. Willingness to learn and outside familiarity with our precepts aside, you are a traditional Guardian, and that presents questions of bias I'm not prepared to deal with in the long term. The truth is, I prefer to have a Zosterian for my Secretary. As Linorio was.''

Liliane tried to hide her dismay. The Arm-trained generally maintained a scrupulous distance from political partisanship or preference, because of the risk such prejudice might taint their work. Nothing in the papers Jolyon had given her had indicated that things in the Northern Orderhouse might be otherwise.

"Master, you need not fear bias in me. I'm Arm-trained. I don't allow opinion or belief to affect my work.''

He shook his head. "I've made up my mind. I'm sorry you've journeyed all this way for nothing, but there it is.''

His gaze was level, his voice neutral, his words as final as a closing door. All at once Liliane was utterly certain that he knew it all—her charge, her identity. She shook the feeling off. All members of the Arm possessed the ability to make one feel they knew everything, whether they actually did or not. If he had really penetrated her deception, he would have gotten rid of her at once, without bothering to go through official channels.

"Unfortunately," he continued, "these things move slowly. It will probably take several months for my request to be approved. In the meantime, we're stuck with each other. I hope we can both make the best of that.''

For the first time Liliane met his eyes directly. "I intend to do everything I can to change your opinion of me, Master, through the quality of my service.''

He held her gaze for a moment. Then, smoothly, he shifted his eyes away and rose to his feet.

"It's time for our meeting. Come.''

He led the way across the court to one of the smaller conference rooms. It was draped with tapestries and fabrics in every shade of red, crimson, scarlet, and maroon; a long table was set at its center, surrounded by six high-backed chairs. The Abbot and his two assistants were already seated. They rose to their feet and bowed when Selwyn entered—the assistants deeply, the Abbot with no more than a slight inclination of his head.

Selwyn took a chair across from the Journeyers. Liliane

seated herself on a high stool in the corner of the room. As the meeting progressed she took notes in the rapid shorthand she had developed herself, transcribing the participants' statements verbatim. Later, she would make two copies. One, with every word complete, would be placed in the Arm-Master's files; the other, with dialogue summarized rather than reproduced, would be provided to the Abbot.

After a brief discussion of routine matters—the progress of those under discipline, a review of the travelers currently lodged at the Orderhouse, a short report by the Abbot on general Orderhouse business—the meeting centered upon plans for the annual mindprobes. While in Pietra's service, Liliane had perfected a technique of doubling her attention; half her mind attended to her flying stylus, while with the other half she scanned and analyzed the emotions that filled the room. The two assistants were uncomfortable in Arm territory. The Abbot, beneath his businesslike manner, harbored a profound dislike for Selwyn—not merely, she suspected, for the fact that he was a Roundhead, but for himself. From Selwyn there was no emotion whatsoever. Now and then the angle of his head, or the motion of his hand, would convey a flash of impatience; otherwise he was blank. Liliane was beginning to find his opacity disturbing. It was as if he were not a man, but the image of one—an effigy substituted for the real Selwyn, who might be somewhere far away, or nowhere at all.

The meeting ended, and Liliane was dismissed. The last she saw of Selwyn was his straight figure moving swiftly across the garden.

She returned to her office. She began her copying, using black ink for the Arm-Master's files and red ink for the Abbot's: for documents sent to outsiders, the authorship of the Arm of the Stone must always be immediately apparent. But she could not concentrate. In her mind she saw Selwyn's face, an image as flat as a painting. The doubts she had put aside, in her room in the nonresident section of the Journeyer Wing, rose up before her again. He was everything she had feared: powerful, formidable, accomplished— and as closed as a dungeon. It would take time to work her purpose against such a man. The six months Jolyon had

allowed her had seemed generous, but given Selwyn's intent
to dismiss her, the time available to her might actually be
much less. How could Jolyon have omitted from her briefing
so important a piece of information as the former Secretary's
Zosterianism? Why had he not added this to the false identity he had so carefully constructed? But Jolyon was a
Roundhead, with a Roundhead's typical arrogance. The
Arm-trained might be Guardians, but in their most essential
definition they were servants—interchangeable, faceless,
their loyalty as entirely assumed as it was rarely noticed. It
had probably never occurred to Jolyon that one Arm-trained
functionary could be much different from another.

Liliane sat back in her chair, laying her pen across the
inkwell. A headache sat behind her eyes. In the main record
room she could hear the muted sounds of work; a murmur
of voices from Tobias's office attested to a meeting in progress between himself and the two scriveners. The little oil
lamps on her desk cast a yellow light across the few para-
graphs she had managed to transcribe.

Her gaze, roving across the surfaces of her office, fell
upon the grille that guarded the Catalogue. On impulse she
rose to her feet, took up her keys, and removed the heavy
box from its place. Laying the Catalogue before her on her
desk, she opened it to the current year.

Since her arrival she had twice been required to make
notations in the Catalogue, but an odd reticence had so far
held her from closer examination. She felt no reluctance
now. Eagerly she turned the pages, moving backward
through time until she reached the year of Selwyn Forester's
arrival in Britannia. Seven years he had been here. Seven
years; twenty pages; forty columns of names, each repre-
senting a child's first entry into Guardian School.

Carefully, moving forward now, Liliane scanned the records of Selwyn's tenure. She ran a practiced gaze down the
columns, searching for the uneven ink-shades of addition,
the minute roughness of erasure, the small irregularities of
substitution. She found nothing. Next, closing her eyes, she
drew her fingers slowly across the pages, seeking through
her skill in divination the small flashing traces of emotion.
Still nothing.

She opened her eyes, sighing. The years of Selwyn's Mastership were blank and perfect, as blank and perfect as Selwyn himself, at least to an initial examination. A more minute search was possible, utilizing a gazing glass and a special wash that revealed writings-over. But she did not expect closer scrutiny to contradict her initial impression. There was no forgery here.

She paged backward again, carefully turning the tissue-thin sheets. She reached the year of Selwyn's arrival, and passed it. Still she paged, not knowing exactly why.

Ten years from her starting point, she found what she was looking for.

It was a page like all the others; but as she touched it she felt something beneath her fingers: a jolt, a spark. She closed her eyes, running her hand down the columns of names. There it was, the very ghost of emotion, like a faint and fleeting scent. Delicately, she brought her power to bear. It might be rage; it might be love. It might be fear. It might be all of those.

Opening her eyes, she put her face close to the parchment. Toward the bottom of the first column, in the section devoted to the Parish of Anadh, she was able to pinpoint the source of her perception: the name Elene Jevalse. Written beside the name was the number three, in black, indicating an average level of fitness; the number was followed by an "X," also in black, denoting that Elene Jevalse did not count among the Gifted.

Liliane dug into the little carved box that held her scrivening tools, and took out her gazing glass. It showed her no indication of alteration. Yet the feeling of change the entry carried was unmistakable. Setting the glass aside, she altered her focus. This time she was rewarded. A semblance had been brushed across the name, tissue-thin, yet enormously powerful. Had it not been for the emotions entwined within it, she might never have perceived it. As it was, she could not get all the way through it, not enough to read what it covered. But as she concentrated her Gift the stain of red seemed to crawl across the paper, bleeding through from underneath.

It was the mark of the handpower-prone that had been

covered up. Blurred though the evidence was, Liliane was completely certain of this.

She put her glass away and closed the Catalogue. She had found forgery, indisputable proof of guilt. But of whose guilt, she could not say. The alteration, in a period ten years before Selwyn had come to the Northern Diocese, need not have been made by him. She had a name, however—Elene Jevalse—and a Parish—Anadh. If she could discover who Elene Jevalse was, she might be able to deduce who had made the change. If it did turn out to be Selwyn, even Jolyon could not wish for better evidence.

Getting to her feet, Liliane replaced the Catalogue in its niche. She returned to her copying. The confidence of purpose had returned to her. What she had found today was as much a mystery as it was a discovery. But if she could penetrate so subtle and delicate a deception, surely nothing could remain closed to her, not even the monolithic blankness of Selwyn Forester himself.

Fourteen

ILIANE PUT down her pen and flexed her fingers to ease them. On the walls of her office the torches burned, straight and unchanging. The oil lamps on her desk, which she used to illuminate close work, guttered slightly in the soft currents of air drifting in from the courtyard.

In the main room, she could just hear the sounds of the Arm-trained leaving for the night, an invariable order of departure that ended every workday. The male clerks went first, separately, followed by the female clerks, in a group. Next were the scriveners, if they were present and not off on assignment with the Investigation Teams. Some time after the scriveners, Liliane departed. Last was Tobias, who remained after the others to complete an inventory of the day's work, reshelve any folios that had been taken down for use, and check that the chests and cabinets that held confidential documents were locked.

Tonight, however, Liliane would outstay Tobias. Selwyn had ordered her to attend him at the nineteenth bell; he had not indicated how late she must remain, but Liliane suspected it would be very late indeed. The annual Progress commenced at dawn tomorrow, and there was much to be done before then.

With a sigh, she returned to her task. She was writing out, from Selwyn's draft, the forty-ninth of fifty copies of the Progress's itinerary. Completed documents, rolled and tied with red cord and sealed with the heavy seal of the Arm of the Stone, lay neatly stacked in a basket on her desk. Tonight, after she had finished, runners from the Orderhouse would set out in advance of the Progress party, delivering the itineraries to all the Resident Journeyers of the Northern Diocese, who were required to post them in a prominent position so that anyone who wished could know where the Arm of the Stone planned to go. Unlike the Raids, with their careful secrecy and reliance upon surprise, the Progress opened itself at nearly every point to the light of public knowledge.

Over the course of the next two months, the Progress party would traverse the whole of the northern half of the Northern Diocese, passing through all the major settlements and many of the more isolated habitations as well. Along the way Journeyer Ordermen would be probed, Resident Journeyers evaluated, the census of deaths and births updated from local records, any changes in the fitness ratings of the pupils of the Guardian Schools emended, the names and classifications of children entering the Schools for the first time recorded, and the orthodoxy of the people and communities of the north thoroughly assessed. The complexity of the journey, and the amount of work it must accomplish, were staggering. Preparation for it had occupied the majority of Liliane's time over the past months.

Though Selwyn required those around him to be fully informed on all relevant issues, he did not consider it his responsibility to provide that information. Beyond his general exposition at their first meeting he had not briefed Liliane on the Progress at all. The huge Progress reports were of some help; for detailed information, however, Liliane turned to Tobias. Despite his distrust of her, he was quite willing to expound on the Progress, and Zosterianism in general. Linorio had not been the only Arm-trained in the Northern Orderhouse to follow Zosterian philosophy: Tobias was Zosterian also, as were both the scriveners.

"How familiar are you with Zosterian doctrine?" he asked her.

"I have a good command of the general principles."

"You know the Substitutions, then."

"Yes." The Five Substitutions were a set of maxims that formed a nutshell manifesto of Zosterian ideology, an expression of the new practice with which the old ways were to be replaced: Participation for Separation. Intervention for Observation. Cooperation for Coercion. Dispensation for Sequestration. Prevention for Apprehension.

"As you've no doubt deduced from the work you've been given, the Arm-Master's goal is to initiate practices throughout the Diocese that fulfill all five of the Substitutions." Tobias's large jet-and-ivory eyes never moved from Liliane's face as he spoke. Because he rarely blinked, his regard possessed a fixed intensity even a Roundhead might have envied. "The first purpose of the Progress is to ensure that the Resident Journeyers are fulfilling this goal. The second is to monitor the orthodoxy of the people without resorting to the terror of the Raids. We want their understanding, not their fear."

"Cooperation for Coercion."

"Precisely. There's a third purpose as well. When Zoster founded the Arm of the Stone, he charged it not only with the enforcement of orthodoxy but with its preservation. Over the centuries, however, the Arm has come to pursue enforcement alone. For all practical purposes, preservation is left in the hands of the Residents. Now even if the Arm had the power to free itself of any part of its charge, does it make sense for such a responsibility to be left to common Journeyers?"

Like all Arm-trained, Tobias had thoroughly absorbed his masters' snobbery. "I suppose not," Liliane admitted.

"The Progress restores the Arm to the whole of its charge. It brings us back into the world and places us among the people, in accordance with the First Substitution. It enables us to monitor orthodoxy at first hand rather than at some distant remove, in accordance with the second. And it makes it possible for us to confront Violation before it occurs, rather than only after it has been committed, in accordance with the fifth. It is this, at least as much as the new methods of governance, that has led to the drop in Violation you have no doubt noted in your perusal of our records."

Tobias was nothing if not acute. Almost from the first, Liliane had been aware that he was keeping a watch on her.

"Is it the same in the other Orderhouses?" she asked. She had been greatly surprised to discover that there were

six other Orderhouses that followed Zosterian principles.
Nothing in the papers Jolyon had given her had indicated
that Selwyn's methods were not unique.

"Yes. Of course, these figures are disputed by those who
fail to understand the new methods, and imagine that Zosterians simply employ leniency in handling error. But that
is not so. The decline is a real one. A few more years and
no one will be able to deny it."

"And then?"

"And then we will bring the Progress to more Orderhouses, and still more Orderhouses, until new practice has
entirely replaced the old. Ten years ago Zosterianism did
not exist. Ten years from now, who knows? Perhaps the
whole world will be Zosterian."

His polished dark features did not change, but in the intensity of his unblinking gaze she read the certainty of his
belief. In the purity of that devotion she could find no trace
of falseness, no hint of duplicity. If there were deception in
the Northern Orderhouse, Tobias was not part of it.

"Of course," he continued, "the Progress is more than
just ideology. It also offers a host of administrative advantages. By conducting the probes on-site we relieve the Journeyers of the burden of traveling to the Orderhouse every
two years. The census and the Catalogue are much more
accurate when updated from the actual records rather than
from the Residents' reports. Requiring the reports themselves to be delivered orally vastly improves their quality—
as you can imagine, information is much more likely to be
accurate when it is presented directly to the Arm-Master.
And conducting the performance evaluations in the Residences means that the Residents can be judged not only on
what they say of themselves, but on the actual state of their
Parishes."

"Aren't the evaluations traditionally the Abbot's duty?"

"Tradition is not our concern. The performance of the
Residents touches very closely upon the people's orthodoxy.
Where orthodoxy is at issue it is more appropriate for the
Arm-Master to be responsible."

"That seems a considerable expansion," Liliane said cautiously, "of the Arm's authority."

Tobias raised his eyebrows, with a haughtiness that was the equal of any of his masters'. "It's high time the guardians of orthodoxy participated more directly in the governance of the Dioceses. Even a traditional should be able to agree with that."

But if this seemed self-evident to Tobias and the scriveners and Selwyn's Roundheads, others were less convinced. Among ordinary Journeyers, antipathy toward the Progress was pronounced. The Abbot in particular was deeply offended by the encroachment upon his rule. But the Arm-Master's mandate exceeded his own, and he had no choice but to cooperate.

"I'm about to lock up now."

Tobias stood in the doorway. Behind him, in the main record room, the mindlight had dwindled to its nighttime level. In his dark robe, with his dusky skin, he seemed to fade into the dimness.

"Is there anything you need before I go?" he asked.

Liliane shook her head. "I have everything here."

"Good speed on your journey tomorrow. And success."

Liliane smiled. "Thank you, Chief Scrivener."

Tobias inclined his head, with the massive dignity that informed all his actions. In the process of working together they had become amicable, but only in the guarded manner of colleagues who are not quite equals. He turned, and was gone.

Liliane put the last word to the last copy, and set her pen upon its stand. Her hand and arm ached with the writing she had done today. Scattering sand to dry the ink, she rolled the parchment tightly and tied it with a length of red cord, to which the Roundhead seal had already been affixed. She placed the parchment in the basket, and then, rising to her feet, began to make her way toward the entrance to the Roundhead quarters. She would leave the basket outside the door. Within moments, the itineraries would be in the hands of the runners.

The nightbound garden and the empty halls seemed strange in their desertion. The door to the foyer swung open as Liliane approached it; it was still standing open when she returned. She did not know how large the Roundhead domain was, or how many people it housed; she had never been beyond this corridor or the garden or the rooms that surrounded it. But it had always struck her as strange that, as many times as she had passed this way, she had never encountered another soul.

She crossed the silent garden, close to Selwyn's door, casting out the net of her Gift as she passed. She felt, as usual, nothing.

In the record room, the night-dimmed mindlight was as faint as the moon. From the shelves in her office she began to gather the folios and parchments she would need for the journey, packing them into wooden carrying boxes. The slash of golden light beneath Selwyn's door hovered at the back of her mind as she worked. The nothingness she had sensed behind it gnawed at her, sharp and unwelcome in its reminder of failure.

In her four months in the Northern Orderhouse, she had come close to fulfilling the first part of her charge. In spite of her crushing workload and Tobias's observation, she had finished her survey of the records and archives, and examined the whole of the Catalogue. The records confirmed the changes Tobias had described: as near as she could judge, Violation rates were four-fifths of what they had been seven years ago, when Selwyn first took office. As Amias had predicted, there was no trace of forgery, alteration, or substitution to contradict this. There might be elision, but that could not be confirmed without access to local records.

She had completed thorough scans of all the Roundheads in the Orderhouse, as well as of the Arm-trained and many of the other Orderhouse personnel. The majority of the Roundheads were Selwyn's men, passionately committed to the new practice to which the Northern Diocese was being shaped. Behind their heavy guards she could detect no duplicity, nor did she find the telltale traces that marked the presence of illegal barriers. The Arm-trained were equally free of deceit, as loyal to Selwyn as the Roundheads were. Selwyn commanded, in fact, a quite extraordinary allegiance from those who supported him, though outside the ranks of his own people he seemed to have attained a level of unpopularity unprecedented even for an Arm-Master. Liliane had heard as many rumors, accusations, and speculations as there were people to give them, most of them motivated as much by personal dislike as by conflict of belief. The few Roundheads who, like Amias, openly opposed Zosterian rule were the worst of all.

But rumors were not fact; accusations were not proof. In four months of effort she had found no hard evidence of Zosterian duplicity, political or otherwise. Until the Progress was over she would not be entirely sure, but she was beginning to believe Jolyon had been mistaken in his conviction of chicanery. She did not look forward to bringing him news of this. But she was confident of her work. A mindprobe, she knew, would prove the thoroughness of her investigation.

The second part of her charge was another matter. Four months of strenuous effort had not gained her entry into even the shallowest layers of Selwyn's mind. She had tried a hundred different approaches, a hundred different techniques, a hundred different levels of intensity. She had long ago abandoned caution, and now routinely utilized the full force of her Gift. But no matter what she did, she could not get through. His defenses repelled her as easily as a wall resisting a pebble. So strong was his guard that she could not even trace its shape.

Nothing like this had ever happened to her before. In the course of her career she had confronted powerful Journeyers, arrogant noblemen, convoluted deceptions. There had not been one that did not eventually yield a chink, a crack, an imperfection; there had not been one, once she knew its nature, that she had not been able to break. But Selwyn seemed to have no flaws at all. She had not been able to discover a single weak point in his defenses; she could not even find an irregularity where her Gift might gain a toehold. By stringent observation she had learned to read the muted language of his body, and to interpret the subtle tones of his voice. Yet these things were on the surface only. All the rest was closed to her. In all her life she had never encountered a person so opaque.

She was aware that the things she had accomplished—the completion of the first half of her mission, the forgery she had discovered in the Catalogue—would mean nothing if she failed to pierce Selwyn's mind. Success in one part of her charge could not absolve or mitigate insufficiency in another. The men who had sent her here did not recognize partial achievement. There was complete success, or there was failure, and that was all.

The Progress offered some hope. It was possible, outside the regimented confines of the Orderhouse, that Selwyn's guard might loosen. There was also a scheduled two-day stop in the Parish of Anadh, which might enable her to discover more precisely the meaning of the altered entry in the Catalogue. But it was just as possible that neither of these things would come to pass, and she would return to the Orderhouse emptyhanded. If that proved to be the case, there was only one option remaining to her, only one technique she had not tried. From the night she met with Jolyon, she had banished from her mind any consideration that her mission could not be accomplished by conventional means. She had made a promise to herself, a resolution she had believed would forever mark the outermost boundary of her duty to her masters. But as time passed and her failure came more and more to seem set in stone, she began to wonder whether principle was a luxury she could afford. Jolyon's words returned to her: *If mindscan and scrivening cannot get you what you need, you must turn to other methods.* In spite of Amias's insinuations, Selwyn had never once, by look or word, indicated the slightest awareness of her as a woman. Yet his guard, which concealed so much, might conceal this also.

A few months ago, even to think of such a thing would have seemed inconceivable. In reality, however, there was only one thing she could not conceive, and that was to come before Jolyon with her mission uncompleted. Risk she could live with, and shame, and compromise. But not failure.

The sound of the bell brought Liliane from her uncomfortable reverie. She gathered up her stylus and tablet and made her way through the murky record room, passing into the deeper dimness of the garden. At Selwyn's door she paused, closing her eyes and breathing deeply, gathering her resolve.

Inside his chamber, all was warmth and light. The torches burned in their stands, and dark red drapes had been let down to cover the glass of the two windows. Selwyn was working, writing rapidly upon a piece of vellum. The candles beside him drew flashes from the metal inlay of his pen and the gold of his Guardian medal. His brows and beard were black brushstrokes across his face. His hair, loose, flowed halfway down his back.

Liliane seated herself in her usual place, facing Selwyn across his desk. He looked up, acknowledging her presence with a nod. Despite his initial coldness, they had developed a cordial working relationship over the past months, so much so that now and then she allowed herself to hope he had set aside his distrust of her. Not that it mattered—Amias had informed her that Jolyon had long ago intercepted and destroyed Selwyn's request for her replacement.

"I'll be done in a moment," he said, his pen barely pausing.

Behind him, the door to his bedchamber stood slightly ajar. Candlelight flickered in the opening, and a shadow moved across it. As Amias had implied, Selwyn's bed was rarely empty; Liliane herself had seen at least three different women, slipping out of his rooms as she made her way to work. She could not help wondering what sort of unGifted woman would willingly sleep with a Roundhead. Or perhaps the possibility of choice had been removed. What would it be like to come so close to someone as closed and controlled as Selwyn? Though in the dark, maybe he was not so closed . . . Her earlier train of thought returned, overtaking her with images she tried, and failed, to push away.

Selwyn finished the document he was working on and set his pen aside. From a covered pitcher on a table behind him he poured two cups of steaming liquid and set one before her. Gratefully Liliane took the drink. She had not eaten since noon. The Orderhouse kitchens made no provision for delivering more than one meal a day to the Arm-trained.

For an hour she took notes from Selwyn's dictation. There were final instructions to the Deputy Arm-Master, who would preside in Selwyn's absence, a note to the Abbot, several letters to be sent by conventional delivery, and a number of short communications, dealing with more urgent matters, for Tobias, who with his farspeaking Gift would relay the information directly to the recipients. In the course of her work Liliane had acquired considerable respect for Selwyn's administrative ability. Violator he might be, but he was also an able leader: precise, decisive and thorough. He demanded a great deal from those who served him, yet he also owned a keen sense of their ability, allowing them considerable latitude in judgment and rarely interfering in their decisions. It was this, perhaps, that accounted for the Orderhouse's organized and cooperative atmosphere, the absence of the edgy tension that marked other groupings of the Arm of the Stone.

"That's all, I think," Selwyn said at last. "Is there anything I've left out?"

"Jostin Mallowmere," Liliane said. "The Southern Arm-Master has requested information on him. He recently moved to the Southern Diocese from one of the northern Parishes, and has applied for a commission as wheelwright."

Selwyn made one of the quick gestures she had learned to interpret as annoyance. "I'd forgotten about that. Take care of it, will you?"

"Yes, Master," she said, making a notation on her tablet, trying not to think of the additional time it would take to search the records properly and compose a letter of reply.

"Is everything ready for tomorrow?"

"Yes, Master. The kitchens have bundled provisions and the storeroom has assembled supplies. This morning I checked the items against the travel inventory and arranged for everything to be transferred to the stables. I confirmed arrangements with the stablemaster; the horses and mules will be saddled and loaded before first light. I also spoke with members of the party to make sure there's nothing more they need, and gave final instructions to the castellan. I've already started packing the documents and records you requested. I'll see to their loading myself."

Selwyn nodded. "Good. Very good." He seemed to hesitate. "I want you to know, Madelaine, that I appreciate your efforts. The smoothness of this year's preparation owes a great deal to you.''

''I'm gratified to hear you say so, Master.'' It was extremely rare for him to offer any kind of praise. Liliane was surprised to find how much it pleased her.

Selwyn pushed back his chair and crossed slowly to the hearth. His hands were clasped behind his back; his black robe swung about his red boots. Though he disdained the ostentation of ornament, his taste for luxury was in its way as highly developed as any Roundhead's. His clothes were of the finest brocades and wools, with black embroidery about the hems and cuffs. The black shirt he wore, its high collar rising above the neck of his robe, was silk. His scarlet belt was a wide strap of buttery leather; his boots, crafted to the precise shape of his foot, were never marred by scuffs or unevennesses in the red dye. The chain that held his Guardian-medal was of a restrained yet pleasing design, more attractive in its simplicity than the thick ropes of gold favored by other Roundheads.

''You've served me well these past few months,'' he said, staring into the flames. His aquiline profile was edged in light. ''The work we do, especially the Progress, has little similarity to the traditional procedures you're used to. Yet I don't think you've given me any less diligence than you'd show someone of the old school.''

''I told you when we first met, Master, that I don't let ideology affect my work.''

''No, you don't, do you,'' he said. ''It's an odd thing. You make a better Arm-trained than most of those here, in the strict sense of the term.''

''Master?'' said Liliane, puzzled.

''Never mind.'' Turning, he paced toward his desk. His smooth black hair had fallen forward over one shoulder; he tossed it back, a quick, practiced gesture. All his motions were like this, strong and graceful, a balance of perfect ease and absolute control. He seated himself again, straight-backed, his hands clasped with precise symmetry on the arms of his chair.

''However open-minded you think you are, you'll find what follows much more difficult,'' he said. ''Standing eye to eye with change is very different from dealing with it on paper. Even confirmed Zosterians find some of the principles I advocate hard to accept. You, being traditional . . .''

"On the contrary." Liliane sensed an opening. "I'm looking forward to it. These past four months . . . when I first arrived, all I knew of Zosterianism was what I'd read. But reading can't convey the . . . the vitality of what's happening in the Northern Diocese. I'm impressed by what I've seen here. I welcome the opportunity to see more.''

"Really?" He watched her with his long dark eyes. "Your resumé doesn't suggest such flexibility.''

"I have no control over my assignments, Master. Where I've been doesn't necessarily reflect who I am.''

He smiled a little. "That's a neat statement. Perhaps you'll use it in your next posting, when your new Master voices his concern over your stint among Zosterians.''

"I hope you don't think me so facile, Master.''

"Of course not, Madelaine. I'm well aware that you're never less than perfectly sincere.''

He was needling her. He did this now and then, as if it gave him some sort of private amusement. It pleased her, in a brief reversal of the balance between them, to refuse a response.

"I meant what I said, Master," she replied quietly. "My service is to others, but my thoughts are my own.''

"Of that," he said, "I am not in any doubt at all.''

As she often did when she was with him, Liliane felt herself thrown off-balance, in a way she could not satisfactorily define. She dropped her gaze, fixing it on the surface of his desk.

"Well," he said. "If you're really interested in the changes we're working here, there couldn't be a better opportunity than the next two months to learn about them. The Progress, more than anything else, lies at the heart of our endeavor to take Zosterian reform out of the realm of theory and into action.''

"Tobias tells me that the six other Progress Orderhouses show results similar to yours.''

"Yes, though they haven't been in operation as long. Of course, the fact that all the Zosterian Orderhouses are located in forsaken corners of the world like Britannia makes our success easy to ignore. Then again, places like these offer a freedom that wouldn't be available elsewhere.''

''I should think it would be hard to argue with a one-fifth reduction in the Violation rate. Not to mention the marked decrease in incidences of rebellion and sabotage.''

He looked at her. ''As always, you have complete command of the facts.''

''Not complete enough, Master.''

He raised his eyebrows. ''How so?''

''As I said before, my knowledge of Zosterianism is only a book knowledge. But I want to change that. I've been anticipating the Progress, as a chance to gain real understandings to put in place of theoretical ones. I want to be able to serve you as your Secretary should, Master. As Linorio did.''

His expression tightened. Beneath the control of his manner, Selwyn's moods shifted unpredictably, like conflicting currents beneath the surface of still water. Liliane could not feel the alterations, but she had learned to read them, in the drawing of his brows, the flick of his glance. What she saw now told her she had misstepped.

''I don't think you need to be concerned with that.'' His voice was formal. ''Such learning, in any case, will hardly benefit you in your future career.''

Liliane bowed her head, recognizing closure. ''Yes, Master,'' she murmured.

''Well. You have work to do, and so do I. You'd better go.''

Liliane got to her feet, making the slight obeisance that was customary. He acknowledged her with a brief nod, bending once more to his writing. The scratch of his pen followed her as she moved toward the door. She sensed, as she often did, the completeness of his dismissal—as if, once their business was done, she simply ceased to exist. Tonight, for some reason, this evoked in her a startling flash of anger. She felt, obscurely, that he should not be able to ignore her so completely, as if she were no more than the Arm-trained Secretary she pretended to be.

Dismayed at her own irrationality, she sought her office.

She dropped her tablet and stylus on her desk and, despite the mountain of papers that waited for her, sat for some time staring at the tapestried wall opposite, disciplining her mind to meditation. Like the pause before she knocked on Selwyn's door, this had become a habit—it helped dim to bearable levels the acute sense of inadequacy any contact with him produced. Tonight calm was difficult to find. It was a long time before she picked up her pen and turned her mind to work.

Many hours later, her head buzzing with weariness, she blotted the final words, cleaned her pen, and rose to her feet. Gathering up her work, she took it into Tobias's office, placing it on his desk where he would find it and deal with it tomorrow. In the moonlike dimness of the mindlight she passed through the record room and out into the garden. The air was moist, touched faintly with the scent of roses. The light beneath Selwyn's door showed he still worked, laboring even later than she.

Pausing, she listened, with her Gift and all her senses, reaching deep inside the weight of quiet that lay upon the courtyard. Almost, she could hear something, faint and distant, like the sighing of the ocean. Her mind seemed to approach it, like someone moving through trees toward the water's edge.

She closed her eyes. She laid the length of her body against the wood of Selwyn's door, turning her cheek against its chilly surface, spreading her fingers across its rough planks. With all her strength she reached out, not really knowing if what drew her was Selwyn, or simply the mutter of others' emotions that filled the Roundhead quarters. She was no longer aware of the solid surface she leaned upon; she seemed to have passed through it and into a wider space. It had been a long time since she opened herself so fully, abandoned so entirely the guard with which she normally bounded her Gift. Perhaps it was weariness that made it possible now. But exhaustion sapped her control. Instead of ranging out she felt herself falling toward the dark place at the center of her being, pulled irresistibly toward a refuge she had not known she needed.

As she descended, into a quiet more perfect than any

physical silence, she felt . . . something. Not emotion, not feelings, not any gleaning of her Gift, but a presence. A wall. Huge and dark, without chink or crack or crevice, it seemed to reach up and out forever, like the stretch of the Fortress across its alpine meadow. This wall too cradled at its heart a pulse of power, a current of light, a blaze of being . . . she could sense it clearly, even through the adamantine stones. . . .

Selwyn?

But it was gone, the wall and what it held, like a glimpse through a window passed and left behind. Dizzily she pulled back. It was a struggle, for she had gone very deep. Emerging, a strange wild longing gripped her, a reaching of her soul, for what she did not know. It swept through her like a wind, and then was gone, leaving her empty and close to tears.

For a moment, too weary to move, she leaned against the door. The silence of the night enfolded her, deep as the sky. When at last she pulled away, she saw that the illumination beneath Selwyn's door had vanished. He had doused his candles and gone in to his mistress.

It was cold the next morning as the Progress party gathered in the stables, and dark, for the sun had yet to rise. Liliane huddled in Costares's cloak, shivering, as Selwyn performed a meticulous predeparture check of baggage and equipment. Pale and severe in his black traveling cloak, he looked as if he had slept the whole night through, rather than only an hour or two or, perhaps, not at all.

At last everything was disposed to his satisfaction. The party mounted and clattered toward the gates, the horses' hooves echoing hollowly off the cobbles of the courtyard. Though the sky had paled with the coming dawn, the earth was still drowned in darkness; Liliane could barely see the horse in front of her. But Selwyn, in the lead, rode unfalteringly over the rising hills and out onto the moors that washed like a shallow ocean against the back walls of the Orderhouse. By the time it was full light, Liliane could see that they followed a narrow road, more a track than a thoroughfare, winding among the hills and hummocks. Most of their travel during the next two months would be along such ways. The level stones of the Guardian Roads—and civilization itself, if Marya and Lithhilde were to be believed— ended at the Orderhouse.

The night before, exhausted beyond words, Liliane had made her way to the Cloister Court, where Amias was waiting, chafing at her lateness. She had come to dread these meetings, not simply because of the difficulty of the reports—she could not allow Amias to know how unsuccessful she was in regard to Selwyn himself, nor did she wish to hand over to him her only discovery, the name of Elene Jevalse—but because of Amias himself. Since their first meeting, he had behaved toward her with ever-increasing familiarity, as if his knowledge of her supposed history gave him license to stand too close to her in the darkness, to stare openly at her breasts and hips while she reported to him, to allow his mindspeech to stray into inappropriately intimate modes. At their last meeting he had forced her to walk with him along the pathways of the Cloister Court, pinioning her arm under his and pulling her close against his side, careless of who might see them. Had it not been important to his view of himself that he remain true to the Celibate Rule, she had no doubt he would not have stopped there. Even so, knowing she was a heartsenser, he did not attempt to disguise the salacious pleasure he took in touching her—as if, having done what she supposedly had done, she had lost the right to object to such attention.

She had no choice but to endure it. Amias was her only contact with Jolyon, and a great deal depended on his goodwill. Also, at least in the beginning, his interest in her had served to distract him from the slim content of her reports. But for all his egotism, Amias was not a stupid man. Hints about inconsistencies in Selwyn's behavior, tedious details of her questioning of other Guardians, and excuses about the heaviness of her workload had ceased to satisfy him. For the past month, he had been growing more and more impatient.

<A disappointing report,> he thought when she had finished. Once again they were pacing the paths of the Cloister Court, her arm locked in his, his hip brushing against her

with every step. <Surely after all this time you should have more to tell me.>

<I've used the past four months to crystallize my suspicions, Master, and confirm the directions in which I need to work. The Progress should make things much clearer. I believe I'll discover something important.>

<And what might that be?>

<I'd prefer not to say until I'm certain. I'm sure I'll have a great deal to tell you when I return.>

And pray the Stone that would be true. She could feel Amias's sour annoyance.

<Make sure you do,> he thought. <You have little time left. The Progress marks the limit of your stay here.>

<That's only six months, Master. Master Jolyon told me I could have eight, if I needed them. And . . . there's a possibility it might take even longer.>

<Longer?> He came to a halt, pulling her round to face him. <What do you mean?>

<You know better than anyone the difficulties I face, Master.> It was an effort to keep her thoughts compliant. <Selwyn Forester is an extraordinary man. The methods that work on ordinary Guardians are too crude for him. These things have slowed my progress.>

He glared at her. He was gripping both her arms now, his fingers digging into her flesh. <Are you telling me you cannot enter his mind?>

<No, Master, I'm not. I'm just saying that it's more difficult than I expected. If I'm to complete this mission as it should be completed, I need more time.>

<This request doesn't please me. It won't please Jolyon either.>

<I'm sorry, Master. I wouldn't make it if it weren't necessary. I know how important this mission is. I share your sense of urgency.>

There was a pause. She could feel suspicion turning behind his flat face, as gray as week-old bread in the moonlight. She forced herself to stand still in his grip, to return his pop-eyed gaze with guileless innocence, though she felt as if her loathing of him would tear her apart.

<I'll relay your request to Jolyon,> he thought at last. <We'll see what he has to say.>

<I'm grateful, Master.>

She tried to pull away. But his fingers tightened. He bent his head, bringing his face within inches of her own.

<I don't have your Gift,> he thought. <But I'm not a fool. I can tell when someone's trying to lead me around by the nose. The Progress had better yield what you say it will. I won't be so easy to persuade the next time.>

Liliane took several deep, silent breaths. <I understand, Master,> she thought, when she felt able to project the proper degree of subservience.

He let her go then, and she returned to her room, feeling as if an hour in scalding water would not be enough to free her of the feeling of his touch. Riding along the narrow track, she could still recapture the shadow of the desperation that had descended on her. It was not Amias she feared— she could resist him if she had to. But she must have something to resist him with. The Progress must yield something. It must.

There were twelve in the party. They rode along the track in single file, Selwyn in the lead. After him came the Investigation Team Primary, a tall man named Colmagh who was native to Britannia, and wore his red hair wound up in the topknot favored by the people of the North. Next rode the members of Colmagh's Team, five Roundheads who had worked with him since leaving the Fortress fifteen years before. Liliane followed, the scrivener Anselm behind her. The servants, with four packmules on a link-lead, brought up the rear.

The overcast dawn had risen into a bright, windy day. The sky was blue and high above the endless moors; clouds crossed the face of the sun, their shadows racing before them across the heather. The party stopped briefly for a meal at noon, eating from hampers the Orderhouse had packed. The Roundheads arranged themselves in a tight circle, away from Liliane and Anselm and the servants, conversing softly in some unknown tongue. Once, startled by a burst of voices, Liliane looked toward them and saw them laughing, as if at some kind of jest—even Selwyn, his head thrown back and all his teeth showing. In the time she had worked with him, she had not once seen him laugh. It seemed very strange.

By late afternoon they had reached the first stop of the Progress, the village of Locvar. Locvar was a small habitation of no more than one hundred people, its dwellings huddled around a packed-dirt clearing that served as the central square, with a well and a pillory-post at its center. Poor as it was, it was the largest village of its Parish, home to the Resident Journeyer and his staff, and to the Guardian School. The Residence and the School were housed in a single building, Guardian-built in the customary massive style, casting an afternoon shadow wider than the village itself.

The Resident Journeyer, a mountainous man with a head as bald as an egg and tiny piggish eyes, stood ready to greet the party. Liliane could feel his apprehension, as sharp as the stale smell that emanated from his shabby robes. He was not, she sensed, a supporter of Zosterian principles. He made a short speech of welcome, which Selwyn and the others endured, clearly impatient. Supper, served in the Residence refectory, was a lengthy meal, with more speeches and some ragged entertainment by a group of villagers. The Roundheads accepted it all with the bare minimum of courtesy. Afterward, they were shown to their quarters. Since it was an all-male Residence, Liliane found herself with the female servants. A bed had been hauled into a corner of the room and screened with hangings, to provide her with accommodation more fitting to her rank.

The next day the work of the Progress began. The probes and evaluations were first: Selwyn and Colmagh closeted themselves with the Resident, while the remainder of the Team took the other Journeyers in turn. Liliane spent the morning in the Residence library with the census lists, checking the heavy vellum scrolls against her own folios, adding the names of children born to the Parish during the past year, marking a black line and a date through the names of those who had died. She finished quickly and, alone with the Parish records, took the opportunity to glance through them. The rates of Violation in this Parish seemed to have held steady over the past few years. Cross-checking her own notes, she saw that Selwyn's records agreed.

That afternoon, while Selwyn and his men met with Locvar's headman and representatives from other, smaller villages in the vicinity, Liliane was ushered to the Resident's office, to receive the information she needed to update the Catalogue. The Resident sat behind his desk, his massive bulk squeezed between the arms of his chair, his hands folded upon his belly. Liliane could feel his simmering resentment. Evidently his evaluation had not gone well.

"I was expecting Linorio," he said, watching her as she took out her writing implements and unwrapped the scroll onto which she had copied the records of the Catalogue for the past ten years.

"Linorio is dead," she said shortly.

"Ah." His voice held no regret. His beady eyes slid over her, small as poppy seeds in the doughy mass of his face. "It isn't often you see a woman in your kind of occupation. When I first saw you ride in after the Arm-Master, I thought . . . well, I thought your presence might not be entirely professional."

Liliane controlled her annoyance. This man was her equal in rank; she did not have to tolerate such treatment. But perhaps his incautious overtures might lead to something. "Oh?" she said. "Why is that?"

The Resident looked uncomfortable. "Well . . . he's not celibate, you know."

"Yes, I know." Liliane arranged her face into an expression of distaste. "I knew before I came here that Zosterians don't follow traditional rules, but I had no idea of the extent of it."

"You're not a Zosterian yourself?"

"Certainly not."

He eyed her. She could feel his curiosity. "I'm traditional, too. I was at the Fortress for a long time, in administration. All this is quite a comedown for me." He gestured toward the village, the Parish, the whole of North Britannia. "Heretics and savages, dreadful food and rotten wine and filthy weather. It feels like a prison sentence sometimes."

"I can imagine," Liliane said sympathetically, wondering

what failure or infraction had led to his posting here.

"Not that I neglect my duty. One serves the Stone no matter where one is."

"Of course." She pretended to hesitate. "I wonder if I might ask you, as a traditional, what you think of the Progress."

"The Progress." The Resident practically spat. "Give me a good Raid anytime. These dogs of peasants are heretical by nature—they obey only if they fear. And what's to fear in a Progress? We Journeyers rely on the Arm of the Stone to keep the people in line. If they don't, how can we?"

"I see your point."

"You must have seen a Raid or two. You know what I'm talking about. Zosterians." He turned the word over in his mouth like a piece of spoiled food. "Breathing down my neck, prying into my papers, probing me right here in my own Residence, dressing me down in front of my men. The Arm-Master took me to task for not unblocking a well. A well, can you imagine?"

"A well?" Liliane repeated, puzzled.

"Yes. One of these miserable hamlets had a well that was fouled by falling earth. The Arm-Master believes we Journeyers should fix that sort of thing—sick animals, bad soil, dried-up springs, crippled babies. Participation for Separation, or maybe it's Intervention for Observation—who can keep it straight? But I ask you, how will unblocking wells and fertilizing soil hold the people to the Limits? How will paying them visits and listening to their troubles protect the Stone? Our job is to see they're educated and to catch them if they Violate. By the Stone, we're Guardians, not nurse-maids! In the days of the Raids, a Resident made his own decisions. He answered to the Abbot, not the Arm-Master. He didn't have to worry about performance standards or goal plans or the Five cursed Substitutions!"

The force of his emotion had pulled him forward in his chair. He was staring at Liliane as aggressively as if she were Selwyn himself. "I couldn't agree more," she murmured soothingly. "It must be dreadfully frustrating for you."

"It's more than frustrating. It's humiliating." He sat back

in his chair, sighing. "But what can I do? The Northern Diocese is a long way from the Fortress, and not just by land. No one cares what goes on here."

"There's something I've heard . . . well, maybe I shouldn't say." She pretended uncertainty. "It's just a rumor, after all."

"A rumor?" She felt his eagerness. "Go on. You can say anything you want to me. It'll go no further than this office."

"Well . . . the records indicate that Violation in the north has declined over the past few years. I've seen that for myself. But I've heard some people say it isn't really so. That the records may be . . . inaccurate somehow."

The Resident leaned forward. His voice dropped to a whisper. "Not just inaccurate. False. The records are forged."

Liliane allowed her eyes to widen. *"Forged?"*

"Forged." His tiny eyes darted back and forth. "Selwyn Forester and his men are altering the records to support their cause."

"But how?" Liliane sent out her Gift, probing for truth. "How can they do that?"

"Well . . . there are many Residents, especially north of here, who have agreed to submit false reports, to hide errors and ignore complaints of Violation. Zosterian sympathizers, the lot of them."

"But that's shocking. Horrifying. Do they do this on their own, or does Selwyn Forester instruct them?"

"He instructs them, of course."

"You know this personally?"

"Well . . . not personally. But I have the information on the best authority. The very best."

Liliane sat back, trying to control her disappointment. The fat man knew no facts, only hearsay. Her Gift showed her only the tangled network of his prejudice. In the ten years she had been in the world, she had frequently found herself dismayed by the poor quality of the Journeyers she met. She was aware that the Novice Examinations were not everywhere administered with equal rigor; she had seen for herself how the Fortress teachers turned a blind eye to

Apprentices' shortcomings so long as their annual probes confirmed their basic fitness. The sad truth was that the world's need for vast numbers of Journeyers often forced the primacy of quantity over quality.

The Resident would have been happy to complain for the rest of the afternoon, but Liliane was tired of the game, which, it was now plain, would yield nothing of value. Firmly, she returned to the business at hand. For the next half hour she took down names and amended notations, which the Resident read to her from a report compiled for him by the Guardian School's head teacher.

"Perhaps," the Resident said as she packed away her writing implements and rolled up her scroll, "you would allow me to give you a tour of the Residence gardens. I'm quite a horticulturalist, you know."

Liliane offered him a smile. She could not imagine this ponderous man nurturing plants or sowing seed. "That's very kind of you. But I have such a lot of work to do. And I've a meeting later today with the Arm-Master." She lowered her voice a little. "If I'm not perfectly prepared he becomes very angry. You can imagine."

He was easily manipulated. His poppy-seed eyes rolled over her, regretfully. "I understand."

Early the next morning, their work in Locvar complete, the party mounted up for the next leg of the journey. The Resident saw them off, his Journeyers behind him. Liliane could feel their collective relief; the dull murmur of their resentment was also very clear. Meanwhile, in the village square, the townspeople went about their business, paying little attention to the gathered Guardians, for all the world as if the Arm of the Stone were not just a few feet away. The people of Locvar seemed to fear Selwyn and his men far less than their fellow Guardians did.

After he had made his obsequious good-byes to Selwyn, the Resident came over to Liliane, holding up to her a small bundle wrapped in roughweave cloth.

"For sweet dreams," he said. "I grew the plants myself."

Liliane took the gift, surprised and, in spite of herself, touched. Later, unwrapping the bundle, she found six delicate sachets, smelling delightfully of lavender and other herbs.

Halfway through the morning Selwyn dropped his horse back to walk by hers. "You received a present this morning."

Liliane felt herself flushing. "Not really a present, Master. A token."

His dark eyes rested on her face. "The Resident wouldn't have been pressing you to make your copy of his evaluation slightly more favorable than mine, would he?"

"If it had been that kind of gift, I would have refused it, Master." She met his gaze squarely. The color in her cheeks was no longer from embarrassment. "We spoke about his garden. He gave me some of his herbs."

"So this token is merely an indication of personal regard."

"I suppose so, Master."

"I see. Well, be mindful of what you accept in future, Madelaine. We'll be seeing a great many Residents over the next few weeks. If all of them give you tokens, we'll need an extra packmule to carry the weight."

And he rode away, leaving Liliane uncertain whether she had been rebuked or, improbably, made the subject of a jest.

Fifteen

 LITTLE over a week into the Progress, the party left the moors behind and entered a region of rolling mountains, with green slopes cut by scree-strewn gullies and runnelled with the many streams that hurtled down from the heights. Sinuous valleys ran between the peaks, cupping lakes whose narrowness belied their depth. Their waters, dark and smooth as glass, mirrored a sky occluded constantly by clouds, now clumped like clots of cream, now trailing in ragged mile-long ribbons, now sweeping like a turbulent river toward the edge of the horizon. The weather shifted from overcast to downpour to misty sunlight in the space of hours, as if each day encompassed a whole year of changing seasons. Sparsely populated as the moors had been, this land was even emptier. There were no roads, only narrow tracks meandering faint and unmarked through the lowlands. Villages were few, with an occasional small croft or shepherd's hut the only sign of human habitation in between.

Travel, though not difficult, was tedious; the many lakes and streams forced frequent detours and often took the party miles out of its way. Residences in this wild place were sometimes several days apart, and most nights now were spent in the open. The servants pitched tents and built fires and cooked travel rations, doing what they could to make the party comfortable, though the vagaries of the weather made comfort difficult to achieve. Liliane had done much traveling in her life, but it had always been Guardian-style, in easy stages along Guardian roads, with comfortable nights and ample meals in Guardian post-houses. Not since her Novice journey had she slept on the ground in damp blankets, or eaten food that tasted of the smoke of campfires. It did not have to be this way: the Roundheads could have placed a binding around the group to keep it dry, or raised shelters and created fires by power, or employed distance-walking, which would have carried them between Residences in the space of hours. But Liliane had seen, in the Orderhouse, how Selwyn and his men measured their power, never accomplishing through their Gifts what could be done by hand. Here it was the same. Except for a binding if the cold or rain grew severe, or the assistance of power to part the waters of a stream or bridge a treacherous gully, the party of Roundheads journeyed much as ordinary men and women did.

The major part of the Progress's work was devoted to the Residences and the Schools. But the party frequently paused in the smaller settlements as well, and also when they encountered one of the crofters' compounds and shepherds' huts that dotted this empty landscape. The people of the wilderness were of a different stock than the fair folk of the villages, small and dark, wild in the way of those who possessed no amenities beyond the barest tools of survival. The low stone huts in which they dwelt, thatched with bracken or fern, were rarely more than a single room with a firepit in the center, in which humans and animals lived tumbled together.

The poverty of these little people was no worse than the wretchedness Liliane had seen in the crumbling slums of Osman; their ignorance, however, was beyond anything she had ever encountered. Her first scan of a crofter family showed her that, astonishingly, neither parents nor children had ever attended Guardian School.

"It's true," Selwyn told her when she brought the matter to his attention. It was his practice each evening to dictate a record of the day's travel; they were in his tent, Liliane with her tablet and he with his own notes, sitting on either side of a glowing brazier that seemed to lend more smoke than warmth to the damp air. Because of the chill, he wore his cloak, the hood pulled up. It cast a shadow across his face, as if the place he sat were dimmer than the tent itself. "You'll find it's the same across much of this northern area. The distances here are often too great to make School attendance practical."

"But Master, if the people don't attend School, how can they know the Limits?" She could not understand his apparent unconcern. "How can they avoid Violation? I've checked my lists. They aren't in the Catalogue either. It's as if they don't exist. They could Violate every day and no one would be the wiser."

"*I* would be the wiser." His tone was sharp. Since they had reached the mountains, an odd irritable mood had invaded these sessions. He was often abrupt with her, in a way he had not been since the first days of her arrival; she could feel him, sometimes, rushing the business they did together, as if trying to cut their meetings as short as possible. "Don't forget, my men and I visit them every second year, which is more attention than they ever had before I came here."

"Of course, Master. But the uninterrupted care the Residents could provide—"

"The Residents!" He made a gesture of disgust. "You've seen how little the Residents are willing to do. It's hard enough to get them to take care of people who live across the square, never mind those who are more than a day's journey away."

"It's a matter of law," Liliane said stubbornly. "It's one of a Resident's primary duties to see that his Parishioners receive a proper education."

"The law and those who deliver it are two different things. This isn't something unique to the Northern Diocese. There are lax and lazy Residents everywhere. All across the world names go unrecorded—thousands of them, whole missing generations."

Liliane stared at him, shocked.

"It isn't the danger you might think. You've seen how primitive these people are, how poor. They have barely the ability to scratch a living, let alone contemplate Violation. And if by some chance they did manage to Violate, their extreme isolation virtually guarantees there would be no contagion.''

Liliane dropped her eyes. It was very difficult for her to accept what he told her. From childhood she had been taught that the safety of the world depended on the assurance that everyone—everyone—knew the Limits.

"Shall I record the names, Master?''

"No. It's not the Arm-Master's duty to classify people for entry into the Catalogue. And I won't have you doing the Residents' work for them.''

There was a brief silence.

"Well," he said. "I have no more business. Have you?''

"No, Master.''

"I've written up the coming week's itinerary.'' He took from his document case a sheet of parchment, heavily lined with dark penstrokes. Selwyn was an impeccably organized man; his tent was always in perfect order, his horse and tack in flawless trim, his hair and clothing immaculate even under the most difficult of outdoor conditions. The documents he produced, however, were chaotic, tangled webs of crossed-out words and inserted sentences, so thickly written they were sometimes almost indecipherable. "See that Anselm gets a copy this time. He seems to think you're trying to slight him by exclusion.''

"Master, I certainly didn't mean—''

"Of course not." He waved away explanations. "Anselm is touchy where you're concerned.''

"Touchy, Master?''

"Yes." He looked at her. "I told you when you came. You have the place he believed was his.''

She had been reaching for the parchment; involuntarily, she drew back. Leaning forward, he placed the parchment on the ground between them. The light of the brazier pierced the shadow of his hood for a moment, glowing redly on his cheek and temple, casting his features into sharp relief.

"Go now," he said.

Liliane retrieved the parchment and left his tent, seeking the chilly shelter of her own. By the light of a small portable oil lamp, she wrote out the necessary number of copies of the itinerary he had given her. Despite the cold, Selwyn had gone to sit with his men about the fire that burned at the center of the camp. She could not understand what he said, for it was the Roundheads' habit when they were together to converse in the vernacular of Britannia, but he sounded animated, careless, as if he had never turned on her, a few moments before, a look of ice.

She thought of the crofters, of all the other unrecorded people—the forgotten of the earth, lost in outer darkness. Her heart ached for them, for the generations that would follow them, deprived of the Guardian protection that was their birthright. Much as Selwyn's dismissal of the situation troubled her, she was aware that his indifference did not stand alone. She had seen enough to know that his assessment of the Residents of the north was entirely accurate. Selwyn, at least, was attempting to care for those within his reach. Few others did as much.

The Progress was now close to midpoint. Liliane had found nothing to shed doubt on the veracity of the Order-house records, or to support the accusation of collusion made by the Resident of Locvar. She did not believe, now, that she ever would. Whatever Jolyon might think, the changes Selwyn claimed for the Northern Diocese were real. Everywhere, rates of Violation had either dropped or held steady. Everywhere, the people appeared both content and cooperative, a signal alteration in this place long known for its population's inclination toward rebellion.

Selwyn and his men behaved toward the villagers and crofters with a businesslike civility that was totally unlike the cold contempt that formed such a basic component of Roundhead and even Journeyer treatment of the unGifted. They were always prepared with the names of the village headmen, the kin-lines of the families, the local customs and history; they never left a habitation without offering some service of their Gifts—Dispensation for Sequestration, the Fourth Substitution of the Zosterian Rule. There was never any doubt, of course, of what they represented. Selwyn was not tolerant of transgression when he found it, nor did he hesitate to call upon the full power of the Arm of the Stone. But he and his men seemed, in a most unRoundheadlike way, actually to care for the people among whom they journeyed. And though the people feared them, with the awed and reverent dread of those confronted by powers beyond their comprehension, they did not hate them.

The same could not be said for the Residents. Selwyn did have his supporters—not surprisingly, it was in these Parishes that Violation rates had dropped most dramatically—but the majority of the Residents employed his methods only under protest. In contrast to the civility he offered the villagers, he treated his fellow Guardians with boreal coldness. His rigorous performance evaluations, against standards established during previous Progresses, nearly always found their subjects wanting. No excuses were allowed, no mitigating circumstances considered. The penalties imposed for failure were harsh; for success there was the briefest of acknowledgments, followed by a long list of new tasks and goals.

Liliane, copying out performance reports from Selwyn's dictation, writing up goal plans from his scribbled notes, often marveled at the inflexibility of his judgment. In a way, she admired the singlemindedness of his determination to bring change to the Northern Diocese. Yet it was not just change he was seeding, but hate. The dark and simmering resentment that surrounded the Progress's work was remarkably uniform from Residence to Residence. For those who did not support its principles, Zosterianism was a bitter pill to swallow. Selwyn, laying the foundations of his vision across the Northern Diocese like iron bands, made no effort to administer it gently.

Civil toward the villagers, harsh toward his fellow Guardians, toward his men Selwyn turned yet another face. Alone in the wilderness with Colmagh and the rest, he was clearly more at ease than in any other setting. There was little trace, at such times, of the cool formality of his professional manner; he laughed and spoke, moved and gestured, not like an Arm-Master, but like any man. All the Roundheads, in fact, seemed to have abandoned much of the constraint of their ordinary behavior. Physically diverse as they were, in the Orderhouse their guarded demeanor had made them seem much alike. Now the distinctness of their personalities was fully evident. Colmagh was methodical and patient, a man who looked much and said little. His second, Merillion, was quick-tempered and impulsive. The others were serious and mirthful, impatient and calm, and every permutation in between. When they gathered at night about the fire, talking and arguing and often laughing, they might have been any group of companions engaged upon a difficult journey. A stranger coming upon them in the dark, when the shadows made all robes black and the shifting firelight obscured the telltale Roundhead red, would not have suspected that here was the feared and dreadful Arm of the Stone, scourge of Violation, cleansers of the earth.

Liliane herself was not included in this relaxed cameraderie. She did not expect to be. Her inferior status, as well as her non-Zosterianism, guaranteed her exclusion; beyond that, she had long been aware that Selwyn's men mistrusted her. Since they had reached the mountains, however, something more had come into play. The occasional impatience, the slight chill she had first sensed in Selwyn during the evening sessions in his tent had hardened, over the passing weeks, into a glacial distance. Now, halfway through the Progress, there was no longer any trace of the fragile cordiality that had grown between them in her first months at the Orderhouse. When they met, he maintained a stiff courtesy that was more remote than silence, broken only when she attempted to ask a question or make a comment not strictly related to the business at hand, at which point he cut her off with a brusqueness just short of outright rudeness. He spent not a moment more in her presence than was absolutely necessary; he seemed, in fact, actively to avoid her, moving round the edge of the campsite rather than cross her path, turning a corner rather than pass her in an Orderhouse corridor. She was aware sometimes, not from any released emotion but from the language of his body, of his abhorrence of her physical presence. He could not bring himself to approach her even through the indirect medium of papers or books, laying them on a table or chair, or even the ground, rather than putting them into her hands.

She could not think what might have caused this change. The quality of her work was as it had always been; her efficiency had not declined, nor her manner altered. She did not believe he had pierced her disguise—surely he would not allow her to continue to work for him if that were the case. Whatever the reason, she knew with leaden certainty that it spelled doom for the second portion of her charge. Despite the apparent loosening of his guard, she was no closer to mapping his mind than she had ever been. Now, with his sudden dislike, there was no longer any possibility of following the opportunity that had seemed to offer itself in the Orderhouse just before they left, of winning his trust through portraying herself as a potential convert. And in his obvious distaste for her person, she had a conclusive answer to the feasibility of Jolyon's final option.

For her part, she was as sensitive to his physical presence as he seemed to be to hers, though for different reasons. Because of her lack of any inner sense of him, his corporeal self had become the sole focus of her observation. She had been watching him for so long, and with such intensity, that his face and body sometimes seemed more real than her own. In the course of the Progress she had hardly seen a mirror; she kept her hair smooth by touch and her clothing neat out of habit, and beyond that scarcely thought of how she looked. Yet she could call to mind without effort the exact shape of Selwyn's face, the precise darkness of his eyes. She could predict with accuracy, at any given time, how he would move, how he would sit, how he would speak. She was aware of him even when she could not see him, a sense of his presence almost as accurate as sight.

These things meant little, of course. She had mapped him only from the outside; the detail of her charting pointed only to the magnitude of unknown territory within. Still, she watched—as he rode at the head of the Progress party, as he sat across from her in his tent, as he joined his men about the fire at night. Her exclusion, always partial, was now complete, for the Roundheads echoed their leader's behavior in all things. Even Anselm would not come near her. Yet even from so much distance there was a thing she saw, a thing only a heartsenser could perceive. A profound trust linked Colmagh and his Investigators, born of many years of shared labor. Their devotion to Selwyn was even stronger, an allegiance far more encompassing than had been apparent in the Orderhouse. But what Selwyn gave them in return did not go nearly as deep. The man he seemed to be in the firelight—younger, more impulsive, openly swept by the full range of mercurial emotion Liliane had only suspected before, stirring behind his Orderhouse mask of cool control—was no more than the topmost layer of his self. Below, the largest part of his being still lay concealed.

The mountains gave way to moor once more, a northern heathland even more desolate than that of the south. But the wide track the party followed, closer to a road than any they had encountered since leaving the Orderhouse, was the main passage to the port towns of the extreme north, and there was more traffic here than they had seen anywhere in their travels. At the first sight of the party's black garments, travelers urged their mounts away from the track, waiting with their heads bowed until the Roundheads had passed by, their fear a dark taint upon the constant wind.

In the sixth week of the Progress the party reached the apex of its journey, a sizeable town on a rocky seacoast, from which the ocean spread out gray and sullen toward the ice at the top of the world. This place was a major port, for trade with the cold lands to the northeast. The Residence and the School were the largest the party had yet encountered, and it was three days before their work there was complete. On their final night the Resident organized a banquet, to which all the town's notable citizens were invited. The Resident, one of Selwyn's sympathizers, kept a mistress, a native unGifted woman by whom, it was said, he had several children. Because she sat beside him at the table there was not the objection there was in other Orderhouses to the presence of outside females; several of the Roundheads had women at their sides, including Selwyn.

Liliane had been aware of his assignations along the way of the Progress, sometimes in the Orderhouses, sometimes not. Never before, however, had she actually seen him with one of his paramours. From her place among the female Journeyers, and from the distance of her own exclusion, she watched him, trying to glean what it might be like for a woman on whom Selwyn's fancy fell. She did not watch for long. The way he turned his head, the way he looked into the woman's face, the way she looked back at him, unsettled her in a way she could not comfortably define. She had never before felt strongly about the choice of celibacy among Roundheads, but now she knew: it was not proper for those engaged in the most serious endeavor in the world to pursue the distractions of the flesh.

It was in the seventh week of the Progress, near the end of their journey, that they came at last to the Parish of Anadh. Anadh was sizeable, comprising the village in which the Residence was located and six smaller hamlets. The party entered the first of these just before noon. Selwyn and his men met briefly with its people, shared a meal with them, and moved on. When they reached the second hamlet, however, it was immediately apparent that something was wrong. The fields had not been plowed or planted for the summer just past; there were no animals in the pens and pastures. All the houses and buildings were marked by signs of neglect, fast deepening into decay.

Selwyn halted the party in the middle of the track that straggled through the settlement. With a gesture he sent Colmagh to investigate. Colmagh pushed open a door with his riding crop and looked inside. He returned, shaking his head.

"Empty," he said. "No people, no corpses, no furnishings."

For a moment Selwyn sat very still upon his horse. Then, without a word, he spurred the animal forward, and the party resumed its interrupted progress.

A few hours later they arrived in the village. They were greeted by the Resident, a thin, twitchy man whose fear of Selwyn was very apparent. He exuded a strong sense of guilt—something he had done, or had not done, Liliane could not tell which. The party was fed and accommodated in the usual way. For once Liliane had her own chamber, a tiny cubicle that probably belonged to the Deputy Resident. After so many nights of communal camping or sleeping behind a curtain in the female servants' dormitory, the privacy seemed deeply luxurious.

The following morning she began her work, as usual, in

the library. Arranging her papers and writing implements as if for the census, she set about looking for Elene Jevalse. It took only a brief search to find her. Aged twenty-one, she lived outside the hamlet of Cors, together with her father, Simeon, her mother, Merriam, and her siblings Comyn and Annis. Simeon was a blacksmith; Comyn was apprenticed to his father. Cors, it seemed, was the deserted hamlet the party had passed through yesterday. With the sole exception of Elene and her family, a black line was drawn through the names of every one of its inhabitants. The cause of death had been written in and then heavily crossed out, with the word "contamination" inserted above.

Liliane noted the information down, tucking the slip of parchment away in her belt. No sooner had she done so than the library door was flung open with such force that it rebounded off the wall. Reflexively she leapt to her feet, slamming the census folio closed. She turned, with a pounding heart, to see Selwyn, striding across the floor toward her. For an instant she was possessed by certainty that he knew what she was doing and had come to stop her. But he swept past as if he had not seen her. He was visibly agitated: raw emotion—anger—poured off him in waves. She stood staring at him, forgetting herself in her astonishment. What on earth could have so disordered his control?

Reaching the window, he turned. His face was drawn with rage; his dark eyes seemed to boil. "You have your tablet? Good. I will dictate a report."

Selwyn's anger, it turned out, was for the deaths in Cors. The previous spring the hamlet had been struck by what seemed to be a virulent and fatal sickness. The Resident of Anadh had ordered Cors and its environs quarantined, sending Journeyers to barrier an area several miles about. Not until weeks later did he order an investigation. By then every villager had died. The investigation revealed that the deaths had not been caused by plague at all, but by fouling of the stream from which the villagers got their water.

In accordance with the Second Substitution—Intervention for Observation—an investigation should have been undertaken as soon as word of the plague reached the Residence, and appropriate action taken to halt the sickness' course. But

the Resident of Anadh had not intervened; worse, by bar-
riering the area and preventing those who were still healthy
from leaving, he had greatly increased the death toll. As
punishment, he was to be dismissed from his post at once.
One of the Roundheads would escort him back to the Orderhouse, where he would await further judgment.

The report completed, Selwyn dictated a letter to the Abbot, briefly outlining the situation. He also dictated a commission, temporarily assigning the Resident's post to his
Deputy. Lastly, he issued a series of instructions for the
Roundhead who would be accompanying the defrocked Resident.

Liliane took frantic shorthand; it was a struggle to keep
up with the flow of Selwyn's words. He paced as he spoke,
back and forth across the cramped library, his body taut as
stretched wire, his hands white-knuckled behind his back.
Anger poured out of him, the flow of it battering Liliane's
extended Gift. Even as she wrote, she found time to wonder
at his loss of control. The Resident of Anadh had failed in
his responsibilty, but there had been other failures along the
path of the Progress, some of them almost as great, and none
had come close to cracking Selwyn's perfect guard. Could
it be that he feared for Elene Jevalse, who lived so close to
poisoned Cors?

''That's all for now,'' Selwyn said at last. He had stopped
his pacing; he stood by the window again, his hands still
clasped behind his back. ''Bring me fair copies within the
hour.''

''It may take me a little more time than that, Master.''

He turned from the window and fixed her with an icy
stare. ''Within the hour, I said. Someone of your excellent
credentials should be capable of understanding such a simple instruction.''

Over the past weeks he had treated her with reserve, with
coldness, with distaste. Never, however, had he turned upon
her the cutting contempt he reserved for the Residents. All
her self-control could not prevent the blood from rising to
her face. Lowering her eyes, she gathered up her materials
and turned to go.

Halfway to the door, his voice stopped her.

"Madelaine."

She turned. His face had changed. It was no longer angry, though she could not read the ghosts of expression that informed it.

"That was uncalled for. If it takes more than an hour, so be it. I know you'll give me the work as quickly as you can."

"I'll do my best, Master," she said.

"You always do." He moved away from the window, toward the table set at the center of the room. His emotions had subsided, though Liliane could still feel, like the tumult of an underground river, the low mutter of his anger. He leaned both hands upon the back of a chair. "I'm sorry I took my anger out on you, Madelaine." He studied her, his eyes resting on her face in a way they rarely did these days. "You're only doing your duty."

"I know your anger wasn't directed at me, Master," Liliane said softly. She was barely breathing. She sensed a shifting in him, the turning toward her of a face she had never seen. The moment in which they stood was a knife-edge of possibility. One false move, one wrong word, and it would be lost.

"You're so pliant. So calm. That's your strength, isn't it? I could almost envy you." He sighed, a completely uncharacteristic sound. "Anger is a useless emotion. I used to think it a source of strength. But really it's just self-indulgence."

"You have every cause to be angry, Master. All those lives, needlessly lost."

Something surged within him—deeper than rage, more painful, like thunder rolling round the edges of his soul. Liliane heard in it echoes of the dark passion she had sensed so long ago, in the Fortress. His guard had cracked. She knew it, with the certainty of instinct she had learned in Pietra's court and honed in Costares's. She focused her Gift like a lancet, bringing every ounce of her strength to bear, probing for the breach.

"It's the indifference of it," he said. "As if those villagers' lives matter less than . . . ours. Why is it that those who are charged with guarding the world care so little for it?"

"How will you punish the Resident of Anadh?"

"I haven't decided yet. But whatever his sentence, he'll never hold another Residency." He looked at her. "You think I'm too hard on them, don't you? The Residents."

"It's not my place to judge, Master."

"No?" He cocked his head slightly. "But I think you do."

She felt herself flush.

"Tell me. How would you have dealt with the Resident of Anadh?"

It was not a challenge. He sounded as if he really wanted to know. Scanning the Resident the previous night, Liliane had sensed the man to be not so much indifferent as cowardly. The guilt he felt seemed to argue that he regretted his action, although he would have greater cause to regret it in the future.

"I think I'd have made more allowance for an error in judgment, Master."

Selwyn pressed his lips together. "An error in judgment that cost thirty lives. Perhaps more."

"Yes. But it's possible this Resident has learned from his experience, and will never make such a mistake again."

"Do you think I should leave him here and risk it?" He shook his head. "No. My methods weren't new to him— he knew the standards I require. Yet at the first sign of difficulty he fell back into the old ways. A man like that will never be anything but a stranger to change."

"Change is difficult, Master. Especially for people who've never had to change before."

"True enough." He pulled the chair out and sat down at the table. "But that's one of the advantages of being Arm-Master. They can't disobey me, much as they'd like to." He smiled faintly.

"Do you know how much they hate you?"

"Oh yes." He nodded, his face grave now. "Yes, I know."

"They might be more cooperative if they hated you less."

"If I was kinder to them, you mean? If I moved more slowly, praised more readily, forgave mistakes more generously?" He shook his head. "I've seen the way you charm them, the way you draw them out and make them trust you.

But I don't have the time for that, Madelaine. Nor the inclination."

"But shouldn't the Zosterian principles you practice toward the people be extended toward Guardians? Cooperation for Coercion. The Third Substitution."

He scowled. She waited. But though she could feel his anger flare briefly, there was no trace now of that deeper emotion.

"Cooperation is indeed a tenet of Zosterianism," he said. "But I don't see any need to extend that principle to Guardians, where they fail the people. For centuries these Journeyers have been abusing their Parishioners—hoarding their power, hiding their skills, standing back, like the Resident of Anadh. What good is a Gift that's turned inward and benefits only those who already have it? What justification can there be for our withdrawal from the misfortunes of the unGifted—as if we were not just human beings, but something better? No." He shook his head again. "Power carries a duty with it, a responsibility. We Guardians have imposed an order on the world; the very least we can do is to remedy some of the terrible misery we have created thereby. It's time, and past time, to call these Residents to account. If they won't comply, then they must be swept away."

His words were passionate. Yet even as he spoke them he was regaining control, his guard healing. Liliane reached out, striving to throw a wedge into the diminishing breach.

"But that goes beyond reform. Or at least, beyond Zosterianism as I've learned to think of it."

He looked at her. Something stirred, and then dropped away; she felt it, as final as the closing of a door.

"What you've learned," he said quietly, "I can't say. But I'm sure it isn't sufficient to allow you to form judgments of that kind."

He pushed the chair back and got to his feet. He was blank now, as blank as he had ever been, the chilly distance of the past weeks covering his features like a veil. Liliane turned her face away so that he would not see what must show in her eyes. Her disappointment was like a physical weight. The chance had been so close.

Selwyn moved toward the door, circling her more widely

than was necessary. Returning to the table, she set her papers down, returning her mind to the familiar tedium of work. Behind her, she heard his voice.

"You'll need this."

She turned. She must have dropped her stylus; Selwyn was holding it toward her. She stepped forward, reaching out to him. For once he did not pull away, or place the stylus on another surface rather than give it to her directly. Their gazes met. Nothing in his face changed; no shutter flew back behind his eyes. But briefly, as clearly as a call and as close as a hand laid upon her skin, she felt the heat of his desire.

Liliane was shocked. She felt blood flood her face. For a moment she was rooted to the spot. Then, woodenly, she pulled her stylus from his fingers and turned her back, hiding her telltale face. She heard the soft sound of the latch as the door closed behind him.

She stood beside her chair. The blood pulsed in her cheeks, at her temples, in her throat. Her mind spun in circles. What gripped her, what held her motionless, was not the strangeness of that moment, or even its breathtaking unexpectedness, but the depth of her own response.

That night, lying in her bed, Liliane confronted things about herself she would rather not have known. She understood that what she felt had been there for some time, just beyond the reach of her own self-knowledge, gathering mass and heat like a hidden infection. The failure of her judgment, of her will, horrified her. How could she have been so blind? Yet how was she to identify what she had never before experienced? The only man she had ever known was Pietra. The only response she had ever felt was disgust.

Amias had been wrong. Clearly Selwyn did not desire a liaison with a subordinate—why else would he have turned on her over the past weeks such icy looks, such cold rejection? In her mind she heard Jolyon's voice; the image of his bitten fingers possessed her memory. She knew precisely what he would want her to do with her new-found understanding of Selwyn's feelings. But as close as the circumstance of her failure had moved her, in the past weeks, toward consideration of such a solution, recognition of her own feelings now put this strategy beyond the bounds of possibility. She was a heartsenser. She could not come so close to her own longing and survive.

The bell rang for midnight, for one o'clock. Liliane lay sleepless. She stared at the ceiling of her cubicle, plastered in a relief design of small flowers and leaves. Her eyes followed the twining stems, a labyrinth as tangled as her thoughts.

Then, at the very edge of perception, she felt something. It was approaching; it was outside her door; it was past. She sat up in bed. It had been Selwyn. She knew it without question, with that strange sense of his presence she had developed during the Progress, stronger now than it had ever been before.

She leaped out of bed and ran to her door, opening it a little and looking out. To her physical eyes, the long corridor was empty. The eyes of her Gift, however, knew otherwise. He had drawn up a semblance to make himself invisible, but she saw him even so, cloaked and booted for outdoors, rounding the corner to the stairway leading down to the main floor.

Not questioning the instinct that drove her, Liliane flung on her clothes, seized Costares's cloak, and left her room. Stealthily she moved along the corridor. She reached the wide flight of stairs and ran down it. Selwyn had already disappeared, but the sense of his presence lingered, as visible to her Gift as a trail of footprints would have been to her eyes.

She followed, to an unbarred door at the back of the Residence, to the village's main street, to the road by which the Progress party had traveled in the day before: the road to Cors. The night was bright with moonlight in a nearly cloudless sky; every surface was touched with pearly radiance, every hollow and turning painted with inky shadow. Liliane could feel him, far ahead, still wrapped in his semblance. She kept to the road's verge, hugging the shadows of trees and hedges in case he should look back. Not for the first time, she gave thanks to the Stone for the lack of nearspeech that made it impossible for him to sense her presence.

Just short of Cors itself he turned off the road, onto a

narrow track leading into a wood. The track ended in a sizeable clearing. By the time she reached it he had already entered the cottage that stood at its center. The cottage was large and stoutly built, its whitewash glowing in the moonlight, its thatch dark as velvet. Adjoining it was a blacksmith's forge. The forge doors stood open, and Liliane could see the dull glow of the fire, banked for the night.

She knew whose cottage this was. The moment Selwyn had set his feet on the road to Cors, she had known where she would find herself. She would have found a way to come here on her own, had he not led her.

Stealthily, she circled through the woods to the cottage's rear. She crept across the clearing, past a frost-ravaged garden and a stone well that explained why this family, out of all the families of Cors, had survived. She pressed herself against the wall of the house, straining to sense what was going on within. She could just feel the presence of people, but the walls were too thick for more; she could glean no emotion, nor even tell how many were in the house. Between the shutters the window openings, covered with greased parchment, released nothing but the glow of light within.

Returning to the front of the house, she settled herself in the underbrush to wait. The ground was thick with fallen leaves, so sitting was not uncomfortable, but it was very cold. In spite of Costares's cloak she was soon chilled and shivering. Above her, the sky was pale with frost and vapor. Between the clouds the stars followed their paths about the earth, and the moon drifted slowly toward its setting point.

At last, hours later, the door to the cottage opened. Golden light fell into the night. Selwyn emerged, carrying a bulky cloth-wrapped bundle. Behind him followed a young woman with long red hair, clad in a nightrobe and a shawl. Selwyn turned, setting down his burden. The girl stepped into his arms. Very dimly, muted by distance, Liliane could sense their emotions: simple sorrow from the girl, something more complicated from Selwyn. His guard was down again; but though she reached forward with all her strength, he was too far away for detail. She could feel completion, and love; there was also, perhaps, fear. That was all.

The girl murmured something into Selwyn's neck. He pulled back, smiling down at her. He reached out and tucked her hair behind her ears, cupping her face between his palms for a moment. Then he spoke one word. Liliane heard it plainly.

"Elene."

They separated. Elene withdrew into the cottage, closing the door behind her. Selwyn took up the bundle and moved toward the forest, his steps swift and silent, drawing the semblance over himself as he walked. As he passed, Liliane stretched out her Gift, but there was no feeling now, not even a quiver.

She waited for some time before getting stiffly to her feet and making her way to the road. The mystery was solved. It was Selwyn who had altered the Catalogue for Elene Jevalse, who was his lover. Or rather, another of his lovers. Yet surely she must be more than that. It did not make sense for him to put everything he had and was in jeopardy for this woman, unless he truly loved her. If that were so, he was a Violator in more than deed—in his thoughts, his very soul. How else could a Roundhead love an unfit woman?

What was the evil in Elene Jevalse's mind? Was it hidden still, or manifest? Was she aware of what Selwyn had done for her? There was no way to know, nor did knowing matter. The facts were plain. Selwyn was a Violator. Liliane could prove it now.

She plodded along the road, her steps slow with exhaustion. The moon had set long since; the sky held only stars now. It was near dawn, and dew had fallen. Already, in the chilly air, it was turning to frost, a glittering and ghostly blanket across the world. In her mind Liliane saw Elene as she flung her arms around Selwyn's neck, as Selwyn embraced her in return, his face turning against her hair. The desire she had sensed from him today meant nothing. It had been an instant, a reflex, a thing any man might feel. Only as she realized this did she understand her own willful and impossible wish for more.

Yet in what she had discovered tonight lay change. Her

knowledge of Selwyn's transgression must inevitably replace all other feeling with the repugnance the fit naturally extended toward the Violator. Whatever she felt now, she would soon be free.

Sixteen

THE PROGRESS party returned to the Orderhouse almost precisely two months after they had left it, on a brilliant afternoon in late October. Colmagh, who possessed the ability for farspeech, had sent ahead to announce their arrival. When they rode into the courtyard the grooms and servants were waiting to take their horses and relieve them of their baggage.

Marya and Lithhilde and Chloe welcomed Liliane back with their usual deferent courtesy. Unable to speak in public of the work of the Progress, they spent the evening meal chatting about various Orderhouse events that had taken place during Liliane's absence. Liliane did not pay much attention; her responses were the minimum required for politeness. Along the Progress there had been no time for weariness, but now she felt as if all the exhaustion she had denied over the past few weeks descended upon her at once. She could think only of sleep. But when she returned to her room she found a note from Amias, directing her to meet him in the Cloister Court. Sighing, she fed the note to the fire and set her tired body to wait for midnight.

She dreaded this meeting. The apprehension she felt as she sat waiting was akin to nausea. She had made Amias a promise; if she did not keep it he would be furious. She could not yield to him what she had found in Anadh; it was her trump card, the one thing she had to hold against her superiors' judgment of her failure to complete the second portion of her charge. That left only the nonfindings of the

Progress. She had done good work, she knew; the case she
had built to refute Jolyon's charge of forgery was solid and
compelling. But she did not think Amias would be satisfied
with it.

At the midnight bell she made her way to the Cloister
Court, through darkened corridors sharp with cold. She was
lightheaded with exhaustion, a little unsteady on her feet.
The sky was clear tonight, the moon full; the pathways of
the court seemed very bright. Amias was waiting, as usual,
in the shelter of the cloister.

<Let us walk,> he thought as she reached him. Without
giving her a chance to answer he took her arm and tucked
it under his. Liliane had endured this before, but tonight the
pressure of his body, the feel of his thoughts, were too much
to bear. She pulled free, with more force than she intended,
causing him to take a step backward. She felt the sting of
his surprise, swallowed almost at once by anger.

<Master, the moon is very bright,> she thought, trying
to put a better face on her reaction. <I fear we might be
seen.>

<No one is about at this hour. I know this Orderhouse
and its ways.> He was scowling; his small mouth was tight
with insult. <But very well. If you want, we can stand in
the shadows.>

Briefly, Liliane closed her eyes. The meeting had just begun, and already it was going wrong.

<Well?> Amias demanded. <Give me your report.>

Liliane did, in phrases she had rehearsed many times. He
edged closer as she discoursed, his eyes roving over her—
an assessment even more open than usual, as if her physical
rejection gave him all the more license to touch her with his
eyes. It took him a moment to realize she had finished. She
felt his attention withdraw as he considered what she had
said.

<I told you when you first came that your searches for
alteration would gain you nothing,> he thought sourly.
<Where there's collusion, there's no need for forgery.>

<Respectfully, Master, as I told you, I found no evidence
of collusion in my scans of the Residents.>

<Scans can be mistaken. You said yourself that the fall

in Violation seems tied to the Residents' Zosterianism. If that's not collusion, what is?>

<My scans are never mistaken, Master.> It was an effort to keep her mindvoice from expressing what she felt. <And I found only one Resident who was openly Zosterian.>

<Semantics.> He made a dismissive gesture. <This information is quite comprehensive. I'll relay it to Jolyon at once. Now, what about the rest of it? You haven't said anything about the Arm-Master's Violation.>

Liliane's heart sank. <I've made good progress, Master. I'm on the track of important evidence.>

<Not the same evidence you mentioned before you left, I hope.>

<No, Master. But I don't want to go into detail until I'm absolutely clear on what it means.>

<That's almost exactly what you told me two months ago. How long does it take for you to be clear on something?>

<What I told you two months ago, Master, was that I expected to discover something significant during the Progress. And I have. But I need to research certain things here in the Orderhouse, and to complete my scanning of the Arm-Master, before I can make a full report.>

<That won't do.> He was angry again. <It's not your business to withhold information from me. If you've found something, you must tell me now.>

<Master.> Liliane poured into her mindvoice all the deference she could muster. <I need more time. Not long— just until I'm sure. Surely someone of your experience can appreciate the need for thoroughness in an investigation.>

<Are you daring to compare yourself to the Arm of the Stone?>

<Master, I'd never presume—>

<Enough,> he thought. <I've had my fill of your vagueness, your allusions, your hints at discoveries that somehow never turn into actual facts. Do you have something for me, or not?>

<Master, I—>

<There isn't anything, is there. You've failed. You can't get into his mind.>

<Master, if you'd just let me explain—>

<Or maybe it's something else. Jolyon briefed me on you before you came here—he told me about your talent as a barrier-breaker, your reputation as an illusion-piercer, your secret conferences and confidential missions and undercover identities. Now, is it really credible that a heartsenser of so much skill and experience could fail to enter the mind of one man, even if he is an Arm-Master, and strongly guarded? Could it be that this is not an issue of skill, but of will?>

<What are you implying?>

<You were a long time along the Progress.> His bulging eyes rolled over her. <All alone in the wilderness—the only woman among so many men. Perhaps something happened on one of those cold dark nights. Something that, shall we say, weakened your devotion to your charge.>

"What?" Liliane gasped aloud. But of course some part of what he said was true. She heard, horrified, the admission that undercut the outrage in her voice. An expression of triumph spread over Amias's face.

<So that *is* it. Is it him? Or one of the others?>

She stared at him, speechless.

<It's him, isn't it. Well, no one can say I didn't see it coming.> His mindvoice held a kind of vicious satisfaction. <I told Jolyon. I said, you can't trust a woman who employs her body for personal gain. I told you, too. Didn't I say, when you first came here, that you couldn't use him as you had used others?> He laughed, his spite tearing at the silence of the court. <Do you think you'll reap some kind of benefit from attaching yourself to an Arm-Master? You won't, you know. He eats women up and spits them out like cherry pits. Two weeks from now he won't remember you exist. Or maybe it's not so cold an intent. Perhaps you think he cares for you. But he cares for no one, only for himself. All you'll gain from this betrayal of your purpose is the discipline you deserve. Jolyon will know of it this very night—>

<Stop.>

Liliane projected all her strength into that single thought. It struck Amias like a blow, shocking him into silence.

<I have not betrayed my purpose,> she thought, force-fully. <You have no evidence of the thing you accuse me of. And even if you did, what grounds would you have to assume it meant abandonment of my trust? Who are you to denounce me because my methods of investigation don't suit you? Who are you to tell me how to conduct a mission your superior has personally charged me to carry out?>

<You . . . what . . . > Amias was so enraged his thoughts fragmented. <How dare you bespeak me this way, woman? I am *your* superior! I am Arm of the Stone!>

<And I am a heartsenser!> Liliane abandoned herself to fury, to all the rage and humiliation she had felt and hidden in the months of her enforced subjection to him. <Do you understand what that means? If it comes to a choice between you—a mediocre, aging, dirty-minded Roundhead relegated for life to one of the most undesirable postings in the world—or me, a heartsenser whose promise and skill has been recognized by the Arm of the Stone itself, whom do you think your superiors will choose? Before you accuse a heartsenser, be very certain you are correct. Be very certain you have proof. For if you're wrong, make no mistake about it—Arm of the Stone or no, you will be ruined!>

Amias had fallen back under the onslaught of her fury. Any guard he might have had was gone. She felt his outrage, snapping like a weasel in the small cage of his mind.

<I will inform Jolyon of your disrespect, woman.> His mindvoice was uneven. <I don't need to make accusations to tell him that you haven't accomplished the second portion of your charge.>

<That wouldn't be wise. Because you don't know for certain, do you? What if I really do have evidence? What if I really can prove Selwyn Forester's Violation? What will Jolyon think of your judgment then?>

He did not reply. His pop-eyed regard was as baleful as a snake's.

<When my work is done I'll come to you as Jolyon ordered, and you can bespeak him as if it were all your doing. In the meantime I will conduct my mission as I see fit, in my own way and according to my own schedule. Do you understand?>

<I understand.> She felt his hatred. <I understand more than you think, you traitorous whore.>

Without thinking, Liliane stepped toward him. He fell back. She sensed his sudden fear. Never before had she relished the advantage her Gift gave her over others. But in that moment, in the shame that followed upon his involuntary release of emotion, she felt the full power of it, of knowing the very thing a person most wished to keep hidden.

<Don't ever insult me again,> she thought, very slowly, forming the words like projectiles in her mind. <Don't summon me again either. If there's something you need to know, *I* will summon *you*.>

He was getting control now. His rage was changing, becoming something calmer and more cold.

<Very well,> he thought. <You win—for now. Don't make the mistake of thinking you've beaten me, though. I'll be looking for the proof you mentioned. If I don't hear from you by December's end I'll bespeak Jolyon, evidence or no. We'll see which of us he listens to then.>

Liliane did not bother to reply. She wanted nothing more than to put distance between them. Turning, she began to cross the Cloister Court. She felt his regard as she moved away: not the prurient heat of other nights, but something much uglier.

In her room she fell onto her bed, weak with reaction. She had made an enemy tonight—not a particularly powerful or influential one, but tenacious and, if she read him right, capable of real viciousness. Had she pushed him too far? Yet she had had no choice. If she had done otherwise, he would be bespeaking Jolyon even now.

How long would it be before he thought it over, before he saw that neglecting to inform Jolyon of his suspicions of her failure would put him in as bad a light as accusing her if she succeeded? Not long, she thought. Certainly well before December. She had even less time than she had thought.

Liliane slept badly that night. As she braided her hair before the mirror the next morning, she saw the paleness of her cheeks, the dark circles beneath her eyes. She had not looked at herself carefully in weeks. Her face in the mirror seemed unfamiliar, thinner than she remembered, shadowed as if by illness.

Passing through the red doors of the Roundhead quarters and into the false spring of the glass-roofed garden, she felt routine closing round her like a vise. She paid her respects to Tobias before beginning work. He greeted her courteously, and they spoke for a while about the Progress, as well as Orderhouse happenings during the last two months. There had been two full-scale Investigations, and a dispute involving a pair of Ordermen; beyond that, the weeks of the Progress party's absence seemed to have been singularly uneventful.

In her office, Liliane opened her work-chest to find a note from Selwyn, directing her to present herself in his office at the seventeenth bell. She did not pick up the paper, but read it as it lay, in the bottom of the chest. She had discovered, over the past days, the danger that waited for her in anything he had touched.

Without enthusiasm she unpacked the documents she had taken with her on the Progress and began the task of amending the Catalogue according to her Progress notations. The noon meal was brought by the clerks, but she could not eat. Steadily she worked through the afternoon. When the seventeenth bell struck she picked up her tablet and stylus, and made her way into the garden.

Though the afternoon was darkening toward evening, Selwyn had not yet lit his candles or kindled his torches. He rose from his desk as she entered and went to stand before one of the windows, as if trying to put distance between them. The way he moved conveyed restlessness, though his guard was firmly in place and Liliane could feel nothing from him. It had been that way since the afternoon in the library.

On the night she had seen Elene Jevalse, Liliane had truly believed her understanding of Selwyn's Violation spelled the death of her disastrous feeling for him. In the days that followed, however, she discovered this to be untrue. Whatever it was that drew her to him stood face-to-face with her knowledge of his transgression, and refused to yield. She was afraid to look at him, lest he see some telltale sign in her face. At the same time she longed to gaze at him and could not stop her eyes from turning constantly in his direction. She could scarcely concentrate on her work; she missed whole sentences of dictation and was forced to guess at them afterward. Even the papers he gave her, imbued as they were with the sense of his presence, were treacherous. She had only to lay her hands on them, and it was as if she were touching him. It was difficult to recall the days when they had been nothing more than paper and ink.

She had wondered, on that dark night, how a Roundhead could love a woman who was unfit. But she was worse, for she was infatuated with—no, obsessed by—a manifest Violator, and even her knowledge of what he had done could not turn her from him. Was she a Violator also—unmanifest, latent? It was her childhood fear, returned to haunt her. At the very least there must be some failure, some falling short, some lack of purity. Surely Selwyn could not otherwise have gained such a foothold in her soul, nor would she be so incapable of dislodging him.

The silence stretched out. She waited, her heart beating. The extension of her Gift was habit now, something she could do despite her distraction and distress. At last, his back still turned, he spoke.

"You can put your tablet down," he said. "I haven't called you here to work."

She placed her tablet on his desk, clasping her hands in her lap. There was something strange in his voice. She felt, suddenly, afraid.

"I've heard from the Fortress," he said. "Word was waiting when we returned. Your posting here has been terminated."

Liliane was struck dumb. She had hardly thought of this in months. She had assumed Jolyon had taken care of it once and for all.

"There's a party of Journeyers leaving the Orderhouse in two weeks. They're going all the way to the Fortress. I've arranged for you to travel with them. How long will it take you to finish up your pending work?" He turned to face her. For the first time, she saw the haggardness of his appearance. "Well? Can't you speak?"

"I . . ." Liliane swallowed. "That is . . . I didn't expect this, Master."

"You knew I intended to replace you. I didn't hide it from you."

"Yes, but you didn't say anything more about it. I thought . . . I thought you'd changed your mind."

"No."

The single word was like a stone dropping from a great height. Liliane rose to her feet. She did not try to analyze the desperation rising within her. Distantly, she was aware of her fingernails cutting into her palms.

"Master, I don't understand why you'd want to send me away now. I've made an excellent adjustment to this assignment. I served you well along the Progress. You've always seemed satisfied."

He gestured, a quick, impatient motion. "I told you before, it has nothing to do with your performance."

"But that's what my superiors will think. They'll believe you were displeased, or that I couldn't fulfill my duties. It will reflect on my career."

"No." He shook his head. "I've written a recommendation for you. It praises you in the highest terms and endorses you for further duty. I made sure to emphasize that your dismissal was not motivated by any action or omission of yours, but purely by politics. I want a Zosterian for my Secretary. You are not a Zosterian. It's as simple as that."

"Why should it matter if I can do the work? What difference does it make to the work if I'm Zosterian or traditional?"

"I've made up my mind." His voice was very cold. He turned back to the window. "There's no point in discussing it further. Two weeks should be ample time for you to complete anything still waiting on your desk. If you finish before that, you don't need to report for duty. Now go."

She stood looking helplessly at his back. Against the murky twilight outside the window, he was a column of solid black. Only his red boots and belt broke the monochromatic flow of his figure—and his white hands, clasping and unclasping behind his back. She was reminded all at once of the first time she had ever seen him, in the Novice Wing. Now, as then, he was a mass of conflicting signals: the coldness of his voice, the aversion of his stance, the agitation of his hands.

As if feeling her gaze, he turned. His black brows were twisted into a scowl as ferocious as any he had ever directed toward an erring Resident.

"Go!" he said. But his voice was not the shout she expected. And she felt it again—desire. Not a swift touch this time, but a flood of wanting, raw and painful and profoundly unwilling, rolling over her as irresistibly as an ocean tide.

Conscious thought deserted her. She stepped forward, into his arms, feeling them enclose her, sliding her own around his neck. He bent his head to kiss her. The rush of his released feeling was so intense it took her breath. The strength went out of her all at once; she felt her legs give way.

He lifted her up and carried her into his bedroom, kicking the door closed behind them. He laid her on the bed; she felt his fingers, unlacing her gown. He stripped off his own clothes, hurling his golden medal carelessly to the floor. His body was parchment-pale, the skin stretched tight over muscle and bone; he was not cool to touch, as she had imagined he would be, but hot as fever. He kissed her so she could hardly breathe, his black hair falling across her face, a darkness more complete than her own closed eyelids. Her body opened to him, her Gift helplessly extended. She could not tell his feeling from her own, a doubling of sensation almost too great to bear. She would break, she would fly apart under the weight of it. But she was beyond caring. The world around her had dissolved. She was rising into another, far past any point of return.

Yet for just an instant, in a small clear corner of her mind, it seemed to her that she was not rising at all, but falling, plunging into a pit. She saw its depth; she grasped the violence of her descent. And she understood, with the certainty of impact, the impossibility of surviving such a fall.

Seventeen

ILIANE CROUCHED behind the fountain at the center of the Roundhead garden. Above her the glass roof framed a sky thick and cold with stars, a strange contrast to the mild warmth and faint flower-scents that permeated the air. It was soothing, drowsy. She longed for sleep; she had had little enough of it in the past days. But she had slept earlier. Now she must wait.

She had sent word to Tobias this morning, via the clerks, that she was too ill to work, knowing that Tobias would tell Selwyn and that Selwyn would therefore not expect her to come to him that night. In the interest of authenticity she had visited the Orderhouse Infirmary; the doctor who examined her told her she was suffering from malnourishment and exhaustion. He gave her a sleeping draught and packets of powders to be taken with her meals, and ordered her to spend the day in bed.

She returned to her room. After some hesitation she took the draught and slept deeply until the twenty-second bell. She woke only a little refreshed. In the mirror her face looked haggard and unhealthy, her eyes bruised with fatigue. She had lost more weight during the past week; her ribs formed grids of shadow beneath the skin of her breast and sides. Turning away, she pulled on her clothes and dressed her hair. As she dragged her comb through its stubborn tangles, her thoughts turned, irresistibly, to Selwyn. The comb became his fingers, pulling straight her curls, releasing them to spring back to their accustomed shape. She had never

outgrown her childhood ambivalence toward her hair, but
Selwyn had told her he found it beautiful.

As the midnight bell echoed through the Orderhouse, Liliane crept out into the darkened corridors. Stealthily she
slipped through the shadows of the court; silently she entered the quarters of the Arm of the Stone. Ordinarily the
red doors registered the passing of anyone who was not a
Roundhead, but Selwyn had set them to ignore her touch so
she could come to him in secret. Secret from him too now,
she drifted like a ghost into the garden. The light beneath
his door told her he was still at his desk, filling with work
the dark hours that, for the past seven nights, had been filled
with her.

She had wept the first time, unable to help herself, the
intensity of the experience, the horror of what she had done,
overwhelming her all at once. With a gentleness she would
not have expected, Selwyn gathered her in his arms. He held
her, stroking her hair, until her weeping ceased and they
made love again. And again. So much lovemaking—her
body ached with it, was bruised and sore with it, inside and
out. Yet even now she had to fight the craving that urged
her to abandon her vigil, to burst through his door, to thrust
herself into his arms and lose herself in the need whose
depth seven nights of frantic indulgence had not come close
to plumbing.

She leaned her head against the stone of the fountain's
coping and closed her eyes. She was aware that this raw
and terrible wanting, quite outside anything in her experience, did not all belong to her. Incapable of shuttering her
Gift when she was with Selwyn, she was forced to bear the
weight of his passion as fully as her own. It possessed her
now even when they were not together. There was no longer
a moment when she did not think of him—his black hair
like a veil across the pillow, the curve of his lids above his
clear dark eyes, the texture of his skin and the way it folded
close around his bones. He was thin almost to gauntness,
all juts and angles, no softness anywhere; she could count
his ribs as they rose and fell with his breathing, trace the
path of each muscle and vein. There was no longer a moment when she did not feel his touch—his fingers, his

warmth, his breath, his weight. It was as if the sense of him, which she had found first in his footsteps, then in everything that passed through his hands, had imprinted itself upon her very skin.

So it was for heartsensers. In each the madness took a different form. Some lost their minds, some their wills.

She had only herself to blame. It was in full knowledge of the consequences that she had stepped into Selwyn's arms, the power of her resolve, for the first time in her life, insufficient to sustain her on the path she knew she ought to walk. In her heart, she despised herself for her failure. She detested the abjectness of her subjugation even as she yielded to it again and again. But she could not help herself. Like the protagonists of the cautionary tales her Mentor had told, she was lost.

Ironically, had the pursuit of her mission rather than her own weakness brought her to this point, she knew now how little good it would have done her. When they were together in the dark, Selwyn's desire filled the room like fog. But it was only feeling he released, nothing deeper. He had pulled aside a door for her, but a hundred more lay beyond it, sealed tight shut. Love had burst them all open, in the library at Anadh when he feared Elene Jevalse dead; hunger, clearly, did not possess such power. All she had gained by her disastrous choice was a place in the long procession of his women—an answer to the persistent question of physical need, or perhaps a little more.

Yet there was one thing. Selwyn, she had discovered, went somewhere at night, a destination secret enough that he felt it necessary to bind her into sleep while he was gone. The binding caught her by surprise, the second time they were together, but the following evening she was ready. She retreated to the dark place within her mind the moment she felt his power stir. Breathing deeply in pretended sleep, she felt him rise from the bed. She heard the rustling of his clothes as he dressed, the click of the latch as he left the room. He did not come back until just before the dawn bell. Returning to bed, he passed his hand gently across her eyes, lifting, as he thought, the binding. Sighing, she pretended to wake, winding her arms around

his neck to distract him from any suspicion that her unconsciousness was less deep than he intended. He brought
an odd odor back with him: oily and metallic, somehow
subterranean.

He set her to sleep each night, or so he believed, though
he did not always leave the room. Unnervingly, on the
nights he stayed, he remained awake for hours, watching
her. She could hear the mutter of his feelings, like the flow
of an underground river, overlapping currents of indecision,
regret, and inward-turned recrimination, all threaded through
with a kind of angry tenderness. Whatever else he felt for
her, it seemed clear he regretted their union as much as she.
Sometimes he touched her—her hair, her eyelids, her shoulders, her breasts. It took all the strength she had to lie still
beneath his hands, not to betray the secret of her wakeful-
ness. For she was determined to follow him. Wherever he
went, whatever he did, it could not be merely Roundhead
business. If it were, he would not take such trouble to ensure
her ignorance.

Time was short, she knew. The consciousness of her re-
scinded posting was always with her, a shadow deepening
with each day that passed. Forcing herself to wait and watch,
until she was certain of the pattern his excursions formed,
had not been easy. But she had done it. Now, kneeling behind the fountain, she concentrated upon the readiness
within her, a lifeline of purpose against the currents of her
own weakness. She did not allow herself to consider the
rest: the danger of her situation, her terrible longing, the
question of whether she would be strong enough, when
the time came, to do what must be done. Since their first
night together, she had known that delivering Selwyn up to
Jolyon meant delivering herself as well. In her soul, she did
not feel like a Violator. But the fevered landscape of her
obsession could leave no doubt. Her will, which had not
been enough to keep her from Selwyn's arms, was strong
enough for this at least: to follow her mission to its end.
Eyes closed, cheek against the cold stone coping, she waited
not just for her lover, but for the moment in which she could
speak what she knew, and free the world of them both.

*   *   *

Selwyn emerged at last, just after the striking of the second bell. His open doorway was an arched rectangle of tawny light. For a moment he was silhouetted against it before the door swung closed and darkness returned. Shadowy among the shadows of the court, he left the garden.

Liliane waited a little before she rose and followed. Though he was nowhere in sight, her sense of him was like a beacon. It led her along the main corridor, down one side passage and then another, threading a complicated path through a labyrinth of halls and chambers where she had never been before. It was very quiet in the granite passages, a strange hush that did not buzz or hum like ordinary silence, but stopped the ears like the weight of water. Mindlight hovered above like luminous smoke. She paused at every turn and archway to make sure the space ahead was empty; she glanced behind her frequently to be certain she was not followed. She was fearful of becoming lost, but she did not dare leave signs to aid her journey back—she was skilled enough to make them invisible to an ordinary Journeyer, but not to a Roundhead.

Selwyn's trail led her to a blind corridor, its end closed by one of the ubiquitous red doors. Carefully she pressed her hands against the wood, extending her Gift. She sensed only emptiness beyond. She lifted the latch, wondering, now that it was too late to take back the action, whether Selwyn had set all the red doors to ignore her touch, or only those she habitually passed through.

Before her a flight of stairs curved downward into dimness. There was no mindlight here—torches lined the walls instead, each with a black plume imprinted above it. Liliane was reminded sharply of the Fortress. She almost expected to see, at the bottom of the stairs, a herd of shivering Novices, chivvied along by silent white-clad robes. Instead, she found herself in a wide basement. Floor, walls, and ceiling were faced with great slabs of speckled granite. The low roof was supported by massive square columns, with torches affixed to all four sides. The flames flickered in a breeze that could not be felt, sending shadows scuttling over every surface. Everywhere, haphazardly scattered, were piles of objects, some covered by sacking, some exposed, prosaically, as bags of grain or boxes of candles and other supplies. Along the full length of the right-hand wall were stacked barrels of ale and wine, condiments and salt meat.

There was no sign of Selwyn, or of anyone else. Cautiously, Liliane stepped out into the open space. Selwyn's trail led to the center of the vast room, turned abruptly, advanced toward the wall of barrels—and stopped dead. It did not move left or right; it simply disappeared, as if he had dropped through the floor.

Puzzled, Liliane stood still, extending her Gift and all her senses. Had he turned about and retraced his steps? That was impossible—she would have encountered him. But where else could he have gone? She had no idea, yet within herself she felt a growing conviction. The wall of barrels was a dead end. There was nothing here she needed to investigate. It was time, and past time, to take her search elsewhere.

She had actually begun to step away before she realized the discrepancy between what her mind told her, and what she could still feel: the unmistakable pull of Selwyn's presence. Closing her eyes, she refocused her Gift. It was difficult, for the desire to turn away was very strong. But he *was* here, she was certain of it—here, and very close.

She opened her eyes. She understood now what was before her. A semblance held this wall—a very good one, not only creating a convincing image, but effectively deflecting attention away from itself. Had it not been for her particular connection with Selwyn, even her knack for illusion-finding might not have been enough to penetrate the falseness of the message her mind sent her. Even now it was difficult to resist the diffusion urged upon her attention.

Narrowing her focus to a pinpoint, Liliane reached out with both hands. The illusion was true to all the senses: she could feel the barrels beneath her fingers, solid and splintery, and beyond them the stone of the wall, damp with condensation. She gathered her strength. Then, deliberately, she withdrew her belief. Illusion endured only so long as it was accepted. She had learned that, long ago, in her hazing days.

A moment passed, another. The coldness beneath her hands began to change. Suddenly she was touching not stone but wood. Drawing her fingers lightly downward, she found iron studs, the long bar of a hinge. A door. And beyond the door, a room; in the room, Selwyn. She could feel him even through the thickness of the wood, the volume of the air between them, as closely as if he were just beside her. There were others, too, though she could not tell who or how many.

She turned back to the basement. A quick search of the stacks of supplies located a gap between two large boxes draped in sacking. She crept beneath the fabric and wedged herself into the space. With her fingernails, she picked a tiny hole in the coarse material and set herself to wait.

After a little while her legs and feet were numb. The monotony of the view through her peephole was broken only by the odd shadows that swept the room, or the more solid form of a rat scuttling across the floor. Even down here she could hear the bells that tolled through the Orderhouse to mark the passing of the hours; she counted them, one by one, becoming increasingly uneasy as the night drew toward an end. She could not stay much beyond the dawn bell. The Orderhouse day officially began an hour later, but early risers were common, especially among the Arm of the Stone.

Just as she had decided she could not remain a moment longer, the occupants of the hidden room emerged at last. There was no sound or sign; they simply appeared, passing through the apparently solid wall as if through a veil of mist. Selwyn was in the lead, followed by Colmagh and the second Investigation Team Primary, Renart. After them came several other Roundheads, some of them Investigators, some not. Silently they passed through the room and up the stairs. Liliane heard the distant sound of the door as it closed behind them.

She waited a little, and then, wincing at the pins-and-needles pain of her cramped legs, crept out of her hiding place. It was much too late now to explore the room. She sighed with frustration, feeling again the press of time. But Selwyn had not, in her limited experience, left his bed two evenings in a row. If she pretended sickness a second day,

and returned tonight, she should be able to work uninterrupted.

Swiftly she retraced her steps along the silent corridors,
terrified lest she encounter an early-rising Roundhead. She
had carefully counted doors and turnings against the possibility of becoming lost, but because Selwyn had again preceded her the way was easier than it might otherwise have
been. Gaining at last the places she knew, she quit the
Roundhead quarters and entered the safer territory of the
court. The sentry saw her as she slipped through the shadows along the walls. But he had glimpsed her on too many
other nights, hurrying from Selwyn's bed to her own, to
question her presence now.

On reflection, it did not seem wise to stay away from
work a second day. She decided to report as usual and pretend a return of sickness later on. Accordingly, she sat at
breakfast in the chilly company of the clerks—since her
rescission, the Arm-trained staff had become distant and un-
friendly—and then took her way to her office. She was
nearly done with the work that had been pending when she
returned from Progress; Selwyn had sent her nothing new,
using Anselm for whatever dictation he needed. Two days,
or perhaps a little more, and she would be finished.

Just after the noon meal she received a message from
Tobias, requesting the Arm-Master's accounts for the month
of August. The book that included that period had gone to
Selwyn the day before, via one of the clerks, so that he could
check her completed entries for the Progress. Leaving her
office, she crossed the court and entered Selwyn's rooms—a
thing she would never have done had she not known he was
absent. Despite what happened between them after dark,
during the day he maintained his professional rejection of
her, and she was aware that she was not welcome here. She
retrieved the book and carried it to Tobias, waiting while he
searched out the information he needed, crossing the court
once more to put the book back where it had been. As she
stepped away from the desk a wave of dizziness overtook
her. She had not slept at all last night, and very little for the
seven nights before; exhaustion seemed suddenly to weigh
like a cloak of lead on all her limbs. She sank into the chair

before the desk, bowing her head, waiting for her equilibrium to return.

Something—not a sound, but a sense—alerted her. Looking up, she saw Selwyn, standing in the open doorway. She could not control her physical response to him; her heart began to pound.

"I'm sorry," she said. She gripped the arms of the chair, but somehow could not rise. "I was just going."

He waved away her apology. He did not seem angry to find her here. "You're very pale," he said. "Is something wrong?"

"I felt dizzy. I'll be all right in a moment."

He closed the door and came toward her. Stooping, he put his hand to her forehead, then to her cheek. His fingers, as always, were dry and very warm. "You seem feverish. You're still ill. You shouldn't have come in today."

"I do feel weak." This was more opportune than she could have hoped. "Perhaps you're right. Maybe I should go back to bed."

"Yes, that would be best. Come." He straightened, and held out his hands. "You can stay here. Sleep as long as you like; I won't disturb you."

Liliane stammered, caught off guard. "I should . . . I think I ought to go to my own room. I don't want to inconvenience you . . . and Tobias and the others . . . they should see me leave."

There was a pause. Unuttered meanings hung between them.

"You're right, of course," he said.

His hands were still extended. She put hers into them and allowed him to pull her upright. Instead of letting go, he drew her into his arms. Startled, she stiffened for a moment, and then relaxed against him, her face turned against his chest. She could hear the steady beating of his heart. The clean smell of him surrounded her. He was as fastidious as a cat, even to his clothing; he never, as so many did, smelled of sweat or unwashed cloth.

"I missed you last night," he murmured.

Surprised beyond words, she lifted her head. His eyes, dark and clear, moved across her face. Leaning down, he

kissed her—not with the urgent demand of their nights together, but with an unhurried tenderness that made her dizzy
all over again. Something rose in her she could not name.
She closed her eyes and let the world dissolve. She felt she
could stand forever, just this way.

At last he drew back. Placing his hands on her shoulders,
he pushed her gently away.

"Go now," he said. "If you're not better in the morning
I'll have the Arm's physician take a look at you."

Liliane nodded, not trusting herself to speak. Everything
in her longed to yield, to tell him she would stay. It took
all the will she had to remain silent.

She glanced back as she pulled the door closed. He had
seated himself again behind his desk. A folio was open before him; he was intent, absorbed in what he was reading.
He had already forgotten her, moved beyond this moment
and into the next. A surge of emotion shook her, dark and
wrenching. It was unjust that she should think of him every
second, and he be able to put her aside as easily as a turned
page.

Crossing the garden, she felt the spell of his physical presence fall behind. With every step, the weakness that had
urged her to remain diminished. The stage was fully set for
what she planned to do tonight. It remained only to go forth
and do it.

Liliane went to her room and slept for several hours.
When she woke, she felt surprisingly calm. At the ringing
of the midnight bell she returned to the garden, keeping vigil
for more than an hour after Selwyn's light went out, leaving
her post only when she was certain he would not emerge.
She retraced her steps through the empty hallways, finding
her way easily despite the fact that she no longer had his
trail to guide her. Now, standing before the wall of barrels,
she felt more like herself than she had in some time. The
habit of purpose, banished in the turmoil of the past weeks,
had begun to reassert itself the night before, as she resumed
the familiar patterns of her profession. Its solid certainty was
with her now, and she embraced it with relief.

She closed her eyes, reaching out as she had done before,

feeling the semblance surrender reluctantly to the reality of the door it hid. Running her hands over its surface, she found the latch. She had feared it might be locked, but so certain were Selwyn and the others of the power of their illusion that the door opened easily to her touch. The last of the semblance vanished as it did so. She could see the door clearly now, and the room beyond.

She stood at the threshold, cautiously surveying what lay before her. Mindlight, triggered by the opening of the door, revealed a large, low space, faced and columned in the same stone as the basement, furnished with long tables and high drafting desks. The tables were cluttered with a strange jumble of objects and papers. Several of the drafting desks had large parchment sheets affixed to them, covered with spidery lines that suggested diagrams or maps. On the far wall, obscured by shadow, a collection of metal objects was dimly visible, lying on shelves or hanging from hooks. There was a smell in the room—the same odor Selwyn brought with him from his nighttime excursions, musty and subterranean, metallic, strange in a way she could not readily identify.

Liliane had not known what she might find in Selwyn's secret place. Somewhere within herself, however, she had assumed there would be documents of some kind, secret writings or hidden records. But this looked more like an artisan's workshop. She set her feet across the threshold, passing from the shadowed dimness of the basement into the pale clarity of mindlight. She felt her heart beating, as if she were afraid. Yet she was not conscious of fear, only of intent.

Turning first to the chaos of the tables, she discovered a miscellaneous welter of hand-tools, artisan's equipment, pens, tablets, folios, papers, bottles of ink and other liquids, and boxes and packets of powders. These things revealed little beyond the fact of their disarray and the obvious frequency of their use. Passing her hands across them yielded only the vaguest of sensations, flickers of feeling too faint to identify.

Shifting her attention to the parchments on the drafting desks, she found herself utterly mystified. From the precision of their composition and their neatly lettered keys and labels, they were plans or schematics of some kind. But for what, she could not guess. The labels were all in some kind of code. Both Pietra and Costares's courts had hosted licensed Modifiers, and what she saw now reminded her of the plans they had produced. Yet she had never heard of a Roundhead following that profession.

Reaching out, she placed the tips of her fingers gently on one of the parchments. At once a tremendous jolt of feeling ran up her arm, a wrongness so palpable it seemed to cast a veil of darkness across the room. She snatched her hand away, unconsciously cradling it against her breast, as if it had been burned. There was Violation here—major Violation. She could not identify it, or quantify it, or classify it, as a Roundhead could have; her limited expertise did not allow for that. Yet she recognized it, with a force of conviction absolutely beyond question.

For a moment she stood motionless. Already, without knowing exactly what she had found, she knew that she had discovered more than she had bargained for. The impulse to turn away, to leave the final work of determination to others, was very powerful. Yet even as she thought of flight, she knew she would not flee. She had come too far not to complete what she had begun.

She turned, slowly, to the wall of metal objects. Their contours were alien, like something glimpsed in a dream; it was impossible to decipher their purpose. Yet there was something within them that evoked the ghosts of familiar objects—changed, elaborated almost beyond recognition, but there, a base from which these fantastic creations had sprung. Taking a breath, she moved closer, her arms held out before her. She did not want to put her hands on these things, for she already suspected what they were. But touch would confirm what sight could only estimate. She could not leave without knowing exactly what she had found.

In the end, touch was not necessary. The purpose of whoever had forged the objects was strong. Its essence, trapped within the metal, breathed out an aura as cold and deadly as the air of another world. Liliane backed away, her hands still outstretched. These things were tools—but not tools the

Limits would recognize. There was not just one Violation here, but hundreds.

She stood in the center of the room, trembling. This was the stuff of nightmares, of legends. It was the sort of thing that one was told could happen, but never dreamed it possible actually to encounter. No ordinary human Violators had made these things—Roundheads had made them, the Arm of the Stone, purifiers of the earth, preservers of the powers of the mind, final bulwark against the perversion of the hands. It was a thought to unravel reality. In all her speculations as to the nature of Selwyn's unfitness, Liliane could not have conjured up anything so appalling, so abominable, so depraved as this. How could such rottenness be hidden? How could her Gift have failed to sense it? She had given herself to this man. She had desired him so much she was sick with it. She had longed to stand forever in his arms. Cold with horror, she closed her eyes.

"I underestimated you."

Slowly Liliane turned. He stood in the doorway, exactly as if her thoughts had conjured him up. She had not felt his approach. The sense of Violation around her was strong enough to eclipse even the dark currents of her obsession.

"I dreamed of you," he said softly. He was dressed for sleep, in a nightrobe and garnet-colored overgarment. His hair was loose around his shoulders, his eyes like pieces of coal in his pale face. "I woke alone and knew myself for a fool. That story of sickness—you followed me here last night, didn't you?"

Liliane's tongue seemed to have frozen. She could not speak. Strangely, she felt no fear. Selwyn's presence carried the inevitability of dreams, or of an understanding formed far below the pathways of conscious thought.

"What did you do, steal into the garden and watch my door till I came out? But how did you know? How did you know to watch?"

Still she did not speak.

"You may as well tell me. I know you're Jolyon's spy."

Liliane's false calm trembled. "What?" she whispered.

"I've known from the start. Who you are. What you're here to do."

She struggled to absorb this. Abruptly, Selwyn advanced into the room. The sudden motion banished her dreamlike passivity. Instinctively she stumbled backward, into the hateful aura of the abominations behind her. She froze, unable to move further. Selwyn halted too, his hands against one of the long tables. He fixed her with his glittering black eyes. Terror gripped her now, battering helpless insect-wings inside her chest. The air was thick, difficult to breathe, overloaded with the stench of Violation and her own fear.

"How . . ." Her voice was a croak. She swallowed hard. "How did you find out?"

"I have my sources. Just as Jolyon does."

"But then . . . why did you let me stay?"

"If I'd dismissed you outright, Jolyon would have known I'd seen through his little ruse. I never imagined you were any real threat. I never thought you'd get beyond your industrious digging among my records." He smiled, the very ghost of an expression. She knew the ugliness within him; she should not still find him pleasing to look at. Yet she could not force her eyes to see him otherwise. "I told myself that even if you dug to some effect, you wouldn't have enough information to put what you found in context. There was nothing that, if pressed, I couldn't blame on subordinates. But I was wrong." The smile was gone. "I should have followed my instinct and gotten rid of you at once. I realized it while we were on Progress. I would have dismissed you upon our return even if your revocation hadn't arrived. Although I don't suppose that would have changed what's happened." He stared at her. "It was at Jolyon's instruction that you came to my bed, wasn't it?"

"Yes."

She saw the muscles tense around his eyes. "Just that? Nothing more?"

She did not reply. After a moment he turned his head, abruptly, breaking their gaze.

"It was all there for me to see." His voice was bitter. "I knew your reputation. I knew about your . . . special skills. It's an unnatural thing, a heartsenser who consents to be a whore for her masters."

This was not a man, but a monster. Why should she care

what he thought of her? Even so, she felt the sting of his words. "You didn't have to take what I offered," she said. "You could have turned me away."

"I don't need you to remind me of my lack of judgment." His face had hardened. "You never answered my first question. What made you watch me last night? What made you think I would leave my rooms?"

There was no point in lying. After all, there could be only one outcome to this confrontation. Yet Liliane could not bring herself to tell the truth. The existence of her inner refuge was a thing that, since Goldwine, she had shared with no living soul.

"Your binding didn't work," she said.

"Didn't work? That's impossible. How could it not work?"

"I don't know. All I know is that it didn't set me to sleep. I was awake when you left; I was awake when you came back."

"And when I stayed?"

"I was awake then, too."

"Scanning me, no doubt?"

"Yes."

His face twisted. "Was there never a moment when you were not a spy?"

"It was my charge. What else would you expect me to do?"

Suddenly he was moving again. Liliane dodged sideways, intent on keeping distance between them. The wall came up hard against her shoulder, jarring her to a halt. Selwyn was close enough now, and the Violation-objects were far enough away, for her to feel him. His guard, she realized, was well and truly ruptured. Feeling poured from him, as least as strongly as in Anadh. Yet she did not reach forward with her power, as she would have even an hour ago. She drew up her guard instead, as tight and close as she could.

"Are you scanning me now?"

She could not meet his eyes. "No."

"No? Why not?"

"I don't need to."

"What do you mean, you don't need to? You've never

broken my guard, that much I know. Isn't it part of your charge, to get behind my guard, to map my mind?''

"I've seen this room. It's all the map I need."

He closed the distance between them. His hands gripped her shoulders. She could feel his anger. "This room is just a fraction of what I am. Look inside me—go on, I'll make it easy for you. This is what you wanted, isn't it? Look!''

"No." Liliane struggled in his grip, putting her hands out to push him away. She felt his skin, smooth and warm; her fingers tangled in his silky hair. She could not help herself. Against reason, against knowledge, fear, and horror, the feel of him affected her as it always did. Her Gift, beyond her control, arrowed forward, futilely seeking union—the curse of the heartsenser, the pursuit of an impossible joining.

He was all around her now, open, for the first time since she had known him. The places where his guard had been were blank spaces in his mind, but their contours were clear in the very emptiness they left behind—more defenses than she had thought it possible for one person to maintain, some of them illegal, some of them not. Each had sheltered a different layer of anger, a different well of grief or loss, a different structure of purpose. Unconfined now, these things flowed together, an unbearable turmoil nearly impossible to interpret. Yet clear above it all, like an eye gazing down upon a stormy ocean, his intellect floated free, and his ambition, his arrogance, the questing restlessness of his soul and its constant turning toward what was forbidden. The darkness in him too was clear, the foundation of his being, wrapped up in words and phrases whose cadences held the wonder of childhood. And, at the very center of his mind, one last barrier. It was massive, black and huge as the Fortress itself. But it was neither high nor thick enough to fully conceal the heart of brilliance it guarded, a pulsing power like the sun . . . like the Stone . . .

"Enough."

He let her go. With the withdrawal of his touch her Gift also withdrew. For a moment the emptiness of it was overwhelming. She covered her face with her hands. Her knees gave way, and she sank to the floor. She felt tears streaking her cheeks. Never had she seen so deeply into another person. It had been more like a mindlink than any use of her Gift she understood. The absoluteness of it, the loss of control, terrified her.

Even so, her training had been at work. There was a map of him now inside her mind, just as Jolyon had ordered. His barriers and defenses, in miniature, wound their convoluted paths within her, like a walled city glimpsed from above. Its tiny inhabitants, a thousand snippets of restless emotion, struggled uneasily against their confinement. And his Violation—that was within her too, the heavy ground on which the city rested, the murky light in which it bathed. She had done her work too well. The corruption that gripped him was now part of her. By whatever road she came to it, the ending of her story was the same. In the achievement of her mission lay her own condemnation.

Selwyn had turned his back. He was leaning with both hands against one of the tables, raggedly attempting to rebuild the complex architecture of his inner self. Emotion still poured from him, but the flood was rapidly losing its force; soon he would be closed again, inviolate.

"What did you see?" he said at last. His voice was quiet, his back still turned.

"See?"

"Yes." He turned. He looked drained and haggard. "I don't know any more what's inside my soul. You're proof of that."

Liliane felt anger jolt through her, powerful and surprising. "How dare you ask me that?"

He was taken aback; she could see it in his face. "What do you mean?"

"You force me into your mind against my will. You make me share what no sane person should be made to touch." Her voice was shaking. Somehow she had gotten to her feet. "And then you dare to ask me what I've seen? You know what I've seen—Violation. And now it's mine as well as yours. You've passed it to me, like a disease. . . ."

Her voice broke; abruptly, the tears were falling again. She willed them away, but they would not stop. She put her hands over her face to hide them. She heard Selwyn's voice.

"You're wrong." Oddly, he did not sound angry. "How

can I explain to you how wrong you are? Even if there were such a thing as Violation, it wouldn't be contagious. You can't be corrupted by anything in me. Seeing is not the same as being.''

"You are a Violator," she wept. "Everything you say is a lie.''

His tone was harder now. "But it's what you wanted. All I've done is to give you freely what you spent every minute of your time with me trying to take by stealth. Do you think it would have been different if you'd succeeded without my knowledge?''

"Of course not!" She tore her hands away from her face. "That's the point, don't you see? This was never a real mission. Jolyon sent me here to fail.''

"Madelaine—" He spoke her false name. Through her tears she saw him step forward, his hands moving as if he meant to reach for her. She pushed herself back against the wall.

"Get away from me!" she cried. "I never want to feel your touch again. You revolt me!''

He fell back. His face had smoothed and hardened, like setting porcelain. He was angry now, she could feel it. "You aren't worth my compassion," he said. "I showed myself to you. There's not one other person in the world who has seen so much. But you're as blind as the rest of your kind. I gave you a sphere, and you saw only a plane.''

"I never asked you to give me anything.''

"True. But now that you've told yourself half the story, I'm going to tell you the rest. For . . . completion's sake.''

Liliane pressed her hands to her ears. "I don't want to hear this. Why are you doing this?''

"I don't think I'll tell you about my childhood," he said, ignoring her. "Or how I came to be a Guardian. Suffice it to say that when I first became a Roundhead Apprentice, it was . . . well, under false pretenses. Once on the sixth floor, I became the protégé of a powerful Roundhead named Marhalt. You've heard of Marhalt?''

He glanced at her. He had moved away from the table; he was pacing, moving slowly back and forth, his hands clasped behind his back. She did not reply.

"Well, it doesn't matter if you have or not. Marhalt was—is—not like other Roundheads. He detests Jolyon's kind. He values deliberation over zealotry, wisdom over suffering. Under his guidance, my understanding of the world began to change. Though it was never possible for me to be a Roundhead like Jolyon, it did seem possible for me to become a Roundhead like Marhalt.

"After years in the Fortress, I returned to the world, as a Field Monitor. Everywhere I went I saw misery. The Northern Diocese is a paradise compared to some of the places I've been. And my views changed again. I began to remember what I knew in childhood, and had forgotten in the Fortress—that injustice isn't just a matter of harsh Investigations, of Interrogations that leave their subjects mind-dead, but of people starving and suffering and dying while those with the power to change such things do nothing more than watch. Some of my colleagues agreed with me, and the result was Zosterian philosophy. None of us imagined, when we started, how successful we'd be. We never thought we'd become strong enough to put our principles into action. But we did."

He had stopped pacing. He stood silent for a moment, his face intent and inward.

"I came to the Northern Orderhouse to implement the Progress. But Zosterianism wasn't my only motivation for choosing Britannia. There's someone here, you see. A man. My brother. My brother is what you would call a Violator. For much of his life he has experimented with tools and mechanical objects—he created most of the things you see in this room. I came to Britannia with the intent of confronting him. I wanted to save him, to make him understand how terrible his actions were. But when I found him at last, it wasn't he who changed, but me.

"I was ready for it, I know that now. I was restless; for a long time throwing myself into my work hadn't been enough. I didn't yet understand that the Roundhead path I walked was just another aspect of the persona I had grafted onto myself back in the Fortress, a false garment that never really fit me. When my brother and I came face-to-face, I had my arguments ready—I had thought out everything I intended to say. In the end I said none of it. It was he who talked. His words horrified me. All the same, I felt their power. It was as if he were telling me truths I already knew.

"I couldn't admit that to myself at once, of course—any more than he could believe, when he saw me for the first time, that the Roundhead at his door was really his brother. Accepting such things is like picking the world apart and putting it back together in a different shape. It was my brother's daughter, in the end, who provided the key. She's a maker, the most Gifted I've ever known. When I first found my brother, I still believed that mindpower and hand-power were entirely inimical. I could not understand how my brother's pursuits and my niece's mindstrength could coexist so easily, like two leaves on the same branch. Why hadn't my brother's tools and machines long ago killed his daughter's Gift? It seemed an impossible riddle. But it's the question itself that is the riddle. It must be asked the other way around. Once I understood this, I grasped the truth of what my brother has known for most of his life: that mind-power and handpower are not enemies, but two halves of a divided whole."

Liliane could stand it no longer. "Stop," she said. She was sitting at the base of the wall again; she had folded herself as small as she could, her knees close against her chest. Her hands were pressed to her ears, but they were not enough to block his voice. "I can't bear it. Please stop."

He moved over to her and crouched down. The rich over-robe he wore pooled around him like spilled wine. He was so close she could smell him: the chalkiness of the ink pow-der he mixed himself, the aromatic residue of sandalwood from the press in which he kept his clothes, the herbal oil he combed into his hair, all unified and transformed into something else, something uniquely his own, by the dry heat of his body.

"When you've seen what I've seen," he said softly, "you begin to understand that the evil in our world goes far be-yond anything identified by Zosterian philosophy. Our whole way of life is wrong. It's all a construct, a false vi-sion—Violation, the Limits, all of it. The Split didn't come from the pursuit of handpower. It came from the loss of balance. Balance, real balance, is equality. In a perfect world, the two powers would be conjoined, inseparable, like the right hand and the left.''

Liliane shrank away from him. ''This is blasphemy,'' she whispered. ''How can you say such things?''

''You live in a world where there is no truth beyond the need to perpetuate the power of the Fortress. What do you care for the suffering of the people of the world, for their starvation and disease and death, as long as the structure of Guardianhood remains intact? But I care, I and my men. When my brother was just a boy he invented a plow with a double blade that would have done twice the work with half the effort. If every tool in the world was modified just that much, can you imagine how much better life would be? That is what this room represents. In this room, my companions and I are working toward discovering exactly how much misery it is possible to wipe out. When we know, we will unleash our knowledge upon the world.''

Liliane stared at him. She felt a kind of sick fascination. ''You don't really believe you can do that, do you?''

''Who will stop me? You?''

''Jolyon will send someone to replace me. And someone else and someone else, until he succeeds.''

''He will not succeed. You've taught me a lesson, Madelaine. I'll never again underestimate someone as badly as I did you.''

''You can't hide what you're doing forever. Someone will discover it.''

''Perhaps.'' He watched her steadily. ''But this isn't a new endeavor. We may be the first Roundheads to walk this path, but not the first people. Right now, across our world, there are more secret workshops like this one than you can begin to imagine.''

They stared at each other. There seemed to be nothing more to say. After a moment Selwyn rose and paced a little distance away. Liliane too got to her feet, on legs that felt numb and heavy. She watched his back. She knew what must come next. She could not seem to muster any emotion, not even fear. Everything had been wrung out of her.

''All my men are Zosterians,'' Selwyn said, softly. ''All

I had to do was to remove the barriers of their indoctrination; it was never difficult, after that, to convince them of the truth. But that would not be possible for you. And a mindwipe . . . that risks leaving something behind. No. It's too dangerous. There's no other way.''

His head was bowed. His hands hung by his sides, his fingers loose. Everything about his stance suggested reluctance. And it came to her that though he knew he must kill her, he did not want to. The will for life, flattened into nothingness beneath the press of the night's events and the understanding of how they must end, rushed up through Liliane with irresistible force. The evil of what she had heard, the horror of what she carried within her, fell away like ugly garments. All that mattered was the possibility that she might not have to die.

''Maybe there is another way,'' she said. She took a step toward him. Her legs still felt weak, but she was no longer numb. Fear and desperation possessed her, and hope, trembling along her limbs as if she had woken from a long, feverish sleep.

''What do you mean?''

He had turned. His suspicion was plain, but he made no move to evade her as she approached, step by slow step. She kept her eyes on his, willing into her features all the conviction of which she was capable.

''This night has changed everything.'' She swallowed, to keep her voice steady. ''I won't pretend that I'm not . . . horrified by what you've told me. I won't pretend the things in this room don't disgust me. You wouldn't expect me to feel otherwise. But . . .'' She swallowed again. ''I've . . . realized things tonight about my presence here that make me question everything I was sent to do.''

''Don't insult my intelligence. I didn't tell you what I did because I thought I could change your point of view.''

She was very close to him now. His guard was disordered again; she sensed his skepticism, his distrust. But in his eyes, dark and clear, fixed upon her face as if they would never leave it, she saw a thing he had never let her see before: her own power. He did not believe her. But he wanted to.

"It's not what you told me," she said softly. "It's what I understood for myself. This mission was as much a way to force me to fail a Test as it was a real assignment. There was never any possibility of my surviving it—either I wouldn't find your secrets, or I'd condemn myself by doing so. I have no allegiance to this mission any longer. I have no wish to betray you now. I don't want to give that to Jolyon, I don't want him to gain anything through you or me. Can you understand that?"

He watched her as if mesmerized. "What are you saying?"

"I won't tell you I can ever accept what you believe. But maybe it doesn't matter. What happened between us—it wasn't pretense. It wasn't planning. I didn't want that to be true, but it is. You have to have felt it." She stepped forward again, close enough to feel his heat. "Don't you know what that means for a heartsenser? What I said to you before—I only said it to hurt you. It isn't true." She reached up to place her hands upon his chest, absolutely confident that this time she would feel nothing but her own strength, her own hope, her own will to survive long enough to carry her secrets out of the Northern Orderhouse. "I want to stay with you. Please, just let me stay with you."

Perhaps if she had not said the words . . . perhaps if she had not touched him. . . . She saw his face change, and knew she had lost him. He jerked back, away from her hands. Anger clamped across his features, like a veil falling down.

"No," he said. The muscles of his throat worked with his breathing. "No. I won't let you do this to me twice."

He was moving toward her. He was going to kill her now, right now. Liliane fell back, stumbling over her own feet. As she came up against the wall she felt his hands close around her throat. His fingers were like bands of fire. She felt her airways close, her lungs collapse; she struggled, her chest heaving. But there was no breath to be had. Even when his hands left her neck and moved up to her forehead she could not breathe. His power, that bright thing she had sensed inside him, was unfettered now. It was coming for her, widening like the sun, filling up the entire universe of her consciousness. Instinctively she retreated, pulling back inside her mind. He was gaining on her, almost close enough to touch her. Desperately she dived, down and down into the dark place at her center. The blackness overtook her so quickly she did not see if he had followed.

The
Stone

Eighteen

SMALL oil lamp burned on the table beside the bed. The light it cast was not strong enough to pierce the darkness that held the corners of the room, or to dispel the shadows that pooled in the folds of the bed curtains and the coils of the sheets, but it was sufficient to lay a dim radiance across the bed itself, and the body of the sleeping woman upon it.

She lay on her back, one arm flung above her head. The weak light drew glints of gold from her tumbled hair; it described the arch of her closed eyelids and the plane of her cheek; it filled her cupped palm with shadow and poured darkness along the folds of her linen shift. The clotted fabric disguised the curves and hollows of her body, making her seem as slight and sexless as a child. She was deep asleep, completely motionless but for the shallow rise and fall of her breathing.

Propped on his elbow, Bron watched her. Still and waxen as she was, it was almost possible to imagine that he had succeeded at what he had set out to do—that his resolve had not deserted him, as he looked into her terrified eyes and felt her struggle to breathe, that he had not removed his hands from her throat and called up his power instead. He had intended only to destroy her memory of the night, of all the nights they had spent together. But he had acted in haste, without proper preparation. When she awoke the next day it was apparent that he had taken too much. She could move; she could dress and feed herself; she could hear and follow spoken commands. Beyond that she seemed entirely empty, without memory of herself or him or anything else. She sat all day without moving, staring at nothing, her hands softly folded in her lap. At night she lay down to sleep, obedient as a child.

He locked her in his bedroom; no one but he knew she was there. He informed Tobias that she was temporarily absent on an errand to one of the nearby villages. Cloaking himself in invisibility, he went to her room and removed her travel bag and some of her clothing to make sure of the deception. Each day he worked in his office, as if nothing were amiss. Each night he lay awake beside her, watching as she slept. Sooner or later, he knew, his interrupted action must be completed. Even mindless, she was dangerous. It was possible that a skilled Interrogator could extract enough shadows from her empty memory to reconstruct what she had seen—and she had seen too much, not just the room and what it held, but almost the whole of his secret self.

Yet three days had come and gone, and still he had not summoned up the will to kill her.

In a life lived constantly upon the cusp of risk, Bron had early identified the roads along which danger might approach him. Self-betrayal, treachery, the malice of others, political fiat, chance discovery, simple bad luck—anticipating these, guarding against them, had long ago become as natural as breathing. The tie that bound him to Serle and Serle's family posed a different sort of danger, for it was the one thing that reached behind his barriers and touched his true self. But in all the world, there was no one else who compelled him in such a way. He had had friendships since his days in the Fortress, some of them close, but there had not been one he could not have abandoned if expediency dictated. He had had lovers, many of them, but he had never cared for any of them enough to matter, nor kept them long enough for that to begin to change.

He was aware that this woman was not like the others—in the profound unwisdom of their liaison, in the inexplicable intensity of feeling she had evoked in him. There was also the fact that, in all his career as a Roundhead, he had never with his own hands taken a human life. Yet these things, concrete as they were, failed to illuminate the core of his difficulty in performing what he knew to be a necessary act. Since the age of twelve necessity had ruled his life. In all that time he had never once failed to follow where it led, forcing himself past fear and feeling and preference alike, subordinating the heated turmoil of his deeper self to the ice-clear understandings of his intellect. It should not be different now. And yet it was.

For some time before Madelaine arrived—though he knew her real name, he could think of her only by the false one—he had expected her, or someone like her. Jolyon's hatred had outlasted their Investments; he had kept track of Bron through all his various assignments, just as Bron had kept track of him. For a long time he had done no more than watch. But little by little, as his influence grew, he began to act. He had planted at least one agent among the Roundheads of the Northern Orderhouse. Britannia's new Field Monitor was almost certainly Jolyon's man. There had been a series of suspiciously observant merchants, a parade of too-curious travelers, even a few visiting Roundheads posing as Zosterian sympathizers. When Linorio died, Bron had not been deceived by the apparent naturalness of his death. When he learned that Linorio would be replaced not by the scrivener Anselm, as he had requested, but by a stranger, he had known at once that the stranger must be Jolyon's agent.

He contacted his sources in the Fortress, and received, smuggled in by special courier, a dossier detailing the agent's identity, career, and charge. After some thought he took Colmagh into his confidence.

"He must have powerful support, to carry out a thing like this," Colmagh observed when he had finished reading the dossier.

"Yes," Bron replied. The Zosterian philosophy he and his colleagues had conceived and codified went a considerable distance beyond the reforms originally envisioned by Marhalt, not only in its scope but in its abandonment of the secrecy Marhalt firmly believed was essential to the success of his cause. Marhalt had opposed their commitment to bringing it to the world. Well-known to be a moderate, he had maintained his separation from the Zosterian movement even as many of his colleagues became converts. Yet he had never severed his connection to Bron and the others, and it was in part the powerful shield of this protection that had enabled Zosterianism to come as far as it had. To move against Bron, or any of Marhalt's pupils, was to move against Marhalt himself. Jolyon's prestige was considerable, his personal following within the Suborder substantial, but no Orderman had the clout to oppose a member of the Council of Six. "He must have backing from one member of the Council, at least. Although I doubt this is an open action. Jolyon has always preferred to work behind the scenes."

"This could be a serious threat to us." Colmagh's fair brows were creased with concern. "This woman is extremely skilled. By repute, she's one of the best heartsenser agents now working. And her behavior in the Midland Sea makes it clear that she's ambitious. An assignment like this could set her up for life."

"Only if she succeeds. And she won't, I promise you. Conventional espionage won't get her anywhere, and there's nothing in this dossier to indicate she has the power to threaten our barriers."

"I can't help wondering why Jolyon has picked this particular time to act. And why this particular agent?"

"I don't think the timing's mysterious. I'm sure the only reason he hasn't acted sooner is that he couldn't talk anyone into backing him before now. As for the agent . . . actually, she seems an odd choice. She was one of his pets while she was an Apprentice. Still, the secrecy of heartsensers is fairly impenetrable. He might not have known who she was until after he picked her."

Colmagh was looking at him, a strange expression on his face. "You know this woman?"

"Only in the sense that I know all Jolyon's victims. We made it a point to keep track of them, my companions and I."

"There's nothing between you? No connection?"

Bron frowned. "Connection?"

Colmagh seemed to hesitate. "Nothing Jolyon does is random, you know that," he said. "This heartsenser is unusual in many ways, not least in her departure from the

Celibate Rule. She's evidently used that . . . ability to some effect already. It wouldn't surprise me to learn she had been instructed to use it here."

"On me, you mean? Jolyon knows me very little if he thinks he can trap me that way."

"I think he knows you very well." Colmagh's gaze was steady. "It occurs to me to wonder whether he might have some particular reason to think she could succeed."

Bron felt a flash of temper. "Do you really think I'd be stupid enough to sleep with Jolyon's agent? Even if I did, do you truly imagine that's all it would take to break my guard?"

Colmagh's gaze did not waver. "I think you should block the appointment."

"Why? Because you have no faith in my willpower?"

"I have a bad feeling about this. Call it a premonition."

One of Colmagh's Gifts was divination; it sometimes spilled over into prescience. "I've appealed her posting through official channels," Bron said. "If I do more Jolyon will realize I've seen through what he's trying to do. I don't want that, at least not yet."

"It seems to me the lesser of two evils."

"I don't agree. It may be risky to have her here, but it would be far more dangerous to refuse to play the game. She'll be gone in six months. Maybe less."

"A week might be too long. You don't know—"

"Enough, Colmagh!" Bron raised his voice to carry over the Primary's; he used, not the casual between-colleagues tone in which they had been conversing, but the formal voice of his rank. "Your concern is noted. But I've already made up my mind on how to handle this situation. I don't intend to change it."

Another man would have lowered his gaze and held his tongue. Colmagh did neither. "This may be meant for you, Selwyn," he said. "Jolyon is only our enemy because he first was yours. But if you fall into his trap, so do we all."

Outside his family, there was not one other person Bron would have allowed to speak to him in such a way. But of all his men, he was closest to Colmagh; he trusted him as much as he trusted anyone. He knew, in any case, that the

Primary's words stemmed not from defiance but from dedication.

Knowing the foolishness of overconfidence, Bron took no chances. He strengthened the semblance that bound the tool room. He reviewed the files and records. He ran rigorous tests of his men's barriers; though he did not tell them Madelaine was a spy, he did inform them that she had been assigned to him against his will and was not to be trusted. He even looked to the Catalogue and the binding he had placed across Elene's name. The binding was as strong as he knew how to make it, which was very strong indeed; despite Madelaine's reputation as an illusion-piercer, he had little fear of discovery from that direction.

He knew very well the pointlessness of speculating upon Jolyon's convoluted motives, and so wasted little time in thinking about his enemy. Colmagh's words about connection stayed with him, however. He had not been entirely forthright with the Primary, for he had never forgotten the punishment he and the heartsenser had shared. When he received the dossier and realized who she was, it had come flooding back, a vivid sensory memory—the sun on his shoulders, stone against his knees, the flash of sea-blue eyes through a veil of unbound hair. He could still recapture his sense of the contrast between her apparent pliancy and the strength he sensed beneath it, as if he had somehow perceived her Gift, though he had not known its nature until he read her file.

He could not explain why time and experience, ruthless cullers of memory, had left this particular incident intact inside his mind. Perhaps it was the weight of the enmity they shared. She, no less than Bron, had been enshrined in the pantheon of Jolyon's hatred; though he had never stopped a punishment of which she was a part—he and his companions had abandoned their attempts to interfere with Jolyon's pursuits once it became clear that he had the protection of certain powerful Masters—he had made it a point to keep track of Jolyon's actions, and had known each time she was singled out for persecution. Or perhaps there was a simpler reason. The courtyard had been his last penance before he left the Novice Wing—a line drawn across three years of misery, a thing never to be forgotten.

The punishment had been Jolyon's doing. Knowing the minuteness of his memory, it was possible that he recalled the incident. There was no reason, however, for him to assume that Bron did. And if he had chosen her for her skills alone, in ignorance of her identity, the entire issue was moot. The thread of memory that bound him to this woman was nothing more than coincidence. A connection, perhaps, but not the kind Colmagh feared.

Irrationally, Bron had assumed she would be much as he remembered her. His first sight of her, when she arrived at last, was a shock. The woman before him, slight and self-effacing in her drab Journeyer gown, her hair skinned painfully back from a pale, plain face, seemed a far cry, not just from the calculating seductress Colmagh had invoked, but from the riot-curled, blush-cheeked girl of his memory. Only the sea-blue eyes were as he recalled—he saw that the first time she raised her gaze to his—but she looked at him so rarely this was easy to forget. Before the reality of the woman, the image of the girl withered like a flower petal in a frost. Within a week the memory of the sunlit courtyard was gone, vanishing back into the realm of imagination from whence it had risen.

Madelaine quickly proved herself to be as competent as her dossier had suggested. She was an excellent scrivener—intelligent, efficient, never less than flawlessly prepared. She possessed not only a thorough knowledge of Arm procedure, but a mastery of Orderhouse and Diocesan history. Her assumption of the manner and methods of the Arm-trained was as perfect in its authenticity as it was unflagging in its consistency. Wisely, she had not attempted to fabricate a Zosterian background for herself, but her easy familiarity with its principles might have led an outsider to think her a sympathizer. She deployed her Gift with skill and discretion; she was certainly scanning him whenever they were together, but there was not the slightest sign of it—no telltale pauses or lapses of attention, no surreptitious glances or unguarded gestures. And she behaved at all times with the utmost propriety. There was never any indication that she was attempting to call upon the skills she had employed in the Midland Sea. Bron sometimes thought about the minister whom she had seduced to gain her position in the Osman Empire, and wondered what desperation or profligacy of taste could have been tempted by such an absence of charm.

In addition to Colmagh, Bron had identified Madelaine to Tobias, who kept an eye on her and reported regularly on her activities. She was conducting a systematic search of the records and also questioning Orderhouse personnel, including the Arm-trained and Bron's own Roundheads, proceeding with impressive speed and efficiency, given the enormous amount of material to be gone through and the fact that she was up to her eyes in legitimate work. She met regularly with Amias, whom Bron had long known to be Jolyon's agent; Amias, no doubt, relayed whatever information she gave him directly to Jolyon. Bron took a certain pleasure in imagining how these reports must frustrate his enemy. There was nothing for her to find—nothing in the records, nothing in the minds of the ordinary Journeyers, nothing in the minds of the Arm-trained, certainly nothing in the minds of his men, to whom he had taught barriers of his own design. As for himself, though his lack of near-speech made it impossible for him to sense her use of her Gift, he would have known if she pierced his guard. She never did.

She was failing, as he had known she would. By now, he thought, she must perceive this. The consequences must be looming very large in her mind. The official censure the Arm of the Stone would give for failure would be terrible; it would ensure that, heartsenser or not, she never held a decent posting again. If she were wise, however, it would be Jolyon's vengeance she feared. He would see to it that she paid the price of failure not once, but over and over, for the rest of her life.

Unable to succeed, unable to fail; an unenviable position, even a desperate one. But if she felt desperation—or dread, or frustration, or indeed any emotion at all—there was no sign of it. Watching her, one could easily imagine her one of those dull functionaries so common among the Arm-trained, whose devotion to detail was the most compelling fact of their existence. But Bron had come to realize that her colorless persona was not exactly what it seemed. Whether natural to her or deliberately assumed, it was clearly the principal weapon in her arsenal of espionage. Her silent ways, her precise and careful correctness, the very plainness of her appearance, served to direct attention away from the fact of her person as effectively as a semblance. Sitting with her in a room, it was easy to forget she was there. When she spoke, the neutral tones of her voice made everything she said seem unexceptional. When she listened, the selflessness of her focus urged a speaker to say much more than was wise.

Altogether, she was a good deal more formidable than he had anticipated. Had he not known what she was, he would probably never have suspected her as she pried her way through his unrevealing papers and chipped futilely at the monolith of his secret life. It was fascinating, in a way, to watch her in action, for the dichotomy between what she was and what she seemed was so great. More and more he found himself searching for some hint of that other self—a flash of calculation in those downcast eyes, a stirring of intent behind that relentlessly tranquil face. He could not stop himself, sometimes, from needling her a little, trying to push her into an unguarded reaction. There was no disguise in the world so perfect it could not slip: if there were anyone who knew that, it was he. But she never slipped. Even failure was not enough to make her crack.

From the beginning he had watched her—as closely, perhaps, as she watched him. He was aware that the way he thought of her had changed over the passing months, partly out of his growing respect for her professional ability, partly because, spy or not, she was one of the most competent assistants he had ever worked with. But it was not until the Progress, with its cramped quarters and lack of distraction, that he grasped the presence of a different alteration. One day he turned to her and realized that he had ceased to find her plain. Her skin, which he had thought colorless, now seemed to glow with a dozen translucent shades of ivory and rose. In her features, which he had dismissed as unremarkable, there now appeared a delicacy very close to beauty. The curves of her slender figure, which he had thought meager, now suggested more to him, in their very slightness, than more obvious endowments less left to the imagination.

From that moment, looking at her ceased to be a neutral act. His eyes began to linger on the contour of her cheek, the smooth sweep of her throat, the shape of her breasts beneath the heavy fabric of her dress. He was stunned by the change, so complete, so consuming. Where had it come from? He could not trace the process of alteration; it seemed to have descended from one day to the next, a bolt from the blue, an earthquake of transformation. Yet that could not be. Even an earthquake was the endpoint of a long chain of events, the culmination of a thousand shifts below the ground. What had happened must have been taking shape for some time, out of reach of his conscious awareness. It was deeply unlike him to so lose track of the processes of his inner self. Perhaps there was more at work here than a failure of will. Perhaps the change in her was some aspect of her professional skill; perhaps this was how she had trapped her minister in the Midland Sea. Yet when he asked Colmagh, who possessed the ability for both near and far divination, to monitor her for semblances or bindings, the primary discovered nothing. In Colmagh's face, as he reported his findings, Bron saw a host of unasked questions. He provided no explanations. He did not wish to admit to the other man that any portion of his premonition had been correct.

He strove, through coldness, to undo what had happened. He met with her only when it was absolutely necessary, going out of his way to avoid her at other times. When they were together he treated her with the utmost brusqueness, speaking as little as possible and looking at her as infrequently as he could manage. He kept space between them, refusing even to receive papers from her hand. But the more he tried to kill desire, the more desire grew. The more he tried to banish her from his thoughts, the more he thought of her. He saw her in his mind when he was with other women. She came to inhabit even his dreams.

Distracting as it was, Bron told himself, it was only lust, with lust's peculiar characteristic of feeding more strongly on denial than on fulfillment. It was only because desiring her was so perverse that he wanted her as he did. If he could not undo what had happened, he could at least refuse to yield to it. The moment they returned to the Orderhouse he would dismiss her, whether or not his official request for her removal had been granted. Once she was gone, he would be free.

Bron was no stranger to the suppression of impulse. Of his own will, he would never have reached out a hand to touch her. But when she walked into his arms that day in his office, the drowning passion in her face caught him utterly off guard. Whatever he had expected, it was not this. It did not seem possible to counterfeit such an expression, nor to respond as she did except from a hunger as deep as his own. It captivated him, swept him away with a violence he could not have anticipated. Afterward, as she wept into his shoulder, he knew he had been right. Whatever reckless impulse had prompted her to throw herself into his arms, it was more than just a desperate effort to stave off her departure. The tenderness he felt surprised him. He stroked her hair and face until her tears were gone, until she lifted herself up and kissed him with such unguarded passion that he was swept away all over again. He had heard the stories about heartsensers. Even so, he would not have imagined her capable of such fierce carnality.

In daylight, looking back at the night just past, he felt as if he had gone mad. He wrote an order for Tobias, changing the instruction he had originally given, ordering him to implement her immediate departure. But he worked all day in his office without dispatching it. And when she returned that night, as he had told her to do in the hours just before dawn, he saw that same expression on her face, and his will died within him. Daily, the cycle repeated. Every morning he told himself that the night just ended had been the last. Every night she passed in secret through the corridors of the Roundhead quarters, the red doors opening before her like eyes, and came into his bed, pressing her body so close to his it seemed sometimes their skins must fuse. In the dark she abandoned her cool disguise, giving herself to him more completely than any woman ever had. He felt like a man dreaming, fully aware of the unreality of his state yet powerless to wake. It was like leaning over the crumbling edge of a precipice and speculating on how it would feel to fall. It was like lowering a hand toward a flame and wondering exactly when the skin would catch fire. He was not certain, if he could have resisted, that he would have wanted to.

She was a spy. That had not changed. Yet even so close to the heart of danger, it seemed possible to control the risk. She had failed in her charge—the shift in their relationship could not alter that. In two weeks, she would be gone. In the meantime, though his body might yield to her, his barriers were proof against anything she might bring to bear. The sleep-bindings kept her harmless when he was not there to watch her, and his keying of the doors ensured she came and went in secret. The danger of her position ensured her own discretion. He had been deceiving himself, of course, and about more than risk. He realized that the instant he saw her in the basement room. Not once in his life had he underestimated someone as profoundly as he had underestimated this woman. Not once in his life had he been so misled by another. She had duped him as thoroughly as if he had never known her purpose. She had manipulated him as ruthlessly as any Roundhead used an Interrogation subject—and she had extracted an equal amount of truth.

Beside him in the lamplight she moved, turning toward him on her side. A line of light described her neck, her shoulder, the hollow of her waist, the arch of her hip. He thought of the other tool rooms that might be brought down by the discovery of his own. He thought of the painstaking process by which the Zosterian movement had been built, of the swiftness with which it could be dismantled. He thought of his vision of change—in his own lifetime, through the alteration the new philosophy forced upon the Guardian system, in the lifetime of others, through his careful exploration of the world beyond the Limits. He thought of Marhalt, whose secrets he still guarded. He thought of Colmagh, whose instinct in this thing had been truer than his. He thought of Jolyon. All these things, all these people, all these consequences, turned upon his will. Upon a single act of his hands.

Reaching out, he wrapped his fingers around her neck, fitting his thumb to the hollow of her windpipe. He felt the smoothness of her skin, the warmth of the blood that flowed beneath it. She had no mind, but her body was the same; after all that had happened, he still wanted her. The thought of making love to her as she had become had seemed repugnant. But why should it be? She had used his body to work her purpose; why should he not use hers? Desire and anger swept him, so closely joined he could not tell which was stronger. He removed his hand from her throat, drawing it along the curve of her hip, across her belly and up to her breast. He felt the nipple tense beneath his palm—the animal response of the flesh, deeper and more enduring than intellect. He pushed her onto her back, pulling up her shift.

Under him, she stiffened. Her hands came up against his chest. Her eyes opened. For an instant there was something in them, as if she might be coming back to herself; but she blinked, and it was gone. Her arms relaxed and dropped away. She lay passive, her face as blank and distant as the moon.

All Bron's lust had vanished. He wanted, suddenly, nothing more than to be away from her. He left the bed and pulled his velvet overrobe over his nightclothes, feeling her empty gaze at his back. He left the bedroom, closing the door behind him, and went to sit at his desk. It was close to morning; the room was gray with the murk of the dissolving night. The shapes of his possessions, the chairs and tables and candlesticks, bulked in the shadows, oddly unfamiliar in their nighttime aspect. Across from him, the windows were like two dim eyes. He sat watching as night gave way to dawn, as the outlines of the garden took shape beyond the glass, waiting for the dawn bell to deliver him into another day.

With the coming of light, Bron pulled himself together. He put on unwrinkled clothing, bathed his face and eyes in icy water, combed and rebraided his hair. A servant brought breakfast on a tray. He did not eat, but took it all in to Madelaine, who still lay sleeping. He set the tray on the little table by the chair where she sat during the day, and

left the room. Out of the corner of his eye he glimpsed the
welter of sheets and quilts that covered her, the tumbled
torrent of her hair, one arm flung free.

Seating himself at his desk, he turned his attention to
work. It had been some time since he had been able to bring
his usual concentration to bear; the meditations and disci-
plines he employed, which allowed him to survive on very
little sleep, were not enough to offset the intense wakeful-
ness of recent nights. He suspected that his distraction was
beginning to be visible. In the past days he had felt Colmagh's eyes on him.

He was paging through a folio, searching for a reference,
when he became aware of an oddness in the air around him.
He looked up, instantly alert. At first he saw nothing amiss,
but then, as his eyes fell upon his office wall, he perceived
that something strange was happening between the windows
that looked out upon the garden. The color of the stones was
odd, lighter than it should be; their texture too was not quite
right. As he watched, they seemed to lose their rigidity. The
lines of masonry between them began to writhe like stretching rope. With a strange groaning sound the entire wall
shifted, bowing inward, as if some vast pressure had been
brought to bear against its other side.

Galvanized into action, Bron leaped to his feet. He had
not gone more than a step before, in a huge implosion, the
wall folded in on itself, vanishing, sucked backward into
nothingness. Where it had been a vortex spun, a boiling
cloud of silver matter confined within a perfect circle of icy
blackness. Bolts of cobalt lightning cracked within its
depths, lashing the pale stuff to billowing frenzy.

With a scream of tortured air, the center of the vortex
dilated, creating a round space like the pupil of an eye. The
figure of a man took shape within it, rushing forward at
incredible speed. Almost as he appeared he had arrived,
pitching out of the vortex to land awkwardly on one knee.
Behind him, the vortex's eye had already conceived another
man, and behind him, another.

All this took only seconds. By the time Bron had reached
the corner of his desk ten Roundheads stood in his office,
their clothing smoking slightly, blue sparks crackling in

their cropped hair. One of them raised his hand, lifting a long slender tube to his lips. Bron felt something, a tiny sting just below his ear. All the feeling in his body disappeared. The floor came up to meet his face.

He lay, unable to move or even blink, his stunned mind trying to absorb what was happening. He could see the boots of his captors, moving to and fro across the floor. Some of them disappeared beyond his field of vision; he heard the door to the garden open. Abruptly his perspective changed. Two Roundheads were lifting him, their hands under his arms. They dragged him across the floor, depositing him in his chair like a sack of grain. He was aware that he was awkwardly turned in the seat, his legs twisted at a strange angle, but he felt no discomfort, nor indeed anything at all.

A third Roundhead, a stocky man with heavy features and small, cold eyes, produced from the air a set of shackles, their metal glowing with the power that had been forged into them. He took Bron's helpless hands and inserted them in the cuffs; he fastened the neckpiece about Bron's neck, and the belt about his middle. Finished, the Roundhead shoved Bron roughly back against the chair, grasping his hair and pulling his head back, so that he was forced to look directly into the man's face. For a long moment the cold eyes rested upon his. Then, with a twist of his lips, the man removed his hand, brushing it down the front of his black robe as if it were dirty. He turned away.

"There's only the one door," he said. He gestured to his two companions, pointing in the direction of the bedroom. "Try it."

The three men moved out of Bron's field of vision. They had placed him so that he faced the vortex, which still fumed and spat with light. It was a Gate—not a natural one such as those that existed between the worlds, but Guardian-made, created deliberately to serve a temporary purpose. Bron had heard this could be done, but he had never seen it. There must be men of enormous power on the other side, holding it open. They must want him very badly to expend this kind of effort.

Now that the moment had come, the moment he had dreaded and anticipated and evaded for so long, he under-

stood that somewhere within himself he had never really
believed it could happen. The black-clad Roundheads and
the glowing shackles and the silver Gate confronted his involuntary gaze; his stunned understanding encompassed the
certainty of betrayal. Yet the experience seemed closer to
dream than to reality, a conjuration of his strained and exhausted mind.

Had one of his men turned traitor? He could not believe
it. With his own power he had removed the strictures of
their Guardian training, placing within their minds the germ
of his purpose and teaching them to build new barriers to
hide what he had done. He was as certain of them as he was
of himself. Could it be that Jolyon, who had waited patiently
for so long, had decided to act even without the evidence
he had expended so much guile to gain?

Evidence or no, soon he would have Madelaine, and
whatever shadows remained in her empty mind. He could
hear the Roundheads rattling the latch of the bedroom door.

"It's locked," one of them said.

"Burst the lock, then," another replied.

There was a sound, as of a small explosion, and a crash,
as of a door flying back against a wall.

"I'm ready."

The sound of that voice turned Bron's soul inside out.

"Show us," he heard one of the Roundheads say.

"It's in the basement."

"Then lead us."

Everything in Bron struggled for motion: his mind, his
limbs, his Gift. Of them all, only his mind could move. Not
until that moment did he understand that whatever they had
done to his body affected his power as well. His Gift had
been struck into sleep, its fires encased in transparent walls
of binding, like an insect in a shell of amber. He battered
at them but could not break them, any more than he could
stir a muscle of his useless body.

A pause, and then they emerged into his field of vision:
the two Roundheads, Madelaine between them. She was
dressed in her gray Journeyer dress, her red-tasseled sash
wrapped about her small waist, her green-lined cloak across
her shoulders. Her golden hair was pulled back and tightly

braided. Her back was straight, her hands neatly clasped before her. Her face was pale, but no longer empty. She passed Bron by without a glance; an instant, and she was gone. Her footsteps crossed toward the open door and faded away into distance.

Upright in his chair, helpless as a corpse, Bron felt himself possessed, for the first time since he had discovered he was not to be a Speaker, by despair. His mind returned to childhood, to the moment when the Arm of the Stone had resurrected Serle's plow from the earth. This moment was the same. It was not a change, or a shift, or a transformation. It was an ending.

The other Roundheads began to return. They had rounded up servants to help them; one by one they carried in Bron's men and the Arm-trained, all paralyzed like himself, shackled with the same glowing chains that confined him. The servants' eyes were wide with terror; they trembled as they laid the bodies on the floor, side by side like so much cordwood. When they were done, twenty-eight men lay upon the stone flags—twenty-five condemned by the secrets they shared, and three by nothing more than loyalty.

A little crowd of onlookers had gathered in the garden. Prominent among these was Amias. Bron could see him through one of the windows that still existed on either side of the vortex, craning his short neck to get a better view. One of the captors moved past; Amias stepped forward and touched the man's arm. They spoke a few words, then the captor nodded and moved away. Amias disappeared from Bron's field of vision. After only a moment he reappeared around the corner of the desk. He planted himself in front of Bron's chair. His flat face was animated by an extraordinary mixture of triumph and malevolence. Bron had not suspected this dull and lumpish man was capable of such intense emotion.

"You never had much use for me, did you, Selwyn Forester," he said, his voice acid with hatred. "You knew I was Jolyon's agent, but you never bothered to do anything about it, because you never believed someone as high and mighty as yourself could be threatened by someone as low as me. Well, here's something for you to think about while you're waiting for them to take your mind, and I hope it keeps you awake every night you have left to live. This is my doing. Mine. I'm the one who brought you down. When you're dead I'll still be here, wiping away the changes you've made. You're nothing, Selwyn Forester. A bad dream, an evil thought, a few seconds of interruption in the long flow of Guardian rule. In ten years there will be no trace of you in the Northern Diocese. There will be no sign you ever lived at all.''

He leaned forward and spat in Bron's frozen face.

One of the captor Roundheads—the man who had set Bron's shackles—appeared behind Amias. He reached out and took the smaller man roughly by the shoulder. ''These are Violators,'' he said. ''They can be approached by authorized persons only.''

Amias turned on him a look of rage. ''Don't you know who I am?''

The Roundhead contemplated him. ''I know who you are.''

''Then you know I'm the one who summoned you. You know I'm to be the next Arm-Master here.''

''I know you summoned us.'' The Roundhead's voice was very cold. ''But it was the heartsenser who summoned you. As to the rest, you're mistaken. *I* am Master now.''

Amias's face seemed to collapse with surprise. The Roundhead turned him about and pushed him forcefully away. He paused a moment, looking into Bron's face, as he had before. This time his heavy features were set in an expression of disgust. Abruptly he turned and was gone.

The paralysis was wearing off. Bron found, with great effort, that he could move his eyes, enough to fix his gaze on the open door, through which Roundheads and servants still moved. At last Madelaine and her escort returned. She no longer walked freely between them: they had her gripped by the upper arms, as if supporting or restraining her. They halted just inside the entrance. As they did so Madelaine glanced toward Bron, a swift blue flash, gone the instant her eyes met his.

The Roundhead who had identified himself as leader stepped forward. ''Is there anything else?'' he asked her.

"I've shown you everything I found," she said clearly. "The rest is inside me."

"Very well then." The Roundhead produced another set of shackles. Without protest, Madelaine held out her hands to accept the cuffs. She lifted her chin to receive the neckpiece; she turned about so that the waistband could be closed at her back. At last she stood fully bound. Her lids were lowered over her blue eyes. Her face was white as linen, entirely without expression.

"You will be first," the Roundhead told her. "Go."

Obediently Madelaine moved forward, stepping round the bodies of Bron's men. She approached the Gate. For an instant, at its mouth, she hesitated. The winds of power stirred her cloak; sparks leaped out of the cloudy tides of matter to spit blue radiance across her hair. Bron saw her body tense; he saw her shoulders pull inward, rising and falling with the deep breath she took. She stepped forward. The vortex seized her. With breathtaking speed she shot away. She had not looked at him again.

The leader snapped his fingers toward the servants, who huddled in a little group on one side of Bron's office.

"Their turn now," he said. "Pick them up and throw them into the Gate. Headfirst is best. Be careful not to get too close."

In a trance of terror, the servants obeyed. Two at the shoulders, one at the feet, they picked up Bron's men as if they were logs. They swung them a little backward, and then tossed them forward into the silver maw of the vortex. One by one they shot away; because they had lain facedown, and were removed headfirst, Bron never saw their faces. Tobias was last. He was so heavy the servants could barely lift him. He managed to turn his head as they did, twisting it painfully around to meet Bron's eyes. For an instant their gazes held, then Tobias too was gone, a mote of dust upon the Gate's distant eye.

The leader looked at Bron. "Now this one."

Two servants came forward and hauled Bron to his feet. They dragged him to the edge of the vortex. Close up, he could see the depth of it, the impossible distance of the black opening at its center. The awesome forces it contained traced eager fingers across his skin. Bolts of cobalt lightning writhed and crashed, inches from his face.

The servants stepped away, but he did not fall. Someone's power, not his own, held him upright. A pause; then, with an enormous blow, he was propelled forward into chaos. It took him like a whirlpool, tumbling and twisting, a vast universe of nothingness. One of the lightning bolts struck him, square in the center of his chest. Still he fell, until suddenly the silver clouds were gone, replaced by cold still air. He tumbled, helpless, fetching up hard against a solid surface, striking his head, losing consciousness at once.

Nineteen

**RON OPENED** his eyes to light and silence.

The light was sourceless, a muted shadowless radiance that lay equally across every surface. The silence was so soft and thick it seemed the air was filled with feathers. A pale surface floated some distance above him—as his eyes focused he saw it was a slab of milky material that resembled neither plaster nor stone. On all four sides were walls of the same substance; below him, the floor was a mirror image of the ceiling. The six surfaces combined to form a cube, its dimensions sharp and perfect: a room, or more accurately, a cell. But for himself, it was empty.

Gingerly, Bron pushed himself to a sitting position. The whisper of his clothing, the crackle of the pallet on which he lay, barely ruffled the pall of quiet that lay upon the room. His fall through the vortex had evidently done some damage, mostly on the left side of his body—there was tenderness along his cheek and jaw, a painful cut upon his temple, and mottled bruising across his shoulder, side, and hip. Sharp twinges as he moved indicated cracked or broken ribs. At some point he had been attended to, for the laceration had been stitched, and his chest neatly taped. His Roundhead robes and Guardian medal had been removed, replaced by prisoner's clothing. His feet were bare. About his neck had been welded the collar of long-term captivity, a metal band with a loop at the side for attaching a chain, and bindings forged into its substance to facilitate the conduction of pain. As a final touch, his head had been shaved.

He ran his hands over the unfamiliar contours of his naked scalp. If he had been in the least uncertain of where he was or who held him, this last detail would have banished all doubts. The petty meanness of it spoke of Jolyon, as clearly as if the man himself had been present to whisper his malice directly into Bron's ear. The clothing and collar did not distress him, but the theft of his hair did, an anger that surprised him in its intensity.

The room was furnished only with the pallet on which he sat—thin, covered with roughweave cloth, bare of pillows, sheets, or blankets—and a slop basin in one corner. There were neither windows nor door nor grates, nor any other kind of opening. Placing a hand on the wall beside him, he discovered it to be smooth to the touch, with a tensile flexibility like stretched metal. A soft pulsing was just perceptible beneath his fingers. When he drew them downward he could see the trail they left behind, the faintest bluish glow, vanishing almost as it appeared.

The room was power-bound—walls, floor, ceiling, perhaps even the air. Cautiously, Bron reached for his Gift. His power was no longer inwardly constrained, but there were definitely external baffles at work. The more force he attempted to exert, the more he felt the soft bright air and the muffling silence as physical, rather than aural or visual, sensations. It was like trying to swim against a heavy current. What force he could muster the pearly walls simply absorbed, like blotting paper soaking up ink. Faintly, he felt them react beneath his hands, tightening to receive what he brought against them, relaxing once they had assimilated it, like the digestive system of some enormous animal.

After a few moments he abandoned his efforts. His strength had not yet returned, and the pain of his injuries distracted him. It was pointless to try himself until he was more recovered. He sat back upon the pallet, leaning his shoulders against the softly thrumming surface behind him and drawing his knees up to his chest. He folded his arms atop them, staring at the wall opposite. Its featurelessness was so perfect that watching it seemed, after a while, like being blind. After a time the light winked out and darkness took its place, a transition so abrupt and total that it was as if he had gone blind in truth. Unable to do anything else, he lay down on his uninjured side and slept.

The room, he was to discover, was fully automated. Light and dark followed one another in precisely equal periods. The slop basin cleared itself immediately upon being used. Food and water materialized periodically in one corner; if he did not remove the dishes within a few moments of their appearance, they vanished again. Anything placed in that part of the room, in fact, would after a little while disappear, though whatever was responsible was keyed only to inanimate objects. When he substituted himself for plates and cups, nothing happened.

Sooner or later, he knew, he would be taken for Interrogation. He also expected at some point to see Jolyon, who would surely be unable to resist the opportunity to gloat over a fallen enemy. But the cycles of light and dark came and went without sign or trace of human presence. He kept count of time's passage, raveling a long thread out of the covering of the pallet, tying a knot to represent each change. His ribs healed, his bruises faded. His hair began to grow out. The scab that had formed over the laceration on his temple fell off; he picked out the stitches that had closed it so they would not grow into his skin.

Every light cycle he tested his power against the bindings that held the room. Unyieldingly, it resisted. He could not even discern what material composed the walls, or the nature of the power-matrices that made them what they were. His body told him he was regaining strength, but the manifestation of his Gift was only slightly easier than it had been when he was still weak. Certain channels were entirely blocked, mostly in the area of making. Clearly, his captors had devoted a good deal of ingenuity to the issue of holding him. There was no one, he knew, who suspected the magnitude of the power he hid within himself. Even so, he began to wonder whether they had succeeded in creating a prison so strong even he could not break free.

One thing he did accomplish. He managed, after a few days, to split the seam of his prisoner's collar and remove it from his neck. He set it in the corner of the room where he left his used dishes; obediently it disappeared, not to return. A childish gesture, perhaps, but no more so than the action that had put it on him in the first place.

As his strength returned, he found his incarceration more and more difficult to bear. All his life he had desired solitude, but the loneliness he loved was of open spaces, untenanted wild expanses unfettered by walls or bindings. The emptiness of his cell, barely wider than two bodylengths, was much too small to be anything but claustrophobic. The desire to move at will, to run long distances, to exercise his Gift without restraint, gripped him so strongly sometimes he could hardly endure it. Knowing he must be observed, he forced himself to stasis, sitting unmoving on his pallet even when need battered most strenuously within him. At such times it seemed almost possible that his craving for motion might by sheer urgency do what skill could not, and catapult him to freedom.

It was a long time since he had spent the daytime hours in anything but work, or used the darkness only for sleeping. He had nothing to do but think, and his thoughts hounded him. The despair that had come upon him in his last moments in the Orderhouse was with him still. His wrecked plans passed again and again before his inner eye. When he thought of the labor that had gone into their making, the care that had been lavished upon their execution, the lost promise of their fulfillment, his soul rocked within him. Only by bowing his face upon his knees and clenching his hands until his nails pierced his palms was he able to stop himself from weeping, from shouting, from hurling himself at the milky walls of his cell until he fell unconscious. Fifteen years of work and experimentation, vanished like a blown-out candle. Everything he had meant to do, the whole arching pathway of the dream to which he had intended to devote a lifetime, shattered. It was, as Amias had said, as if he had never lived at all.

The faces of his men, Colmagh and Tobias and the others, haunted him. He saw them as they must have become, blank and empty with the removal of their power, cast out to freeze to death beyond the walls. Over the winter snow would cover them, ten feet deep. When spring arrived they would emerge again, preserved so perfectly by the cold it would seem they had died only moments before. During the brief season of warmth the mountain birds would feed upon their flesh. What remained at summer's end would be gathered up by the servants and thrown into the midden behind the prison annex, a vast pile of human bones, the leavings of a thousand years of punishment and death.

Madelaine haunted him also, though in a different way. Even now, he knew, she must be tracing for her masters the contours of his mind, the shape of which he had recklessly, foolishly given her. Even now she must be receiving the honors and accolades due to one who had brought so great an evil to justice. In the pitchy darkness of his cell he dreamed of her. He stood again in the basement room with his hands about her throat, and this time he did not flinch or falter, but held her until she was dead. He did not ask himself how she had escaped his power. He did not ask himself how she had so convincingly feigned the blankness of partial minddeath. Those things no longer mattered. In the end, he had only himself to blame. He had known what he must do, and he had not done it.

The architecture of his downfall was clear to him now, as only hindsight could make it: the missed choices, the postponed decisions, stacked one upon the next like a set of stairs, all bordered by an ugly chain of ifs. If he had been less confident, more cautious. If, failing that, he had resisted seduction. If, yielding, he had turned her away the second night, or even the third or fourth. If, unable to turn her away, he had thought to suspect her illness. If, taken in by her lie, he had killed her once he found her in the basement room. If, unable to kill her then, he had killed her later. At each step, a single action might have broken the web of risk, but he had never paused long enough to act. Instead he had dashed headlong forward, as if in eager pursuit of his own destruction.

For nine years in the Fortress, and fifteen years outside it, Bron had maintained unfalteringly the mask that guarded his true self. To it he had added other masks, other deceptions. He had kept secrets and spawned them, followed old purposes and made new ones, abandoned the dreams and vows of childhood and replaced them with others more encompassing and more binding. He had become mighty among the powerful, a leader among those who led. He had achieved things he could not have dreamed when he was fifteen, a new-made Novice eaten up with the need for vengeance, shivering with hatred in the cold hallways of the Novice Wing.

But he had been too successful. He had grown arrogant; he had come to believe he led a charmed life. Others might slip, but not he. Others might betray themselves, but his years of subterfuge and deception in the hallways of the sixth floor had made him immune. He understood fully the risk that threatened what he did, and those who helped him do it, but over the years he had lost that understanding for himself. He had mislaid the knowledge of his own vulnerability. And in that lay the true shape of his destruction.

Bron had experienced before the pain of self-knowledge gained in hindsight—too late to be acted upon, capable only of lacerating the soul with a relentless catalogue of chances missed and choices botched—but never like this. The understandings that came to him between the milky walls of his prison cell were the most terrible of his life.

It did not seem likely he would be forced to live with them long. Each test of his power only confirmed the strength of the bindings that held the cell; the possibility of breaking free was coming to seem more and more remote. Even if he were successful, he would still have to find a way to escape the Fortress alive, and if he managed that, there would be the mountains to contend with. It was just conceivable that, during the Interrogation sessions, a chance might present itself. In view of the extraordinary precautions they had taken so far, however, that seemed unlikely.

Bron did not want to die. His whole soul rebelled against the finality of death, the waste of it. Yet if such a price were inescapable for himself, he intended to make certain his family did not have to pay it. He had given almost all his secrets to Madelaine, but there were some he had held back, including this one, and he would make his own death rather than allow the Interrogators to take it from him. He loved Serle, his wife and children; he knew his brother would carry on the work they had shared. But it was more than that. He had long ago discarded his mother's beliefs and his childish vow, taking up arms in service of a wider battle, setting himself to seek redress for a greater wrong. He had long ago recognized as myth the narrow strictures of the Tale—powerful, embedded with a core of truth, but myth no less for that, in its too-small vision of the Stone, its cramped ancestral dream of revenge and restoration. Yet the talismans of his childhood—his heritage, his Ancestor, the long years of exile, the words spoken in firelight—remained, as deep within him as his Gift. Serle and his children were the last of their kind in all the world. If they vanished there would be no others, ever.

The knots in the thread Bron had pulled from the pallet showed that twenty-two cycles had passed since he woke to his cell. His hair was more than stubble now, and the nails of his fingers and toes were growing. His beard and mustache had long ago escaped their neat sculpted shapes to cover his cheeks and chin. His body was dirty, and his clothing stank. It had begun to seem possible that they had sealed him up here forever, that even Jolyon would not come. He imagined himself in a year's time, in ten years, in twenty. He saw himself at half a century, caked with his own filth, his hair falling in knots to his waist, his nails curled and yellow as the horns of rams.

It was in the twenty-third cycle, a cycle of light, that Jolyon appeared at last.

Bron was sitting as usual upon his pallet, shoulders against the wall, knees drawn up, arms draped across them. One moment the pale surface before him was the featureless blank it always was; the next a door had appeared upon it. It was a prison door, heavy wood reinforced with iron, with enormous hinges and a small grating inset at its top. Bron stared at it, his eyes slow to focus upon any sort of change after so many cycles of sameness. It began to open, swinging outward. The vista of jet-black, mica-strewn stone beyond told him that his cell was located not in the Fortress proper, but in the prison annex attached to the Wing of the Soldier Suborder.

Framed within the rectangular opening was a man: Jolyon. His black robes blended with the stone upon which he stood, so that he appeared to be nothing more than a pale face, a red sash, two white hands hanging on the air.

He stepped forward, into the cell. The door fell to behind him, vanishing into whiteness the instant it was fully closed. He glanced around, swiftly, his features creasing in distaste. He raised a hand and snapped his fingers. A filigreed silver pomander winked into being upon his palm. He set it to his nostrils. Above it, his eyes were steady on Bron's face.

It had been more than ten years since Bron had seen his enemy, but he did not seem to have changed at all. The spiky hair, the smooth and brooding face, the heavy eyes and bitten nails, were all the same. He wore more jewelry than a courtesan at a ball: rings were stacked upon his fingers, bracelets circled his wrists, heavy golden hoops pulled at his earlobes. The intricate rope of gold from which his Guardian medal hung was thick enough to double as a set of manacles. Even his clothing was embellished, the fringes of his sash strung with tiny beads of garnet, the toes of his red boots encased in silver and the ankles bound with chains of gems. On his right shoulder he wore an unfamiliar insignia, a circle of red enamel pierced by a black lightning bolt.

The silence drew out. Bron recognized it as a contest of wills. But he could play that game, and much better than Jolyon, whose strong suit had never been patience. Sure enough, after only a little while Jolyon could stand it no longer.

"So. Are you comfortable in your new home?"

Bron, unwilling to waste words on such a question, did not reply.

"A lot of thought and effort went into making it, you know. It's an ordinary cell—you may have guessed that when you saw the door—but it's been overlaid with bindings, as you see. Thanks to the heartsenser, they are keyed to the exact shape of your mind. As you've probably already discovered, they greatly impede the use of your Gift. Anyone else"—he made a gesture with his free hand, and something sprang into being in the air before him, tumbling down to land on Bron's pallet—"has no difficulty."

Bron glanced at what Jolyon had conjured up. It was the

prison collar, split and all. Anger shuddered briefly within him.

"You've done well for yourself," he said. After so many cycles of silence, his voice was strange in his own ears.

"Yes," Jolyon replied simply.

"Even better now, I imagine."

Jolyon smiled, his eyes falling almost closed. "Not everyone agreed with my methods, but no one can argue with my results."

"What's been done with my men?"

"They've already been probed, sentenced, and cast out. Very clever, those barriers you taught them to build. If we hadn't known they were there it's possible we might have missed them."

"Even the Arm-trained?"

"Even the Arm-trained. Really, we didn't need to bother, but we didn't know that when we started." He shrugged. "They were only Journeyers."

Bron bit down on his rage. "When am I to be Interrogated?" he said, when he was certain he could speak calmly.

"You are not to be Interrogated at all."

"What do you mean?"

"Just that." Jolyon waved the pomander back and forth in front of his nose. "After much deliberation, the Council of Six has decided to forgo the pleasure of looking into your mind."

"I don't believe you. In all of recorded history the Arm of the Stone has never once passed up the chance to pound a Violator's mind to pieces."

"Believe me, it wouldn't have been my decision. But the Council, in its wisdom, has determined that the magnitude of your corruption makes you too dangerous for mind-contact even by the Arm of the Stone. They've decided to base the charges solely on the physical evidence and the heartsenser's testimony. They'll proceed to the taking of your Gift without spending time even on mouth-to-mouth questioning. The ceremony will be three days from now."

"Three days?" The words sprang out before Bron could stop them.

"Oh, I'm sorry." Jolyon spoke with a kind of vicious

satisfaction. "Did you think you had more time? Have you become so attached to your prison that the thought of leaving it distresses you? I suppose even the worst life must seem desirable, compared with death. On the other hand, since death is inevitable, does the timing really matter?"

Bron breathed deeply. He knew what Jolyon wanted. But, filthy and disheveled and beaten as he was, he refused, as he had when he was a boy, to give it to him.

"What are the charges against me?" he said, quietly.

Jolyon frowned, cheated of the spoils of his goading. "There are a great many of them," he said. "Violating the Limits, obviously, through the things you made in that . . . room. I didn't actually count the number of Limits involved, but the list runs to several pages. That's one." He began to count off on his fingers. "Inciting others to Violate the Limits. Breaching mental privacy—your men's, that is, with whatever it was you did to brainwash them to your point of view. Maintaining illegal barriers. Teaching others to maintain them. Betraying the charge laid upon you when you became a member of the Arm of the Stone. Breaking the vows of your Investment. Adhering to a designated heresy, in defiance of the orthodoxy you were sworn to defend—"

"Wait a minute. Zosterianism has never been designated."

"It has now." Jolyon's pleasure was plain. "The Council of Six has officially decreed Zosterianism too dangerous to tolerate. After all, if you could use it as a cover for your Violation, others could too."

"What my men and I did stands alone. No other Zosterians experiment in such a way."

Jolyon laughed. "Do you really expect anyone to believe that?"

"Do *you* have any idea how widespread the movement has become? Designating it means you'll have to get rid of a quarter of the Arm of the Stone, and a substantial number of Journeyers as well. Zosterian principles have also become very popular among the unGifted. Are you ready to deal with them, and their disappointment, when you rip all that away?"

"Those are arguments only a Zosterian would make." All

Jolyon's affected levity had disappeared. "No one will miss a few heretical Residents. No one will shed a tear for the unGifted, if you are right and they have to be put down. One action by the Soldiers, and they'll be competing with each other to see how quickly they can bow their heads and become good citizens again. As for the Arm of the Stone, we'll be better for the loss. You and your kind diminish us more than culling our ranks ever could. You make us weak. You make us . . . not ourselves."

His eyes were fully open now. His lips were wet with the intensity of his words. For the first time his hatred was plain, a fire burning up through the surface of his skin, a boiling conflux within his unshuttered gaze. Bron looked away. He had hoped against hope that something might survive. He knew for certain that nothing would.

Jolyon had pulled himself together. His face was smooth again. "Shall I go on?"

Wearily, Bron shrugged. He had lost heart for this encounter.

"Oh, now you don't care? Would you be more interested if I told you that you were charged with spoiling a heart-senser, in egregious disregard for the rarity and value of that Gift?"

"What are you talking about?"

"She has been spoiled by her contact with you. She's corrupted, no longer fit for Guardianship." He paused. "She's also pregnant."

Bron's head snapped up. "What?"

"You didn't know." Jolyon smiled, gratified; the points of his teeth showed, like a cat's. "Well, how could you? It was only a week you spent together, isn't that so? It was the mapping of your mind that did it—corrupted her, I mean. We saw it when we probed her. We don't entirely understand why it happened. Perhaps it isn't possible to stand so long before something so foul and remain untainted. Perhaps she hid a secret flaw. Or perhaps her infatuation with you overtook her will. Why else would she have allowed you to get a child on her? Even a heartsenser knows how to prevent such a thing." The smile was gone now. "Even if her mind had been clean, that would have condemned her. The child of a Violator like you could not possibly be suffered to live. Nor the mother who consented to its conception.''

Bron looked away from the gloating face of his enemy. A child, he thought. His child. The idea was too strange, too new, for feeling. Had she known? Certainly she had known what waited for her in the Fortress. She had told him, though he had not believed her. And yet she had returned. What kind of will was required for such an action, for following a purpose achievable only through self-immolation? He seemed to see her in his mind, crouching in the basement room and weeping at the shape of his hidden self, standing in his office and reaching out her hands to accept her shackles. Perhaps she had been as eager as Jolyon to rid the world of his child.

''I must admit, for all her flaws, she was an extraordinary woman,'' Jolyon said. ''I really never expected so much from her. Nor, I might add, from you. I've always known you were a Violator, Selwyn. But who could have anticipated such . . . magnitude?''

Bron turned his head and met Jolyon's gaze. ''Has it occurred to anyone,'' he said softly, ''that it was you who spoiled this heartsenser? It was you, after all, who instructed her.''

Jolyon raised his brows. ''I acted in good faith. Her qualifications fitted the mission. Her probes said she was fit. How was I to know she was flawed? How was I to know there was a seed of Violation inside her that would blossom once it came in contact with yours?''

''Your argument is circular. If she was unfit to begin with, she couldn't be spoiled.''

Jolyon shrugged. ''With so many charges against you, what's one more or less? Oh, and there is one more. The matter of your mistress.''

''My mistress?'' Bron said blankly.

''Yes, you had a number of them, didn't you. But only one, I think, for whom you altered the Catalogue.''

Bron felt everything within him come to a halt.

''I've surprised you twice.'' Jolyon smiled his slow smile. ''I feel quite a sense of accomplishment.''

"What did you—" It was hard to breathe. "How did you—"

"The heartsenser pierced the binding you put on the name. She even found out where the woman lives. Lived, I should say, for she is no longer there. Nothing is. We blasted the place to dust, and then we barriered it, to prevent contagion."

Bron bowed his head to his knees. He clutched with both hands at his cropped hair. It did not matter any longer what Jolyon saw. Nothing mattered now. Nothing.

"So I was right," Jolyon said. "This woman was more than just a passing fancy. I confess I'd wondered what could lead you to do something as stupid as altering the Catalogue—and whatever you may be, Selwyn, you're not stupid. But they do say love robs a man of his wits—"

Bron could bear no more. With all the force he had held pent up inside himself for the past twenty-two cycles, he leaped to his feet. Reflexively Jolyon jumped back. The gloating expression dropped off his face like a falling garment.

"Get out of here." Even to Bron's own ears, his voice sounded unhinged. "Get out."

"You're in no position to give orders." Against the wall now, Jolyon had no choice but to stand his ground. His fingers around the silver pomander were white. "There's something I came here to do, and I haven't done it yet."

"Then do it!" Bron had abandoned control. "I'm sick of your Stone-cursed game. Do what you came to do, and leave me in peace!"

Jolyon looked at him. His eyes were unhooded again, like embers in his thin face. Slowly he lowered the pomander. There was a pulse of light, and the little object vanished from his palm. Simultaneously, Bron felt power flashing toward him. It struck him in the chest, knocking him to the floor. He lay, gasping.

"That's just a reminder," Jolyon said coldly. "You have no power in this place. I do."

He moved forward and knelt at Bron's side. His eyes were hotter than coals, but around them his features were without expression, smooth and perfect as a statue's. It was the face of a sleeper, of a person in a trance. His voice, when it came, was very quiet.

"My superiors fear you," he said. "In all the history of our world, there are few who have Violated as you have. So they have chosen the coward's way. They will not reach into your mind. They will never know the true shape of your soul. But *I* don't fear you. I know you—I've always known you—but I don't fear you. And so I will do what my masters are too craven to try. I will probe you." He reached out and grasped the front of Bron's tunic, using his power to lift Bron to a sitting position. His voice had dropped almost to a whisper. "You have power no one suspects. You have secrets no one knows. I could never break you down enough, when we were Novices, to see. But now"—he leaned forward, inches from Bron's face—"I will."

Even as he spoke the words, his power punched into Bron's mind. Crude as a battering ram, it ripped through the layers of outer guard, toward the final core of concealment. But Bron had discovered some time ago that the bindings of his cell, which blocked the outward manifestation of his Gift, did not reach into his mind. Within himself, he was still free. Jolyon's power was a juggernaut, but it was blind as a mole; by itself it could not recognize anything he chose to hide.

But he did not choose to hide. Jolyon thought he knew what was there; very well then, let him see it. Let him understand the true shape of the guard that had thwarted his spite for so many years. Let him grasp, if he could, his own defeat. For that outward shape was all he would ever know. Bron understood now that he was the last of his ancient line living upon the earth. With his death, his heritage would vanish as if it had never been. He intended to take all its secrets with him.

Deliberately, he dropped his many guards. He let the veils of illusion fall. He allowed the high black wall that shielded his ancestry, the Tale, his Gift, the things that made him most truly himself, to stand naked before Jolyon's gaze. He felt the touch of his enemy's power, taking the measure of the barrier. With all his strength Jolyon attacked, falling upon the massive enclosure with an impact that echoed the length and breadth of Bron's mind. Again he struck, and again. But though he strained to the furthest boundaries of his resource, the barrier did not break. It did not even tremble. He was no more capable of breaching it than a bird, dashing itself against the Fortress walls, could mark the stones.

After a long time he withdrew. His face was wet with sweat, his spiky hair plastered to his forehead. His chest heaved with effort. He let go of Bron's tunic, and of the power that had held him. Slowly, bracing his hands on his knees, he rose to his feet.

From the floor, half-lying on his elbows where he had fallen when Jolyon released his grip, Bron looked up at his enemy.

"You never were the strongest of us, were you, Jolyon?" he said softly.

Jolyon's face seemed to collapse with rage. His lips drew back from his teeth. He advanced a step, his body bending forward, his hand rising. For that instant Bron was certain he would kill him, right there. Time seemed to arrow backward. They were boys again, eye to eye in the shadows of the Novice Wing.

After a moment Jolyon straightened. He stepped back. He was breathing hard. With the forefinger of the hand he had raised, he pointed at Bron's chest.

"You will have darkness now," he said, his voice uneven. "No light—only darkness, until they come for you."

He made a gesture. The door appeared, already swinging open. He strode out, not looking behind him. The light dimmed as he went, as if he drew it behind him, attached to the heels of his red boots. The flashing mica of the floor outside was the last thing Bron saw. The door clicked shut, and the blackness was complete.

Bron pulled himself backward, onto his pallet. The petty triumph of his enemy's humiliation had already leaked away. His hand fell on something hard: the prisoner's collar. He hurled it away from him; it struck the wall with a muffled thud. He drew his knees to his chest and abandoned himself to pain.

* * *

Jolyon had appeared in light: Marhalt, when he came, arrived in darkness.

Soon after Jolyon left, Bron had thrown himself with all his strength upon the bindings that held him. He strained until his senses dimmed and red lights burst behind his eyes, phantom firestorms that did nothing to dispel the thick darkness that surrounded him. When he pulled back at last, drained and trembling with effort, he knew for certain that what Jolyon had said was true. He could not escape this place. The pearly bindings, a portrait of his mind painted by Madelaine for her ungrateful masters, were capable of receiving all he had to give and more.

He lay down then, in search of unconsciousness. He had been dozing more or less continuously ever since. Each time he rose toward awareness, he willed himself away; the terrible dreams that waited for him were less agonizing than the thoughts he would be forced to think if he allowed himself to wake. But he was not truly sleeping, and so he sensed, distantly, when someone passed through the walls of his prison and knelt beside him. Light began to rise, the faintest glow against his closed eyelids. He did not stir, or indicate awareness. Sooner or later, whoever it was would either speak or leave.

But whoever it was did neither. At last, reluctantly, Bron opened his eyes. A small globe of mindlight floated just above his chest. Beyond it, a little distance from the pallet, was the dark bulk of a robed figure. Bron pushed himself up on one elbow. The light moved with him, falling upon the face of the man who had woken him.

"Master," he said, surprise bringing the old title to his lips.

Jolyon had looked the same. Marhalt did not. He was allowing himself, as most Roundheads refused to do, to become old. The dark hair had grayed. The ascetic features were bracketed by deep lines, the thin shoulders slightly stooped. His topaz eyes were the same, however, as were his fingers, loosely folded upon his knees: large-jointed, spatulate, stained with ink.

Of all the people in the world who might come to him,

Bron would least have expected Marhalt. It was close to ten years since he had seen his former Mentor.

"Why are you here?" he asked now.

Across the small diameter of the cell, Marhalt regarded him with the level gaze that passing years had robbed of none of its power. "It did not seem right to let you go without speaking to you," he replied. "Without asking you why. Why you did this thing."

Bron turned his eyes away. Of all Roundheads, only Marhalt would think of asking such a question. "You already know the answer."

"If I did, I wouldn't be here."

"I'm a Violator. I lost my mind to the lure of handpower. What other explanation do you and your kind need?"

There was a pause. "You know I don't share the view of Violation so many of my colleagues take," Marhalt said softly. "Violation and purity are not preordained—they are a choice, a choice we make a thousand different times in our lives, a thousand different ways. The seed of weakness lives equally in all of us. The fact that you fell into the ways of hands means only that you could have chosen not to. I know you. I know your Violation. What I do not know is the nature of your choice."

"I made many choices." Marhalt no longer had any ability to compel him—all that had been left behind with his Apprenticeship. Yet the pale glow of the mindlight was much like the candlelight of Marhalt's chambers, all those years ago; now, as then, Marhalt's gaze pressed for the release of secrets. "I chose to join you. I chose to leave you. I chose to create my own beliefs. I chose to make them real. It's no single choice that brought me to this moment, but a host of them. And there isn't one I wish to describe to you."

"What is the point of secrecy now? In two days you'll die for your choices."

"I've gone so far beyond the structure of your understanding that to speak of them would be like talking to you in a foreign language. You could not possibly grasp what I would say."

Marhalt's voice was hard. "I don't have to ask, you know. I could probe you and get the answers I want. There are no rules of privacy for a Violator like you.''

"You aren't afraid of me? Of the power of my corruption?''

"Nothing in you can touch me unless I allow it to do so. On that score I have no fear whatsoever.''

"Others aren't as confident as you. I understand the Council has refused to venture inside my mind at all.''

"Who told you that?''

"Jolyon.''

"He was here?''

"This darkness was his gift to me.''

"I might have known.'' In the dim light, Marhalt's face was angry. "Contact with you has been expressly forbidden. This cell was created so you could be entirely isolated until the moment of your punishment. There are not even guards posted.''

"Yet you're here.''

"I am a member of the Council of Six—I can do as I please. But Jolyon, however important he thinks himself, cannot. He may have the secret support of Council members, but even he cannot disobey its expressed unanimous will. I will make sure this becomes known.''

Bron looked at the older man. One of the things they had most truly shared, during the years of Bron's uneasy adoption of Marhalt's purpose, was their distaste for Jolyon. "He was wearing some kind of insignia. I've heard rumors about a fellowship of some sort. Is it true?''

"Yes. They call themselves the Reddened. Clever, isn't it, with the reference to unfitness? They hold ceremonies—the things they do would make even you sick to hear. They are few as yet, for there aren't many who will put impulse to action the way the Reddened do, thank the Stone. But there are, unfortunately, a large number who agree with the ideas behind their association. Jolyon has gained the ear of the Staff-Holder, and it affords him a substantial amount of protection. His responsibility for your arrest has increased his prestige enormously.'' He hesitated. "I must tell you that there are those among us who would have preferred to see him fail.''

"And leave me free?" Bron laughed. "Don't ask me to believe that."

"You understimate the danger of exalting a man like Jolyon." In the pale mindlight, Marhalt's eyes were intent. "Understand this, Selwyn. You are one of the worst criminals our world has ever known. Even the handpower rings I destroyed were not so bad as you, because you were sworn to protect, to your dying breath, the holy Limits you Violated. But the way you follow disturbs the order of things. You could not possibly have remained free. I would have had you caught the right way—not Jolyon's way, not through secrecy and subterfuge and the service of personal ambition. What Jolyon wants to do to the Suborder threatens the world as much as anything you have done, because it threatens the Suborder itself. The evil you would have accomplished in the few years left to you could not have been worse than the evil that will come from the advancement your capture has given to Jolyon's purpose."

Silence fell. Marhalt sat motionless in the mindlight, his eyes steady upon Bron's face. Bron thought of how he had feared, and then respected, and at last grown to love this stern man who had chosen him for his own. He had left those things behind long ago, as he had left behind so many of his former Mentor's teachings and beliefs. Even so, Marhalt stood at the root of what he was. The Roundhead had done what few others in Bron's life ever had: he had changed him. In that change lay the seeds of all the rest. Accepting the path Marhalt had given him, he had taken the first steps along the way that led him to this prison cell. That was the answer to Marhalt's question. But it could not be said. The gulf between them, of belief and intent, was too great.

"So you will not answer me?" Marhalt said at last, his voice quiet.

"No."

Marhalt watched him a moment longer, and then sighed. "Well. I won't compel you."

He rose to his feet, with the economy of motion he brought to everything he did, and stood looking down.

"I don't know," he said, "if it still matters to you, the

work of change we swore to bring upon the world. From your activities over the past years, I would say it does, despite the . . . other ways you chose to follow. I want you to know that I will continue my work. I will not allow what has happened to affect that.'' He paused, as if waiting for Bron to reply. When Bron did not, he continued. ''I know you still carry things hidden inside you. Things you did not give the heartsenser. Perhaps, if you had been Interrogated, they would have been discovered; but you are not to be Interrogated, and so they will remain unknown. Don't think I'm unaware of the benefit this brings me. I came here to question you, but also to thank you. For keeping the secret of my purpose.''

Bron stared at the pale glow of the mindlight. ''I've kept secrets all my life. The only ones I ever betrayed were my own.''

''You were my finest pupil, Selwyn.'' There was something in Marhalt's voice Bron had never heard before. ''I had such hopes for you. Now . . . I know you are a Violator. I know the evil you have made. Yet when I look at you all I can see is the waste of it. You had it in you to follow another path. All my life I will wonder why you chose so wrongly.''

Bron closed his eyes. An image of the little globe of mindlight, caught behind his lids, winked upon the darkness there. ''If I could have followed you, Master,'' he said softly, ''I would have. I mean that. But I am not a follower. I saw a larger truth. It called me. If I had it to do over, I would not choose differently.''

There was a long silence. When at last Marhalt spoke, his voice seemed to come from a great distance.

''Now I know,'' he said, ''that you are truly lost.''

Turning, he approached the wall. Softly, like a man falling into a bowl of milk, he passed through the bindings of the cell. The last Bron saw of him was the heel of his boot, the hem of his robe, a black blot shrinking, then gone.

He had left the light. Bron stared at it, caught once again between sleeping and waking, between terrible nightmares and the horror of his waking reflections. He reached out his hands, cupping them around the little hovering sphere. It had no warmth, for it was not a physical object, but its spectral presence could be felt nevertheless, a faint vibration against his palms. Radiance leaked through his fingers, moving as he moved, casting strange shadows upon the walls. He imagined the bindings gone; he imagined the darkness of his cell as the expanse of the universe, the light between his hands as the sun, or some distant star. He gazed into its golden heart, willing himself beyond his body, beyond his mind, to a place where he would not have to think or dream.

Perhaps because of the fierceness of his desire, it worked. For the first time since his imprisonment he felt his thoughts sinking away as they did in sleep, but without dreams to trouble him. His muscles loosened. His breathing deepened. It was not peace, but it was close enough.

When they came for him they sent light before them, bursting upon the room like a thunderclap. The pale walls trembled and vanished, leaving bare the mica-encrusted stones upon which the bindings had been fixed. The heavy door flew back with a crash, shocking after so much silence. A Roundhead strode through the opening, two Soldiers in tow.

Through sheer reflex, Bron sprang to his feet. The little globe of mindlight, which he had held cupped in his hands since Marhalt left him, went flying into the corner of the room. Even as he gained his full height he felt the familiar sting, at the base of his throat this time. Feeling left him: the floor shot up to meet his face. There was not the slightest sense of impact. He could do no more than stare, with wide fixed eyes, at the glittering flecks embedded in the stones against his cheek.

The two Soldiers hauled him to his feet; he knew this by the way his perspective changed, for he could not feel their hands. For a moment they held him motionless, facing the Roundhead. The man, whom Bron recognized as the Roundhead Staff-Holder's Second, looked into Bron's eyes, his own very cold. Bron felt the swift, telltale chill of mind-touch—assuring, no doubt, that he was fully bound. With a quick gesture, the Second stepped aside. Bron's perspective

changed again: the Soldiers were carrying him out of the
cell and into the black corridor beyond.

He had never before been in the prison annex, and had
no notion of where they were taking him. Wrenched too
suddenly from the long empty contemplation he had maintained since Marhalt's departure, he was dazed and groggy,
a condition not improved by his utter lack of any sense of
his body. Even when he had made himself invisible or transported himself through the air he had not felt like this, a
disembodied gaze steered by forces he could not feel. Walls
rushed past him; turnings approached and dropped away to
right or left. Archways swallowed him like open mouths.
Each opening passed, each corner rounded, each hallway left
behind, brought him closer to the moment of his death. As
in the Orderhouse just after capture, he could not quite believe it.

They came at last to a dead end, a dusky wall set with a
pair of metal doors. The surface of the doors was heavily
embossed with figures of men and horses—scenes, no
doubt, from the history of the Suborder of Soldiers. Beside
him, Bron heard one of the Soliders bark out a series of
words in a strange tongue. Soldiers had their own power-
language, which they used to assist them in battle; it was
something outsiders, other than the unfortunates upon whom
military attention was turned, rarely heard.

Silently the doors swung inward. A great square chamber
lay beyond, its walls swathed in heraldic tapestries and its
ceiling thick with mindlight. Mica glimmered across the surface of the floor, like a mantle of stars tossed across an inky
universe. At the far end, forming two halves of a semicircle,
twenty-four robed, sashed figures sat: the Councils of Six.
At their midpoint stood the Staff-Holders, the cloudy mindlight flashing from the precious metals and gems of their
ceremonial rods. Lifted above the rest on a high dais was
the Prior. His long white beard flowed over his chest; his
robe swirled about him, a heavy fall of polychromatic silk.
The twisted length of his staff rose high above his head, so
thick that his ancient fingers could not quite close around
it.

The room was empty of anyone but these: the Councils,

the Staff-Holders, and the Prior. It was to be a private ceremony, then. Even Jolyon would not witness the branding of the man whose destruction he had overseen. If he had been able, in his dazed and paralyzed state, Bron would have laughed. He could not recall any precedent for depriving the Fortress of the spectacle of an Expulsion ceremony. It seemed that Jolyon had not exaggerated their fear of him.

The far end of the room, with its motionless frieze of observers, began to approach: the Soldiers were dragging him forward again. They halted about twenty paces from the dais. He heard their footsteps retreating, the sound of closing doors. He did not fall; some power held him upright, rigidly suspended upon the air.

The Roundhead who was the Staff-Holder's Second came from behind, positioning himself directly in front of Bron. By his motions he was unrolling a parchment. In a measured voice he began to read the phrases of Bron's indictment. They were as Jolyon had described, but couched in much more elaborate language and buttressed by many learned references to scholarly discourses on the Limits. Lacking his other senses, Bron's sight and hearing seemed to have grown unnaturally acute; he was aware of the faint shifting of light and shadow as the mindlight above him rippled and stirred, of the reflections that slid along the rods of the Staff-Holders, of the weave in the fine black cloth of the Second's robe and the uninflected flow of his voice. How long had it taken to compose this lengthy document—to research it, to find the references, to draft it and correct it and copy it fair? Did the Roundheads who had created it think it unjust that only the Councils and the Prior would ever hear the product of so much labor?

He became aware that the flow of speech had ceased. The Second moved forward and stooped, laying Bron's Guardian medal upon the floor. He moved aside. Now the Staff-Holders were turning, bending their heads, uniting their gaze upon the small golden circle. A moment passed. The faintest trail of smoke rose ghostlike toward the ceiling. All at once the metal glowed red; it seemed to ripple and shift, then to crumple. The Staff-Holders withdrew their gaze. A misshapen lump lay where the medal had been, charred and smoking, unrecognizable as gold. The Second stepped forward. Using his sleeve to shield his hand, he picked it up and stowed it in the pouch at his belt.

The preliminaries were done. The Prior rose to his feet, pushing heavily upon his staff and the arm of his chair. Slowly he descended the steps of the dais, pausing on each one. The Prior was older than a century and a half; he had headed the Order for nearly a hundred years. His skin was like soft ivory cloth draped loosely across his bones. The frailty of his body was evident in his motions, though his hawklike features showed no weakness at all. His eyes were milky with cataracts, but Bron could see the power in them, like a light burning behind a clouded window.

The Prior halted less than an arm's length away. His blind eyes were fixed to Bron's. The mindlight fell across his hair and beard, white as mist; it caressed the shifting colors of his robe and the twisted strands of his staff. All Bron's disbelief was gone. In the ancient face before him he saw his own ending, as close as his next breath. Inside himself, he struggled. Inside himself, he shouted denial. But his paralyzed body and rigid throat betrayed nothing, and his frozen eyes could only stare. For the first time in his life, he wore a mask not of his own choosing.

The Prior stretched out his hand, placing his palm flat upon Bron's forehead. His touch was deeply cold, a knot of ice set against Bron's skin.

''I, Percival, Prior of the Order of Guardians, call the Stone to witness.'' The Prior's voice was low and whispery, the voice of the Speaker he had been before acceding to the Order's highest office. ''I call it, that it may know how we defend it against those who would do it harm. I call it, that it may see the face of its enemy.''

Power was present now. Bron could feel it, seeping up between the stones, curling through the air like fog: the Stone, responding to the ancient call whose wording had not altered in all the thousand years of Guardian rule. Power filled the room, torrents of it, rivers and waterfalls of it, shaking and buffeting Bron's helpless body. Though it had been more than a decade since his Gift had followed the ways of the Stone's knowing, he had not forgotten the feel of that vast alien force. Behind the walls of binding that cased it he felt his Gift stir, flashing in recognition, battering against the stasis to which it was bound. He realized that he was aware of himself again, his arms and legs and head and chest—but not from his own understanding. It was the Stone's sense of him he felt, one tiny spark of knowledge culled from its complete and inhuman contemplation of all that *was*.

"In the name of the Stone, I kill your Gift." The Prior's voice resonated with the power he had invoked; it seemed to sound inside Bron's head. "In the name of the Stone, I mark you with the Sign of Violation. In the name of the Stone, I cast you out. You are banished from the Order of Guardians, and from the Fortress, and from the world, and from the paths of the living, forever."

A colossal bolt of force punched into Bron's mind—the Prior, his own power amplified enormously by the power of the Stone flowing through him. Though Bron could feel his body, he still could not move. Though the fires of his Gift spat and roiled, they could not break free. The force closed, homing in the barriers that enclosed his inmost self. It was nearly there, nearly there. . . .

It struck. The massive guard that had thwarted so many attempts shattered like glass. Debris shot out, blanketing Bron's mind. The stasis that held his Gift vanished. His power leaped forward, like a man sprinting toward a closing door. It had become again as it had been only a handful of times in his life—a separate entity, an independent will, acting for its own purpose, its own survival. Bron felt his mind pulled after, flying in the wake of his Gift. He was with it when it plunged itself into the fiery currents of the Stone, so much like them in its raging flight that it could not be distinguished for what it was. The fires of existence enclosed him. Briefly, he felt the exhilaration of dancing amid the flames.

Within him the bolt of the Prior's power reached its target: the well of soul at the center of his mind, where his truest being lay in darkness. It exploded like a dying star. It lit up all the places that had been hidden; it leveled every structure inside his mind. Separated from his body, he was yet bound to it. Along the cord of that connection he sensed his own distant agony—his limbs convulsing, his head snapping back from the Prior's hand. The dominance of flesh asserted itself. Pain reached up for him, narrowing the gulf achieved through flight. He felt the first breath of the inferno's killing heat. The flames he sheltered in now could not burn him, for he was of their substance. But the fires inside his head would consume him utterly.

There was an ending, abrupt as a slamming door. He did not know, in that final instant, whether it was fire or darkness that took him.

Twenty

**NOW FELL,** a galaxy of drifting flakes. Watching them was like moving, like being propelled at tremendous velocity through a forest of stars. Beyond lay the sky from which they came, high and distant, black as infinity. The whole was enclosed in a hush so deep it seemed not simply silence, but the death of sound.

Though Bron recognized what he saw, he did not know how to interpret his recognition. Was this some strange prelude to death, a final flash of awareness before the end? But time stretched out; awareness persisted. He realized that he could blink, that he could move his eyes. The sense of his body trickled back to him: his shoulders, his arms and chest, his hips, his thighs and knees and calves. He was lying on his back in an awkward position, his head higher than his feet, half-sunk in some cold and yielding substance. Snow. Around him was a field of snow, faintly luminous in the darkness, its edges swallowed by night and the storm.

Darkness. Silence. Snow. Understanding rose, impossible as a dream. The ceremony was over. He was outside the walls.

In the thousand years of Guardian record, no Violator had ever emerged from the ceremony with an intelligence intact. What had been done to him should have rendered him no more than a lump of witless flesh. Yet here he was, or seemed to be—still alive, still himself. His mind, sluggish with unconsciousness, struggled to fit itself to the truth of this. Perhaps it was only a momentary hiatus, a brief pause between the final instant of consciousness and the first moment of oblivion. Perhaps only his stillness held him to clarity. But, unprotected in the snow, he was deeply cold. Shivering wracked him, making a mockery of his efforts at immobility. If he continued to lie here, he would certainly die. It would be worse than ironic to escape the ceremony, only to freeze to death outside the walls.

Experimentally, he moved: his fingers, his hands, his arms and shoulders. When darkness did not descend upon his senses, nor his thoughts slip away into blankness, he maneuvered his elbows under his body and raised himself to a sitting position. Snow slipped from his shoulders and chest as he did so—he was covered with it, a glittering blanket of white. An intense wave of dizziness took him as he came upright. His sight dimmed; he felt oblivion rushing toward him, an enormous wave ready to break. But the dizziness passed. Oblivion receded. Consciousness endured, strong and steady.

As far as he could tell, he was uninjured, though his head felt like a ripe melon ready to burst, the channels of his mind as raw and ravaged as beaten flesh. A throbbing ache upon his forehead separated itself insistently from the generalized pain. Reaching up, his fingers encountered a tangle of weeping welts. He did not need to see it to know what it was: the symbol of unfitness, the physical stamp of the fires that burned away the Talent of the Gifted—a message to the people of the world, in the unlikely event the Violator did not die, of the nature of what once had hidden there.

What had delivered him? There had been no interruption, no intervention; the presence of the brand on his forehead made that clear. Nor had there been any failure of power. The echoes of the colossal force the Prior had sent against him still whispered at the limit of his senses. He could still feel, faintly, the ashy remnants of the blaze that had raged inside his mind. Yet he remembered also the flight of his Gift—bursting free of stasis, leaping urgently beyond the confines of flesh, plunging toward the power of the Stone. It was his Gift that had saved him. Or rather, its willfulness, that strange and separate volition that had puzzled him all his life. Had it recognized its peril? Or, face-to-face with the Stone after more than a decade of absence, had it merely followed one more time its affinity for the tides of the Stone's contemplation?

Bron drew up his legs and wrapped his arms around them. He had closed his eyes on death; it was not easy to shake so deep an understanding of ending. He bowed his head upon his knees, striving, with all the intensity of which he was capable, to believe in the impossible fact of his own survival. Through the pain of his abused mind he embraced the consciousness that endured within him: the miraculous workings of his thoughts, rising in clarity with each moment that passed, the riotous conflux of his senses, their messages of cold and pain welcome for the evidence of life they offered. With a return of practicality he reached for the warm spark of his Gift, to make himself some refuge from the cold.

The spark was not there.

He forced himself to be still, to breathe deeply. Destruction of a Gift destroyed intelligence as well—the fact that his intellect survived had to mean his Gift had survived also. Beyond a general assessment of his thoughts, he had not yet surveyed his inner landscape with any degree of care. It was possible that the immense fires the Prior had sent against him had damaged him somehow, or at least left behind some lingering after-effect, temporarily obscuring his Gift from sight.

Carefully he reached inside himself. The voice of fear urged him to arrow directly to his center, to thrash and struggle until he found his Gift. He ignored it, beginning instead at the periphery of his mind. At once he saw the damage he had feared, damage which, in the confusion of his waking, he had not truly apprehended. The landscape of his inner self had changed almost beyond recognition. Once a bounded territory bristling with fortifications, it now lay flat and open, bare of enclosures of any kind. His barriers were gone—all of them, even the original barrier of his childhood—blown to dust and rubble by the impact of the Prior's power. The debris of his many guards choked the well of soul where he had kept his secret self. Above the ruins his thoughts floated free, at the forefront of his mind for anyone to see or take.

But not his Gift. His Gift was nowhere to be found. Where its spark had been, there was only darkness. Where its banked fires had lain hidden, there was only ash. Where its light had burned, a bright eye turned always toward him, there was only wreckage.

At last Bron abandoned his efforts. He sat slumped in the snow, his arms loose at his sides. He no longer felt the cold; he was lost in an arctic darkness much deeper than the wintry night. Throughout the events that had stripped him of all he had and all he loved, he had never ceased to desire survival, for as long as life remained it was possible to find new purpose to replace the old. But survival was meaningless without his Gift. Without his Gift there was no way to purpose at all, not even any means, now that his barriers were gone, of concealing who he was. Without his Gift he was a shadow, a cripple, an ordinary man. He could not imagine how to live like that. He did not wish to try.

The snow had stopped. High above, the clouds had pulled apart; the rising moon poured down a flood of silver light, scattering ghostly diamonds across the snow and laying shadows behind the drifts. A little distance away, one of these shadows seemed unlike the others—more irregular, more solid. It was possible, watching, to make out the contours of a human body. One of his men? But they had been cast out well before himself. By now they must lie beneath a foot or more of snow.

Bron could not have said what it was that moved him from his stasis, what brought him to his feet and launched him forward through the snow. He was clumsy with cold, deeply weak from his ordeal; the snow crust was not firm, and he floundered up to his hips in powder as soft and white as goosedown. Still he persisted, doggedly, until he reached the shadow he had glimpsed and, looking down, saw that it was Madelaine.

She was sprawled on her back, sunk deeply in the snow as if she had been dropped from a height. Like him, she wore prison clothing; like his, her feet and arms were bare. A collar was clasped about her neck. Her hair spread in a tangled mat around her head. Upon her forehead the brand of unfitness twisted, raised and livid. She was covered with a fine dusting of snow; it glittered coldly in the moonlight, a cocoon spun by ice-spiders.

Painfully he lowered himself to crouch beside her, reaching out to brush the powder from her face. Her features were as still as a dead woman's, her skin bluish in the pale illumination of the moon. Yet he could see the slow, almost imperceptible rise and fall of her breathing, and even through the numbness of his fingers he felt her lingering warmth. She was alive—a survival as useless as his own, the persistence of a body no longer animated by a mind. She was as empty in reality, now, as she had once pretended to be.

There should have been some satisfaction in this thought, some pleasure in the sight of her, the spy trapped in the icy web of her own actions. But as he looked at her, still and helpless in the snow, he could no longer find it in himself to hate her. She was the instrument of his annihilation, of the annihilation of the only people in the world he had ever truly loved. Yet it was not she who had nurtured the hatred that had brought him here. It was not she who had mapped the shape of his downfall. She was only a tool, struck down now by the very spite she had served so faithfully. Out of all the passages of both their lives only these moments on the snow remained, a pause between the sentence of death and its completion. In the clear suspended silence of that waiting, the world of desire and deception, in which they had confronted and destroyed each other, seemed as distant as a dream, less real than the long slide into sleep that followed dreaming.

Bron felt something turn over inside him. He reached down and gathered Madelaine into his arms. Under her weight he sank further into the snow; it embraced him now nearly to his waist. He bowed his face against her neck, against her fading warmth. Grief tore through him, shattering, irresistible. He did not weep; he had not wept since his family died, more than twenty-six years ago. But he mourned—for the years of struggle, for the hope gone and the striving wasted, for Serle and Elene dead in some unmarked grave, for his men cold beneath the drifts, for his unborn child, dying as the woman in his arms slipped slowly out of life. And for himself. For his vanished power, his shattered dream, his pointless death upon a field of snow.

Once before in his life he had crouched on the ground among the dead, his past destroyed and his future erased, drained of hope and hatred, empty of all but grief. Then, he had heard a call and turned to look within. This time, light as a breath, he found himself journeying outward. His consciousness rose up above the snow, above the twinned shape that was himself and Madelaine. He saw the life that flowed in them—the net of blood, the web of breath, tangles of light against the darkness. The light was dwindling, yielding to the cold. Yet even as she grew dim, he continued to shine. Below the luminance of life a second core of brilliance showed within him, a blue-white effulgence unlike anything he had ever seen, not fading with the imminence of death but holding steady at his center. As if his observation gave it strength, it stirred—expanding, flowing out along his darkening limbs like a dammed river released to fill its bed: a strange man-shaped echo of his outer form, a being composed of light. Still it expanded, larger than his body could contain, drifting from his pores, wreathing about his mouth and nose, making beacons of his open eyes. It spilled into the night, lighting the world around him like a fallen star and striking glory from the snow.

It was his Gift. From outside himself he recognized it, with the solidity of primal understanding, though it was nothing like the power he had always known. It was vastly enlarged, entirely transformed, no longer bounded and confined but infinitely and fully present within him. This was why he had not recognized it when he first awoke. He had been searching for it as he always had: behind walls, beneath barriers. But his barriers were gone. There were no longer any boundaries within him. His Gift filled him as light fills the day, as darkness fills the night. It filled him as air fills the world: perceptible not in itself, but only through the act of breathing.

He fell through the freezing dark, back to his dying body. His skin was as frigid as the snow, his blood slowed almost into ice, yet within him fire danced: the fire of his Gift. Instinctively, now, he found the proper channels of perception. It was no longer a reaching inward, but a spreading out. It was not like dipping a hand into a narrow well, but like raising a gaze on a shore with no horizon. Here at last was the power that had come to him when he was twelve years old: the power that had halted time, the power that since then he had never touched except in the presence of the Stone.

Out of it, he spun a thread of heat. He wove it into a thick fabric of warmth, drawing it about himself and Madelaine like a blanket. He forced heat into his shuddering limbs, gasping at the pain as his hands and feet awoke again to feeling. He poured heat into her, gently, until the fluttering beat of her heart grew steady; briefly, before he pulled away, he made out the shadow-pulse of the child within her. He banished their prison clothing, dressing them both in thick wools and heavy leathers. He drew his hands across his face, undoing the ravages of his imprisonment; he held his palm against his forehead, willing his tortured flesh to wholeness. These acts of making required the merest iota of the force that lived within him. And he knew that, if he wanted to, he could bring warmth to the whole of this place. He could melt the snow all the way to the horizon, make the grass grow and the flowers bloom, so that when the Guardians looked out over their Fortress walls they would know that they had not destroyed him, but only made him stronger.

In that, in what he could do, he saw what he would do.

He sat straight now upon the snow, which he had made hard so it would bear his weight. The pain of his abused mind had vanished, together with his grief and despair, his confusion and disbelief. The currents of purpose ran strong within him, already charting the new shape of his resolve. He was himself once more.

Somewhere out in the night, he felt a stirring. He cast forth the net of his awareness, seeking the source of what he had sensed. From the west it came, from the direction of the Pilgrim Pass: power, moving toward him with steady purpose. But not Guardian power. He could feel that clearly. He waited as the travelers drew closer, as they entered the bounds of his human perception. There were three of them, bulky with wrappings, with flat meshed paddles on their feet to keep from sinking into the yielding snow. Two drew a long sled, heaped with furs; the third, in the lead, was unencumbered.

They halted a little distance away, the two with the sled still slightly behind the third. They were so heavily draped in furs and leathers they looked scarcely human. Their overhanging hoods completely concealed their faces.

"Who are you?" he said into the silence.

The closest of the three raised its mittened hands and pushed back its hood. It was a woman, with a broad stern face, dark hair cut short, and large eyes that glittered in the moonlight.

"We are the people of the mountains," she said.

"There are no people of the mountains."

"We keep ourselves secret." Her eyes were steady. Her breath puffed out in little clouds as she spoke. "The better to fight our secret war."

Bron understood. "You're the bandits. The bandits who break the bindings of the Fortress Passage. Who disguise themselves as Journeyers and kill themselves before they can be Interrogated."

"We prefer to think of ourselves as revolutionaries."

"Revolutionaries." It seemed a grandiose term for such a hopeless cause. "Why are you here?"

"For her." She gestured toward Madelaine, cradled in his arms. "I've come to give her the refuge she needs."

"How did you know she needed refuge?"

She looked at him, her face grave. "I saw this moment, many years ago. I've been waiting for it ever since."

"You're prescient?"

"Yes."

Bron felt he should be surprised. And yet he was not. There was an inevitability to this, to all of it, as of a vast circle slowly closing.

"Bring her now," the woman said. "The Guardians may be too complacent to bother looking over their own walls, but it's still dangerous for us to be here."

Bron got to his feet, Madelaine in his arms. He settled her gently on the sled, pillowing her head upon the furs.

She looked like a sleeping child, her small body lost inside the bulky clothing he had given her. The two who had drawn the sled came forward. They began to bind her with restraining straps and to pile her with coverings.

"Where will you take her?" Bron said to the woman, who stood watching her companions.

"To a safe place." She turned her stern face to his. "She'll be well cared for."

"She's with child."

"I know."

"And her mind is gone."

She shook her head. "I know what was done to her. But she has . . . there's a place she goes, within herself. A place where her mind can rest. A place others can't touch. Her mind is intact."

"You've seen this through your Gift?" Bron said, half-disbelieving.

"Yes. But I'd know it even if I hadn't. I knew her once. I know what she can do to protect herself."

"You knew her? How?"

"We were Novices together, for a little while."

"You were a Novice?" Bron said, astonished.

"Yes." She looked at him, unblinking. "That's who we are, we who you call bandits—failed Novices, lapsed Apprentices, those who have been cast out, those who have run away, those who have defected. The flotsam of the Fortress, turning back to prey on what discarded it."

"How many of you are there?"

She smiled. "That's a thing many a Soldier would give a king's ransom to know. Right now, more than a thousand."

"A *thousand*?"

"Why are you surprised? You were a Roundhead. You know the number who disappear in the course of a year, over and above those who are expelled or punished. What do you think happens to them? Why do you suppose the ground out here isn't littered with their bones?"

"I never thought about it," Bron said truthfully.

"No. Nor do most Guardians. That's what makes it possible for us to survive. So it has been, for as many centuries as the Fortress has existed. We're your shadow, which you do not see, for you're too arrogant ever to look behind you.''

"And you. Were you cast out?''

"I ran away. In the first year of my Novitiate. I had a vision of the mountain people, of the place that waited for me there. And of the two of you, resting on the snow. It's all connected, you see, a single line of possibility. You and she and the child, myself and my fighters and the cause we follow.''

"Your revolution.''

"Yes. Through which we will overthrow the Guardians and restore the balance of the world.''

Her level gaze held power, and her voice—Bron could sense it, the power perhaps of her Gift. But her words fell into silence, leaving behind the cold and the night and the walls that had been there before they were uttered. What could a thousand, Gifted or otherwise, do against those things? What could ten thousand do against them?

The woman's companions had finished arranging the sled. Only Madelaine's face was visible now amid the heaped furs.

"We must go,'' the woman said.

"I would like—'' Bron stopped. The words were ready for his lips, yet they seemed extraordinarily difficult to articulate. "I'd like to ask a favor of you.''

"A favor?''

"There's something I want to give you. For the child. It's inside my head. But I haven't much nearspeech. Would you be willing to reach into my mind and take it?''

Her face showed no surprise. Bron wondered if she had seen this also, through her Gift. She moved forward, pulling off her mittens, holding out her bare hands. "I must touch you to do it.''

Bron took off his own gloves. Her skin was rough and warm against his own. He closed his eyes, gathering the Tale together in the forefront of his mind. He felt her Gift, easing along the edges of his consciousness—alien, shaping itself to currents he did not recognize, but clear and strong for all that. After a little probing she found what he held out to her. Very gently she took it, folding her mind around it and withdrawing into herself once more.

She stepped back, looking at him. He could see, behind her face, that she was examining what he had given her.

"I'll see the child receives this," she said. Then, with something like wonder: "I've never seen a power like yours. It's beyond anything I imagined. I thought . . . sometimes my Gift is hard to read. But now I know I read it right."

"Does your Gift . . ." Bron hesitated. "Does your Gift show you what will become of the child?"

"She'll be like you, in her face and form, in her determination and her will. She'll be like her mother, in her strength and steadfastness. And she'll be like me also, for she will grow up at my side and learn to share my cause. More than that . . . more than that I cannot tell you."

"And Madelaine? What do you see for her?"

"Liliane," she corrected. "I see her with me. I see her bearing the child, I see her nursing her. Beyond that . . . beyond is only shadow." She hesitated. "I'm sorry. I know you cared for her."

Bron glanced away from her steady gaze. "I want her to be comfortable. She and the child. Make sure of that."

"Haven't I told you I will? You aren't Arm of the Stone any longer, to be giving orders to those who already know what to do." But there was no anger in her voice. "You don't ask for yourself?"

"I have no need of prophecy. I already know what I will do."

"Then you're not like most men. Even so, there's something I must say to you. I've seen myself saying it a thousand times, in my visions of this moment—I don't know if I say it for you, or for myself, or . . . for some other purpose." Her face was intent. Her voice took on the resonance of power. "You will pass through the Fortress walls. You will take the Stone. You will carry it through a Gate, and into another world."

The Gift in her was clear, a light shining up through her skin. For a moment she glowed gold in the moonlight. Bron looked at her, awed. The certainty in her voice was like the weight of passed time. He had known, before she spoke, what he would do. Now he knew he would succeed.

The power died all at once, like a torch going out. She was an ordinary woman again, her features drawn and weary. She drew on her mittens and pulled her hood forward over her face.

"Good-bye, Bron of the ancient name," she said. "Your child will remember you. I'll make sure of that."

She gestured to her companions. They leaned forward into the traces, bracing themselves against the weight of the sled.

"Wait."

The sled-pullers paused. Bron stepped forward and looked down on Madelaine's moonlit face. Her lashes fanned softly upon her cheeks; her features were relaxed and smooth, her lips slightly parted with her breathing. Not mindless; merely sleeping. He stooped, reaching down with his ungloved hand, setting it against the furs above her belly. He thought of the shadow-pulse he had so briefly perceived, when he brought her back to life: the last inheritor of the ancient line, going from him now, into the wilderness.

He straightened. "What is your name?" he asked the woman, who stood silent, waiting.

"Goldwine," she said, from the darkness of her hood. "You may use it, when we meet again."

She turned, setting off with the high-kneed gait forced by her snowshoes. Her companions followed. The sled moved smoothly behind them, printing twin grooves upon the drifts. Bron stood looking after them, until he could no longer see anything but the night.

Solitude enclosed him, limitless as the sky. The silence was absolute, the cold like a knife turning slowly in the bones. He turned to face the Fortress. The walls were a black scar between snow and sky, a colossal dam holding back the stars. He and Madelaine had been cast out some distance away, for the unfit must not sully the home of the Stone by lying even within its shadow. Even so the eye could not encompass the whole of the walls' length, nor divine the enormity of their mass.

He was aware of the irony of the moment in which he found himself. From the time he had first found his power he had rejected the trajectory of the Tale—first because he could not bear to surrender to the press of destiny, later because he had come to understand his destiny in a different way. Yet now he found himself at its penultimate instant, as if he had walked its pathways all along. The familiar phrases, which he had tonight given to an outsider to give in turn to a daughter he would never know, stirred inside his mind—a mythic history which retained more than a ghost of its childhood power, a summons from the hereditary depths of memory. But though he stood within the Tale's frame, it was not the Tale's voice he answered by what he planned to do tonight. To take the Stone . . . to bring the Order of Guardians down . . . to complete in the space of moments the work to which he had been prepared to devote all the years of his life . . . these things he would accomplish. But not because it was destined, or because he was called, or because long ago he had bound his life to an impossible vow. He acted now as he had acted all his life: out of himself, out of his own will. Because it was right. Because he wanted it. Most of all, because it was possible.

He laughed, a rich sound amid the cold. It was to the Prior he owed this moment, to the Arm of the Stone. It was they who had broken his barriers, who had given him the full measure of his Gift. Would they understand, afterward, what they had done?

He set aside thought. He breathed deeply, readying himself.

He reached toward the Fortress—not with his own vision, but with the vision of his Gift. He saw the walls and courts and buildings, dark inanimate stone and wood; he saw the lives they enclosed, brilliant stars of consciousness, flashing brighter here and there with the play of power. He saw the Stone, from which all light seemed to come, into which all light seemed to flow—the center, not just of the Fortress, but of the world.

He called upon his Gift. Power poured from him like a river, coursing out above the Fortress, a torrent of binding as wide as the walls themselves. He dropped it like a net across the court, across the Novice Wing and the Apprentice College and the wings that housed the Suborders, across the whole of the Fortress. At its touch, all within were cast into sleep. He saw the minds as they winked into darkness, a thousand candles extinguished by a single breath.

Despite the vast amount of power Bron had released, far more remained. Summoning it, he began to move, passing through the walls like light through water, never disturbing the massive stones. All around him, in the halls and atriums and rooms and refectories of the Fortress, its occupants slept—Apprentices and Guardians, Novices and servants, suspended between one breath and another, one motion and the next. When they woke they would not at first recognize that time had passed. Though they might come eventually to understand what had held them, the hours passed in stasis could never be regained.

At last, slipping through the final barrier, he settled softly upon the grass of the Garden of the Stone. The scent of flowers and wet earth enclosed him; air currents moved gently against his skin. The moon's light was like falling water. High above, at the top of the binding that held the Garden, hung a perfect circle of clear sky, framed in restless clouds: a jewel casket filled with stars.

He moved forward through the trees, his boots pressing dark prints upon the dew. He could feel the closeness of the Stone; his Gift trembled, yearning. But for the first time in his life his human will and the will of his Gift were in accord. For the first time he could approach the tides of the Stone's knowing and refuse to join them.

In the clearing, he stopped. The Stone's prison shimmered in the moonlight, lustrous as a pearl. Fresh from his own imprisonment, he saw in it what he had not been able to see before. These pale walls and the artificial milky slabs that had entrapped him were of the same substance. This was not a physical structure at all, but a binding.

He reached out with his mind, seeking the pattern of illusion. He found it easily. It was not designed to thwart a power like his, only to exclude the eyes of the unGifted and the lesser Gifts of those who were not Speakers. Carefully, he inserted fingers of unmaking into the lattice of the binding's fabrication. There was a moment of resistance; then the binding disintegrated. The milky walls collapsed like subsiding cloth and vanished.

Where the false building had been lay a flat dark circle, composed neither of earth nor rock nor any physical material Bron could identify. At its center, upon a pillar of silvery matter, rested the Stone. It was a shimmering mass of brilliance, more golden than the sun and almost as bright. It pulsed and shifted like a distant storm; at its heart played all the colors of the spectrum. It did not seem a physical object at all, but a gathering of fire, a concretion of light.

Bron reached out, testing the odd darkness before him. Even through the armor of his Gift he felt the shock of power. By destroying the walls he had removed only a portion of the Stone's imprisoning. This circle, concealed within the false structure, was the rest—no ordinary binding, but a strong and ancient making, the work of a very great Gift, its roots reaching deep into the structure of time and existence. He was not certain that even he had the power to undo it.

He set his boot inside the circle. It felt as solid as the mountains themselves. Slowly he shifted forward. The instant he was fully inside the dark boundary his perspective altered. The circumference seemed to rush away, suddenly a dozen times as wide. The Garden disappeared, swallowed by roiling mists. The Stone, on its silver pillar, seemed impossibly distant. The bright flow of its power was gone, cut off as if a door had slammed shut; the brilliance of its physical form had also vanished, so that it appeared to be nothing more than a large lump of translucent rock.

Shocked, Bron stepped back. At once all was as it had been: the moonlit Garden, the inky circle, the clear and quiet night. What was this thing, that it could blot out the power of the Stone? He had sensed ancientness in the binding, and strength. But not like this.

He stood for a moment, gathering himself. Then, in a single swift motion, he launched himself forward. The alteration of perspective, now he was ready for it, did not seem quite so shocking. He began to move, with what his muscles told him were rapid strides. But for all his exertion, he seemed to cover little ground. The Stone and its silver pillar seemed to dwindle, as if they fled his approach. The dark stuff beneath his feet was oddly variable, as if it were not a single surface but many surfaces in succession—now dressed stone, now packed earth, now heaving water, now a core of ice punching through the heart of the mountains. After a few moments he ceased to watch the vertiginous changes, fixing his eyes instead upon the Stone.

One moment it was distant, its pillar smaller than his little finger; the next, with the same dizzying shift of perspective that had accompanied his entry into the circle, it was no more than an arm's length in front of him. It was possible to see, now, a little brilliance in the heart of the dull rock it was in this place, but there was no echo of its power. Like the floor, the silvery column on which it sat was not quite what it seemed—striated and cloudy, it resembled smoke, if smoke could be molded and concentrated into a solid substance.

Bron reached out his gloved hands and, gently, curved them around the Stone's pitted, irregular contours. Touching it, he could sense its power, but only as a small echo of its true song—a great thing made small, like a map that reduces to tiny scale the country it depicts. He understood now the purpose of this place—it was the answer to a question that had puzzled him all his life, of how the Gifts of Guardians could touch the Stone and survive.

Out of his vast reserves of power he spun a gossamer thread of force. Slowly and with infinite care, he allowed his Gift to flow outward, wreathing it about himself like an armor of light. When he was ready he reached toward the roots of binding that held the Stone in place, touching them, testing them, tracing their shape.

He closed his eyes. He breathed deeply. He tightened the grip of his hands. With the strength of his physical body and the strength of his Gift, he lifted.

The Stone resisted, immovable as a mountain. Still he pulled, using all his power now, his muscles and his mind stretching to their utmost limits. Abruptly there was a change—a loosening, a shifting. With an enormous tearing, the Stone came free. The force of it caused Bron to stagger backward. Unable to recover himself, he fell, the Stone cradled against his chest.

The ripping that had accompanied the Stone's detachment did not end with its release. It was as if glaciers were being torn from their beds, as if the weave of the world itself were pulling apart. It was the binding that was tearing, its fabric irretrievably breached by removal of the Stone. It was possible to see the Garden now, blurred behind the walls of mist. The Stone's voice was rising, and fire flickered at its heart. Bron pushed himself to his feet. Stumbling, he began to run toward the circle's distant edge. The tides of unmaking tried to hold him where he was; he could feel the forces of dissolution wrenching at his bones. Strange images followed him, changing with every stride—hallucinatory forests and shadowy cities, vast plains and empty deserts, soaring mountains and heaving rivers, as if each step took him to the heart of another world.

He reached the boundary and threw himself across it, piercing the dissolving walls of mist, rolling over on the grass. The sudden tranquillity of the Garden was like a blow. He turned, gasping with the exertion of his flight, looking back at the place he had escaped. It was destroying itself. The black substance of the circle billowed like an angry ocean. The pillar that had held the Stone was quivering, the forces that made it solid visibly falling away. As he watched, it burst its bonds. A huge cloud of silver smoke flew out, larger than the circle that had contained it. For a moment the cloud struggled, disorganized. Ponderously it began to spin, forming itself into a vortex, like the Gate the Arm of the Stone had created in the Northern Orderhouse. Faster it whirled, and still faster, a wheel of silver matter pierced from edge to edge by cobalt lightning. Its motion propelled it upward, toward the boiling clouds that marked the highest limits of the Garden's binding.

With a huge percussion, the vortex and the binding met. Both were instantly obliterated. The clouds rushed inward, free at last of the manmade bonds that had restrained them, overtaking the stars. A blast of arctic air punched down, dark and glittering, raining ice like tiny diamonds. It struck the ground like a fist. From the point of impact a shimmering veil of frost rushed out, engulfing the paths, the grass, the flowers and the bushes and the trees. The sound of freezing was like the shattering of a million mirrors.

At last it was over. Spring lay vanquished beneath winter's weight. Every surface gleamed with milky ice, as if the Garden had been remade in spun sugar. From the victorious clouds the first flakes fell, drifting down upon a place that had not felt their sting in a thousand years. Only the black circle, dark as the night sky within the ghostly whiteness, was untouched. It was impervious to frost, as it was to any change. This was what remained when the human making was gone: a much older power, born of the earth itself.

Slowly Bron got to his feet. Every motion shattered a hundred glassy blades of grass. The Stone was still close against his chest. He lowered it to the ground, setting it amid the sparkling frost. Freed from binding, it coruscated like a tiny sun. Its song poured out, encompassing the world. For a millennium no one had seen it thus. He stood for a moment, marveling. He was scarcely able to believe what he had done. He had known he would succeed. Yet, looking back, it seemed impossible.

From his stores of power he conjured up a thick leather bag. He slipped the Stone into it, tying the drawstrings at the top. He left as he had come, moving like a spirit through the sleeping Fortress. When he came to the walls, he made to pass through them as he had before. But something had changed—in himself? In the world? For the rest of his life, he would never be quite sure. As he touched them, the black stones shattered. A galaxy of dust shot upward toward the stars; a thousand tons of rubble came cascading down. The roar of disintegration was like the ending of worlds. It shook mountains and collapsed snowfields leagues away. Lost in their enchanted sleep, the Guardians did not stir. But they heard. When they woke the sound of that destruction would be with them, deep in the place where the darkest dreams are born.

Bron found himself upon the snow, unscathed. Stunned, he turned to look on what he had wrought. Half the length of the walls was gone. The broken edges gaped, jagged and irregular, as if some gargantuan beast had bitten them away. Debris blackened the snow—dust, mortar, shattered stone, slabs still partially intact, tumbled about like giants' playthings. He had not willed this. He could not guess why it had happened. Yet he felt the rightness of it. It was the final passage of the Tale, falling into place with an inevitability he could no longer question.

The Tale was done. The Stone was free. Before he set aside his childish vow, Bron had believed this moment must change everything, the breaking of the Stone's enslavement irrevocably and immediately shifting the balance of reality in a way that could be concretely felt, like the Split ten centuries before. Even tonight it had seemed to him this must be so—how could the ending of the order of a thousand years fail to echo out across the earth? But standing now in the fathomless silence that followed on the heels of the walls' destruction, he could perceive no sign of metamorphosis. His senses, wider and more encompassing since the rebirth of his power, as if his awakening had gifted him with a ghost of the Stone's perception, told him that the world was still the same. Unchanged, its currents flowed into the Stone; unaltered, they flowed out again. And in that recognition he saw the truth. The hand of man had bound the Stone; those bindings were now gone. But the hand of man had bound the world as well. The Fortress lay transformed—a lightless eye within its broken walls, its core removed, its center gone. Yet the web of temporal power that issued from it, as the web of the Stone's power issued from the Stone itself, was still wrapped tight around the earth.

He had not worked the transformation he had sought. Yet from what he had done tonight, change would come. He had cut the guy-rope, removed the foundation. Centerless, the edifice of Guardian rule could not endure. It had been a long time in the building; it would be a long time in the unraveling. But it would unravel. It was Goldwine and her kind who would make it so. And then, perhaps, the currents of the world would shape themselves to something new.

As for himself . . . though the world around him had not altered, he stood in a different place. By his actions tonight he had given the Tale an ending. But in ending it, he had also passed, finally and irrevocably, beyond it. He bore no weight of heredity now, no mark of destiny, no lingering encumbrance of vows. There was no man or woman to whom he owed any burden of love or hate or obligation. Like the Stone, he had been unbound. For the first time in his life, he was truly free.

Gathering his power one more time, he sent it outward, laying a final binding, a message of sorts. He was careful with it, for he wanted it to last. Finished, he turned away. Despite the strength he had expended tonight he felt strong, as weightless as light. He began to move, the Stone held gently in his arms, slipping through time as well as space. The binding that held the Guardians would endure for some time. When it broke, it would be much too late for pursuit. All they would see, when they looked outside their broken walls, was the empty indentation in the snow where his body had lain. And beyond it, a world transformed by spring—a season out of season that would abide forever, and forever remind them of what they had lost.